The Blue Pool

Tom Nestor has written many short stories published to acclaim
and was a prizewinner in the Ian St James Competition.
He has also written plays for RTE and BBC.
His last book, *The Keeper of Absalom's Island*,
was a bestselling memoir.

Here, traveller, scholar, poet, take your stand
When all those rooms and passages are gone,
When nettles wave upon a shapeless mound
And saplings root among the broken stone ...

W.B. Yeats, 'Coole Park', 1929

Chapter 1

I was a child of the mountain. It nurtured me and I hearkened to its moods. It called me in the wind and whispered dreams and legends to me. For 400 years it did likewise to every Dawley ever born. The child became a man and the mountain owned my soul. And today I am the last. In a few moments I will drive down to Barton Hall and give the mountain away, the part that is mine to give. We have reached the end of our time, the mountain and I.

Through the open windows of the conservatory I could hear the gurgle of the Morning Star as it meandered through the gorge. For a few moments the sound was shot through by a flock of chirruping goldfinches, which bobbed overhead and then dropped on the profusion of thistle-tops that sprung from the disturbed ground by the side of the gorge. Thistles are a weed of cultivation, a relic of ancient planting.

The conservatory was my father's favourite room; we had built it some twenty years before he died. It looked west, holding the molten afterglow of the setting sun. There was a portable television in one corner and, scattered throughout, a suite of wicker bought at an auction in Adamston. Above the television was the framed print of my father being presented with a cup at an athletics meeting. He looked gauche and bewildered, with a lopsided smile that seemed wrung from him under great duress.

From the window looking due west, all the slope of the tier and a swath of Barton demesne were visible across the river. I could see the cattle track that skirted the Black Castle and the overhang of evergreens that led to the walled garden. Barton Hall presented its front perspective from where I stood: the terraced stonework, the granite balustrades, the network of box hedge and the topiaries in yew and cypress.

Beyond the terraced lawn a crescent of gravel had been hewn from the grass. A cavalcade of cars came in through the main gates. I waited until the Mercedes that flew the tricolour cruised up the avenue and was directed to park before the front steps.

A young government official ushered me straight in and put me sitting with the row of invitees in the front seat of the Long Gallery. The Barton ancestors looked down on me and my eyes flitted from portrait to portrait. I could place them all in my mind without ever looking because I had stood on the mosaic floor many a time and studied them: Richard, Godfrey, William Grantham, Geoffrey, Amos. And in the middle, like a flowering poppy in a field of winter grass, unexpected and wondrous, was Absalom Grantham, the Methodist preacher, his face a liquid pool of compassion and humanity. A man of the cloth, Lionel used to call him, the black sheep in the family of pirates and adventurers. Last of all came the portrait of Lionel himself, looking like a young Lord Byron, the open-necked lace shirt displaying a delicate show of manly chest, dark hair sprinkled with slivers of grey, the leonine head thrown back in haughty Barton pose.

The Minister for Arts and Culture framed silent words with her lips that told me she was about to begin. The audience caught the signal and a hum and shuffle of expectation began to gather strength. I looked towards the front seat where the dignitaries sat, searching for familiar and supportive faces. And then I saw her. She was sitting in the middle, wedged between Carew's widow and Luke Heaney. Mona! My heart leaped and thudded, but I managed to force down the flood of emotion gathered in my throat. We Dawleys, the Irish side, never displayed our feelings in public. She blew a kiss and formed the shape of an embrace with both her hands.

'Ladies and gentlemen,' the Minister began, 'if you'll forgive me, I'll dispense with protocol. This is too warm an occasion to lumber it with formality. I am here today, in this beautiful pastoral countryside, to officially open one of my favourite projects. There is nothing as redolent of our history, and as pertinent to our future, as the bringing together of two great traditions – once diametrically opposed to one another – in what we now know as the Glenorga Theme Park. When the originators of this idea, John Carew, Lord have mercy on him, Luke Heaney and Roderick Dawley, first outlined this concept to me, I was immediately taken with its relevance and potential.'

Liar, I heard myself say. You never wanted to meet us. We were three country yokels wasting your time with a half-baked notion of turning a landlord's estate and a former tenant's home and farm into a theme park.

'Ladies and gentlemen, in a few moments, you will be treated to a first-class interpretative audio-visual show about the Theme Park, put together by Roderick Dawley, here beside me. It tells the story of Mount Fierna, from the time it rose from the sea, the effect of successive ice ages, the coming of its first inhabitants, the arrival of the Celts. The story goes on to trace those moments in history that brought the Dawleys to Mount Fierna and the Bartons to Barton Hall. It is a story of cruelty and degradation, of man's inhumanity to man. But it is also relevant to the present day, demonstrating the propensity of the ordinary person, on both sides of the divide, to rise above the legacy of history and strive for a better place in the dawning of a new day. Ladies and gentlemen, let me introduce you to Roderick Dawley.'

Mona gave me the thumbs up and smiled her encouragement. The little knot of my former workmates from Lackaroe began to stamp the floor in their enthusiasm until the young official stifled it with a dismissive sweep of his hands. A hush replaced the spasmodic applause and beyond the window I saw a rook alight on the statue of a Roman wood nymph and peck at the blank recess of the statue's eye.

'Ladies and gentlemen, some of you will have known my brother Felim. About the time that I began to write the script for this project, I had a great stroke of fortune. I came across a paper that Felim had written as part of his research for a university assignment. Wherever you are, Felim, I thank you profusely because I have lifted whole sections of it to become the script for this presentation.'

I closed my eyes and listened to my own voice. I wished it were Felim doing the voice over. I had a vision of him then, in that exaggerated oratorical stance, standing with his legs planted wide as if reciting poetry in our mother's parlour.

Roderick. The Minister called me Roderick. My mother would have liked that; she and Lionel Barton were the only people from the mountain who used the full version of my first name. I wonder what she would have made of this day? Perhaps it would be a great disappointment to her, for it bore no evidence of a flight of freedom above the ramparts of primal civilisation. Mount Fierna was a prison, she told us, a living tomb. The only way out was over the mountain, catching the currents that rode the slipstreams to a new world.

I am Roderick Jackson Dawley. I came into this world 343 years after the 1601 battle of Kinsale, a seminal event in Dawley tradition since my ancestor went south with O'Donnell to fight that defining battle. As the army traversed Mount Fierna, it was attacked by Barton's men and a renegade force of the O'Brien. O'Donnell drove off the attack and decided to leave a small detachment behind to guard the route on his return journey. But he never returned, the Irish were smashed at Kinsale, the old order was overturned and Ireland as a nation would not emerge for 300 years or more.

We would never admit it, certainly not my father, but we were invaders too, but of a different hue. Long before the garrison from the north dug in on Mount Fierna – the Donnellys, the McRedmonds, the Heaneys – the mountain had witnessed a succession of migrations. Before the creeping spaghnum had created the Bog of Allen from a lowland lake, Neolithic farmers had hunted and gathered on its shores. Several waves of Celts had farmed and worshipped beside Lough Cutra, the Vikings had raided and pillaged, the Norman barons had wrested their demesnes from the successors of the Celts and brought a new economic order. And then the Bartons came.

The Bartons had settled in the village of Grantham, Essex, in the time of William the Conqueror. Richard, the founding father in Ireland, was an Elizabethan adventurer, who enlisted in Sir Nicholas Malby's army in Ireland and was granted the de Val estate. De Val was scion of another Norman family now grown more Irish than the Irish themselves and therefore opposed to British rule in Ireland.

The Barton régime began with a reign of terror. Richard set up his headquarters in de Val's Black Castle and cleared the land of its ancient clans and their followers. He leased more than half of it to English tenants at nominal rents but on condition that they would support him in arms in the spirit of feudal fealty. As a result he always had a small army at his bidding and, whether through fealty or pleasure, his underlings were more than willing to indulge the excesses of their overlord.

I was weaned on stories of Barton terror. I would wake up in the middle of the night, sweat on my brow, and jelly in my bones, as Richard galloped through my nightmares on his mettlesome warhorse. My father would tell me the stories when I brought him tea in the meadow, or sheltered from a rain shower under a blackthorn bush. De Val had built a chapel of ease beside the castle so that his retinue, family and tenants could have church services brought to them. Richard Barton burst into the church with his band of ruffians and temporarily spared some of the congregation so that they could witness the torture of their priest. He was thrown into an iron cauldron filled with melted grease and butter and roasted over a fire until the flesh fell off his bones. When Tighe MacAdastair refused to give Barton a valuable horse, he was fastened to a pair of Barton's chargers until his legs were torn from their sockets. In the dead of night Barton would send his thugs to raid the mountain hovels and procure for him a selection of young women for their collective amusement. It is not surprising that when Barton died the vault was broken into; his body was removed and left in a secluded place on the summit of Mount Fierna where the birds and the beasts picked it clean.

The hatred that stirred in the hearts and minds of mountain men was willed from generation to generation, growing strength in its passing so that it seemed to be born from the genes and cemented in memory banks. Less than 200 years after the battle of Kinsale, Godfrey Grantham Barton built Barton Hall. It was erected on the shore of Lough Cutra, commanding an aspect that the first Gaelic-speaking migrants would have composed a paean of poetry for. It looked southwards across the shimmering water, down to the lowland plains. Its back was to the mountain; the great dining room oversaw a vista of tiered slopes, glens and dales, and the toiling of dispirited tenants in whose souls rebellion lurked.

William Grantham Barton built the west wing of Barton Hall and planted stands of beech and elm. His son Geoffrey drained Lough Cutra and built the causeway to Knock Na Sidhe. He added the east wing, the front porch with its Doric columns, the courtyard, stables and the ornamental garden with its Roman statuary and box hedging.

Geoffrey's son Amos erected the flax mill beside the bridge where the pike road crossed the Morning Star. Then, 70 years after the Great Famine, in a hovel on the valley floor of Glenorga, on Christmas Eve, Joanna Dawley gave birth to a son. He was the first born. They named him after the ancestor who had come south with O'Donnell. Hugh Dawley was my father.

Joanna Dawley gave birth to ten children. By the time Hugh was 25, he was the only one remaining. My father was a dyed-in-the-wool Dawley; he would not emigrate but would make his home on the mountain as his ancestor of the same name did, for my father had a dream. The mountain was his birthright. Once his ancestors had held their land from de Val. One day, with his sons around him, he would wrest from the Barton interloper what was rightfully his.

Grandfather Dawley was a tenant of Geoffrey Barton, one of 13,000 landlords, 800 of whom owned half of Ireland. By the end of the nineteenth century the Land League movement had wrested some concessions from their overlords. Barton offered to sell the mountain land to his tenants who would have availed of the scheme if it were not for Grandfather Dawley. The mountain land was not Barton's to sell, he argued; it was never included in the de Val estate and Queen Elizabeth's grant document would prove that. A specially convened land court upheld my grandfather's claim but threw a sop to Barton that would salt the wound in Dawley resentment for another generation. All the mountain tenants would henceforth hold legal ownership of their land, but Barton and his posterity would maintain hunting rights over the mountain slopes and its valleys.

Hugh Dawley, my father, was a spare, angular-looking man, almost six feet tall. His sparse frame and thin, pinched features gave him an awkward, even fragile appearance. He had inherited the flame-coloured hair of his maternal ancestors who carried Norse blood in their genes. When he had reached his mid-twenties, he was almost bald except for a titian circle that spread over his crown like a tonsure. The same wispy hair grew profusely on the back of his hands and in tufts from his ears. His enormous hands hung from his angular shoulders in a kind of simian perspective. My father was proud of those hands; they were the engine of his strength, his driving force. From dawn to dusk, in all weathers, he moved earth and stone in a welter of activity.

My father was 31 when he met my mother. Every third Sunday in August, pilgrims flocked to the holy well at Manisterluna, which was reputed to have miraculous powers. The water cured ailments and pains and restored sick animals to health; it made barren women fertile, and in that convoluted fashion of providence, caused lovelorn souls to find each other.

Beth Cartor and her brother, Roderick, cycled to Manisterluna in August 1937. Their parents, schoolteachers, taught in the school in Adamston. They were radicals at a time and place that worshipped at the altar of religious convention and the force of its behavioural legacy. In his soul, Philly Cartor was a watercolour artist, but if he followed that calling he would have starved. So he took his easel and his palette and wandered the roads every spare moment he could. It was absurd, a grown man in a land of poverty, indulging himself in a frivolous activity when his fellow man was bowed with the rigours of subsistence living.

Mona Cartor was just as eccentric. She played the piano; the music of Chopin and Bach wafted through her parlour window in the still evening, and people shook their heads in silent judgement. When neighbours had reason to call, they would find the family seated at opposite ends of the kitchen table, deep in the pages of their books. In the Cartor household seven to nine o'clock each evening was reserved for reading.

And there was more and worse to it. Philly Cartor would disappear for days and weeks, and then return and resume life as if nothing untoward had happened. In summer, in the throes of reaping, harvest and rents due, the Cartors would tramp the roads of France and Spain, visiting strange exotic places that the folk of Adamston had never heard of.

Then, in Beth's sixteenth year, tragedy struck. While gathering blackberries on the railway line at the rear of her house, Mona Cartor was killed when struck by a passing train. The disaster drove Philly to drink; he lost his teaching post and was reduced to hawking his watercolours for the price of a bed and a couple of drinks. His presence in the home became more erratic than before and son and daughter were left to fend for themselves. Whilst in her teens, Beth went to work as a nursemaid to old Phoebe Jackson, widow of Brigadier Jackson, who had settled in the glebe house after long service in India. In time she became companion and confidante to the old woman, and loved it because it had echoes of the lifestyle she had been brought up in.

Roderick opened a drapery shop – an outfitter's for gentlemen and their sons, as he styled it. His customers were in short supply and Roderick was to discover that the few gentlemen who graced his shop were as slow to pay their debts as were their tenants and their labourers. The shop closed; Roderick moved to a midland provincial town as a draper's assistant, returning home late on Saturday and leaving again on Sunday evening.

It was Roderick's absence that made Beth take stock of her situation. She was 27 years old, an age when most young women had married and borne children. She had never contemplated marriage; in fact she would have regarded her state as nigh perfect without any of the complications of a marital union. But when Roderick left, she had a vision of her future life and it shocked her; it stretched out interminably, loveless and meaningless. Mona inveigled her brother to accompany her to Manisterluna, as she had heard somewhere that the saint took a hand at matchmaking, yet she was sceptical of the complex fashion by which he brought people together.

But it happened that way. They paid a visit to the holy well, said the customary prayers, drank the water and hung a piece of cloth on the nearby bush to signify their intentions. Then they cycled past the lake, crossed over Barton's causeway and climbed the hill of Knock Na Sidhe. At the summit, Beth turned to scan the landscape and saw Glenorga in the valley below.

'Look, Roderick, look. It's our father's painting.'

Philly Cartor had found Glenorga in his wanderings. The watercolour he created of it was one of his favourites. It had hung above the fireplace in Adamston until he was forced to sell it, leaving a smoke-stained impression on the wall. On that clear August day, with the clouds banked out on the horizon like an alpine range and shadows racing along the valley floor, Glenorga looked majestic, magical, as if it had suddenly materialised, fresh and new, out of the mountain landscape. The Morning Star weaved its sinuous way along the valley floor, the scatter of whitewashed houses shimmered in the sunlight, and the little green fields glistened as if newly painted.

'Let's cycle down there,' Beth said.

They had come abreast of the Dawley house when Roderick's front wheel punctured. While he was repairing the inner tube, Hugh came from the house and offered help but Roderick brusquely refused it. Joanna appeared at the doorway, wiping her hands on her bib as she always did when she greeted a visitor. She smiled at Beth and was glad that the house was looking so well. A new coat of thatch had been recently fixed on the roof and the roses were in full bloom. Many years before, when she had been walking past Barton's kitchen garden with my grandfather, Joanna had admired the trailing roses that were spilling over the wall. Her husband returned in the last month of autumn, took some cuttings and planted them beneath the front windows and at each side of the doorway. When they grew, he fashioned them like an archway to the whitewashed wall.

'Walk a little way with her, Hugh', Joanna told her son; 'show her the valley and when ye come back we'll make a drop of tea.'

And that's how it began: its roots, like all great epics, in a simple trivial event. Beth took up Joanna's invitation to revisit, but next time and for evermore she came without Roderick, who had taken an instant dislike to Hugh. 'We don't need him', Roderick advised her; 'you don't want to waste your life on someone like that, a country gobshite, without manners or grace and a house like a pigsty.'

The dislike was mutual. Everything about Roderick rubbed Hugh the wrong way: his speech, mannerisms, especially the way he drank his tea with the little finger of his right hand sticking out in an exaggerated gesture of refinement. 'That fella should have been a woman,' Hugh told his mother.

In later life, in those soft frail moments when the drawbridge to our feelings was let down, we would probe my mother about her courtship. We always mistook her reticence for tactic, as if it were a safeguard against exposing such private hoarded memories from the scrutiny of tactless children.

'What did you see in him? Go on Mam, tell us,' Mona cajoled.

'It was hardly his flowing golden hair and the handsome cut of his face,' Felim observed.

'Tell us Mam, please,' Mona persisted.

My mother sighed. 'If you must know. It was his passion for things.'

'His passion?' Mona echoed in mock surprise. 'Roddy, close your ears, you're too young.'

They had climbed up to the top of Mount Fierna, to a place called Knocknastumpa, the hill of the stumps. It was almost a year since the pair had first met. The summit was now covered in blanket bog, but where the mountain men had harvested peat, relics of ancient forest were still evident.

'Hugh, you haven't said a word since we left Glenorga. What are you thinking about?'

He swung his great hand in a circle, his index finger pointing the route of its travels. 'See out there, all the way to the Shannon and up here.'

'Hugh, I know. You told me.'

'Aye, I did that. But you don't hear it. Not like I do.'

'It's become a great passion with you.'

'That's the word all right. A passion. My father had it and his father before that. An' I think it's a great thing to have in a man's head. Otherwise we'll never get it back. So let me tell you again.' He swung his hand a second time. 'Out there, all the land you can see, that was Irish land. Until the Normans took it and the Bartons took it from them. That's Barton Hall, down there in the trees. They were bastards, seed, breed and generation. You have no idea what they did to my family and other families in the mountain, right down the years since the first one was planted here in 1585.'

'Hugh, it was all such a long time ago. It's time to forget those things.'

He reddened in sudden anger. 'Does that make it right?

13

Aisy for you to say that I should forget it.'

Beth looked at the intense set of his jawline, the flush that had darkened his forehead and within the tonsure circle. It worried her. 'Hugh, listen to me. Let us make our own life; don't let us be sidetracked by what happened long ago.'

He seemed not to hear. 'We'll best the Bartons yet. The pair of us.'

'The pair of us?'

'You'll give me lots of sons, that's the answer. Turn around. Look down there at the slated house above Waller's Point.'

'I see it.'

'That's Vinny Donovan's place. I remember Vinny when he hadn't an arse to his pants, nothing but a few scrawny fields with rocks and thistles. But he had ten children, eight of them boys. They all stayed together, grew up to be strong young men, mad for work, the harder the better. They made fields out of swamps that only snipe would live in; they rented land here, bought fields there. You know how much they have now? Over 100 acres. That's the way of it, woman. An' that's how we'll do it. We'll walk down there to Lionel Barton one day, me and my own around me, and buy the two big fields that bound on ours.' His gaze was fixed firmly on Barton Hall amid the beech, his lips pressed in a thin line of fierce determination.

'Hugh Dawley, I want you to know this. I am not a brood mare.'

'Ah, now,' the words were a conciliatory whisper. 'I never said anything like that.'

'But you did, Hugh. Is that why you're marrying me, to make me pregnant, year in, year out, until I'm all dried up?'

He shuffled his feet in the heather. A little shower of

seed husks crackled and took flight in the breeze. 'You make it sound all wrong. I never meant anything like that.'

'Then tell me, why are you marrying me?'

The red flush returned to his face. His eyes dropped. 'Because, because, I'm very fond of you. You know that, woman.'

Beth shook her head and sighed. Then in a little surge of affection, she stroked his arm and leaned towards him.

'Do you love me? Tell me.'

The question seemed to grasp him with visible discomfort. He shuffled his feet more vigorously and looked out over the valley. The word *love* and its import were an embarrassment to him, belonging to a world and a lifestyle he had no experience of, and if he had, would never be expressed out loud. Only within a religious context could he frame and speak the responses that spoke of love. In the house he had grown up in, love was never expressed as a declaration of affection. Love, Grandfather Dawley used to say, never saved hay or planted turnips in garden drills.

'Tell me, Hugh.'

'Didn't I tell you, woman? What more do you want? I'm terribly fond of you.'

'I won't marry you, Hugh, unless you tell me you love me. And another thing. Stop calling me "woman". I have a name.'

In Adamston, as long as Beth could remember, they had held what her mother called family conferences, though her father was seldom present. The three of them would sit around the table in the parlour, free their emotions and their problems and speak their aspirations out loud. It was there that Beth first heard about her father's philandering, his eye for a pretty woman and his addiction to the demon drink. As she approached the time set for her wedding, Beth wished that those days were with her again, a time to explore the misgivings and the doubts. But she knew that if she opened up to Roderick, he would seize the opportunity to tell her she was stupid to waste herself on the bogman. Beth turned to Phoebe Jackson.

'The Brigadier,' Phoebe said, 'was a man well travelled and well bred. One would think that such a man, with all his social graces, would have little difficulty about expressing his emotions. But, my dear child, the times he told me that he loved me were few and far between. And when he did, it was with an ulterior motive. You know what I mean, child, don't you?'

Beth smiled and nodded.

'My dear, be careful about love. You see, romance is an invention of us women. It's a fantasy state we build for ourselves when reality sets in and the veil lifts on a humdrum existence. Do I disappoint you?'

'Love is important to me.'

'And to me,' Phoebe responded. 'I hope you find it some day. But first, dear child, find yourself a good man, someone who will care for you and watch over you. And Beth, love might grow from there.'

They were married on Shrove Tuesday in the spring of 1938. Hugh, in his blue serge suit and new brogues, was stricken with a numbing awkwardness. He fumbled and mumbled, tripped over the hem of her wedding dress and banged his knee on the altar tiles when he missed the kneeler. When the ceremony was completed, Joanna Dawley returned home to her chores and Paddy MacAdastair, Hugh's best man, drove them to the railway station to catch the Limerick train. They spent two days in a hotel in the city and sat for their wedding photograph. No amount of cajoling would ever tempt Beth to talk about that two-day honeymoon.

The wedding photograph stood on the mantelpiece above the fireplace in our parlour. The room was a monument to my mother: it contained all the things, material and spiritual, she had inherited from her Adamston home. It was once a partitioned bedroom when Joanna's children were overflowing the cramped house, and when they had gone, was used for storing harness and corn. Over the years my mother had renovated it. The walls were plastered to hide the rough building stones and wainscoting fixed to their lower portion. A window was opened up to look out on Knock Na Sidhe and finally, in the year I was born, the embossed wallpaper, with its Venetian canal scenes, was hung. The paper was a present from Phoebe Jackson.

The woman who looked at me from the sepia-toned photograph on the mantelpiece was beautiful. Even in the picture, with its sombre tones, you could see the sallow skin that lightened the blue eyes and radiated them outward. She was like a Spanish countess, cascading black hair surrounding an oval-shaped face. My father, though he towered over her in the portrait, had no other presence in the room. The moment I walked in, I felt that I was in a hallowed place, a sanctified shrine to my mother's former state. It represented the genteel woman from a different culture, who thought, dreamed and had experiences in a world that was beyond our knowledge. Everything my mother held dear was in that room: the dining table with its claw legs and the inlaid rose pattern in the centre, a pair of Venetian glass bowls, a silver tea service on a tray, and a pair of elephant-shaped mahogany book-ends that stood together because they had nothing to hold between. The table had a hidden drawer; it provided the only reason for my father to enter the room because he kept his money there.

I would sneak a look at her as I passed the window. She was sitting at the table, either reading a book or her bowed head resting on the pillars of her hands. Now and then her eyes would lift and follow the curving canals through the streets of Venice.

Hughie was my parents' first-born. It was tradition that the first son would be named after his father; the diminutive form of the name would be used to distinguish the son from the parent. By an extraordinary coincidence – one that my father would interpret as a sign from the Almighty – Hughie was born on December 24, 1939. That was the day, in 1601, on which the Battle of Kinsale had been fought and lost; it was also my father's birthday and that of Lionel Barton, who now occupied Barton Hall. It was too remarkable to be a mere coincidence, my father would tell us; it was a sign the days of the Bartons were numbered. Those they dispossessed would supplant them. It was the grist in the mill of God's justice grinding out His nemesis.

From where I stood, even as a child, Hughie was the embodiment of maturity. He never talked to me in riddles or mocked my feeble youth, as did Felim. There was an intent look of seriousness about him: in the landscape of his face, in the furrowed brow, the deep-set soulful eyes, the thin-lipped mouth. But until anger swarmed over him or the pain of hurt, he was the gentlest of souls whose loyalty was worn like a cloak, evident and all-embracing. It seemed that he had inherited a set of fundamental values that were as steadfast and unbending as if they had been laid down like old sandstone strata from the beginning of time itself.

Felim, who arrived in February 1941, was our court

jester; he turned our sad sombre moments into ridiculous interpretations of another hue; so ridiculous that we would be forced to smile, not always at his wit but at the gross impossibilities of the analogies he drew. Felim loved to play the fool but was gifted with awesome intelligence. The absorption of learning and the abstraction of knowledge were as easy and natural to Felim as if he was born with those gifts already in place.

He brought with him the flowing golden hair of the ancestral Dawleys. He had the face of a Botticelli model, beautiful and innocent: the physical attributes of a young Greek god, an extraordinary lust for life and the graces to exploit it to the full. How I envied that collection of gifts. When I complained about my shortfall to my mother, she offered me little solace. You had, she said, to play the cards you were dealt with, though all the trumps had been dealt elsewhere.

When I had the sense to make childhood judgements for myself, I concluded that the Dawley family should have been complete when Mona arrived in June 1942. I always knew it would be a struggle for me to find a foothold of my own like the others did. When Mona was born before me, it aggravated my problem. From the day she could reason, Mona placed herself firmly in my mother's corner. She would become the custodian of Cartor values and behaviour, the link from our mother's circuitous route to our hearts and minds.

So close was their relationship, it seemed to me that Mona and my mother were one person. I could sense the way my father tried to puzzle it out, for I think that his affection for his daughter, though sparsely displayed, was greatest. She resembled him most: she had his titian hair colouring and the hard set of his features. Mona inherited his stubbornness, too, and his obdurate allegiance to principle and value. It was all so ironic, for it was those same armaments that she opposed him with and, true to her nature, she went into skirmish and outright battle when the wiser counsel would have been to remain silent. We learned early, as all growing families do, to discover and exploit the potential of sibling foibles. Felim was very adept at that and when he wanted to annoy Mona, he would say in passing, 'You'll never be mistaken for a neighbour's child'.

I would never be a leader in the kingdom of Glenorga; it was my destiny to follow. I became aware of it first when Olly Donnelly and I had a verbal slanging match after a fracas in the schoolyard. He called me the runt of the litter and made it sound as if I had been born with a deformity. I checked it out with Hughie, who berated me for not busting Olly's head and then advised me that, because the world was full of idiots, I should let it in one ear and out the other. Felim, however, had no such diplomacy; he told me in graphic detail what the words meant. The runt of the litter, the dregs left over after the prime ingredients had been used up, was me.

I didn't stack up too well compared to my siblings. I had inherited none of my brothers' physical attributes, the flowing golden hair, or the square-shouldered strength. That early comparison and the shortcomings that I concluded from it would grow to haunt me for years, filling me with self-doubt and dread. It never occurred to me that my mother was right. I simply wished that I had been dealt a different set of cards, and I blamed myself, finding fault with my inadequacies.

The fear was the worst. It could never be expressed in my household; it was a heretical concept in the heroic Dawley inheritance. I was afraid of the dark, fearful of confrontation, frightened of any activity that would lay bare my faults. So I grew up lurking in the verge of the Dawley family, and built for myself a tenuous world of pretence and make-believe. I was alone in the dark sad spaces of my own creation.

The brave seldom suffer. It is a state of confidence and glory, fuelled by recognition and adulation. But the fearful are prone to hazards and are visited by misfortunes. I was a sickly child, thin as a reed and ungainly. I had inherited my father's long arms and his short stubby fingers. I suffered the complement of childhood ailments and a yearly visitation of colds and tonsillitis. My father would look at me with that beetled brow every time I took to the bed and wonder out loud what had gone amiss with my biological composition. Dawley children should not be sickly, but brave, strong and robust. Felim, the eternal comedian, would advise my mother when rumour of some spreading infection had reached Glenorga. 'Put Roddy to bed, Mam, and put sandbags before the door.'

By the time I was six, the routine of our young lives had been established and so too had our individual responses. We were then all at school in Newtown, crossing the flat green field in front of our house called the Nursery because generations of Dawley toddlers had tumbled and learned to walk there. At the end of the field were the stepping-stones over the Morning Star. Mona and Felim skipped over them, agile and sure-footed as mountain goats. Hughie held my hand, guiding my faltering journey from stone to stone. Don't let a drop of water near him, Felim would counsel, or he'll catch pneumonia. When the river flooded and the stepping-stones became immersed, my father would load us on the cart and ferry us over.

There was no road to Glenorga, only a track where horses, carts and people had worn a passage in the ground and exposed the rough stones. We climbed along its margin until we reached the top of the ridge. Then we looked back. Down on the valley floor, my mother was still in the doorway, keeping a distant vigil. We searched the fields until we found where my father was working. He was bent to the soil, our journey unnoticed. Where it tumbled into Lough Cutra, we crossed the stream again. Here there was a makeshift footbridge, a pair of pine logs laid side by side, with a single strand of wire for a handhold. Beneath it the water ran dark and evil. This was Waller's Point were Barton's agent had long ago drowned in his drunken stupor. 'Accident, me arse,' Anton Donovan would later tell me. 'The boys from the mountain got him. Your grandfather and mine amongst them.'

We went along the shore of Lough Cutra; Felim and Mona ahead, Hughie monitoring my progress from the rear. Barton Hall appeared and disappeared in the grove of beech. We kept Knock Na Sidhe on our left-hand side, and dropped down to the village of Newtown where the grey stone school stood gaunt and forbidding under the shadow of Amos Barton's mill. When we crested the ridge and saw the village below us, the fear had returned to me. Every time Miss Horgan asked me a question, though I knew the answer before I had come to her school, a cloud of self-doubt obliterated my reason, words disintegrated into sibilant mumbling and then melted away. I hung my head in token of ignorance.

Once the bell rang, a silent rigorous command took hold of us. It drew us straight to Glenorga and my father's régime of work. It never bothered Hughie for he was a farmer born;

the land was his element. The act of physical labour was like a soothing lullaby that sang to the rhythm of his frenetic hands. It seemed to bother Felim; he would moan and mutter when Hughie hurried us along, but once he was settled to his tasks, the work possessed him too. Mona went to chores with my mother in the farmyard, following the pattern that old Joanna had laid down. But unlike Joanna, neither would ever go to the fields. It was a hard-won dispensation, which my father would dispute time and again, and it led to bitter words and long, rifting silences.

I hated that work regimen. It filled my soul with misery. My hand ached; the pain seared into my brain, but worse was the way my father voiced his silent complaint when he came to check. I had no feel for the chores I was allocated, or strength or skill for the higher order tasks that would relieve the boredom. I would fly myself away in some flight of fancy, make mistakes, miss patches of work, stop altogether with my arms dangling when the fancy wafted me off in its trance. My father would shake me into reality, pull the lobe of my ear or cuff the back of my head. At times I could have hated him, but he was my flesh and blood and hating one's own was a terrible sin. When he left the fields to help with the milking, my heart soared.

We rode home on the workhorse, Hughie driving and I perched in the middle lest I fall off. 'Did he do those things to you and Hughie when ye were my age?'

'Not as bad,' Felim told me.

'Why does he treat me like so?'

'God only knows. Don't worry about it, little brother, we'll all be gone one of these days.'

Hughie reined the horse to a halt. He swivelled round to face us, steely resolve in the clenched jawline. 'No,' he said fiercely. 'We won't be gone. We'll all be here, working this land together. Some day we'll own all the fields down there,' he swung his free hand in the direction of Barton Hall. 'So stop talking about going away, Felim, you hear me?'

Felim cackled in derision. 'Well bless my soul, but we have another one. Another believer in that ould fairytale. I thought there was only one madman in our house.'

Hughie's face paled as if it were an undercoat for the sudden onrush of blood red that replaced it. 'Felim, don't you mock our father. Don't make fun of what he believes. And something else, smart man, don't you worry about Roddy. I'll take care of him.'

Hughie looked softly at me and winked as if the moment was for us alone.

Chapter 2

Once a week my father crossed the stepping stones to MacAdastair's where neighbours gathered to play cards. On Sunday evening he walked to Luke Heaney's public house in Newtown and returned as the wall clock was chiming the midnight hour. Every other night he went to bed when he had eaten and had checked the animals in the outhouse.

Once he had gone, it seemed a veil had lifted from the kitchen. Wednesday was family conference day and we sat around the table in the parlour. On these occasions, I felt I was in a magical cocoon of warmth and affection, in the embrace of my mother's smile and her gentle words. It was a place without chiding complaint or silent criticism; I could feel its tentacles loosing the bindings that fettered me to fear. My mother retraced for us the journeys of Cartor summers and told us it was our duty to follow in her footsteps. We journeyed with her to the Loire Valley: the bull-run in Pamplona, Lombardy Plain, the rumbling cascades at Rhinfalls. And we always finished in Venice, riding a gondola across the pattern of her wallpaper.

But it was more a journey of mind and soul, not a lesson in geography. Its intention was to give us wings, to open up other vistas for life than that single vision of my father's perspective. My mother never criticised him, or cast an aspersion on his scheme for us. She simply presented the obverse of the coin, shining and pristine. It was the Cartor way of smelling the roses: music, books, verses of poetry, knowledge and the way of truth.

'Mam, what's my real name?'

'Roderick. You were christened Roderick Jackson Dawley.'

'You shouldn't have done it, Mam,' Felim interrupted. 'Making him go around with a name like that.'

'Never mind Felim, Roderick. They are wonderful names, borne by two great people.'

'There were many other names you could have chosen from,' Hughie said quietly.

'Phoebe Jackson was a dear friend. I honoured her the only way I could.'

'But, Mam, if my name is Roderick, why does everyone call me Roddy?'

'Because we're afraid,' Felim answered. 'You see Roddy, our father never liked Mam's brother. It was he who started to call you Roddy because he couldn't bear to say the full name. And none of us had the guts to do anything different.'

'I'm not afraid,' Hughie said.

'Then if you're so brave, why do you call him Roddy?'

'Because Mona, I don't like the name Roderick either. No Dawley, as far back as you can go, was ever called that name. Satisfied?

'No. You're going against Mam and the rest of us. We're supposed to stick together.'

'I've a mind of my own.'

'Of course you have, Hughie,' my mother agreed. 'It's important for all of us to understand that. We have to be tolerant of each other, Mona, and appreciate different points of view. But we must also support each other, love each other. And when the time comes for all of us to leave Glenorga, we will have laid down here in this parlour the principles for life and living that will help us cope with the world outside.'

We walked to mass on Sunday mornings, the same route as travelled to school. We would start together but as we climbed the ridge above the Morning Star we were strung out like weary remnants of a vanquished force. My father, with his long steps and sloping gait, was almost 100 yards ahead by the time we arrived at the village. The same pattern would be repeated on the way home. By the time we arrived in the kitchen, my father was heading to the fields in his working-day garb. I would hail him when the midday meal was ready and once he had eaten he would go to bed.

It was that Sunday pattern that first alerted me to what seemed amiss in my parents' relationship. Sunday was family day; the folk of the mountain and the people in the lowlands observed it with all its Sabbath overtones. They came to church in the bosom of one another, husbands and wives side by side, their children around them. My father was abed when his neighbours were cycling to hurling matches, taking the trap cart to visit relatives, or walking their fields.

'We'll climb up to Knocknastumpa,' Mona said, 'and pick wild strawberries.'

'And watch people going the road,' I added. 'We can count the bicycles and the trap carts.'

'Can't wait,' Felim sighed. 'Mam, why don't we have bicycles like everybody else? Then we could go on all the trips that you and Roderick used make.'

'Wouldn't it be lovely?' my mother replied wistfully. 'But who knows, Felim, maybe some day.'

'Oh sure. Some day we'll wake up and they'll be waiting for us outside the front door.'

'You'll pass yourself out some day, Felim, you're so

bloody smart,' Mona told him

'Mam, can I go swimming?'

When the weather was warm, we returned from Knocknastumpa by the head weir. It was built to contain the silt and the sand that the Morning Star collected on its way from the summit of Mount Fierna and was another of Barton's projects during the famine relief schemes. The ice age river had forged a ravine through the sandstone; its walls rose twenty feet over the water level, and above the weir, had formed a deep pool that was shot with slanting sunrays and was the colour of gunmetal. We called it the Blue Pool. Generations of mountain folk had bathed there in the warm evenings of summer. In the generation before mine, Robert Kilraish had drowned there. His body was never found.

'I worry about you all when you go swimming there. Something about that Blue Pool unnerves me.'

'Don't worry, Mam,' Hughie said. 'We're all good swimmers. I'll teach Roddy. 'Tis time he learned.'

'Yeah, Mam,' Felim added, 'let him go. His health is much better, he hasn't been sick for a couple of hours.'

'Okay, we'll go to Knocknastumpa first. Then we'll return by the pool. Now who learned the poem?' My mother transcribed poetry from memory, laying it out in copperplate handwriting.

'I did,' Felim said.

'Good man. Now don't gallop through it. Slowly, Felim. The rest of you listen to the music of the words and the rhythm. Try and imagine what the poet describes. Off you go.'

The words came tumbling out; Felim's mind had travelled to the next piece of imagery, before he had fully voiced the one before.

'I bear fresh showers for the thirsting flowers ...'

'Stop, Felim, stop,' my mother said. 'Announce the poem, please, and the author.'

Felim looked to heaven. He then stood up, adopted an exaggerated oratorical pose and a dramatic accent.

'"The Cloud," by Percy Bysshe Shelley:

I bring fresh showers for the thirsting flowers
From the seas and the streams;
I bear light shade for the leaves when laid
In their noonday dreams.
From my wings are shaken the dews that waken
The sweet birds every one,
When rocked to rest on their mother's breast
As she dances about the sun.'

The times we swam together in the Blue Pool were the closest we ever were. In the beginning, until we had developed skill in the water, my mother watched us from the knoll above the pool. I wondered why she feared it because it was such a beautiful place. We swam in the nude. It seemed a natural state, like when one of us was bathed in the zinc tub on Saturday night and the rest gathered around with the open faces of unabashed scrutiny. Twenty paces from the opening to the pool, the clothes would be cast off and the three took off in unison, stalled for a moment in hovering grace at the edge, and then dived headlong into the water. Hughie swam with muscular strokes. Mona headed for the deeper part, turned on her back and floated gracefully. Both were good in the water but beside Felim they looked ungainly. Felim had the quick languid movements of a creature in its natural habitat. The water was his ether and he exulted in it.

29

TOM NESTOR

The water scared the daylights out of me. The Blue Pool, with its dark sheen and the silent malevolence on its glassy surface, filled me with foreboding. When the water reached my knees, the breath froze in my rib cage and my heart stood still in abject terror. I cursed myself for wanting to come there, as if I was lured by the mesmeric pull of yearning. I went because Hughie told me that the only way to alleviate fear was to confront it. And I wanted to emulate the others and to show them that I had graduated from the periphery into the centre of their circle.

I floundered and spluttered and clung to Hughie with the taloned fingers of terror. He fashioned a sheaf of rushes, laid my belly across it and waded me over the steel-blue surface. In time I learned to drive the sheaf with arms and legs and weave a circuitous journey around the rim of the wider parts.

Time came when Mother stopped watching out for us. While we frolicked in the pool, she went by the pathway above the gorge into the woodland that grew along its edge. I wondered where she had gone. Mam needs her solitude, Mona told me; it is her way of escaping, and God knows she has enough to escape from. I didn't understand what Mona meant but the tone of her voice told me not to probe further. It became a further doubt about my parents' relationship.

'Pity we ever have to go home, I feel so happy here. Why can't it always be like this?'

'Because we can't always be happy, Mona,' Hughie told her. 'The world isn't made like that. Grow up.'

'If I could, I'd freeze this moment now. I'd take it with me and live in it for all time. Far away from here.'

'Not me,' Felim said. 'I'd stay here forever and a day. Down there in the pool, under the water. You know, Mona, if I could choose, that is the way I'd die. I'd dive in there,

THE BLUE POOL

down to the very bottom. I'd lie there on my back, feeling the water around me and listen for the music it plays in my ears.'

'Don't be stupid. It's a sin to say things like that.'

'Trouble with you, Hughie, you have no soul. I don't care whether it's a sin or not, that's the way I'd like to go.'

'Felim, you should have been born a fish.'

'Now why didn't the parents think of that?'

'Speaking about parents, Felim, why did we get our father? That God up there. He's supposed to be kind and loving.'

'Shut up, Mona. You shouldn't be talking like that in front of Roddy.'

'Why not? He's going to find out sooner or later. It's funny, isn't it? In all the houses in Glenorga and Mount Fierna, the marriages were arranged. We have the only parents who married for love. Riddle me that, Felim, you who knows everything.'

'Hughie is right, Mona. We shouldn't talk about things like that.'

'Okay so. Then let me tell you something very embarrassing.'

'You couldn't embarrass me, Mona.'

'Bet I could. I love you all. I love you, strong brother Hughie, smart brother Felim, small brother Roddy.'

Hughie lifted his eyes to heaven. Felim looked sheepish. And I felt a tingling warm glow that started at the base of my spine and touched the nerves of my soul.

I broke my leg on St Stephen's Day when I was ten years old. We returned from mass and were having tea in the kitchen when the bugle sounded. My father's face clouded over, he ordered us to follow him. He grabbed a slash-hook from the outhouse, signalled my brothers to where the pitchforks stood and raced across the stepping-stones. By the time we reached Barton's stone wall the beagles were already through and the horses were milling before jumping across. They halted in confusion when we barred their way into our land.

Then Lionel Barton came forward. I had never seen him that close before. He looked resplendent, like a picture of a cavalry officer I had seen in a book that my mother kept in the parlour trunk. He was wearing a red riding jacket with brass buttons; with a pattern of dull stains where the colour had faded. The rest of the regalia looked rich and elegant: the high boots with silver spurs, the silk cravat and gold pin, the frilled shirt sleeves that peeked out from the sleeves of the jacket. But the horse was a disappointing dappled grey. It was more like a charger than a hunter.

'Mr Dawley,' Barton said, 'would you please move out of the way?'

'Barton, you jacked-up ruffian. Come across that wall and I'll cut you off at the knees.'

'An' you'll get this in your guts,' Hughie said.

'Mr Dawley ...' Barton began again until silenced by Felim.

'How dare you patronise us with that Mister shit. Use our surname like your kind always did when you wanted to distinguish one of us from general rebellious scum.'

'Dawley,' Barton dismissed the niceties, 'I have a perfect right to hunt over your land. I insist on it. Otherwise, I'll have the force of law on you.'

My father laughed; it was dispassionate and fearful. He held up the slash-hook and aimed the cutting blade at Barton's crotch.

'This, Barton, is the law. You should know that. This is

what your kind used on my ancestors for 500 years. Now get the hell away from my land and if you ever try and come in here again, I'll sink this in your skull.'

Two other huntsmen rode forward. One was Alfie Osborne, the whipper-in; he looked after the kennels and controlled the hunting pack. The other was Ferdy Grimes, a neighbour from the lowlands.

'Hugh, for God's sake,' Grimes began. 'Stop this nonsense. Let us through.'

'Shag off, Grimes,' my father shouted, 'you jumped up arse-licker. Far away from fox hunting you were reared and your people before you. You're a traitor, aping those who shat down on us for generations.'

'Those days are gone, Hugh,' Grimes dropped the reins and opened his arms in a placatory gesture. 'Lionel Barton is a decent man and a Catholic like the rest of us.'

'Does the leopard change his spots?'

The Bartons had converted to Catholicism in the early 1920s. They were received with open triumphalism by the clergy and all but the folk of the mountain, who condemned the conversion as simple expediency. The great houses were being attacked and burned, the remnants of the landlord class hounded out. The Barton conversion was simply a device to protect their estate. Soon after the conversion, the old church was renovated and pews funded by individual donation. My grandfather donated three pounds, a lot of money in those times; he was granted a seat in the middle of the short aisle. Barton's contribution must have been enormous because their pew was placed inside the altar rails. Then, to chafe the wound further, the Bartons rode to church in a carriage drawn by four matching greys with a dalmatian running at each side of the vehicle. The Dawleys never again donated to a church collection.

Osborne spurred forward to breast the wall. Then he pulled his horse about to face the pack of horsemen. He raised his crop in the air.

'Are we going to stand here and be bested by a country gom and his half-arsed brats? I'm going over. Who's with me?'

A murmur of approval rose from the horsemen and swelled to a roar of accord.

'Say the word, Mr Lionel, and we'll run them down.'

'I don't want this confrontation. Look men, there are over 1,000 acres in my estate. Enough I should think to give us better sport than those paltry little fields. Call back the dogs, Osborne.'

The bugle sounded. Across the Morning Star the beagles churned in dilemma and the pack melted over the wall. The huntsmen followed in their wake. My father threw down the slash-hook and embraced his sons. It was the only time I would ever see him make such a blatant show of affection.

'Good boys, good boys,' he said over and over. 'Hughie, I thought you were going to stick the great Mr Barton. Jaysus, Felim, you nearly knocked him off his horse with those words of yours.' Then he turned to me. 'You cowardly little shite arse. Hadn't a word to say for yourself, did you?'

It was a holy day, so father went to bed after the midday meal. I slipped away and followed the direction of the hunting horn that sounded in the bowl of the valley. The hunt and its dashing riders fascinated me. They were the epitome of splendour and its inheritance of gracious living. It was a glimpse of another world.

My mother had shaken her head in wistful silence when I told her about the morning's episode. We had embar-rassed a decent man, she told me, made him lose face in the company of his peers. Lionel Barton was host to relatives and friends who had come from abroad to spend Christmas in his home. And we, the Dawleys, had shown ourselves to be no more than ignorant peasants.

I ran along the laneway that once led to de Val's chapel of ease. It was now kept open by Barton's cattle, which used the watering trough beside the ruin. Round the bend of the laneway I suddenly found myself ahead of the beagle pack that had lost the scent and was aimlessly sniffing about. The lead dog started to trot in my direction and then the whole pack swarmed towards me. I panicked, dashed back the way I had come, tried to scale the boundary wall and fell backwards. I thought I heard a bone crack before the pain crushed me like a vice and darkness swept it away.

When I awoke again, Barton and Osborne had carried me into our kitchen and had laid me on the table. I could hear someone screaming and then realised it was me. Then my father opened the stairway door and entered the room with a black glower that filled me with fear before the pain drowned its gathering dread.

'It's the femur bone,' Barton said. 'The boy must be brought to a hospital. Osborne and I will carry him down to Barton Hall, and take him there. You will accompany us, of course.'

My father fixed Barton with an icy stare. 'He's my son, Barton. I want no favours from you. I'll do what I think fit. But just tell me this. Where did you find him?'

'We were riding by the boundary wall.'

'Where did you find him, I asked you? Your side or mine?'

'Your side. Must have slipped and fell against a boulder. Look, Mr Dawley, we'd better be moving.'

'Thank you for bringing him home. Now would you

please leave? I know what to do with my son.'

'Oh, for Christ's sake,' Osborne interjected, 'the boy needs medical attention immediately.'

My father spread his palms outwards as if he were shooing the cat from the milk tankard. 'Did you hear what I said?'

'Mrs Dawley,' Barton implored, 'please. At least bring him to a doctor.' Then he took Osborne by the arm and led him away.

I was loaded on the cart and driven to Knocknastumpa. We went down to where Black Pat Farrell, the bonesetter, lived. My father would have none of my mother's pleadings; this was the way broken bones were fixed in the tradition of the mountain. Black Pat was better than any doctor, he said. We finally found him in Heaney's public house, a hirsute, sinewy man with darting eyes.

'Isn't that a strange thing,' he said, 'all the bones that do be broke of a Sundy? A man can't go for a drink, but he's wanted. Bring him into the parlour.'

Black Pat prodded my thigh when they laid me on the table. I could get the sour smell of drink. My mother must have smelled it too.

'Hugh, Hugh,' she began.

'Shush, woman, shush,' my father told her.

''Tis a clean break,' Black Pat pronounced. 'Missus, will you go out and ask Luke Heaney to get me a couple of laths for a splint. An' the tail of an oul' shirt to wrap around them. Now,' he said, when my mother had gone, 'you hould the boy down, Hugh. I'm going to have to pull the broken pieces together and this is going to hurt. Are you ready?'

The pain arched my back and made me scream until the blackness swept it away. The journey home in the cart was a nightmarish trek through a black cavernous country inhabited by ghouls and their packs of slavering dogs whose fangs were tearing at my thigh.

Hughie fashioned me a set of crude crutches and I grew adept at using them. My father spoke little to me in the aftermath of the accident, but I would catch him looking at me in that suspicious way of his, as if some devious action of mine was responsible for my plight. Felim and Mona frequently questioned me about the circumstances of my accident. What side of the wall was I really at when I fell and why would Barton be so concerned for me?

I was alone with my mother for long periods as my leg healed. I had built her up to be a creature of loveliness who blessed our childhood with the pure spirit of her being. But in the times when we were alone, she wasn't like that. Her words for me were as rare as my father's. She sat for long periods at the foot of the table, her head in her hands, a detached, vacant look in her face when she took them away. Then again she would rummage in the drawer of the dresser where she kept her sewing, find a book and bring it with her into the parlour. She smiled little and she crushed her fingers until the joints creaked.

'Mam, Mam, are you sick?'

'No,' she answered me pettishly, 'I am not sick.'

'Then why are you sad?'

'Stop bothering me, Roddy. You don't know what you're talking about.'

I was seeing, I thought, the dark side of my mother's moon. It was a state I never knew existed. It seemed, as I sat with my leg on the milking stool, that she had placed me in the farthest reaches of her orbit, away from my brothers and sister upon whom some rays of brightness always fell.

Mona understood those facets of my mother's moods. She had become like an acolyte that hearkened and responded to every turn and twist of my mother's thoughts and needs. It was Mona who did the work in the farmyard and the kitchen. But more, she did it as if every chore was an outcome of her special vocation.

When the time came to cast away the crutches, the limp appeared. At first I thought that it was the result of my leg's inactivity and it would right itself once the muscles strengthened. But the limp grew more noticeable and, however I tried, I could not stand fully erect.

'Stand up straight,' my father yelled. He would place his great red hand against my forehead, the other against the small of my back and force my spine rigid. But it reverted again as soon as he took his hands away.

'You're not trying,' he shouted.

'He's doing his best,' Hughie intervened.

'Who asked you? Stand up, I said.'

'Hugh, there's something wrong.'

'There's nothing wrong woman, only shaggin' laziness. I broke my leg when I was his age. Do you see me with a limp?'

'We should take him to a doctor. We should have done that in the first place.'

'Oh, have it your own way.'

My mother brought me on the carrier of Maisie Hanley's bicycle to see the doctor in Adamston. He was an old friend of the Cartors.

'Walk up and down the room,' he told me. I watched his face as I made the circuit of his surgery. He looked the picture of kindness. But as I walked, the smile faded.

'He broke his leg, Dr Hughes,' my mother offered.

'I can see that. And ye had it set. Black Pat Farrell, I

presume?'

My mother nodded, and the doctor's forehead became a web of furrows. Then he put me lying on the couch and examined my leg.

'Jesus, Beth,' he said suddenly, 'how could you let that fool Farrell do this.'

'Is it bad, doctor?'

'Bad is hardly the word. Criminal's more like it. I wouldn't let Black Pat near my dog! Sit up, son,' he told me. 'The break has knitted badly. This muscle,' he jabbed at my thigh, 'is wasting. So we now have the right leg growing shorter.'

My mother averted her eyes. 'Don't blame me, doctor,' she pleaded.

'I'm not blaming you, Beth. I'm blaming the credo of the mountain. *Don't go near doctors, they're all robbers. The old ways are best.* Such stupid nonsense.'

'What can we do? Can you do something for him?'

Dr Hughes shook his head, and sat behind his desk.

'Beth, I can't. This is a job for an orthopaedic man. That leg needs surgery now. There is a man in Dublin I know well, an excellent surgeon. I'll arrange it for you.'

I could see my mother struggling with the suggestion.

'Would it cost a lot of money?' I asked.

'Well, there will be some cost, of course, but you'll get some help from the social services. But, Beth, I don't think money should come into it.'

'Easy for you to say,' my mother said sharply, 'you don't know what it's like up there. An' it isn't all about a shortage of money. Doctor, will the limp get worse?'

The doctor nodded and sighed. 'It will get worse. As long as the boy, what did you say his name was …'

'Roderick. They call him Roddy.'

'As long as Roddy's natural body growth is taking place. Then it will stabilise, but the limp will be quite severe by then. If you and your husband decide not to avail of surgery, then I suggest that you have a special boot made for him with a raised heel. It will help to minimise the physical appearance of the limp. Whatever you decide to do, Beth, good luck to you. And good luck to you too, Roddy.' He walked us to the door. 'Bring him back to me in a year's time, Beth. Who knows what medical science might have accomplished by then?'

I never did go back. When we left the bicycle at the gable of Hanley's house, my mother strode towards the mountain, berating me for not keeping up. She cast aside her sadness and my infirmity as if neither existed. Perhaps it was the only way she could cope with our mutual predicament. Once she stopped, turned back to look at my limping progress and said, 'I brought four children into the world. Every one born without a blemish.' I followed on, knowing suddenly that she was telling me it was I who was at fault. I resolved that I would never seek sympathy for my crippled foot; I would compete and work myself back into the core of the circle no matter how difficult it might be. The visit to the doctor was never again spoken of.

A short time later Hughie brought home a letter from Miss Horgan, the schoolteacher. We were finishing off the evening meal; my father had blessed himself and was silently saying grace when Hughie presented the envelope to my mother. She put it in the dresser drawer where she kept her sewing.

'What's the letter about?' my father asked.

'I suppose it has something to do with Hughie,' my mother said.

'If it has, then don't you think I have a right to know? I'm his father.'

My mother retrieved the letter from the drawer and held it out to him.

'Read it, woman.'

She sat at the far end of the table. Felim moved closer while he continued to wind adhesive tape around the grip of his hurling stick.

'Read it,' my father said again.

'Dear Mrs Dawley, I wrote to you a few weeks ago about Hughie and had no reply so I imagine my letter got mislaid somewhere. What I wanted to say is ...'

'Dear Mrs Dawley,' my father scoffed. 'Am I to be shut out when it comes to my children? Go on, woman. Read.'

'As I mentioned to you before, your son Hughie is an intelligent boy and is particularly strong in mathematics. I think that we were more than justified keeping him at school for that extra period. I know the boy's heart is set on farming but I would suggest to you that he remain in education for a few more years. I have no doubt but that he would win a scholarship to an agricultural college or he could enrol in the new Vocational School in Adamston. In either event, further learning would be beneficial to him. I have always maintained education is just as important for persons in farming as in any other walk of life. If you need to talk to me further about it we could arrange to meet again after mass in Newtown. Yours sincerely, Helena Horgan, N.T.'

The silence descended on the room as if it were being lowered by a pulley. I watched my father's face. I saw the titian afterglow spread out and down to his eyebrows, the jawline hardening. I heard the molars grinding.

'The bitch. The interfering bitch.'

41

'Hugh, she's only trying to be helpful.'

'Sure she is. Whose brilliant idea was it, tell me, for Hughie to stay on for another year?'

'It was mine,' Hughie said quietly.

'Was it now, my smart man? Did you suggest it, mister, or were you primed?'

'I was asked and I thought it was a good idea. What difference does a year make?'

'What difference does it make?' He bounded up from the chair and went to tower over Hughie. 'You could be in the fields with me. I was out there, without a sinner to help, and you off wasting in that blasted school.' He turned and glared at my mother, the clenched fists like the maw of a terrible pincers. For a moment I thought he was going to make a drive at my mother; Felim grasped the hurling stick in his favoured left hand.

'There's a pair of ye in it, isn't there? You and the goddamn teacher bitch, plotting and scheming behind my back. That's what you've been doing since the day these children were born. Well, let me tell you this. No one in this house, or in any other house, is going to best me. Understand this about my sons. Their place is out there in the fields beside their father.'

He turned towards Hughie again. My father's face had softened; he stretched out an arm as if he were going to lay it on his son's shoulder. 'Hughie, tomorrow morning, you go down to the school and tell that woman you're finished.'

'Dad,' Hughie began. The word sounded strange, unfamiliar, even uncomfortable. We seldom used it for it carried within it a preface of affection that was never donated to my father. 'I hear you. Now would you listen to me?'

My father's head moved sideways. 'What is it?'

'I want to work on the land with you. But I think Miss

42

Horgan is right. I'd like to go to the Technical School in Adamston because I could learn a lot of useful things there.'

'Stop,' my father dismissed him with a wave of his hand. 'What is there in working the land, only work? Go down and tell her you're leaving.'

'Why don't you listen to him, Hugh?' Mother suggested.

'Listen to him?' my father scoffed. 'Listen to you, you mean, to the things you have planted in his head?'

'No,' Hughie said with equanimity, 'you're wrong. I'll make up my own mind. I want to work on the land but I want to go with the times. There are new ways coming into farming, better ways.'

'What are you talking about?'

'The tractor, other kinds of machinery.'

'Yerra, have sense, in the name of God, what would we be doing with a tractor? Where would we be getting the money?'

'A tractor could do the work of twenty men and ten horses. The two of us could work 200 acres.'

My father stopped glaring and the tension seemed to ooze from his angular frame.

'Where would we get the money?'

'We'll get it. Borrow, work for it, whatever it takes.'

My father never borrowed money. It was a creed cast in rock, like the tenets of his religion. But all principles can be bought for the fulfilment of a great ambition. He had allowed the tractor to pass through the filter of his values and had silently compromised.

'Is it all right so?' my mother asked as my father moved towards the doorway beneath the stairs. He turned around and ran his gaze over his assembled family.

'Have it yeer own way. Who ever listened to me in this house?'

43

Chapter 3

I had always known fear. It had its foundation in the time when I was a sickly child. Then I feared I would die and that my soul would burn in hell for the sins I had committed in the silence of my mind. I was terrified of the dark. Every manifestation of nature's power filled me with dread: thunder and lightning, storms howling around the eaves, floodwaters from the Morning Star lapping our back door.

When I grew older, the fear changed course. I became conscious of my own limitations and wallowed in misery when events proved me right. I think Miss Horgan understood me better than most, apart from Hughie; certainly better than my father, in whose world there was no psychology, or my mother, who acknowledged only the beauty of intellect and mind. Miss Horgan told me that a gammy leg was no excuse for second-rate performance, and it should be the spur that motivated me. Otherwise my fear of failure would always impede the option of winning.

I resolved to compete and the resolution was short-lived. I tried to help in the fields but my father rejected me with a downcast shake of the head as I lagged behind him and my brothers. When I stopped going, he never questioned my absence. But once, when he came into the kitchen where I was studying alone, he pointed to my book and asked, 'What's it about?'

'It's about Leonidas, the king of Sparta.'

'Ah,' he beamed, 'the man who held the pass against the Persians. What was the name of the place again?'

'Thermopylae,' I told him, my amazement prevalent in the word. 'How do you know that?'

My father's face lit up in the manner of a man who has bared some discovery for another. 'It was in my school reader too. An' I never forgot it. Listen, boy, I think you should stick to the books. You are not cut out for the land. Leave that for the rest of us.'

I wanted to follow him out the kitchen door and tell him he was wrong. I had no wish to make my way in a world outside Glenorga. I couldn't really articulate what I felt but the valley and its landmarks filled me with a special yearning. And I was being cast out, all because of my physical handicap.

Sometimes I would accompany Hughie when he worked alone, but he didn't want me either. I slowed him down. He shared my father's summation of my worth.

Whatever ambition I had about becoming a fit candidate to work beside my brothers on the land was shattered by one defining event. We were bringing cattle from our highest field near Knocknastumpa to winter in the sheltered pasture of the valley. An obstreperous heifer, due to calve in the spring, had made several attempts to return to the summit and the company of a few hardy steers.

'Stay close to 'em,' my father kept on shouting at me, 'don't let 'em turn on you.'

We had passed the overhang of the gorge when the heifer made a last attempt to escape. It was well timed for the track had widened and so had the space between the heifer and me. She wheeled and then kicked off on her hind legs, as if this was a ploy well practised. I tried to cut her off, but once out in open space I was no match for her speed. She passed me in a blur, sending clods of earth and sphagnum in her wake.

'Stop her, stop her,' my father shouted; 'run for Christ's sake.'

Before I had reached the peak of my shambling run, disaster struck. One moment the heifer was galloping to freedom. The next she was tumbling in mid-air, as she fell to the bottom of the gorge. I heard the deep thud against the rock outcrop and then the splash as she hit the water.

'Jesus,' I heard my father say, 'sweet Jesus in heaven, what have you done?' He went slithering down the side of the gorge and I made to follow him. 'Stay where you are. Haven't you done enough damage for one day?'

I sat on a boulder, awash in a sea of dread and misery. It wasn't my fault; even Felim or Hughie couldn't have stopped that stampeding heifer. But fear always filled me with self-doubt and a willingness to absorb blame like a spate of mental flagellation. When my father returned, I knew instantly by the black scowl and the clenched teeth that the worst had befallen.

'Is she all right?' I blurted.

'Is she all right? Jesus Christ, what kind of an idiot are you? You saw her fall down there with your own two eyes. Dead. The finest heifer I ever clapped eyes on. Neck broke. Only fit now for the knacker's yard.' Then he suddenly stopped and came back to me. 'I don't blame you,' he said. For a moment a single sliver of hope pierced the gloom. 'I blame myself. What class of an eegit was I to let you help me? Don't ever offer to help me again.'

I wanted to hate him, to give vent to the surge of detestation that welled up inside me. But I had learned that such feelings were sinful and that the person who harboured them would be visited with great afflictions.

Hell. The greatest fear of all. A place of eternal fire, where the souls of the damned writhed in agony for every minute of every day, without end. I awoke at night in a cold sweat for I had seen the raging fires in my sleep. You could go to hell for any mortal sin – like hating your father, thinking unchaste thoughts, straying into the grounds of a Protestant church. The lesser, venal sins – lying, cheating and swearing – deserved a place called limbo, a kind of holding ground where the same fires raged until the suffering had shriven the soul and made it clean again.

By the time I was eleven I knew that things were amiss between my father and mother. They seldom spoke and no longer walked the fields together. But the greatest testimony to their sundered relationship was that they occupied separate bedrooms. Mona slept with my mother; and my father in the room upstairs. The door to my mother's room was kept locked. Sometimes when he came late from Heaney's public house, my father would try to push the door inward with his shoulder and order Mona to go and sleep upstairs.

'I have rights, woman,' I heard him say, 'an' you have your duty. Open the door this minute.'

'Go away, Hugh, you have drink taken. You'll wake the whole house.'

'Shag the house. Every man on this mountain sleeps with his wife.'

Then the pounding would start. But in the end he would tire and I would hear his weary footsteps wending a way as they receded up the stairway to the loft. No one spoke about those visits. Nor would we speak about it in the parlour where all subjects were encouraged and all mysteries open for scrutiny.

The incident with the heifer set me on an course far from my resolution to prove myself on the land. From then on I ran free and followed a pattern of behaviour that was as remote from mountain lifestyle as Mars from Earth.

I took up with Mikey Kilraish, who taught me how to swim. It was easy to learn in his company for I wasn't cowed, as I was in the presence of my brothers and sister. He cast away the raft of rushes, took me out to the deepest part and threw me in. I threshed like a wallowing hippopotamus and discovered that it made me stay afloat. Swimming, Mikey said, was like riding a bicycle. You discover you can balance the machine and you were away. I had finally mastered the fear that used to suck the breath from my body when the water reached above my thighs.

'I want to show you something,' Mikey said when I grew adept. 'See that lump of rock at the far side. Below that there's a cave. Come on. We'll have to swim underwater to get in.'

The great river that flowed down from the mountain and through the gorge had carved a shelf of sandstone like an ancient megalith. Behind the stone barrier the river had eroded inward, making a cavern beneath the sandstone strata. Mikey was standing on the floor of the cavern when I followed him in. He was grinning like a Cheshire cat, as if he had led me to an Aladdin's cave.

I stood there open-mouthed, gaping at this miniature cathedral beneath the sandstone. A trio of stalactites had worked down from the domed roof to the floor like suspended Doric columns. All along the walls the swirling water had pockmarked the stone like the picture of a moon-scape in Felim's reader. I could only stare and wonder at this place, puzzling in my mind why I had been selected to see and appreciate it.

Then Mikey guided me to a rock shelf at the rear of the cave. The light was weaker there and I had to peer forward to focus on what he was pointing to. There on the shelf, fixed in position by a declivity, was a human skeleton. Suddenly the wonder of the place fled my consciousness in a rush of invading fear. This was the reality of dreadful nightmares in the blackness of sporadic sleep, the inside of a tomb. I filled my lungs with great mouthfuls of air, head-ed for the brighter light at the entrance to the cavern and swam back into the pool.

'Scaredy cat,' Mikey said when we were putting on our clothes, 'did you never see a skeleton before?'

I shook my head. My teeth were chattering.

'I seen loads.' Mikey shrugged in mock bravado. 'The Bartons have a big vault behind the house with a wide crack in the door and you can see in. Some of the coffins are broken and the skeletons are falling out. I'll show you if you want.'

'I don't want to.'

'There's no call to be frightened about that oul' skeleton in there. That's only me Uncle Robert.'

'Your uncle,' I echoed aghast, 'and you never told any-one about it?'

'Why should I?' he said sharply, as if he resented the implied accusation. 'All I ever got from that fella was a clip on the ear and a root up the arse. I never liked him.'

''Tis wrong. He should get a Christian burial. His rela-tions should be told.'

'Go along our' that, will you,' Mikey berated me. 'He's

well forgotten by now. An' anyway, haven't you seen the cut of him yourself? He's inside there, lookin' the picture of comfort, and half a smile still on his oul' face.' He wagged a finger at me and moved a step closer. 'An' don't you be tellin' anyone that we found him.'

Mikey was surely bound for hell and because I liked him I made supplication for his mortal soul. He said no prayers, and never went to confession. Once he told me that he had no respect for his father whom he called a right oul' shite. If it weren't for the law that forced him to attend, he would never go to school either. What good would geography and bits of Irish and sums be to him on an English building site?

Mikey had the face of angel innocence and a crop of curling blond hair that tumbled over his forehead. My mother didn't like him. The Kilraishes had a bad reputation among folk of the mountain. The parents had raised a squall of children: fourteen still living, three who had died in childbirth. The first four had been born out of wedlock, and it was only the threats of a visiting missionary priest that persuaded the parents to satisfy and sanctify their union in the eyes of mother church.

The Kilraish house was on the side of Mount Fierna facing north. Until I got to know them better, I thought that the state of constant war that existed between Long Pat and Lena Kilraish was simply a device that emphasised, through deliberate contradiction, their compatibility with one another. They spoke through me, using me as the conduit to poke derision at one another. While he whittled and littered the stone floor with wood shavings, Long Pat would casually tell me that a woman in Newtown had set her cap at him. Lena would whirl from the fire that she was

tending, and dart to where I was sitting, with the light of
battle in her eyes.

'Will you listen to him, Roddy Dawley? Wouldn't you
think that every woman was dropping her knickers 100
yards away from him? An' do you know the truth of it?
He's past it.'

I misinterpreted the banter and the byplay and failed to
see the vicious intent behind Long Pat's façade. It puzzled
me that Mikey saw both his parents as an embarrassment. I
asked why he always criticised his father and never referred
to his mother.

'Is it codding me you are?' Mikey said. 'My oul' fella? I
don't think he knows I exist. He's time for no one but himself.'

'But he doesn't beat or give out to you. You can come
and go as you like. He must be very fond of you.'

'Jaysus, Roddy, talk sense. I don't want him to be fond
of me, you hear me? He's a laughing stock, himself and my
mother. You haven't an idea what goes on in that house
when there's no one to hear them.' Then he smiled, as if he
had knowledge far superior to my probing innocence. 'But
my mother now. She's very fond of you. "That Roddy
Dawley,"' Mikey mimicked Lena's sibilant inflection. '"Isn't
he the grand young man? Do you hear me talking to you,
Long Pat Kilraish? A lovely young boy, quiet and refined".'

'Go way our' that, Mikey.' I could feel my face redden.

'Look at him, blushin' all over. An' you know why she
says that? She fancied your father, long time ago.'

Lena Kilraish had been in service in Barton Hall and,
according to folklore, could have her choice of eligible farmers' sons.

Lena Kilraish and my father though? That wanton

sinner, that bitch in heat, as Felim described her when I sought verification for the stories that abounded. Every Tom, Dick and Harry had had a cut off her. How dare she be associated with my father.

'My father never had anything to do with your mother. He wouldn't look at—'

Mikey wiped his nose with the hem of his jumper. 'Are you saying now that my mother wasn't good enough for Hugh Dawley?'

'I am. I am.'

'Then little you know about men, or women either.' Mikey laid a mollifying hand on my shoulder. '"I'll tell you this much, Long Pat Kilraish. He'd have a better life with me than with that jumped up Cartor wan from Adamston. All airs and graces, looking down her nose at the rest of us. That wan is as cold as a fish".'

Whatever else about my parents, they had married for love; each was the only sweetheart the other had. Now, that most revered icon had smashed and its fall swirled round in my head. My father was part of the rutting entourage that lusted after Lena Kilraish. Anyone but her; the village bicycle that everyone had ridden, according to Felim. I had separated the two facets of her life that I had become familiar with – the woman who spread warmth and fun about her kitchen floor, and the flaring Jezebel. I couldn't think of one anymore without the other rushing to close the gap. Even more painful was the view of my mother held by the sibilant harridan. Beth Cartor, font of elegance, the pure spirit, was a stuck-up charlatan.

'An' wan thing else.' Mikey pointed an emphatic finger at me. 'Don't be taken in by Long Pat. Keep a tight watch on him.'

The Kilraishes lived well, despite their apparent state of poverty. Our stable diet, except Friday, was bacon and cabbage. When that varied, we were like vultures round the table; fighting for a share of the delicacies that sometimes fell our way. Only when the flush of a good cattle sale overcame my father's natural frugality did sausages or lamp chops perfume the kitchen with their exotic promise.

Mikey's hunting prowess filled the Kilraish table. Mount Fierna abounded in game. The monks at Manisterluna had stocked their moat with trout that followed the tributary to the Morning Star. The hazel thickets harboured woodcock and pheasant; the overspill from the river in winter brought flocks of greylag geese, widgeon and mallard. But all were allowed to exist unmolested because the folk of the mountain thought it beneath them to hunt and trap. Only the very poor made do with game.

In the small hours of the night, when the world was asleep, Mikey was going from field to field checking his traps. He showed me how to set snares in the pathways that rabbits had worn under the hedgerows. He knew how to bait patches of stubble in ploughed fields and trap pheasants with lures of grain attached to fishing hooks.

We were almost the same age, Mikey and me, but he left me for dead when it came to canniness and worldly wisdom. Even as a twelve-year-old, he had knowledge that amazed me and made me wonder if I would ever manage my place in the world, so circumspect were my ways in comparison. Every purpose he had was measured in terms of money. Mikey, at twelve, had the ambition and vision of a miser. Money was for hoarding, in mounds.

The mounds grew. Mikey sold his produce to the hawker who parked his horse-drawn caravan on the outskirts of

Adamston, Padden, 'the Soldier Adams', who had fought in the Great War. Mikey dashed to the Post Office and deposited the money in his account. He left his Post Office book with the lady behind the counter, because there was no hiding place in the Kilraish house that he could trust.

I became a partner in Mikey's trade, but I didn't do it for the money. It had occurred to me, as I watched Mikey sell to the hawker, that this was the way to fund the wireless that my mother hankered after. Mikey knew the price of a good second-hand one. 'Three pounds and ten,' he told me, 'and "tis like throwin' money down the drain. What would you want a thing like that for?'

I distrusted the man in the radio shop the moment I saw him. He examined my credentials with a litany of questions, whilst leering at me.'If I were you,' he advised me, 'I'd be buying that wireless while the price holds. Everything do be going up these days.'

I returned a few weeks later and put my money down on the counter. 'The wireless. There's the money. Three pounds and ten.'

The wireless man eyed the coins as if they were poorly wrought counterfeit. He waved a dismissive arm at me. 'Ah no. No. No. No. You'll be buying no wireless for three pounds and ten. That was ages ago. The price is gone up.'

'I was here,' Mikey said. 'I heard you sayin' it. Three pounds and ten.'

'I warned ye. Didn't I warn ye? Ye should have taken it when 'twas going at that price.'

'Then you can stuff it,' Mikey told him. The angelic face suffused with a sudden influx of anger. 'Come on,' he began to gather up the money, slipping it along the counter into his palm with the deftness of a teller in a bank. 'There's more than one radio shop in this town.'

The shopkeeper placed his taloned fingers over Mikey's. The nails were chewed to the quick and the nicotine stain had burned into the tips of his middle and index fingers like the burl in a piece of antique furniture. 'Don't you be the smart man,' he leered at Mikey. He looked at me for confirmation. 'Aren't you the one that does be wanting the wireless?'

I nodded.

'Let this be between you and me. Tell you what. The price is four pounds even. Give me what you have there. Take away the wireless and you can owe me the balance. I'll get you to sign a bit of paper and you can pay me a halfcrown every week for the next four weeks. How does that be sounding to you?'

I knew I was being cheated, but my heart was set on this moment. I had conjured up visions of my mother's joy and the dumbstruck admiration of my brothers and Mona when I unfolded the paper wrapper around the wireless. So I signed the commitment to pay the balance and ignored the whispered admonitions from Mikey.

'What class of an eegit are you?'

The shopkeeper wrapped the radio in brown paper, placed in it a cardboard box and then put the batteries on top. 'The wireless and the batteries, all together, comes to four pounds. Now the aerial wire and the connectors, say five shillings and sixpence. And my own time, going out to the mountain and rigging up the wireless, that will be another ten shillings. All the add ons so, that will come to fifteen and six. Add that now to the balance you owe me for the wireless, let's see now, ah yes, a grand total of one pound, five shillings and sixpence.'

A wave of confusion washed over my befuddled brain. I was so taken with buying the radio and the spillover of joy and admiration that it never dawned on me that there would be ancillary expenses. Any youngster with a rudiment of sense would have known that you could not simply bring a radio home, turn it on and expect it to work without making the necessary connection. I was beaten.

'You have your wet,' I heard Mikey say.

'Well now,' the shopkeeper responded in cryptic lisps of sarcasm. 'The smart man from the arsehole of the mountain agin, is it?'

''Tis an' all, Mikey answered. 'An' if you think we're going to pay you for a twist of wire and a few "chainy" connectors, you must think we came down in the last shower. Come on, Roddy. Take your box an' we'll go.'

We took the long route to Glenorga with my precious cargo, avoiding the perilous footholds above the gorge. It was no big thing, Mikey assured me, to yoke up a wireless. The Nevilles had installed one a few months back and Tommy, the youngest son, who worked in a garage in Dublin, had rigged it up. He came home every weekend and there was nothing he didn't know about mechanics.

I feigned sickness on the Sunday. When the coast was clear, Neville fixed the aerial cable to the ventilation window of the hay barn. He hammered a staple in the gable end of our house, pulled the wire taut, then took it through the frame of the kitchen window and into the socket at the rear of the wireless that I had placed on the sill. Then he connected the dry batteries, all the time keeping up a running commentary of what he was doing. Great changes are coming, he told Mikey and me. This wireless set of ours would be like a dodo in a few years; there was a new model on the way, worked by electricity. All you had to do was plug it in and off she went.

Then came the defining moment when Neville turned the switch and the dial lit up. He spun the dial and suddenly a fanfare of music filled our kitchen: 'The March of the Slaves' from Verdi's *Aida* as I would later learn. Neville raised the volume and the trumpets bounced outward from the walls like the slough of a retreating wave. Even when Neville and Mikey had gone and I was seated before the windowsill studying the geography of the dial, I still heard the trumpets.

Felim and Mona were home before my mother; she had gone her usual solitary way by Knock Na Sidhe and the Giant's Grave. We met her in the front yard, skipped about her in excitement, forced her to tie on a blindfold and be led into the kitchen. I turned the knob and held my breath until the dial lit. Neville had tuned the wireless to the BBC, 'The Light Programme', and what issued forth was a programme of dance music called 'Grand Hotel'. It was playing Glen Miller's 'String of Pearls'.

My mother's head jerked to one side like a startled bird trying to recognise a once familiar sound. Then she pulled off the blindfold and saw the wireless. Her face lit up like a Christmas tree.

'It's a wireless, Mam,' Mona gushed. 'Roddy bought it for you.'

My mother swept me up in her arms and clasped me to her bosom. With a little gasp of wondrous exultation, she whipped off her coat, grasped the back of a kitchen chair and began to dance with it around the room. Then Felim took it from her; stood erect, bowed from the waist and with a great sweep of his arm offered himself in the dance. My mother led him expertly and gently for a few moments until he caught the rhythm and the movement. I remember thinking again how all the skills were stored, semi-complete, in some memory bank in Felim's brain. Round and round the room they swept, my mother's head thrown back, the dark hair cascading across her face. She was ravishingly beautiful as she laughed in the essence of sensual pleasure and, as I watched, they seemed to merge into a single shape, a sculpture of living art, like two figures entwined on the lid of a musical box.

Instinctively the same intent seemed to grasp the dancing pair; they parted for a moment and invited Mona to join. She giggled and blushed but in an instant was swept in by their welcoming arms, and the faltering first steps were nudged into rhythm and shape. Round and round they went. I watched them twirl and turn, read the wonder in their faces and felt the glow of their delight as if it were issuing forth from the depths of some long entombment.

I waited to be beckoned in but no signal came. It was I who had created this moment. I had plotted, schemed and dreamed it. Like an ancient artistic benefactor, I, who had made the art possible, was superfluous in the wonder of its appreciation. But perhaps it was something else. With my shortened leg and ponderous boot, I would be just a vulgar encumbrance to the perfect rhythms of their dancing feet.

A shadow fell across the front door. Without looking up, I knew it was my father; so did the spinning trio, who now stood rooted to the floor. The music still played but we didn't hear it any more. I heard instead a great silence being lowered like a canopy of doom.

'What's this, what's this?'

My mother disengaged from the group and ushered the

others towards the door and their waiting chores. My father stayed the movement with an upraised hand.

'Stop. I asked a question. Am I going to get an answer?'

'It's only a bit of harmless fun, Hugh,' my mother faltered. 'A simple bit of fun, for heaven's sake. What's wrong with it?'

My father's jaw was set in granite; the voice came laden with sarcasm. 'What's wrong with it, she asks me. I come home from the match, a little diversion from breaking my arse at that land out there, and what do I find? My wife and my children doing fancy steps around the kitchen as if it were a ballroom. Isn't it grand people ye are, like the Cartors of Adamston, able to dance and cavort when there's work to be done? Amn't I the lucky man to have married and raised such quality?'

'Ah, come on, Father,' Felim pleaded. 'We were just enjoying ourselves. Okay, we forgot the time, that's all there is to it.'

'Is that a fact now? And did I ask you the question, did I, did I?'

'Oh, for Christ's sake,' Felim began but was silenced by the sudden onrush of my father, who grasped him by the shoulder and swung him round to glare into his face.

'Listen, boyo, as long as you are in this house, you will never take the name of the Lord in vain. Or you'll feel the weight of this hand.' My father pressed his fist under Felim's chin until the white of the knuckles showed.

I watched the blood leave Felim's face. 'Father,' the word was ice cold, 'lay your hand on me, and 'twill be the last—'

'Felim,' my mother implored, 'go to the yard, you and Mona.'

'It's only a bloody wireless,' Felim said from the door-way. 'What's all the—'

'Go Felim, please.'

My father stood gazing at the wireless. It seemed that he was seeing it for the first time and only now was associating it with the music that was still playing.

'Who brought that thing into my house?'

My tongue clung to the roof of my mouth. I tried to moisten my lips to force the answer through.

'Roddy did. He bought it for me.'

'Roddy did. Well isn't that great now? The same smart man who couldn't stop a heifer from falling into the gorge. Tell me, smart man, did you ask me?'

'No, Father.' The words were barely above a whisper.

'No Father, an' may I ask you this? Where did you get the money?'

'From selling rabbits and a pheasant. I sold them to the Soldier Adams.'

'Yourself and Mikey Kilraish, I suppose?'

'Yes, Father.'

He came to where I was sitting at the corner of the table. He made a pincers of his thumb and middle finger and pulled my face around to look him in the eye.

'So, the son of Hugh Dawley selling rabbits like a common labourer. How much did the wireless cost?'

'Four pounds.'

My father whistled. It soared above the music from the wireless. 'Four pounds.' The fingers tightened on my chin. 'Have you an idea what I could have bought for four pounds? An acre of hay, a ton of manure. An' my smart bucko goes and buys a bloody wireless. Listen to it; listen to the rubbish it's playing.'

'Hugh, let him go.' My mother prised his fingers away. 'He bought it for *me*. You know how I love music.'

'Oh, I do indeed,' my father sneered. 'What does a mountain man know about the piano or that fella you're always on about? What's his name?'

'Stop it, Hugh.'

'I have it. Showpan. That's the man. Tell me, bucko, did you pay for the wireless in full?'

I wanted to lie but I knew he would discover the truth. 'No. I owe ten shillings. But I'll have it all paid off in the next four weeks.'

My father rose and towered over me. His fingers formed into grasping talons, closing and opening out again. I turned my head away.

'Look at me, smart man. I'll tell you this. No Dawley ever owed money to a living soul. An' we won't start now. Tomorrow morning you take that wireless and give it back to the man you bought it from. No Dawley catches rabbits and sells them as if we hadn't a penny to our name and couldn't feed ourselves. You know what that means, bucko? If I hear or see you again in the company of any Kilraish, I'll redden your arse.'

When he was gone, my mother took me gently by the arm and led me to the parlour. I waited for the soothing words of compassion that would heal the hurt and salve the wounds, words of appreciation and understanding, the rapture of sympathy for a shipwrecked soul. But none came. She took me through a tour of Europe, halting at cities where the great composers had worked and lived: Chopin, Schubert, Rachmaninoff. As always she finally came to Venice and seated me on an imaginary gondola plying its way along the Grand Canal.

In the morning I took back the wireless. The man in the shop deducted half a crown for the use of the set and gave me back the remainder. I gave the money to my mother and she put it in the earthenware crock where she hoarded the small savings that chanced her way. No one spoke about my father's behaviour; no one offered a token word of sympathy for my plight or appreciation for my grand scheme. I wallowed for days, fighting the filling receptacle of hatred for my father, despising my own stupidity for I should have known better.

And then, a month later, when we were all seated for the evening meal, the man from the radio shop brought in a new wireless set and rigged it up to the aerial that was still suspended from the hay barn. He switched it on; the dial lit up. 'You have a fine wireless there, Hugh,' he said, 'far better than the second-hand set the young fella wanted to buy.' My mother's face beamed like the dial and my father preened in satisfaction.

They looked at him in a new light of wonder.

Chapter 4

The radio opened a corridor to an outside world of great expanse. Electricity had come to Adamston in 1956 and had spun off to little hamlets and villages like Ardagh and Newtown. It had come almost to the foothills of the mountain but was repulsed there. Our mountain kitchen continued to be lit with a paraffin lamp; we cooked on the open fire. There was no running water, no toilet, and no roadway between us and the nearest point of paved civilisation.

Felim acquired a copy of *Peyton Place* and read it underneath the bedclothes by the light of a bicycle lamp. I spirited it out, hidden inside my jumper, and read snatches of it to Mikey Kilraish. Brendan Behan's play *The Quare Fellow* opened in London. The priest in Newtown, Father Morgan Lynch, preached a sermon about Behan and others of his ilk, who were bringing the Catholic face of Mother Ireland into disrepute. The ordinary people of Ireland and Britain should not support his play and have no truck with a man who used the Holy Name in vain and blasphemed his own religion.

Morgan Lynch had come to Newtown in the autumn of 1954. He was then in his middle forties, having spent most of his priesthood as Dean of Discipline in the seminary college in Danesfort. Lynch was a small, wiry man with protruding green eyes and a trembling upper lip that gave his features a fish-like appearance. On his first Sunday amongst us, he stamped on the altar tiles and expounded the basic laws of attendance which would apply in his church: no lateness, no standing in groups at the rear of the church, and no whispering. Felim took an instant dislike to him.

My father received a letter in the post – the envelope had an official wax seal – informing him that the priest wished to see both himself and his good wife to discuss a matter of singular importance. When he arrived, Morgan Lynch was ushered into the parlour. Felim, Mona and I stationed ourselves in the hallway where every word was audible and we could see the figures in the room through the chinks in the door.

'Hugh, let me get straight to the purpose of my visit,' the priest said. 'What plans have you for your boy Felim?'

'I was hoping to keep him on the land, Father. I need the help.'

'Nonsense. You can't keep a boy like that on the land. It's a negation of his God-given talents. Don't you think so, Mrs Dawley?' He never looked at my mother when he directed the question at her. Instead, he fixed his eyes on the wallpaper, and waited for collaboration.

'I have little say in the matter,' my mother answered.

The priest nodded rapidly as if in agreement. 'Hugh,' he commanded, 'your boy must go the college in Danesfort. There's no question about it. And no question either that he must study for the priesthood. Our diocese needs men of talent, Hugh. Are you following me? Are you aware of the honour and the opportunity I am proposing? You may be sending out from this house a future bishop, a future cardinal, perhaps a professor of theology or dogma in a Catholic University. In Rome itself. Are you aware, Hugh?'

My father hawked. He always did when he was wrestling with something in his mind, or when he was cowed by the presence of someone else.

'Father Lynch.' My mother turned her face sideways to catch the priest's attention. 'Felim is not interested in the priesthood, he does not have the vocation. And anyway, we couldn't afford to send him to Danesfort.'

'Good on you, Ma,' Felim whispered.

The priest crossed his legs and brushed imaginary flecks of dust from the fabric of his trousers. He spoke to my mother as his eyes wandered the canals of her wallpaper.

'Mrs Dawley, why don't you let the matter rest between your husband and me?' The blue tint of stubble had turned to a foreboding black and the face that focused on my father's was intense and scowling. 'Hugh, it's a nonsense to suggest that the boy has no vocation. He's merely a youth; and has no sense of what the priesthood entails. He will only know when he mingles with students destined to be the implements of that service. Now, let me tell you—'

'Money,' my father said, 'we don't have the money.'

The priest loosened the grip of his interlaced fingers. 'That's not a problem. I'm certain your son will get a scholarship. If not, the diocese has a bursary for poor, I mean exceptional students. I'll talk to the authorities in the college within the next few days. Now, will you please convey me down the mountain; I nearly broke a leg on the way up.'

I expected that my father would rant and rave about Felim's imminent departure, but he never brought it up. Perhaps he knew more about Felim's predilections than the rest of us. Felim had the genes of a mountain man: he might leave but he would always be drawn back. There was, however, one big row about Felim's choice of college. I heard the fall-out of the dispute when father came late from Heaney's public house and beat a short-tempered tattoo on my mother's door. 'Bitch,' I heard him say as he made his resigned shuffling way up the stairs, 'you've turned the priest agin' me and we won't have luck for it.'

Felim ignored the priest's offer. He sat other scholarship examination, and had a choice of four schools. He chose Villiers Academy in Adamston. Tony Villiers was a nephew of Phoebe Jackson and a star pupil of Philly Cartor. He ran what he called a non-denominational establishment, and offered his students a broad classical education.

In the summer of 1956, Hughie returned from England. He had gone there, almost two years before, once he had completed his stint in the Vocational School. Hughie had cycled the ten miles to Adamston with the same diligence as had marked all his period under Miss Horgan's tutelage. He never liked school; it was a distraction from his love of the land. As soon as he returned from school, he threw the books with gleeful abandon on the horsehair couch in the kitchen and made for the fields.

My mother was hurt severely when Hughie left to work in England. My father told her to have sense: Hughie would be home as soon as he had saved enough to buy a second-hand tractor. I had never seen my mother so distraught. It was a strange reversal of roles, for she blamed him for plotting and abetting in Hughie's emigration. It was a scheme to separate mother and son, she accused him, a cowardly ploy, cloaked in the funding of a tractor.

I had sensed that Hughie and my mother were growing apart. He played a mute role now in our family conferences, as if he had little interest anymore in the web of my mother's ambitions. And yet he didn't appear any closer to my father.

Hughie told me that he had worked every hour God sent while he was in England. In those two years he never came home. There was an empty space beside my mother in the church pew and a vacant place at the Christmas dinner. He returned a stockier Hughie but with a hard, lean face and eyes that brooded as if lost in a vacant reverie.

Within a week of his homecoming, Hughie came riding the rock-strewn track on a green belching monster. The tractor was a second-hand Massey Ferguson, almost better than new, Hughie maintained, because it had done only light work in the level fields of the Turf Board and was always housed at night. Hughie would get to know that machine intimately. He was a mechanic born.

I went to watch the machine at work in the fields and wondered at the incongruity of its place amongst us. In 300 years our mountain ways had changed very little. Man was the single unit of labour and the horse the standard of power. We paid no heed to the advent of new ways or to the signals of encroaching science. Suddenly, through Hughie's intervention, the Dawleys had become quixotic patrons of technology. We, the epitome of Spartan frugality, had a green monster belching in our fields; the Philistines had introduced the wheel

As I looked down the field, I knew I was seeing the future. My brother had reduced my father's ambitions to simple, facile objectives. Horsepower, engineered by vapour oil, had made manpower redundant.

Rock and roll arrived in 1956 and Morgan Lynch preached about it and its originator, Bill Haley. Rock and roll, he said, was the greatest single influence for evil since the dawning of communism. It was a cancer that infiltrated the moral fibre of our youth like a spreading virus. He returned to the theme a few weeks later when he heard that the cinema in Limerick had erupted when the effects of this new primal music worked its way into the hearts and minds of the audience. Fists fights broke out; seats were ripped up and thrown at the screen. We were on the brink of anarchy, Father Lynch said, unless man turned back to God and ignored the evils and the pitfalls that Satan had loosed amongst us.

On the first Sunday in September our neighbours came to hear the broadcast of the All-Ireland hurling final. While the kitchen filled to overflowing, my mother and Mona went up the dirt track to Knocknastumpa. My father fixed a glow on his face when he greeted the first-comer and it remained there, like a frozen fossil, for the remainder of the evening.

The visitors left the kitchen like a pigsty when they departed. Some had come straight from Heaney's pub; they belched and farted, the stink mingled with sweat odours and became amplified in the press of bodies. Cigarette smoke eddied about the kitchen in a swirling vapour trail; it clung to the underside of the ceiling in auger-shaped twirls like the smoke from a thousand genie bottles.

Father's mood suddenly switched, and he went to the milking with a surly face and the lantern jaw was as rigid as if it were bolted down. Felim, who worked beside my father, had become aware of more explicit signals. He darted into the kitchen between trips to empty his pail. 'Batten down the hatches; there's a hurricane brewing.'

And a hurricane it was but this time it blew from both ends. 'Where were you, woman?' my father demanded as soon as he entered the room. 'Our neighbours were here, and no one to make them a cup of tay. You shamed me.'

My mother whipped off her apron, rolled it in a ball and threw it into the middle of the table. Her face was the colour of beetroot, her eyes sparked.

'Neighbours. Pigs more like it. Look at the state of my kitchen. Smell it. Never bring those people in here again.' My mother stamped her foot and moved away from the table to face him, eyeball to eyeball. 'This is my house too, Hugh Dawley. I'm entitled to respect.'

My father raised his arm and bunched his fingers into a fist. Mona moved in front of mother. 'Get out of my way, you little strap,' he shouted at her, 'or you'll feel the weight of this hand.'

'Go on, go on,' my mother spat at him. 'Hit me, act the brute. It's the only thing you know.'

'Bitch,' my father muttered but all the indignation seemed to have drained away. 'You make me sick with your airs and graces. We're not good enough for you, I suppose.' He kicked a chair out of his way and yanked the door open.

'Your tea is poured out,' my mother shouted after him.

'Shag the tay,' he shouted back, 'an' you with it.'

After he had gone, we stood in frozen silence, like petrified characters in a woodcut. Felim was the first to break away. He vented a long drawn out whistle. 'There he goes,' he said, 'the prince of civilisation.'

Mona rounded on him. 'You're a great man for the smart words, aren't you, Felim? But you stood there like a dummy when that man raised his hand to my mother. As for you,' she looked at me as if I were a piece of cowdung, 'you're a snivelling coward. You must have been born without balls.'

'Stop it, all of you!' mother shouted. 'The last thing we should do is fight amongst ourselves.'

In the small hours of the night, I sat in the darkness in our kitchen, my ear glued to the 1,500 metres commentary at the Melbourne Olympics. Ronnie Delaney, an Irish athlete, unfancied and unheralded, came out of the pack at the final bend and spreadeagled the field. The voice of Rex Alston of the BBC became lodged in my head, 'A gold for Eire!' Listening to the post-race euphoria, I failed to hear my father enter the room. When I looked up, he was leaning against the doorjamb, trying to make sense of the excited jabbering.

'Did he win?'

'Yes, yes, he sprinted off the last bend and fooled 'em all.'

'Be God,' my father sucked his lips in admiration, 'you're telling me he bate Landy?'

'He bate 'em all. An' then he knelt down on the track, blessed himself and said a prayer in thanksgiving.'

'Well, that's great an' all. Back to bed now with you. 'Tis all hours of the morning.' My father turned to leave.

'How did you know? I didn't think you had any interest.'

He smiled. 'You'd be surprised. I used run the mile. I took the senior cup in Limerick two years in a row.'

Ronnie Delaney was interviewed on the radio. But I barely heard the interview. Round and round in my head went the refrain 'my father a miler'. He must have been teasing me; I had never heard a single reference about his ability as a runner. I played the Olympic race in my head and it was I, perfect in body and grace, who emerged in full sprint from the last bend.

We played hurling, the ancient game of the Gael, in the Nursery Field. It started when Hughie was eight and my father fashioned him a makeshift hurley from the root of an ash tree that had toppled into the gorge. Long Pat Kilraish supplied the hurley for St Luna's, the Newtown club. But most of us in the field could ill afford the price of a Long Pat, as we called his creations. We made do with makeshift sticks of our own crude design.

Of a summer's evening in the Nursery Field we could muster twenty players. Some came from the village of Ardagh on the other side of the mountain, where there was a hurling tradition going back over 100 years, and 'twas said that an Ardagh man never saw danger or never took flight in a fight.

My mother simply saw it as organised faction-fighting. She cited its inherent violence; its association with drink and raw passion and the spleens between clubs that seemed to slide like lubricated enmity from one generation to the next.

In the beginning I stood on the sideline, hating myself for the iniquitous twist of fate that had left me with a crippled leg. I watched my brothers with envy: Felim shooting scores that belied imagination, Hughie, with his square shoulders, meeting every forward charge with gusto and deft stickwork. Incompetence is always more acute when stacked up against the talents of one's own siblings. Then, one evening, Hughie thrust a stick in my hands and marched me to stand between the pair of stones that served as goalposts. The ball flew passed me, trickled over the head of my stick, ran between my legs. But worse than my ineptitude was the terror that clutched me the minute I stood between the stones. 'Go home, go home,' Ferdy Culhane from Ardagh rasped at me; 'you're useless. Whose idea was it anyway to put a cripple in goal?'

A hand grasped him by the scruff of the neck and lifted him off the ground until his feet dangled. 'It was my idea, Culhane,' Hughie said. 'An' if you ever call him a cripple again, I'll ram my hurley up your arse.'

I practised with Mikey Kilraish in the small paddock behind his house. I had Mikey stand about 30 feet away and aim shots at me. If I positioned myself nearer to the left-hand goalpost and sprung from the platform of my raised boot, my agility improved. I developed the skill of flinging myself across the goal line and parrying the ball away. When I felt ready, I went unbidden to the goalposts in the Nursery Field.

They laughed at me but it turned to a begrudging silence when I dealt comfortably with everything they threw at me. All but Hughie; he shouted his appreciation with every save and once came between the goal line to tousle my hair. But Felim never approached me and I began to suspect for the first time that the vessel of all talents was envious of those with merely a little.

'We have a goalkeeper, a right good one,' Hughie announced when we sat at the kitchen table before bedtime. 'You should have seen Roddy. He's a beauty,' he said to my father.

Father laughed, deep from the pit of his stomach. It was the belly rumble of instant unbridled mirth.

'I'm telling you,' Hughie was quietly insistent. 'He's a good one. Come out yourself tomorrow evening and see.'

My father blew air through his nostrils, a token of his cynical disbelief. 'We'll go out now,' he said. There was still some light left.

'Into goal,' my father ordered. 'We'll see what you are made of.' He took the leather ball from Felim and the hurley from Hughie. He tested the spring of the hurley shaft until it curved like a bow.

'Any time you're ready, Father.'

Father moved back twenty yards from the goalposts and placed the ball on the ground. He held the hurley stick like a natural; he made practice swings that only the correct fusion of grip and wristwork would allow. Then he stood over the ball, rolled it onto his stick until the ball smashed into the stone wall at my rear.

'Throw it back to me,' he ordered. There was something like a leer hovering amid the bristles on his upper lip. 'You'd better see this one 'cause 'tis coming straight for you.'

'Hey,' Hughie started to say but my father dismissed him with a curt look. I watched him bend over the ball and knew instinctively that he was telling the truth; he was aiming the shot to hit me. If the leather ball took me flush in the face, it would tear my head off, so I raised the hurley head to protect me. The ball struck it head on but the impetus of the blow sent me sprawling. I heard him laugh.

'You were lucky there. This time I won't tell you, except that it's going to be either above or below.'

'Stop it,' Hughie shouted, 'you're going to hurt him.'

'He can always duck,' my father said, 'if he sees it in time.'

My father stood over the ball, leaning on the stick. This time the arc of the swing was slow and deliberate. I could see the ball fall languidly to the point where he would meet it squarely. And I saw no more. I heard the ball smash behind me and began to feel the duped outriders of relief before the pain shot through my upper arm. It hung by my side numbed all the way to the elbow.

'I'm a bit off,' my father said, 'but I'll get the hang of it in a minute.'

Mona started to move towards me but Felim tugged her back. Hughie's eyes were fixed on my father in a sort of mesmerised trance.

'Ready! Here comes the cannonball.'

I went into my crouch, holding the blocking stick horizontally. The fear seemed to come from the shaft, weaving along the wood grain. I felt my knees shake and the damaged foot twitch. The hurley stick swung in its spinning arc, the ball fell for the strike and, before the leather smacked against wood, I had turned my back. In an instant the fear blackened to remorse. I sat between the goalposts and I wept.

'He won't make it,' my father's voice grew faint in the distance as he walked away. 'You want balls to be a goalkeeper.'

Hughie sat on the bared red earth beside me. He put out a tentative hand to allay the racking sobs, but I brushed it away.

'Our father is a brute,' Mona said, 'a big thick ignorant brute.'

'Maybe, maybe,' Felim mused, 'but it did prove something. At this moment, Roddy, at approximately 9.45 on the evening of 14 June 1956, you have been discovered to be a coward.' He turned away with an air of disconcerted nonchalance, swinging the hurley my father had handed him, snapping his fingers to the beat of some silent tune in his head.

In the summer of 1957, for the first time in its history, St Luna's won the county minor championship. Hughie and Felim were both on that team. Felim scored one goal and eight points in a final tally of one goal and fourteen. The local newspaper carried an account of the game and a photograph of the team. My mother cut them out and stuck them to the wallpaper in the middle of St Mark's Square.

We were beginning to prosper. At first the signs were barely perceptible, like the gradual build up of the cowherd. That was Hughie's idea. Milk was a regular income and less dependent on the vagaries of weather. I would awake now to the sound of animals passing the bedroom window on the way from the milking byre. The routine had changed; it had gone from a languid start to the day to one of fevered activity. It seemed that Hughie's fervour swept them all along.

THE BLUE POOL

We leased twenty acres of land from Hannah Histon
and the cowherd grew to 25. My father bought a new suit,
his third since his marriage. In that same year he came
home from a cattle fair in Adamston, flushed with success
and the signs of celebratory drink. He took a wad of notes
from the inside pocket of his greatcoat, peeled off a dozen
or more from the bundle and handed them to my mother.

'Go and buy something for yourself, woman.' He went
into the parlour, lodged the money in the hidden drawer of
the dining table and went upstairs to change into his working clothes. The sound of his footsteps on the cobbled yard
and the clanking of milk cans had faded away and yet my
mother was still staring at the notes in muted disbelief. I
don't think she bought anything from that incredible wind-
fall. I didn't know then, nor did any of us, that my mother
had other uses for it.

The beckoning fingers of prosperity coincided with
other developments; perhaps they were part of the reason.
Slowly, like the faint signals of a new régime, my mother's
dominance began to fade. Our family conferences had
become desultory affairs. Hughie sat wordlessly in the chair
next to my mother; Felim fidgeted listlessly through the
tour of Europe when once he had been goggle-eyed with
interest. The thrust of participation fell on Mona and sometimes she would turn on her brothers with peevish annoyance, demand that they contribute and wonder if they both
had grown too smart and clever for their own good. Old
men before their time, she said they were. My place at the
conference table reflected my status. I was placed at the bottom, near the door where the draught came in, and was
seated on a backless kitchen chair.

Then Lionel Barton entered my life. Mikey and I had sneaked over the estate wall to the place where the Barton vault stood. I had convinced myself a hundred times that I would never let him persuade me to go there because the memory of his uncle's skeleton, in the cave of the Blue Pool, still filled my dreams. The vault was built of granite, in the shape of a pyramid with an iron cross at its apex. The oak door was bolted but, because the hinges had rusted, Mikey was able to ease it forward and squeeze himself through the opening.

'Don't be an oul' scaredy cat,' he laughed at my reluctance to enter, 'they are all dead. Won't do a thing to you.'

The air was dry and musty but I wasn't sure if that was why I could feel it catch in my throat. The moment my eyes became used to the gloom, I saw a skeletal hand that had worked free under the rotted lid of a coffin. Then I saw Mikey dart to the rear of the vault. He picked up a skull from the ground and threw it to me with a grin of demonic devilment.

'Here, catch!'

I backed away in horror as the skull dropped at my feet. I watched it bump and settle against the base of the wall.

'Do you know who that was?' Mikey leered. 'That was oul' Richard, the greatest bastard of them all. He doesn't look too tough now, does he, Roddy?'

'How do you know who it is?'

'Because the skull fell out of the coffin up there with a brass plate and oul' Richard's name on it.'

'We should put it back.'

'We should, in our arse. We should bring it up to the Nursery Field and play football with it.'

'You're an ignorant whelp, Kilraish,' a voice said from the doorway. Lionel Barton pulled the door open and strode into the vault. 'Pick up that skull and give it here to me.'

Mikey did as he was bidden with an alacrity that surprised me. Then as Barton put out his hands to take the skull, Mikey dropped it again and bolted. Barton picked up the skull, walked to the end of the vault and laid it on top of the broken coffin on the highest ledge.

'Run if you want to,' he told me, 'but I would rather you stayed a while. I suspect that you have some modicum of decency about you, unlike that Kilraish scoundrel.'

'I don't run very well.'

'Oh, indeed; you were the unfortunate boy that fell from my wall. There now,' he patted the skull affectionately and placed it inside the broken coffin, 'go back to sleep, Richard. You know,' he confided, 'this place is a shambles. I must really find time to put it in order. Look at William Grantham there, falling out again.' He eased the skeleton arm beneath the rotting timbers. 'Have you ever seen a skeleton before?'

I almost blurted out that I had seen Mikey's uncle in his cave in the Blue Pool. 'No,' I shook my head.

'That young Kilraish was right about one thing. They are harmless.'

Barton's face was tanned and a mane of steel-grey hair fell almost to this shoulders. I thought he resembled the stone lion that guarded one pier of the wrought-iron gate to the estate, cragged and rugged. There was a red carnation in the buttonhole of his tweed jacket.

He ushered me out of the vault, steering me through with a plump bronzed hand. 'Let's walk up to the house,' he said; 'we'll take a glass of lemonade. Would you like that?'

I stopped and I could feel the pressure of the hand urging me forward. Barton halted and nodded. 'Ah, I see, that wouldn't go down too well, would it? A son of Hugh Dawley fraternising with the enemy.'

'My mother will be expecting me.' I lied. 'I have jobs to do.'

He smiled. It lit up his face like a beacon and yet it held a knowing insinuation. 'Jobs,' he made it sound incredulous. 'I have heard it said that you do nothing on the land. You run wild all day, yourself and that scallywag Kilraish.' Then he asked, 'Are you afraid of me?'

I shuffled my foot on the dust of the floor. It rose in tiny whirls of pewter-coloured smoke.

'No need to be afraid. I'm not an ogre. Anyway, no one need ever know. Come along. Let me close this door. I really will have to do something about this vault. Can't let it deteriorate any further.'

All along the gravel pathway to the rear entrance to Barton Hall, I was tormented with the conflicting poles of debate that ran round and round in my befuddled head. This was the man my father hated, and his ancestors before him. I was cast in that same mould as them; it was my filial duty to carry the inherited torch as my brothers did. But this man, Lionel Barton, who was the incarnation of generations of brutality and abuse, smiled at me and offered me lemonade.

He led me into the conservatory that had been built off the great dining hall. It looked out over the waters of Lough Cutra and beyond to the tiered fields of Mount Fierna. I could see the outcrop of rock against which my grandfather's hovel had first been raised. Out there was Glenorga. I felt pangs of traitorous guilt. Barton beckoned me to a wicker armchair that was overflowing with cushions and went to tug at the velvet, tasselled cord that hung from the ceiling. I heard a bell sound in the distance.

'This is my only claim to fame,' Lionel Barton was saying, 'this conservatory. In every generation the incumbent Barton added a feature to this house. William built the west wing, Geoffrey the east wing and the front porch. My father, Amos, walled in the kitchen garden and refurbished the library. But it all ends here, young man, in the occupancy of Lionel. After me there will be no more.' He paused, 'Say, you're Roderick, aren't you?'

'Yes.'

'Nice name. And tell me this. How is the leg, the one you broke?'

'It's all right. I can barely run. Sometimes it's hard to walk.'

'Shame. That leg should have been treated properly.' He sighed. 'Ah well, what's the use in talking.'

A woman came through the great dining room and Barton beckoned her in. 'Rose, will you fetch us some lemonade; a large glass for this young man here.' When she had gone he turned to me with a conspiratorial wink. 'Mrs Trenchard is the soul of discretion. Rather like the representation of the three wise monkeys. You know what that is, of course?'

I shook my head. 'I had one in my bedroom when I was your age, a present from my Great Aunt Sophia. Three monkeys sitting on a plinth of wood, one with its fingers over its ears, another with a hand over its mouth and the third covering its eyes. See no evil, speak no evil, hear no evil. That's Rose Trenchard. So don't you worry, Roderick.'

The woman returned with glasses on a tray and stared unblinkingly at me as she laid it down on the table.

'Thank you, Rose.' The words were a dismissal. He waited until her footsteps were muted on the marble floor of the corridor, then raised his glass.

'Here's to friendship.' His brow furrowed at the flush of shock that warmed my face and averted my eyes. 'Yes, I know. It sounds very improbable, doesn't it? We've been bitter enemies, Roderick, the Bartons and the Dawleys, the keepers of stupid, mindless enmities that should have been buried generations ago. But we can't go on forever, can we? All that terrible hate gnawing at our bones? So let's drink to better days.'

Lionel Barton walked me down the avenue of beech trees, flanked by green lawns and statuary of Roman gods. I thought of the starving people in the times of the Great Hunger who had stood there in meek desperation, hoping for a crumb of leftover from the Barton dining hall. Shame lanced through me like an arrow. I kept my eyes on the ground lest he saw the evidence in my face.

'I believe you're a hurler, a goalkeeper no less?' I heard his voice in the distance of my discomfort.

'It's the only position I can play in.'

'Never played the game myself, though I would have liked. It's a great game.'

Curiosity shifted my eyes upwards. Here it was again, the subliminal suggestion of affinity from one who was the epitome of detachment from our station in life. The Bartons had played rugby, the game that characterised their status. To hear him express admiration for our native game was like a link had come apart in the machinery that held the Barton drawbridge in its time-worn place. But perhaps he was simply toying with the witless offspring of his enemy.

'I mean it,' Barton went on. 'I have tremendous admiration for the game. I must have seen every Munster Final over the last 30 years. Now let me ask you this. The lady you just met, my housekeeper. Her son, Gene, is coming to work for me. I understand he is a pretty good player. Do you think there might be a place for him in your Nursery Field?' He stopped, smiled and held his head sideways. 'As a favour?'

'If I ask, won't they know I was talking to you?'

Barton pursed his lips and made a sucking noise

through his teeth. 'You're an astute boy – nobody's fool, young Roderick. In that case, let Trenchard make his own way. Now I want to show you something. Come along, let's take this pathway through the shrubbery.'

The laurel and the undergrowth of briar and honey-suckle had formed a tunnel beneath the stand of beech. I slithered in his wake until we came to a rustic stile.

'See here,' he said, pointing towards Glenorga. 'This lane runs all the way to the estate wall, right opposite the spot where you fell. If you come through this stile, you are almost at the rear of Barton Hall and beside the entrance to the kitchen garden. Let me show you.'

I followed him to the archway that led to the garden. At the other end was the basement window with a flagstone surround. When we reached the window, he tugged at one of the iron bars and levered it out. Then he dragged the bar across its fellows. 'I used to steal out here in the dark of night, when I was your age, and make that noise. The servants were scared out of their wits; they thought it was the ghost of de Val, dragging his chains in his torture chamber. Now, young Roderick, why am I showing you all this?'

I shook my head, feeling his searching glance scrutinise my silence. 'If you ever want to visit me, and I hope you will, you can use the route that I've shown you. It's quite safe; no one will see.' He fixed the bar in its socket. 'A couple of the other bars will come out as well, enough for you to squeeze through. At the other side of the window there's a small flight of steps. It will bring you out on the corridor beside the library door. If I'm at home, that's where I'll be. But one proviso.' He jabbed his index finger at me as if to focus my complete attention. 'Don't come on Sunday. Always people around. Run along now, young man. Nice meeting you.'

Chapter 5

The success on the farm continued and my father basked in the glory of it. It seemed to heighten his passion for work. Hughie was still immersed in his intense love of the land. I seldom saw him anymore, as he had gone to the fields before I was astir and he didn't return until late in the evening.

My father bought land from the Widow Kirby whose fields were adjacent to ours. Neilus Kirby had been found dead between his turnip drills a few years before. Kirby was a drunk who every now and then disappeared from his home for days or weeks. He was reputed to be a violent man who frequently beat his wife. He filled me with an instinctive fear that had no basis in my experience, other than there was something strangely dangerous about the way he looked at me.

In the spring of my thirteenth year, we made a great advance. When the farmers whose land fringed upon the commonage on the lea of Knocknastumpa made a successful petition to the government to have it converted to private ownership, my father was granted 40 acres. He celebrated, as his neighbours did, and when he returned from Heaney's, he made a timorous assault on my mother's bedroom door.

My father never even raised his voice at my mother's refusal, but returned to the kitchen and I knew by the scrape of the chair on the flagged floor that he was settling down before the fire. He then talked to himself for hours. He was generous in his praise for Hughie, who was a Dawley, seed, breed and generation. His soul was cast in the same mould that made his father. Their time was coming; one of these days they would walk down to Barton Hall and buy the two big fields that ran parallel to ours.

My father talked deep into the night. It seemed that he was haranguing us, reminding us of the heritage we had forsaken but still pulsed in his veins and in those of his son. The free grant of land was the turn of fortune; it was history returning the spoils of war, generations later, to those from whom it had been wrested. I heard Mona calling from my mother's room and beseeching him to go to bed, but he carried on. Where were the Bartons now? They had once claimed that commonage as they claimed the mountain. And now the land had come home, back to those who had followed O'Donnell to Kinsale. God had been listening all those years.

Felim was in his third year in the secondary school in Adamston. His role as our court jester was as constant as ever, turning our black moments into flashes of light. Felim was Villiers' star pupil and every school report and every meeting with his mentor lifted my mother to new heights of basking self-indulgence. She sat in the parlour in the aftermath of the compliments, silently staring at the wallpaper, perhaps charting a course for her brilliant son.

Felim returned every weekend and went to the fields with Hughie, although the tractor had made us obsolete except for the son of sons. Everything about Felim, his attitudes, abilities and ambition, decreed that his alignment with Glenorga was over. And yet, every Friday evening when he returned, Felim would inquire where Hughie was working, throw his things on a chair and scurry off to join him. There was a strange bond between them. When I passed I would see them close together; Hughie solid and square on the tractor seat, Felim leaning against the mud-guard in nonchalant ease, hands gesticulating in non-stop punctuation to his words. Their laughter would reach me, as if they had built some private sanctuary, and they alone knew how to enter and abide in it.

My mother spent long hours in the parlour, either read-ing or lost in reverie. I wondered where the books came from since the space between the elephant bookends had always been empty. Once when I entered without knocking, I had seen her hands darting to hide a book in the folds of her long skirt. I had by now stopped trying to unravel the puzzle that my mother had become for me. Her face lit up when Hughie came in from the fields and a wider version of the same smile greeted Felim when he returned from Adamston, whilst Mona was forever in the soft warmth of my mother's sunray. I was in the arid terrain of the dark side.

The distance between us seared the core of my soul, but the more the space between us widened, the more my love for her was formed.

Mona had become boss of the farmyard. She was equal-ly comfortable in the welter of labour as my father and brothers. Mona was first stir in the mornings, and brought the cows home to the milking. Thereafter her day was a myriad of routine tasks and she galloped from chore to chore as if each one was the gift of a new discovery.

Every month the creamery cheque came, regular as clockwork. The day after it arrived, my father cycled to

Adamston. Since it was just another chore associated with the land he went in his working clothes.

'God's sake, Father,' Mona would stand in front of him, arms akimbo, 'you can't go to Adamston dressed like that.'

'Mona,' my mother said softly, 'leave it be.'

'I'm not good enough for you, my lady daughter, isn't that it? There's a pair of ye in it, two women looking down on decent people. Well, we can't all be Cartors. We can't all be reading books and going on tours of Europe. But if you don't like the way I go on, you can lump it.'

Mona bit her lip and went out into the yard. When he returned from the town, Father's mood had lifted. He wore a smug smile as he re-entered the kitchen, but it slowly drained away as he waited for my mother's permission to stash the money in the hidden drawer of the parlour table.

'I have money here. I want to put it away.' My mother made no reply. 'Did you hear me, woman? I want to go into the parlour and put away the money!'

My mother nodded. When he returned, he would give her money. He had started that practice when our upward surge had begun, a closed fist reaching out to her hand in a wordless gesture until she opened her palm to receive it.

'Hugh, I can't take this. It's too much. Give it to one of the others.'

'There's no fear of the others. If they want money, all they have to do is ask me. Take it now. I want you to buy yourself something. A nice dress or a coat. You never bought anything from the other money I gave you.'

'I will, Hugh. Some day soon, when we aren't busy, myself and Mona will go into Adamston.'

I roamed far and wide in the summer of my thirteenth year.

The day that was dawning outside my window was mine alone. I could use it or abuse it any way I wished because I had been judged expendable. From the summit of the first tier above Glenorga, I would stop and let the landscape soak into my being. It was beautiful in the early morning light, pristine and moist-fresh as if it had just emerged from the aftermath of creation.

A spiral of smoke climbed from Kilraish's chimney. The Kilraishes smelled of smoke; it was always wafting or blowing in their faces, either from the faulty chimney in the kitchen or from the burning, discarded wood outside. Mikey's twin, Rosie, sat on a primitive sawhorse beside the pile of wood. She smelled of wood smoke, apple blossom and ripening corn. In that summer, Rosie was an enigma, beautiful and inexplicable.

'Come sit here beside me, Roddy Dawley.' It was a habit, willed from her mother, to use first and second names. I blushed to the roots of my hair and cast my eyes to the ground.

'Are you scared of me, Roddy Dawley?' She was laughing at me again.

'I'm not scared? Why should I be afraid of you?'

'Because you fancy me, isn't that the way of it, Roddy Dawley?'

I tried to put sense and meaning on my feelings for her, yet couldn't tie them down. But one thing I knew for certain: my feelings for Rosie Kilraish were different from any sentiment that I had ever known before.

I sat beside her on the sawhorse and she entwined her legs with mine. She moved closer, tracing her fingers along the nape of my neck. She sent pulses of shock, like ripples of electric current which surged to my brain and turned it into a desert. She had reduced me to a gibbering idiot. I wanted to run away.

'Stay there, Roddy Dawley. You're not leaving until you tell me.'

I knew how she wanted me to answer. She asked me that same question over and over again. It was whispered to me as we left the classroom in Miss Horgan's school, as I stood in the queue in front of her to take communion at Sunday mass, in my comings and goings with Mikey. The same question that made me cringe with embarrassment.

'Are you my boy, Roddy Dawley?'

I slid down from the sawhorse and made for the house.

'You are. You are. I know. I can tell.'

Ardagh was a straggle of houses lying in the hollow of Glendign and seemed always to be cast in gloom or shrouded in mist. If it wasn't the mist that cloaked it, it was the dense fog of peat fire smoke that hung over it.

The shape and structure of the houses embellished the mystic quality of the village. The houses were roofed in the Ardagh style: the thatch advanced over the gables, fell in fringes over the upstairs windows and formed an arch above the lintels of the front door. There was neither system nor order to the siting of the houses; they seemed to have been thrown at random. The dividing street resembled a gigantic saw, with the houses as its teeth. But the overall impression was like a beaver's dam, comfortable, safe and homely.

Martin Culhane owned the biggest house in the village. Culhane was wealthy. According to Mikey, Martin could sell and buy every one of his neighbours. He owned the public house, the grocery and the hardware that spilled onto the pavement.

Mikey was an odd job man for Martin Culhane, a jack-of-all-trades, he told me. He cleaned, swept, arranged the hardware on the pavement and stocked the grocery shelves. Sometimes, when there was an influx of customers, he would help behind the bar; pouring bottles of stout and filling the occasional pint.

Culhane always wore a suit, the image of a successful rural man. Even on the warmest summer day, he favoured a high-necked starched collar and a burgundy red tie. Martin had an ingratiating manner that waxed and waned depending on the range of homage his customers qualified for. His wife, Mag, wore her preferences on her sleeve, plain for all to behold. She was a fluttering bird-like creature, who seemed to hop from place to place as if it hurt to put her feet firmly on the ground.

The Culhanes were exceptional in the tradition of the mountain, as they were wealthy in a community where poverty frequently encroached. Consequently, the folk of Mount Fierna offered them the twin symbols of begrudgery: voluble respect in their company, patent envy out of it. The seeds of that strategy were deep-seated in 500 years of coping with landlords; the Culhanes were simply native replacements of the old order.

Martin seemed to go out of his way to be pleasant towards me, perhaps because he had regard for my father.

I had known the Culhane son, Ferdy, since he first came to play in our Nursery Field. Now in his second year in a Jesuit College in Limerick, he had grown thoughtful and studious and spent long hours in his room. Muirne, Ferdy's sister, was seventeen, ravishingly beautiful, without a hint of parental lineage in body or soul. She reminded me of

Maureen O'Hara, the film star, whom I had seen playing opposite John Wayne in *The Quiet Man*. Flaming red hair fell down to her shoulders, forming a frame for her face.

Muirne was attending an elite convent school in Limerick, the kind that placed more emphasis on manners and decorum than on academic subjects. By now she had lost the vernacular of the mountain. She played the harp and the piano, Irish romantic melodies on the former, classical pieces on the latter.

When I passed by the window of the parlour, she would knock on the windowpane and beckon me in. I was offered tea in a china cup, a piece of toast with dollops of marmalade dripping over its sides, and exotic variations like grapefruit or a slice of melon. Muirne regarded me as a brother or some kind of callow youth whose simple innocence was ripe for exploitation. The housecoat would fall open as she moved about, revealing a vision of anatomy that made me pull my eyes away for it was a sin to see. Sometimes I would catch her watching me with sidelong smirks as I tried to balance the savour of temptation with the onrush of guilt.

In days of mist or incessant rain, Mag built a peat fire in the grate and Muirne entertained me. She played the harp and sang her repertoire of Irish songs: 'The Quiet Land of Éireann', 'She Moves Through the Fair', 'Down by the Sally Gardens'. I knew those songs from late night radio programmes and, much as I liked them then, there was a quality in Muirne's singing that was never captured in the studio versions.

On summer days, when the wind quietened and the heat shimmered like filigree tracework above the cloak of heather, we picked wild strawberries on Knocknastumpa.

We followed the meander of the Morning Star from the cascades above the Blue Pool to its source in the blackness of a bogland spring. I made her a garland of honeysuckle twined round a circle of laurel leaves; she laid wild poppies on a rabbit-cropped patch until they spelled my name. We swam in the Blue Pool in noonday stillness when the only sound was the gentle chimes of the feeding rivulets falling over the remnants of old red sandstone. Muirne, the flower of convent gentility, the drawing room rose, swam in the nude. She threw off her clothes with giggles of luscious abandonment and laughed at my blood red face. I hoped the summer would never end.

I didn't suspect it then and I grew angry when Mikey tried to forewarn me that Muirne played me with the same artistry as she wrought music from the keyboard of her upright grand.

'Are you clever at school, Roddy? I hear you are. Are you as smart as Felim?'

'Oh no. Miss Horgan never taught anyone as clever as Felim. She told my mother that.'

'It must be wonderful to be like that.' Muirne selected a rib of grass and cleaned under her nails. 'I'm useless. I might fail my Leaving Certificate.'

'You're not useless. You won't fail.'

'If I do,' Muirne broke the rib of grass and sent the pieces floating down the current, 'it isn't the end of the world. What's Felim like? People with brains are gloomy and serious.'

'Felim is always making jokes. He's great fun.'

'I'd like to meet him. You could bring him some day with you and have a picnic. The three of us. Wouldn't that be nice?'

'Felim works all day with Hughie. He wouldn't come. You could meet him after mass on Sunday.'

'No, Roddy. I don't think that would be a good idea. Tell me, is it true that Felim doesn't believe in religion?'

The idea filled me with dread. Of all the wrongs a body might do, turning one's back on God was a mortal sin. I had a vision of Felim in consuming flames, his face disintegrating in molten liquid.

'No, no, that's not true. Felim goes to mass with the rest of us. He says his prayers too.'

'Ah sure, it must be only a rumour. What's he going to do when he leaves Adamston?'

'Mr Villiers says that Felim will get a scholarship to the university. Maybe he'll become an engineer, or a doctor, even an artist.'

'An artist? What makes you think that?'

'He talks to my mother about it. About going off to France or Italy and living there.'

'France, Italy, wouldn't that be lovely? Isn't it grand for him to have those notions?' She was silent for a little while, wistfully watching the flow of the water and idly gathering her clothes about her. 'Roddy, will you tell Felim I was asking for him?'

I told Felim. I went to the meadow where he was cutting a swathe of hay along the hedgerow so that the tractor could start the mowing. He was shirtless; the sun had tanned his skin to the waistband of his trousers, leaving a band of ivory just below. He kept on swishing the scythe as I told him. Felim laughed at me. 'Do you ever hear what the man said when he saw the wooden horse in the streets of Troy. *Timite Danoas, dona ferentes.* Beware of Greeks bearing gifts.'

'What does that mean?'

'Forget it. So you're a messenger boy now?'

'She just asked me, that's all. What will I tell her?'

'Anything you like.'

'I can't do that. Felim, she's very nice. Can't you—'

Felim stopped scything and flicked the sweat from his eyebrows. He wasn't smiling anymore. 'Roddy, the likes of Muirne Culhane would swallow you up, spit you out and make a right fool of you. And when that happens, don't come looking to me for sympathy.'

The pedestal I had built for my brother collapsed like a house of cards. Hughie I loved, but Felim was my hero, the golden boy with all the gifts. He suddenly had feet of clay; he was spiteful and dismissive.

'You're a right smart man, aren't you? You think you know it all.'

'Grow up, Roddy, for God's sake. I can't treat you like an innocent babe forever. Now get out of here and leave me to my work. Come to think of it, it wouldn't do you any harm to give us a hand. There must be something useful you could do.'

I could feel the onrush of self-pity. I had promised myself never to revisit that state.

'I tried,' I half-sobbed, 'but none of ye want me. Ye all think I'm useless.'

'Then,' Felim said, 'convince us otherwise.'

Martin was waiting for us where the narrow white road made the first twist to entwine the straggle of Ardagh. Behind him Mag hopped from foot to foot, for once holding her head erect and in her face a fierce fix of anger.

'Jaysus,' Mikey whispered, 'trouble.'

Martin grasped Mikey by the earlobe. 'You little bastard, you bloody hoor's melt, I'll fix you.'

'I done nothing, Mr Culhane, honest to God,' Mikey wailed.

'Hear him,' Mag squawked. 'Listen to me boyo. Give him a clip in the ear, Martin.'

Mikey backed out of reach once the grip on his ear was released. 'I told you I done nothing. You can't prove anything against me.'

'Can't he?' Mag said, 'Well, he can so. There's a man inside there in the grocery, Patsy Barron from Dromtrasna. You short-changed him, you bloody robber. He gave you a pound and you gave him back the change of a ten-shilling note. And you did it to Philly Grimes as well and Jackie Power. We're onto to you now, bucko.'

'Where's the money,' Martin demanded. 'I had to pay back those men out of my own pocket. If you don't give me the money, I'll set the police on you.'

Mikey backed away a few more paces and began to laugh. 'Go on,' Mikey stammered between gusts of mirth. 'Ye haven't proof. The police will laugh at ye.'

Martin scratched his poll. 'You did it so; you're after admitting it.'

'I heard him too,' Mag cackled.

'I admitted nothing. I'll go home and tell my father that ye accused me of stealing and he'll have the law on the pair of ye.'

Martin's shoulders drooped. People of the mountain had an inherent distrust and fear of the forces of justice. The law was for landlords and constabulary and had been imposed like a weapon upon them for centuries. Then there was the threat of Long Pat Kilraish, who was capable of anything in the pursuit of an easy shilling.

'Get out of here,' Mag pointed a finger at Mikey. 'Never darken my door again.' She turned towards the hapless Martin. 'Weren't you the right fool to bring a Kilraish into our house?'

'I wasn't the first Kilraish to darken your door,' Mikey's cackled with glee. 'My mother was here before me.'

Mag was like Lot's wife, frozen in a pillar of shock. When she recovered she swung around and furiously hopped away. Then she had second thoughts. 'Get out of my sight, Kilraish, and take that half-legged Dawley with you. An' don't aither of ye come within an ass' roar of me again.' I saw a flush of remorse flit across Martin's crestfallen features as he looked at me.

'I'm sorry,' he mumbled. 'Sorry.'

Mikey ran ahead of me. He clambered over boulders and heather clumps, pausing every now and then to let me catch up. He halted before the portals of the Giant's Grave. When I reached him, he had lifted a flagstone from the ground and was waiting for me to examine the hollow he had scooped from the earth beneath. It held a dozen bottles of stout, some packets of cigarettes and a mound of coins.

'Christ, Mikey. The Culhanes were telling the truth.'

'What does it matter to the Culhanes? They have loads of money.' He began to count the money, his fingers moving with the deftness of a cashier. 'Seventeen shillings and sevenpence,' he declared, 'an' I would have made a lot more if it weren't for that ould arsehole from Dromtrasna. Here,' he shoved two half-crowns towards me, 'your share.'

I shook my head. 'No thanks. I don't want any part of it. What you did was a sin, Mikey. You should give it back. Otherwise, you'll roast in hell.'

'Hell, me arse. You can believe in that ould codology if you want but you won't catch me at it. All right, I'll tell you what we'll do. We'll take the half-crowns and we'll go to Newtown. Buy ourselves chocolate and biscuits, and have a feast. Are you on?'

'I don't think it's right. The money was stolen. And I don't like it here. People were buried here. Their bones are under the earth.'

Mikey looked to heaven and pursed his lips. 'Sweet Jesus, what will you come up with next.'

''Tis true,' I told him. Barton's name rushed to my lips and I choked it off. 'A man told me. He said that people who lived around here, thousands of years ago, used bury their dead in places like this. It's a kind of sacred place.'

'That a fact? Mikey scoffed. 'I've come in here many a time and nothing ever happened to me. An' I'm not the only one.'

'No one else but you would come in here.'

'Think so? A few days ago I found a book under that flagstone, over there to your right. 'Twas gone yesterday. I was afraid my stuff would be gone with it. But it's all here, every penny and the fags and the porter. Now what do you make of that?'

'What kind of book?'

'What do you mean? A book's a book. It had a red cover and goldy paint all round the edges.'

Mikey removed the bottles of stout and set them in a row. Then suddenly, he picked one up, and smacked it with the palm of his hand. Immediately the froth gushed forth. Mikey quaffed long and strenuously, his Adam's apple popping in and out. He sighed when he took the bottle away.

'Jaysus,' he said, 'that was grand. I was dying with the

drought.' He passed the bottle to me as if it were as natural as sharing a drink of lemonade. I hesitated. On the day of my Confirmation I had pledged to abstain for life from intoxicating drink. I believed that drinking was another arrow in Satan's quiver of temptation. Father Morgan Lynch preached that drink was the scourge of all classes and especially of those whom he called 'my beloved poor.' I took a swallow and gagged. The porter tasted foul, it caught in my breath and entered my nostrils. I coughed, spluttered and heaved. Mikey slapped my back.

'You'll be grand. It happens to all of us. Take a deep breath and then another swallow. You'll be as right as rain then.'

He left me the bottle and opened another for himself. As I drank, the bitter taste was subsumed by a feeling of luxurious exhilaration that soared my spirits to a summit of contentment. Mikey pressed a second bottle into my hand and I experienced a great bond of fellowship between us. I refused the cigarette he offered me because I had tried one previously. It had made me sick and I feared I might spoil this wonderful glow that surrounded me. Then a wave of tiredness settled upon me and lifted me skywards. When I looked down I saw myself sitting between the portals. I fell asleep.

I dreamed that my mother and I were sitting alone by the Blue Pool. She was reading a story to me; the book had a red cover and a golden tinge on the outer margin of each page. Then when I looked again, she had changed into Mikey's Uncle Robert whose eyes leered at me from the depths of his sunken face. He stretched out a skeletal arm, fastened his fleshless fingers on my shoulder and began to draw me underwater to his resting-place in the river's cavern. I screamed, vomit filled my mouth and overflowed into my nostrils. Then it was Lionel Barton who swam before my vision. He was kneeling on the ground and began to wipe away the smears of vomit with a white hand-kerchief. He put me sitting erect and shook me gently. I awoke and knew that he was no dream.

'There now, there, there,' he clucked. His voice was laden with concern. 'You'll be all right now. Sit up.'

My head throbbed; my stomach was still lurching in spasm. 'Mike,' I gasped, 'where is Mikey?'

'I sent the little bastard packing, with a buzz in his ear. You look like death, young Roderick, but I think you'll survive. What were you up to?'

I told him all that had happened. He listened, shaking his head.

'I may have said this to you already. Kilraish will get you into trouble.' Barton spread his hands. 'Now then, how do you feel?'

My head throbbed in hammer blows. There was a seismic disruption taking place in the pit of my stomach. In all the bouts of illness and afflictions that had visited me since I was a child, I never felt as bad as this.

'Terrible. I think I'm going to die.'

'Nonsense. But let it be a lesson to you. What you need is a warm bath and a good cleaning down. We'll have to do something about these clothes too. We can't let you home to your mother in your present condition.'

I knew I should refuse. Misshapen images of treachery strove to form but were aborted in my pain and misery. 'I think I'll go home,' I said feebly.

Barton interrupted me with a dismissive wave of his hand. 'You'll do nothing of the kind. Take the route I showed you. I'll be along presently. Wait for me in the library.'

I hauled myself erect. Slivers of pain, like pinpoints of a thousand knives, lanced through my head and rushed out above my eyes.

'Steady, old boy, you sure you can make it alone?'

I nodded. 'How did you find me?'

'Purely fortuitous. I was passing by, heard you being sick. Off you go now.'

I stood for a long time by the basement window before I removed the iron bar. Once I took it away, I had crossed the Rubicon and entered the lair of our sworn enemy. It was an act of wilful duplicity, a negation of everything I had been weaned on and was expected to uphold. I would betray the centuries of suffering and domination, break faith with the heritage of my forebears. But try as I might, I couldn't see Lionel Barton as the incarnation of evil and cruelty. He had shown me the obverse of the image, the outward signals of a kind human soul.

The remains of a fire still glowed in the library fireplace and a leather armchair stood before it. All around me the atmosphere was laden with symbols of comfort and cheer. I felt tired and drowsy. The chair beckoned me towards it. There was a book lying on the seat. It had a red cover and the pages were gold-rimmed. I turned it over to look at the title. It leaped out at me in embossed letters. *Pride and Prejudice.*

Chapter 6

I never liked Gene Trenchard. He arrived in our Nursery field one evening in June, carrying a brand new hurley. There was a swagger about him even as he waited to be invited to play. He must have been seventeen then, about the same age as Felim, but there was a bluish tinge to his face which suggested that his advent to manhood had advanced more rapidly than the rest of us. Trenchard was taller than Felim and had the body of an athlete.

Perhaps my dislike was founded on the way he moved. He walked on the balls of his feet, springing upwards with each step. In full flow he had the agility of a hare. I avoided walking beside him as the limitations of my deformity were thrown into stark relief beside his lissom grace. What I disliked most was his tactic of cultivating those who suited his schemes and ignoring people who didn't.

Felim occupied the topmost rung in Trenchard's ladder of importance; they seemed to have many things in common. Both were handsome, moulded in that perfect foundry of physical beauty and elegant form. But they were also in rhythm with the beat of each other's minds, with a similar sense of humour and interests.

A few evenings after he arrived my father came out to watch the game and drifted to where I was standing between the makeshift posts.

'Who's the new fella?'

'Gene Trenchard. He came here of his own free will. He wasn't asked.'

My father pulled the lobe of his ear; it was his way of showing that he suspected some hidden implication.

'Did I ask you if you brought him here? Did I? From where?'

'From Barton Hall. He's the stockman.'

'Ah yes. He'll be Rose Trenchard's son. He'll be a Protestant so.'

'That's right.'

'Well, well, what's the world coming to? Barton's stockman, and a Protestant, playing hurling in my Nursery Field, right in the middle of mountainy sons. Isn't that a good one?'

My father started to walk away. At that moment Felim split the ball towards the far end of the field. Trenchard ran on to it, trapped it and in a blur of movement whizzed it past Vinny Staples in the opposite goal.

'He'll be good,' my father said.

I went home uneasily that evening for I thought my father was playing one of his devious games. He would ask a few casual questions about something and give the impression he was satisfied with the answers. Later, however, when one was off guard, he would return to the subject in anger and accusation.

My father should have been in bed when we trooped in after the hurling. But he was sitting before the fire, still with his boots on and the long legs stretched full. He waited until Hughie had sat and then swung round to face him. But the gaunt troubled face suddenly dissolved into ease.

'Isn't that gas?' he said. 'Imagine one of the Barton breed coming up here to play hurling. To my field. Who'd have thought it?'

'Yeah,' Hughie agreed, 'times are changing.'

'No, Hughie,' my father shook his head in slow emphasis, 'we're changing. We're not seen as ignorant downtrodden peasants any more. Isn't that a good one?' A wink of appreciation closed one eye. 'My Nursery Field is good enough for a Protestant. If my father had seen the day, or his father before him ...'

'There is nothing wrong with being a Protestant,' Felim said.

The smile faded. 'Is that a fact? An' what do you know about Protestants?'

'I go to school with them,' Felim answered calmly. 'We shouldn't confuse Protestants in general with the likes of the Bartons.'

My father ruminated as he digested Felim's remark. Whatever Hughie said he always took on face value but he queried Felim frequently. The mood was shifting; the ever-present hazard was emitting signals of caution. We had learned to recognise them.

'He seems a nice boy,' my mother kept her eye on the sock she was darning, 'and a very good player, I hear.'

'Brilliant,' Felim said emphatically.

'Where did he get it from?' my father wondered. 'The likes of him don't grow up playing hurling.'

'He learned it in Adare,' Felim said. 'He went to the Christian Brothers school.'

'I suppose that explains it.' My father was talking to Hughie again. 'He didn't learn it from Barton, that's for sure. That fella wouldn't know one end of a hurley from the other.'

'But he does,' I heard myself saying, too late to seal off

the flow. 'Mr Barton loves hurling; he goes to all the matches.'

The words hung in mid-air in petrified fingers of condemnation. I could feel the eyes burrowing into my wilted soul. I waited for the clap of doom. It came instead in caustic spear thrusts.

'Well, well, *"Mr Barton"*, if you don't mind. Here's a fella who knows his place. It's *Mr Barton*, now is it? An' tell me, you fawning little shit, how do you know so much about the great Mr Barton?'

Hughie, my saviour, spoke. 'I was telling Roddy. I've seen Barton at matches, many times.'

My father pulled at the lobe of his ear and pinched the stubble of his chin. I could feel his gaze swing from one to the other and heard the creak of the chair as he bent to take off his boots.

'Felim, you should ask him in,' my mother said. 'He seems quite a nice young man.'

'Would it be all right?'

No one offered an opinion. The question was aimed directly at my father. He gathered up his boots and contemplated the laces. They were leather thongs and when wet become sodden and slimy. He looked at me.

'You, sir, attend to my laces when the boots dry out. You hear me, Mr Dawley?'

'Yes, Father.'

'Would it be all right?' Felim asked again.

A bone creaked in my father's knee when he stood up. It made my teeth clench. 'It wouldn't be my way of doing things, but sure, whoever listened to me?'

And so Gene Trenchard came amongst us. I wondered at the ease with which he was integrated. None of our neighbours' children ever frequented our home unless bearing a message or running an errand. Friendships were never equal to the challenge of my parents. My mother had raised a barricade around us, as if any intrusion might contaminate her aspirations. If that weren't enough, my father's reputation was like a moat that surrounded the rampart. Even Mikey Kilraish, brash and precocious as he was, would never come within 100 yards of our house.

Yet Trenchard came like a lost soul to the bosom of a surrogate family. He constantly thanked my mother for the courtesy shown him, presented her with bunches of wild flowers, brought little packages of sweets in greaseproof paper. My father received a day-old copy of the *Irish Independent* and back issues of *Old Moore's Almanac*. I had my usual view from the margins. Trenchard had placed me firmly at the bottom of the scale and treated me with disdain when there was no one else about. He called me the Dawley runt.

But I had greater problems to contend with. A letter came in the post. It carried the seal of the parochial house and smelled of old parchment and beeswax. My mother read it out at the evening meal. *Dear Hugh, Please be good enough to direct your son Roderick to present himself at the parochial house at two o clock, on the afternoon of Friday, 14 July. I remain, yours in Christ, Father Morgan Lynch, D. D.*

'What's all that about?' my father asked. 'I hope for your sake, Mr Roderick Dawley, that you're hiding nothing from me.' He turned to my mother. 'Well, is this something else I should have known about?'

'I think it might have something to do with the examination that Roddy sat last month.'

I waited in the parlour while the priest finished his midday meal. An illuminated scroll, framed in gilt and edged with Celtic spirals, dominated the far wall – *Arms and Pedigree of the Lynch Family*. The room smelled like Barton's library, the lingering odour of leather and Probert's polish. Beside the fire was a carved mahogany prieu-dieu. The book of office, with its black calfskin binding and linen page-markers, was lying open on the lectern.

Father Lynch entered with a flourish. 'Roderick. Interesting name. Hardly a name associated with the Dawley clan, is it?'

'I was called after my mother's brother.'

'Oh I see. That explains it. Now let's get down to business. I want to talk to you about the examination you sat in Danesfort. Do you know that I was Dean of Discipline there for many years?'

'No.'

'No what?'

'I don't know.'

'Young man. When you speak to a priest, you should address him as "Father". Now, because of my long-standing association with the college, your results were transmitted to me directly. You did very well. So well, in fact, that the college is offering you a scholarship for three years, which may be extended, depending on the results of your Intermediate Certificate. I presume you understand the import of all this?'

'I think so.'

'I think so.' The thin lips tightened, the fingers drummed on the desktop.

'I think so, Father.'

'Good. Your father will be proud of you. You will be the

first boy from Mount Fierna to attend Danesfort.' The priest paused; a slight frown appeared above his eyebrows. 'You will be taking up this scholarship, of course?'

Danesfort loomed in front of me and I was filled with dread and foreboding. The day I sat the examination, I was overwhelmed by the humourless atmosphere of the place: a gaunt limestone pile, remote and cheerless, standing like a monument to incarcerated souls. The students' dress and speech were so different to my own that they eroded my faltering ego and I knew I would never be comfortable there. I should have yielded to the temptation and deliberately failed the test.

'I suppose so,' I mumbled.

'Young man, do you know what Danesfort is?'

'It's a boarding college, Father.'

'Not *just* a boarding college. The primary purpose of Danesfort is to provide a seminary for students who wish to study for the priesthood. It's a diocesan college. Now, do you realise what I'm saying?'

'I don't know, Father.'

'Have you thought about becoming a priest, Roderick?'

'No, Father.'

'Don't dismiss it like that. I made this point to your brother Felim but unfortunately it fell on deaf ears. When one associates with fellow students who wish to dedicate their lives to God, and with priests who have already done so, one becomes influenced in an almost subliminal way. It happened to me and to many of my colleagues in Christ. The church needs people like you, Roderick, with intelligence and academic prowess, who can compete with our counterparts in other denominations. Do you see what I mean, Roderick?'

'I think so, Father.'

'Good.' He folded his fingers and held them under his chin. 'Roderick, that limp of yours, has it improved?'

'It will never improve, Father.'

'I see. Well, don't let it discourage you. The church needs priests in many lands, not just in Ireland. Oh, I had almost forgotten ... I believe you are a hurler.'

'A goalkeeper, Father.'

'Excellent. Danesfort is a renowned hurling college. You'll be welcomed with open arms. So, that's settled then, Roderick. I will be in touch with the president of the college. In due course you will receive all the data you need. Now I want you to do something for me.'

'Me, Father?'

'Yes. I am concerned, Roderick, about your family's attitude to religion and the church. Your brother Felim, for instance. He doesn't sit in the family pew at Sunday mass. I have seen him several times at the rear of the church. But more recently I haven't seen him in attendance at all. And it has come to my attention that he is gadding about with that Trenchard fellow. You know him?'

'He plays hurling in our Nursery Field, Father.'

'Does he? Indeed. Is your father aware that he is a Protestant?

'I think so, Father.'

'I see. That's a further complication. Anyway, going back to Felim, I will not have that, Roderick. And neither should you, especially now when your credentials must be above criticism. See if you can effect some change in your brother's foolishness, before I have to intervene. Will you do that?'

'I'll try, Father.'

'Do more than try, Roderick. Now, the second thing. I've noticed that your father doesn't pay any dues. He strikes me as a decent God-fearing man, and I don't want to embarrass him. From now on, Roderick, I am going to read out from the altar what each household donates. I think it's right that every man should pay his lawful dues; it's one of the precepts of the church. Do you know why your father does not comply, Roderick?'

'No, Father,' I lied.

'Perhaps I should talk to him myself. That will be all then, for the moment. Look upon me, Roderick, as your friend and counsellor. Should you need any support from me, feel free to come and visit.'

I walked home by the lake, taking the pathway that led to Manisterluna. The ruined monastery threw off the rays of the sun and brightened the grassy mounds and the sandstone flags that marked the graves of mountain generations. Over the top of Knocknastumpa a black cloud was gathering. Long ago, Beth Cartor and her brother came this way and saw the golden valley of Glenorga. On such innocuous little bits of trivia are built the destiny of innocent powerless souls. If they had made a different turn, perhaps even halted at a different site, I would never have entered this world.

A terrible loneliness, dense as the black cloud, sucked me into a miasma of despair. I never wanted to leave Glenorga; it was my home, my special place in the sun. Danesfort was the death knell of an awesome sundering. The great cloud passed overhead and when it journeyed past the avenue of stately elms, Barton Hall emerged in the light.

I found Lionel Barton watering plants in the conservatory. He was wearing a deerstalker with a matching open-necked plaid shirt. 'Lemonade?' he asked.

I shook my head. He fluffed out a cushion on the wicker chair that stood by the French windows and motioned me to sit. 'You look troubled, young Roderick.'

He pulled up a chair beside mine, took off the cap and smiled at me. His face was written all over with the markings of compassion and concern, the same signs I used see in my mother's countenance when I was a sickly child. The words came rushing out in the gushing relief of pent up distress.

'Dear me,' Barton said when I had finished. 'Now where will we start?'

'I don't want to go. That's all there is to it. I'll go to Adamston with Felim.'

'Roderick, I can be honest and tell you what I think. Or I can be a charlatan and tell you what you want to hear. What age are you now?'

'Thirteen. I'll be fourteen in March.'

'That age already? The days of running free are over, Roderick; time you put on the mantle of responsibility. You don't like me saying that, do you?'

'I don't care.'

'Good. Now tell me, what's wrong with Danesfort? I believe it's a fine school.'

'I don't want to leave home. I'm afraid, Mr Barton.' The tears welled up; I blinked rapidly to keep them in check.

'Please call me Lionel. Why are you afraid?'

'I'll be out of place in Danesfort. The day I sat the examination, I saw what the students were like. They are the sons of rich people, from towns and villages and big houses in the country. They have a way of speaking that's different to me. I'll be a laughing stock with my crippled leg and all. I'll hate it. I know I'll hate it.'

For long moments Barton looked out of the window. There was a faraway look in his eyes as if he was seeing something beyond the vista of crag and stunted hazel. Then he slapped his thigh, slid back his chair and bent to open a cupboard door. He returned with a pair of tall glasses and a large bottle with a red label and the name Nash printed in silver lettering. He handed me a glass, poured and waited until the lemonade fizzed to the top.

'Many years ago, Roderick, when I was younger than you are now – I was only ten – I was sent to a public school in England, a place called Amersham Hall. It was the custom of the time; sons of the so-called landed gentry were so despatched. I remember thinking exactly like you now. And when I went there, I discovered that I was exactly right. I was small and reticent, the worst possible ingredients for the mix that existed in that school, indeed in any English public school. But worse, I was Anglo-Irish and Catholic. A papist bogman. And because I expected that reaction to me, I accepted it. It was the worst thing I could have done. I became, with respect, a cripple of another kind, an emotional one. It took me a long time to recover. I still bear some of the scars. But, and this is what I want to impress on you, it was I who was wrong. I should have fought for my crumbling ego, stood up to be counted, and demanded respect and recognition. No one can grant you self-esteem.' Barton stabbed at his temple. 'It must come from up here.'

Outside the window a dragonfly hung suspended as if caught in a vacuum. In the elm trees a wood pigeon cooed and a magpie flung a shrill challenge in defence of its arboreal territory.

'So you want me to go too?'

'I want nothing from you, Roderick. But if you were my son, I would do everything to encourage you to go. How many boys were in that examination hall?'

'About 200, maybe more. The place was full.'

'And how many of those, do you think, were offered scholarships?'

'I don't know.'

'No more than ten. So what does that say to you?'

'I was lucky. The questions fell for me.'

'Oh Christ. Sorry. Don't be so bloody disparaging about yourself. You've talent; you're a damn bright boy. Recognise your ability and fulfil it.'

'But I could do that in Villiers' school in Adamston.'

'You don't have a scholarship there. Anyway, that's my advice. Think seriously about it.'

They were waiting for me around the kitchen table. The meal was over but no effort had yet been made to clear away the tea things.

'So you came home, Mr Dawley,' my father said. 'We were going to send out a search party for you. Well, what did the priest say?'

'I won a scholarship to Danesfort. The results were sent on to Father Lynch.'

Hughie leaned across the table and grabbed my hands below the wrists. He squeezed and I could feel his strength and satisfaction flow into my veins. 'Good man yourself, Roddy. I knew you had in you. Fair play to you.'

Mona hugged and kissed me. 'Well done, little brother.'

My mother moved her head to and fro as if savouring the wonder of it all. Then she came round the table and ruffled my hair. 'I'm very happy for you, Roderick.'

'What does this scholarship mean?' my father wanted to know.

'It means that my fees and board will be free for the first three years. It will be extended for the remaining two if I do well in my Intermediate Certificate.'

Hughie whistled his appreciation. My father was searching for the drawback, some militating factor, yet uncovered, that would reduce the value of the achievement. He pulled his eyes away from the attic door. 'How many boys took the examination?'

'About 200.'

'An' how many would have been awarded scholarships?'

'Ten maybe. Twelve at the most.'

'So you're just one out of twelve. But not bad, not bad.'

'What do you mean, not bad?' Creases furrowed and blackened on Hughie's brow. 'Give Roddy credit. It's bloody great.'

My father made a placatory gesture with his outstretched hands. 'What else did the priest say?'

'He said it was a great honour for me to be accepted into Danesfort. I should be very grateful.'

'I'm very happy for you,' my mother said again; 'it is a great honour.'

A blur of movement appeared in the periphery of my vision. Felim stood bolt erect. He turned the chair front to back and placed his hands on the topmost rail. For a moment I thought he would adopt his oratorical stance and lead into a verse of poetry. *I bring fresh showers for the thirsting flowers, From the seas and the streams.*

'Will you listen to yourselves,' he began, 'talking about honour and gratitude? Who does that pompous Father

Lynch think he is, acting as if we were all serfs and slaves and couldn't be trusted to make decisions for ourselves? He assumes the right to see Roddy's results before we do and bend them to his own design. Roddy, I'm delighted for you, but let me tell you this, that Father Lynch doesn't have any interest in you other than to exploit your brainpower.'

'Sit down, you!' my father snarled.

'I won't sit down.' Felim turned towards my father. 'If you don't listen to me, then let the consequences be on your head. Roddy, tell me, did he ask you if you wanted to go to Danesfort? What exactly did he say?'

'He'll be very angry if I don't go, Felim. I'm sure of that from the way he was going on. He wants me to become a priest; he said that the Church needs people like me.'

'I bloody well knew it,' Felim scanned the faces round the table looking for vindication. 'Who the hell does he think he is? Mam,' he sought my mother's support but her face was downcast, her fingers idly moving the crumbs on her plate, 'for God's sake, Mam, don't let him run our lives. Don't let Roddy go to Danesfort. Let him come to Adamston with me. Let us show that jumped up Father Lynch that we are not afraid of him.'

My father's clenched fist smote the table. The delph bounced and rattled and the hunk of brown bread jumped from the board.

'Sit down, you pup you. I'll have no one in this house, as long as I'm alive, criticise the priest or what he stands for.' My father stabbed an accusing finger at Felim; it was throbbing with anger. 'If I ever hear another word of that carry on, it won't be my finger I'll be pointing at you.'

'Are you threatening me?'

'What does it sound like? You may be a right smart man,

you may be cutting a fine figure down there in Adamston with your fancy Protestant friends, but you won't stand at my table and try and lord it over me. I will not have blasphemy in this house or bad things said about a man of God.'

Felim laughed while he held my father's gaze. 'You should listen to yourself; you're a tough man in your own kitchen but you're scared shitless of—'

'Sit down, Felim,' Hughie said. 'That's enough.'

Felim hesitated. Then he righted the chair and sat down. He tilted back his head, half-closed his eyes and exhaled with exaggerated slowness.

'Father,' Hughie started to say.

'Don't tell me you're going to side with your scamp of a brother.'

'Stop it. Stop it all of you,' my mother implored. 'It sickens me the way we go on in this house. We're like a tribe of wild people, roaring and screaming at each other at every hand's turn.'

'Are you talking about me, woman? If there's roaring in this house, who made it like that? You can't answer me that, can you?'

'Please, Hugh, let it stop. Please?'

'Right, by God, I'll stop it and this is the way I'll do it. As long as I am master in this house, we'll respect our religion and what the priests tell us. Now, Mr Dawley, sir,' the finger stabbed at me, 'I want you to go to Danesfort. Me,' he thumped his chest, ''tis me that's telling you. And I don't want to hear another word about it. That's it, finished.'

My father's feet stamped on the stairs as if pounding out his authority. The canopy of silence descended over the table. Moments later the footsteps sounded on the boards again, softer and less deliberate; he had changed the heavy boots for what he called the low shoes. It took a disturbing event to change my father's routine and we read the signs like a ship's captain watches for sea change. He was going to Heaney's. But he would go first to the fields, choosing a clean pathway along the headlands to keep his shoes dry. The land and the fields were like an opiate to him, they salved his wounds. By the time he arrived in Heaney's his humour would have lifted.

'I would like us all to go into the parlour,' my mother said, after the door had banged in my father's wake.

'Mam,' Hughie said, 'there's nothing to talk about. It's all fixed up. Roddy is going to Danesfort.'

'And I'd like to see Roddy go to Danesfort too; it's a very good school. Don't you think so, Felim?'

'I do not. But I've said my piece and I didn't exactly get widespread support for it. And let me add one more thing, Mam: Roddy will be eaten alive in Danesfort.'

It was cold in the parlour. The fire was seldom lit anymore other than for Christmas day. It had been lit, especially for me, when I was a sickly child.

'Close the door, Roddy,' my mother said. 'Whatever about the others, you and I will have our own conference. Here, take my chair. Now tell me, what's the problem?'

'I don't want to leave.'

'Roddy, look at me. There's nothing in Glenorga for you. Surely you can see that for yourself. Nobody is needed now only Hughie, and if it was up to me, even he would be gone. Do you think I'd have stayed here this long if I had any other option? Danesfort will be good for you; it will make you stand on your own two feet. You need that, Roddy. I want you to be confident about yourself and be able to make your way in the world without always looking over your shoulder. Do you understand what I'm saying?'

'I know what you're saying, Mam. I'm not as important to you as Hughie, or Mona or Felim. I can see how you look at them. It's been like that since I broke my leg. Father doesn't want me either; he thinks I'm useless. So okay, Mam, I'll go to Danesfort. It's what everybody wants.'

Beyond the window a vixen cried from the summit of Knocknastumpa. Our sheepdog barked a warning and it tapered to a growl in the depths of its throat. The room had darkened; it smelled now of aged camphor and old ruined decay.

'Mam, why don't you ever say you love me?'

Shadows lengthened on my soul, sending wavelets of gloom to haunt me. The mood was mirrored in the landscape of Glenorga. The Morning Star exulted no more in its journey through the gorge; the story of its passing was a song of lamentation. Then one evening as I sat on the bank of the Blue Pool, listening to the tinkling cascades below the weir, Felim found me.

'Thought you might be here,' he said as he pulled off his clothes. Hayseeds clung to the matted hairs of his pullover and hid in his eyebrows. The water seemed to part with outstretched arms of welcome as he dived, as if it had embraced its own kindred. For a while I thought he had entered the cavern beneath the eddy, but he suddenly arose in the middle, arching upwards like a dolphin. He crawled up the slope of the bank and stretched on the close-cropped grass.

'Are you mad with me for saying that you'd be eaten

alive in Danesfort?'

'It doesn't matter. I have to face it. You're probably right.'

'I shouldn't have said that. It was wrong of me, and stupid. Roddy, you'll be fine. I know you will.'

'I know I won't. And so do you. Felim, I'll be awful lonely.'

'For what?'

'For Glenorga. I never want to leave here.'

'Oh Christ, you've got the Glenorga bug too? I thought that you were different, Roddy; that you could go away from here and never look back.'

'I thought it was you that was different.'

'Shows you how little we know about each other. Did I ever tell you about the swans?'

'Swans?'

'In Lough Cutra. About a year ago I was walking along the shore and saw them, a hen and a cob and three young ones, almost fully grown. They were all around each other in a circle; they reminded me of us, having a family conference, except the father was present. Then the cob began to attack the cygnets. He went after them viciously, stabbing at them and beating his wings. And then the mother joined in. Finally it dawned on the cygnets that they were being driven away. It was a sad thing to watch; they swam together away from their parents and every now and then one of them would turn back and try to return. They came eventually to Waller's Point, spread their wings, ran on the surface of the water and took off. And such, Roddy, is life. Better to go before you're driven away. Time you stopped being afraid, Roddy.'

He began to collect his clothes, arranging them on the

ground in the order he was going to put them on. 'I'll give you 50 yards' start and race you home.'

'Father Lynch talked to me about you, Felim. He doesn't see you in the church anymore. Unless he does, he's going to speak to Father about it.' Felim shook his head in disbelief and dropped the pullover. 'It's wrong, Felim, not going to mass. If you died tonight you'd go straight to hell—'

'Roddy, you believe what you want. I don't want to disillusion you, but I'm fed up with religion, especially the kind of religion that Napoleon preaches. And that's all I'm going to say. Just in case you become a priest and you put your hex on me and turn me into a pillar of salt!'

'What's hex?'

'A spell, a kind of curse. You wouldn't do that to me, would you, Roddy? I'm your hero, amn't I?'

'OK, you are my hero. But I wish you'd go to mass like the rest of us. Our father will go mad if he hears.'

'Roddy, I won't make you false promises. I'm done with religion.'

But he wasn't. A few weeks later my father came late from Sunday mass. 'You sir,' my father glared at Felim, 'where were you this morning?'

'At mass, Father. Listening to the word of God, or should I say to the man who would be God.'

'Don't get funny with me. I'll ask you once more, where were you at mass?'

'He was with me,' Hughie said, 'in the back of the church.'

'Did I ask you, did I? Once more, where were you, you pup?'

'Okay, Father. Let me confirm what you already know. I

was behind the creamery wall, playing pitch and toss with Josie Costello, Jer Histon, Francie Noonan, and yes, I almost forgot, Gene Trenchard. Now, what do you make of that?'

The fist smote the table; the echo of tortured wood reverberated from the walls.

'Am I hearing this right? You deliberately didn't go to mass.'

'That's right. And I won't be going any more either.'

'Woman,' my father's anger dissipated into shocked disbelief, 'do you hear what that fella is saying? What class of a pup did you rear? We have an atheist, a damn pagan for a son. Christ almighty.'

'Don't look at me, Hugh, I've always encouraged—'

'Encouraged? Encouraged my arse. You, Felim, you go to mass on Sundays or else you get out of this house. Do you hear me?'

'I hear you.'

'And?'

'We'll all be in our pew next Sunday,' Hughie said.

'Speak for yourself—' Felim began.

'I speak for all of us,' Hughie said; 'we'll all be at mass. Come on, Felim, we've work to do.'

My father sat at the table, his head in his hands. His body slumped and seemed to deflate. He murmured through the fingers that pressed against his lips, 'What is happening to this family? What are we coming to, at all, at all?'

Chapter 7

Beyond the stepping-stones I turned and looked back. It was early morning; the sun was burning off the haze, and the summit of Knocknastumpa came and went in the mist. The vale of Glenorga looked new-born and verdant as it must have first appeared to the Neolithic farmers who had settled in its bounty. Mona waved from the doorway; my mother stood motionless beside her.

I lugged a cardboard suitcase that my mother had bought for her honeymoon. It had never undertaken another trip until now. I went along by the gorge, shutting out the song of the Morning Star. I didn't want to hear it for it was a dirge that mourned my passing. Behind me were all the symbols of my lost youth, standing out in the morning light like the ruins of an ancient habitation. Lionel Barton was right: the days of running free were over and buried.

Barton had asked me to call on him before I left. I found him sitting at his desk in the library. 'Damn bills. They're like the head of Medusa: you pay one and three more take its place. So you're off then?'

'I'm going on Wednesday next. I have no choice, Mr Barton.'

'Lionel, please. Friends shouldn't be so formal with each other. Will you write to me?'

'Write to you?'

'I know it sounds preposterous. But I'd relish hearing

from you. Tell me how you're getting on. And if you think I may be helpful to you, please let me know.'

'If you like.'

'I would like it very much. Now I have a few things for you. They are founded on my own experiences, admittedly a long time ago.' Barton opened a drawer at the base of the bookshelves and brought out a slim wooden box. 'You like to read, don't you?'

'Yes, I do.'

He removed an object from the box that looked to me like the pressure handle of a bicycle pump. 'This is a torch. Chances are that the only opportunity you'll get to read is when you go to bed at night. So you put your head under the blankets, switch on your torch, like so, and read away undetected. I think it's rather good, don't you? Oh, there are some spare batteries as well.'

'Thanks very much.'

'There's something else in here. I have this feeling that you're a person who appreciates nature and all its works. This is a book about such things: *Landscape of the British Isles – Formation and Change.* I think you'll like it. A word of caution though. There are things in it that run counter to our traditional notions of how the world and its creatures were made.'

'Thanks again.'

'Okay. Now, Roderick, the reason for this wooden box. I think it would be unwise of you to bring these things home with you. So this is what I'll do. You know that spot in the Giant's Grave where Kilraish hid his ill-gotten hoard?'

'You knew that?'

'I'm an observer, Roderick. I see and hear. Anyway, I'll leave this box and I'll also put this in it.' Barton rummaged in his pockets, frowning as he searched. 'I thought I had it on my person, now where the hell ... Ah, I remember.' He took an envelope from the mound of papers, opened it and extracted a five-pound note. 'This is for you. One never has enough money in boarding school, as I recall.'

'I can't, Mr Barton. I can't take money from you.'

'Thought you'd say that. Rather like beholding oneself to the enemy, eh? It's just a little gift – a token of my interest in you. Look, I'll leave it in the box; if you're that unhappy about it, leave it behind you. But I hope you don't.'

'It's too much money. I can't take it.'

'Of course you can. Well that's it then. I wish you luck. I'll look for you in despatches, Roderick.'

I found the wooden box beneath a sandstone flag. I put the torch and the book in my case and argued with myself about the money. I had never owned that much before. I thought about leaving it under the stone but I decided that it would be an ungrateful thing to do. I pocketed the five-pound note, feeling as I did that it was another act of betrayal. I was a Judas accepting 30 pieces of silver.

All my feelings about Danesfort were prophetic. Felim told me that I would grow accustomed to the place; it was in man's nature to adapt and become resilient, even in the face of the most hostile environment. But I never did grow accustomed; I accepted with growing certitude that I would never be able to adapt.

I was a person without connection. Every other student had some semblance of support; either fellow students or teachers and priests who had come from their native place or its hinterland. Being the first student to attend from Mount Fierna was not the great honour that Father Lynch had foreseen; in truth, it hung round my neck like a millstone. I had no one to turn to.

Danesfort was like a collection of several wolf packs. I was never allowed to enter any of them; Alpha males and the lowest order in the rankings rebuffed me alike. Hopalong Dawley, as they called me, with twisted leg and scholarship, was at best an oddity, at worst a freak. It was perfectly fine that a well-formed boy, from a civilised place where priests and missionaries had been nurtured, should be clever and able. It was ridiculous if he came from a barbaric mountain and walked like a cripple. I would create an isolated world of my own and from there I would fight the wolf pack from an intellectual platform, prove that the mountain freak could match the best.

The day after we arrived, Father Joachim Cordial, the hurling coach, known as Akim, assembled the first years in the boot hall. His surname was a misnomer; he had pinched features, small bleary eyes behind horn-rimmed spectacles and sardonic lips that gave his mouth a perpetual leer. Akim brought sarcasm to a fine art, as if he had discovered that the only effective way to deal with students was to treat them with disdain. He walked up and down the line, inhaling deeply and shaking his head. Then he stood midway and silently surveyed his crop of potential talent. 'Lord, in your infinite wisdom, why do you try me so? Look at what you sent me.' Then he addressed the first boy in the line. 'Name and place of origin.'

'Cronin, Father, from Creeves.'

'Cronin, from Creeves. Now hear this. By the time I've finished with you lot, you'll wish you had never known my name. So let me spare you the effort. Just call me "sir". Is that understood? Answer for your peers, Cronin.'

'Yes, sir.'

'Where do you play, Cronin?'

'Corner forward, sir.'

'Corner forward. If I had a penny, Cronin, for every boy that fancied himself as a corner forward, I'd be a rich man. Are you any good?'

'Don't know, sir.'

'You don't know. Cronin, the good ones always know and aren't afraid to say it. Next?'

'Halpin, sir, from Kilbradern.'

'Ah hah, Halpin. You'll be a brother of Phillip. Where do you play, Halpin?'

'Same place as my brother, sir.'

'Good, good. Perhaps, Lord, you show me a modicum of mercy. Next?'

'Dawley, sir, from Mount Fierna.'

'Are you telling me, Dawley, that the folk of Mount Fierna have put aside their cudgels and their war paint and have taken to hurling? Where do you play?'

'I'm a goalkeeper, sir.'

'A goalkeeper, no less. Are you trying to be funny?'

Halpin tittered and the titter grew as it spread down the line. The boy at the end laughed outright.

'No, sir.'

'Dawley, walk down the line and run coming back.'

As I walked the first outline of a red mist grew like cobwebs around my peripheral vision. It had never happened to me before but I found myself exulting in it. I willed it to deepen in a fiery glow of red-hot anger. I bathed in its exuberance. I found myself exaggerating the limp. I stumbled deliberately as I ran the return.

'Dawley, are you trying to make a fool of me?' The laughter began to swell.

'No, sir. I'm a goalkeeper and a good one.'

'A good one, no less. Hear that, my motley crew. God help you, Dawley, if you're having me on.'

Akim led us to the hurling field. He formed two teams and put me in goal at one end. I took up my usual position, a yard away from the left-hand post. I saw him raise his eyes to heaven and mention something to Halpin, who giggled and went to share the merriment with Stapleton, another who basked in the slipstream of an older brother's reputation. In the first twenty minutes all that came my way was a feeble shot from Cronin. Five yards away he threw up the ball to strike and I shouted at him. He missed the shot and I struck it down the field with nonchalant ease.

'Sir, sir,' Cronin ran to Akim. 'He frightened me. He made me miss.'

'He made a fool of you. This is a hurling field, Cronin, not a kindergarten.' Akim stalked towards me. 'So you're a smart one too, Dawley. Well, let's see how smart you are. Stapleton, come up here. Bring the pouch of balls with you.'

Stapleton had come to Danesfort with an aura of fame surrounding him. He looked as if any moment his body would burst out of his clothes. He had wide shoulders, thighs like tree trunks, great red hands that grasped the hurley as if it were a matchstick. The lore said that when Stapleton struck the ball, it travelled at 60 miles an hour and all the goalkeeper knew about it was when it struck the rigging behind him. He was already on the panel for the county minor team.

Akim placed six balls on the 21-yard line. 'Stapleton,' he asked, 'how many of those can you put away?'

Stapleton looked at me and grinned. 'All six.'

'Right then. Let's see you do it.'

I watched Stapleton place the first ball on a mound of grass. But it wasn't him that bent over the ball. I was back in the Nursery Field: my father stood there, feet planted wide, fierce concentration on his face. I summoned the red mist; I felt it glow like a halo round my head when I remembered the mockery and the failure. The red mist made a gargoyle of Stapleton's face. By the time he rolled the ball on his stick, I knew he was hitting it to the right. I lifted off the platform of my built up boot and took it square on the hurley face, a foot inside the right-hand post. I killed it dead and let it fall into my hand.

'That the best you can do?' I smiled at him.

He went right again and this time I didn't bat it down. I met it full and whipped it down the field. I revelled in the warmth of his anger, drawing it away from him to feed mine. 'Rile him,' Felim had once offered me a tactic, 'make him lose focus. You're a samurai warrior, Roddy, turning the enemy's strength against himself.'

'Come on, Stapleton, really hit it. Move it up to ten miles an hour.'

Stapleton mouthed words at me, out of sight of Akim. I interpreted them to suit the red mist. 'You crippled shit, I'll drive it down your shaggin' mouth.'

It's coming straight for you, Roddy. Plant your feet wide. Remember you once turned your back on a shot like this and felt the shame and the wound. Not now, Roddy. You're invincible.

Just before Stapleton struck, I moved my stick downwards. He caught the movement and angled the ball head high. I caught it in my splayed fingers and held it aloft in my fist. His team-mates behind Stapleton gasped. Akim scratched his poll.

'It's a fluke,' Stapleton appealed to Akim. 'He can't be that good. And him with a bad leg and all.'

Akim pondered and screwed up his mouth until his lips disappeared. 'Go in on him, Stapleton, let's see what he makes of the rough stuff.'

Stapleton grimaced with glee and flexed his muscles.

This is it, Roddy, one on one. He'll throw the ball forward, gain five yards, and by the time he hits it, he'll be breathing in your face. Then he'll follow through on the charge and crease you. Come on red mist. Stapleton is your father; he thinks you're no damn good.

I moved off the line to cut down the angle of the shot. Stapleton saw me coming and took his eye off the ball. The shot was weak and easily parried. My hip caught him off balance and as he lurched past I slapped him on his ample backside with the flat of the hurley. He came roaring like a bull from the back of the net; a foot becoming entangled as he lunged. He fell like a toppled oak.

'Enough, enough,' Akim ran forward. 'Pack it up, Stapleton, all of you.'

'I have more shots,' Stapleton pleaded.

'You've had four,' Akim reminded him. He began to scratch his head again. 'Don't know what to make of it, Dawley. You shouldn't be any good.'

By the next day the word was out. Canon Rufus Childe, the college president, stood by my right-hand post. His voice had the resonance of a foghorn and when he erupted in anger, which he frequently did, his deep, booming voice could be heard bellowing round the college and its grounds.

'Tell me,' Childe said when the play was at the other end. 'I was just thinking. You'll be a brother of Felim

Dawley, the county minor.'

'Yes, sir.'

'We shouldn't have lost him. 'Twas against my better judgement we let Morgan Lynch go after him. He wouldn't know one end of a hurley from the other.' Childe winked at me. 'Don't be telling people now that I said that. Right?'

'Right, sir.'

'You and me'll get on just fine. You're a scholarship boy, aren't you?

'Yes.'

'If you ever want any advice, if you ever get into trouble, come and see me.'

It's the exception that makes the rule. The judgement of society's behaviour is not how the common man is treated but rather how those who don't conform to the standard are. I had academic and athletic ability in a crippled frame, and that was against the norm. I heard 'Hopalong Dawley' being shouted at me from behind tree trunks, from shadowy places in corridors, from the protection of groups.

The odd thing, though, was that it applied only to me. Harry Stuart was a polio victim and his movement was more grotesque than mine, but Stuart had a lifeline that protected him from the pack: he was a first cousin of Attila, Father Karl Roberts, the Dean of Discipline. It was like being Caesar's wife.

Attila was a monstrous concoction of forces whose outward appearance belied the internal web of a cunning mind. He was strikingly handsome in a feminine way. I never saw stubble on his face and it was said that he used cotton wool for toilet paper. Attila occupied the foremost ranking of all the things I despised about Danesfort and its régime.

I found solace in the study hall. Study was the catalyst for the nemesis I craved. I would one day ram down the throats of the wolf pack, in intellectual wisdom and glory, every arrowhead of revenge that I kept in my mental quiver. Every night when I went to bed I trawled through the events of the day for anything worth remembering. When I had completed my mental stock-take, I pulled the bedclothes over my head, switched on the torch and read Barton's book.

The dormitory where I slept had once been the chapel; it had a vaulted ceiling and oaken beams and was Arctic cold. From second year on, students were allocated a room, which was shared with another. When my turn came, I was left in the chapel dormitory. Attila, who organised things according to preference, was well aware that no one wanted to share with me. Fraternising with Hopalong Dawley would bring the ridicule of the wolf pack. But it bothered me not a jot.

I read the book over and over, until I had almost committed it to memory. It kept me awake at night, because the marvel of discovery filled my head. I felt uneasy about it too and it grew as I lay awake in the dark. This new knowledge ran counter to what I had learned at school in Newtown and what Father Lynch preached from the altar. And worse, it was radically different from what my father believed. There was no mystery about creation, no miracle, no hand of God; I had come upon the dawn of scientific truth. I should have built a wall around my discovery and kept it to myself. But I erred.

Jamesy Regan wanted to be a priest. His mother's brother was a monsignor and the bishop's right-hand man. Jamesy had none of the monsignor's brilliance and so, in defiance of the wolf pack, he came to me seeking help. He could not make head or tail of geography, but his biggest problem was Latin because he would need to do well in it to qualify for the seminary. I did some of the written exercises for him and slipped them into the drawer of his desk in the study hall. Then, because he was the only one who had ever sought or professed gratitude for my help, I made the fatal mistake of sharing my knowledge and its source with him.

Geography and history were then a single subject on the curriculum, taught by a layman, John Carew. He stomped up and down the aisle, shooting rapid-fire questions and loosing at barrage of vitriolic shrapnel at every hesitant response. The odour of stale alcohol lingered as he passed; his fingers were stained with nicotine, his eyes bloodshot.

'Dawley, explain the origin of peatland?'

'There are two kinds of peatland, sir. One grows on …'

'Grows, Dawley, grows?'

'Yes, sir. One grows on mountain slopes and is known as blanket bog. That happens because of high rainfall, which does not seep into the ground but stays in stagnant pools in the hollows and forms sphagnum.'

'Sphagnum? Tell the class, Dawley.'

'That's a kind of moss, sir. It takes the minerals out of the water and makes it acidic. As the sphagnum grows over the surface of the water, it shuts out the light and the air. All the dead vegetation is decomposed and compacted.'

'By the cross of Christ, Dawley, aren't you some class of a scientist. Where did you hear all this?'

'I read it, sir.'

'Where?'

'In a book, sir.'

'Name and author?'

'I forget, sir.'

'You forget. Maybe you're right, Dawley.' He stopped pacing and stood in front of me. 'Some books are best forgotten, done away with.' Still looking at me, he barked, 'Rodgers, ports on the Baltic? Now, Rodgers; not tomorrow.'

A few nights later I was about to turn off the torch when the bedclothes were yanked off. Attila loomed over me, the lips pouting in exaggerated triumph, an expectant smile on his soft face. 'May I have that torch, please?'

'It's my torch, sir.'

'It is indeed. But as you are well aware, it is not permitted to read in bed. Hand it over, please. Now, what were you reading?'

I put my hand under the pillow and withdrew my decoy, *An Anthology of Intermediate Certificate Poetry*.

'Very clever, Mr Dawley. Let's stop playing little games, shall we? Let me have the book you kicked down to the end of the bed.'

I rummaged and found the book. I held it in my hand. 'This book does not belong to me, sir. I was given a loan of it. I have to give it back.'

'Perhaps you have. But in the meantime, it is my duty to confiscate it.'

He took the book in his outstretched hand without even glancing at it. 'Put your clothes on, Mr Dawley. I'll expect you in my office in five minutes.'

When I entered the office Attila was testing the flex of a bamboo cane. 'Both hands please. Stretch them out. Over the table.' The speed with which he stood erect and swished took me completely by surprise. The cane cut into the palm of my left hand and, almost before I felt the pain, it came down on the other. He moved from hand to hand with extraordinary agility, six canings on each one and the last across the cramped knuckles because my fingers had involuntarily gone into spasm. I felt the agony along my spine and down to the calves of my legs.

Attila put the cane down and smiled at me like a sadistic swordsman. 'It helps, Mr Dawley, if you squeeze the hands under your armpits. Take a few moments and then sit down. You hate me, don't you? I can read it in your face. That's good. I like boys to hate me.' He joined his fingers and held them to his lips like a picture of a monk at prayer. 'Let me share something with you, Mr Dawley. I don't like you either. Indeed my feelings for you would run deeper than that,' he spread the hands and snapped them together again, 'only that my calling as a priest prevents me from enjoying, let's say, the more basic emotions. You understand me?'

'Yes, sir.'

'Good. I'm surprised our paths haven't crossed before now. In all the time I have been observing you, Mr Dawley, my opinion hasn't changed; rather has my conviction been confirmed. Intelligence, you see, is not a weapon; it does not give you any right to treat the rest of your fellow students as if they were inferiors in the presence of your exalted acumen. What gives you the right to shut yourself off from your peers?'

'I'm not that way at all, sir.'

'Mr Dawley, let me remind you. I'm the one with expertise in student behaviour. I consider your performance to be an exercise in pride and vainglory. Intelligence is granted to you by God.'

'I know, sir.'

'You do not, Mr Dawley, but you shall learn. I promise you that much.' He joined his fingers again. 'Tell me, who is

Rosie Kilraish?'

My heart fluttered and then pounded. I felt the warm glow spread over my face. Even the burning hands beneath my armpits flared in a sudden surge of warmth.

'A neighbour's daughter, sir.'

'A neighbour's daughter. Indeed. Am I to infer then that your relationship with this, ah, Miss Kilraish, is purely neighbourly – all sweetness and light?'

'Yes, sir.'

Attila smiled, pulled open the drawer of his desk and took out a tattered envelope. He extracted a sheet of lined paper, and mimicked a young female voice.

> *Mount Fierna,*
> *Newtown*
> *April the fourteenth, 1957,*
>
> *Dear Roddy,*
> *I hope this letter finds you, as it leaves me, in the best of health. I am writing to tell you that I miss you and the very minute you come home for the summer holidays you are to come to see me. Mikey is gone off to England with Patsy. He says he's never coming home again. My mam and dad are fighting all the time. I'd love to get away from this house too. We could go together and then I'd have you all to myself and I could kiss you all the time. That's it for now, your affectionate girl,*
> *Rosie Kilraish*

Attila tore the letter into shreds, held it aloft over the wastepaper basket and watched the pieces drift downwards. He leaned forward.

'Dawley, I'm sure you have gathered by now that this college is a training ground for future priests. What age are you?'

'Fourteen, sir.'

'Fourteen, and already on the high road to depravity. Do your parents know about this, ah, relationship?'

'Yes, sir. But there is nothing wrong with it. Rosie is just a sister of my friend Mikey.'

'The sentiments expressed in that letter, Mr Dawley, go far beyond the bounds of natural friendship. Everything I see about you points me towards one conclusion. You are a dangerous influence. But we won't let you taint the sound religious principles which our boys are nurtured in. I believe you are good at English, so I assume you understand what I am saying?'

'I understand sir, but—'

'No buts, Mr Dawley. I've met your type before; lying and deceit is second nature to you. Now I want you here again in my office tomorrow morning, just before class. You have further punishment owing due to that letter.' He took up the cane again and pointed its end at my chest. 'I warn you. If you attempt to take your suffering out on some other student, I'll flay you alive. Have you got that?'

'Yes, sir.'

'And one other thing, Mr Dawley. You may sleep like pigs in that place you come from. But here our boys wear pyjamas in bed. We insist on it.'

'Could I have the book back, sir? It doesn't belong to me.'

'You're audacious, I'll say that for you. Who owns the book?'

'My brother, sir. In Adamston.'

Attila peered at the book's cover as if he were seeing the title for the first time. '*Landscape of the British Isles – Formation and Change*. Well, well.' He screwed up his mouth and imitated a public school accent. 'Aren't you the proper little English boy. British Isles, no less. The mere Irish landscape would not be good enough for you? I must read this for myself; see what heresy that godless country is now promoting. We shall speak again, Mr West Brit Dawley. I have no doubt of that. Off with you now.'

Sleep never came that night. I fought against the well of anguish that threatened to spill over and engulf me with tears of sorrow and frustration. Round and round in my wakefulness went the unfathomable dilemma of my place on this earth. I had failed my father; my mother had turned her face against me; here in Danesfort my shortcomings were derided, my strengths interpreted as arrogance.

Next day as we were shuffling out of the geography class, Carew called me.

'Dawley, Dawley, stay.'

I braced myself for a stream of tirade. By now the grapevine would have learned of my encounter with Attila. Carew closed the door and guided me towards his desk. He placed a finger on his lips. 'Why, in the name of all that's holy didn't you listen to me?'

'Listen, sir?'

'I warned you. The other day, remember what I said. Some books are best forgotten, done away with. I thought you'd get the message.'

A voice from the edge of the wilderness, a cry of succour across the black divide, and I had missed it. So much for the clever lad with the stamp of arrogance.

'Sorry sir. It's only now I realise what you were trying to tell me.'

'I had to be vague, Dawley. You understand? You had a bad time, I hear?'

'Bad enough, sir.'

'*Nolle bastardos carborundum*. Don't let them get you down. Okay?'

'I'll try, sir.'

'What's your first name?'

'Roddy.'

'Roddy, let me say this to you and remember that I never said it.' He closed his left eye and winked conspiratorially. 'For whatever reason, you've put yourself outside the fold, and a place like this will never tolerate that. Get yourself back in or the system will beat you. It always does. The second thing, which the system can't tolerate, is any hypothesis that runs counter to the collective view held by this institution or the official church. Do you understand the word radical?'

'Something that is different?'

'Close enough. So, Roddy, keep your radical notions to yourself. And the best of luck to you.'

In the summer of my fourteenth year I fell in love with Rosie Kilraish. I had set out to visit Muirne, but Rosie waylaid me as I dropped down the slope of Knocknastumpa. She was sitting on the makeshift swing, tentacles of woodsmoke drifting around her and her bare feet like burnished bronze.

'You're wasting your time, Roddy Dawley.'

'What are you on about?'

'Your precious Muirne is gone off to some foreign place. A walking tour, if you don't mind. An' you never come to see us now. We're not good enough for you anymore.'

'Ah, don't be talking ould balderdash. Anyway, I shouldn't be here at all; you got me into a lot of trouble.'

Her face dropped. 'I would never get you into trouble, Roddy.'

'You did. You sent me a letter to Danesfort. They opened it and I got caned.'

Rosie slipped off the swing and stood beside me. 'I'm sorry. I thought you'd like me to write to you. What was wrong about what I said anyway? I wanted to tell you about Mikey.'

'That was fine. It was that stuff about kissing that got me into trouble.'

Rosie twined her arms around my neck and kissed me full on the lips. The tip of her tongue forced my lips apart. My heart jumped and the spreading warmth gushed over my face.

'You like that, don't you?'

'No I don't! 'Tis wrong, 'tis a sin. We shouldn't be doing it.'

She pulled away. 'Roddy Dawley, you're a right ould eegit. For all your smartness, you haven't a bloody clue.'

'And you shouldn't be writing me bloody ould letters.'

'Don't worry, you'll never get another one.' Rosie turned away in a swirl of cloth and bronzed legs. A flash of ivory flesh suddenly appeared like a hem above the rim of her dress. 'You're to go into my mother. What she sees in you I don't know.'

Long Pat was sitting in the centre of the kitchen whittling lengths of hazel. The dour dark face and the speed of the flying splinters telegraphed Long Pat's mood. As I walked in, he stopped work and spoke to the hazel rod.

'He's back, is he? Does that fella have anything better to do in his own place?'

'Take no notice of that man,' Lena said. 'He got out of the wrong side of the bed. You'll have a square of apple tart.' It was an order, not a request. Lena's hospitality never contemplated a refusal. 'There 'tis now and shut up.'

She had aged. The hand that laid the plate on my lap continued to shake even when she placed the other on its wrist to steady it. Her hair was the colour of thawing snow in a mud pool. 'Ate that now, I said. Ate it up.'

I ate in silence.

'You must have a heap of new stories now?' Lena asked.

I laid the plate on the table and stood up. I thought that Lena might follow me out to the yard as she often did when Long Pat's impatience had left a story unfinished. But there was a deliberate and final set to her movement as she sat by the fire and rocked. I told Rosie about her father's reaction to me.

'You mustn't take any notice of him.'

'He doesn't like me, Rosie. He frightens me.'

'It gets worse and worse every day.'

'What did I ever do to him?'

'It's not what you did, Roddy. He keeps on bringing up things about my mother. Like she was a slut; the mountain bike. He says that she was soft on your father; he could ride her any time he liked. And a lot of other men as well. Roddy, did you ever hear anything like that? About my mother, I mean.'

I looked into her moist eyes and saw the hurt lurking there. 'No Rosie, I never did.'

'Anyway, let him jump in Lough Cutra. I don't care.'

'Aren't you afraid?'

Rosie laughed. 'Of him? You must be joking. Anyway, Roddy, haven't I got you? You're my boy, aren't you?'

'Will you stop going on with that class of talk, Rosie? Come on, let's get away from the house.'

Rosie was a tomboy. She clambered over rock and crag like a mountain goat, goaded me on, waited for me to catch up and just when I reached her, set off again in a gallop through thicket and gorse. We hunted rabbits, planted snares, baited corn patches for pheasant and pigeon, tickled trout beneath stones in the Morning Star. And we swam in the Blue Pool. Rosie swam in her knickers and bra.

'You know what Mikey told me?'

'Yeah?'

'He saw yourself and Muirne Culhane swimming here and she had no clothes on.'

'No such thing.'

'He did, he swore it. He said that Muirne had big diddies and a big crop of red hair. You know where, don't you?'

'Don't talk like that, Rosie. 'Tis dirty.'

'Listen to him. And I suppose you didn't look at her at all? Are you some class of a saint?'

'Mikey was only having you on.'

'Will you look at the colour of him, as red as a rose. I suppose I'm not good enough for you at all after seeing that Muirne one?'

'I never looked and that's all that's to it.'

'I can't stand that Muirne. Stuck up bitch. Anyway, when I'm her age I'll have just as much as she has. Another thing Mikey said. You had nothing on either.'

'I had so. I had my underpants on. Like I have now.'

'You might as well have nothing now because I can see everything.'

My hands dropped to cover my crotch.

'Look at him,' Rosie giggled. 'What are you trying to hide? You have nothing that I haven't seen before. Come on. I'll race you three times round the pool. You'll have to give me a kiss if I win. And not one of your slobbery oul' pecks.'

In the Giants' Grave, where we sheltered from a rain shower, I showed her the cache where Mikey had hoarded his booty. The earth around the hole was recently disturbed and when I lifted up the covering slab, I found a folded piece of paper beneath it. Instinctively I knew the note was for me but before I could conceal it, Rosie grabbed it from my fingers. She unfolded it and read, '*June 1957, Roderick, I'm taking a gamble that you might find this note. You have been neglecting me. Am very anxious to discover how fares it with you. Please come to chat. You know who.*'

'"You know who",' Rosie repeated, setting her head to one side like her mother did. 'This note is from Mr Barton. You and him are friends, aren't ye? You needn't try to fool me. Your father will kill you if he finds out.'

'You won't tell a soul, will you, Rosie? Promise me you won't.'

She placed a finger on her lips, moistened it and pressed it against mine. 'I won't breathe a word. But you're a funny man, Roddy Dawley. Sometimes I don't understand you at all. I wouldn't go next or near the likes of Barton. He's not our kind.'

'He's a very nice person when you get to know him. Far better than many of the people I've met.'

'Maybe he is, but I wouldn't want to find out. He's always coming in and out of this place. That's scary. Maybe he's in league with the devil. I'd never come in here on my own. But he's not the only one that does that, I've seen—'

'Seen what, Rosie?'

'Nothing. I was thinking about something else. Come away, Roddy. This place frightens me.'

TOM NESTOR

In Barton Hall the light shafted through the window and illuminated the books on the library shelves. It brightened gold lettering on leather-bound volumes and on the family crest that decorated their spines. We had talked for over an hour, or rather I had talked and Barton had listened.

'You should have written to me,' he said. 'I would have found a way to intervene.'

'No. I'm glad I didn't. They read the mail and they would have found out about you and me. It could be a lot worse then.'

'Second thoughts. Yes, you were right to be prudent. The way you describe it, Roderick, it sounds like we are still back in the days of the Inquisition. You know, I have always held that two great evils have been inflicted on mankind: denominational religion and the British Empire. And I think the former is the worse. Are you going to continue?'

'Oh yes. I can't give up now.'

'You're a brave boy, Roderick.'

'I'm not. Most of the time I'm scared stiff. But the really funny thing is, they think I'm arrogant and big-headed, above them in some superior way. I'm afraid to answer questions in the classroom in case I say something that comes straight out of my head and not from the textbook.'

'Dear, dear, dear. I should never have given you that book.'

'I'm very glad you did. I'm the one who's sorry because they confiscated it. I'll get it back, I promise you that. They have no right to keep it.'

'Okay. Let's forget college for a moment. I did something a few months back, which I should have done a long time ago. I made a will. Now why should I concern you about that?'

'I don't know, Mr Barton.'

'Mr Barton again. You'll really have to try harder, Roderick. I made a will because if I didn't, everything would go to pay my creditors, and I couldn't bear to see some of my prized possessions falling into the hands of the Philistines. Do you follow me?'

'No, sir.'

'First Mr Barton, now sir. *Lionel,* please! I trust you, Roderick, as a friend. So let me tell you something in confidence. My estate is encumbered. That, in a nutshell, means that I am seriously in debt. I may have to sell off portions of my land in order to pay my creditors. I suppose if I live long enough most of it will go. However, I will never part with the house. But, in truth, there is a very limited market for it. It's very impractical now, and costs a fortune to maintain.'

'But you're rich, Lionel. My father says that there is no end to your wealth.'

'Idle talk, Roderick. The fact is I inherited the greater part of the debt. My forebears were wantonly extravagant. It cost a fortune to get this house into its present shape. Every Barton that ever was had to leave his mark on it; it was almost rebuilt anew several times over. And then, of course, the lavish lifestyle. It took 24 tons of coal a year to heat this house and more than a dozen trees. At one stage this estate employed over 80 people. The landlord entertained and was entertained in return. It was not unusual for 100 guests to sit at tables in the dining room and the Long Gallery when the huntsmen met on the lawn. And I inherited the debts of all that. Come, let me show you something.'

Barton took my arm and led me to the window overlooking the lawn and the avenue of elms. 'Notice anything?'

It took me some time to recognise the bare patches

where the Roman statues had stood. All along the avenue, at both sides, the squares of red earth stood naked and sparse like some ancient earthwork pattern. 'The statues. They're all gone.'

Barton guided me back to my chair. 'All gone. Sold, plinths and all, to an antique dealer. Grandfather Geoffrey brought them from Italy as evidence of his Grand Tour. Never liked them very much.'

'I'm sorry you had to sell them.'

'Don't be. If they were important to me, I'd have made other arrangements. Which brings me to what I started out to tell you. There are some very nice things in this house and I want to make sure that they fall into the hands of the right persons. Roderick, I have bequeathed my library to you. I would be honoured if you would accept.'

For a single moment my heart soared, filled with the benevolence of this gentle soul who had offered me nothing but affection since our paths had first crossed. But then the implications of the gift routed the wash of good feeling.

'I can't. They'd find out. My father would know.'

Barton smiled and nodded. 'I have made provision for that. In my lifetime the books will remain here and then, after my demise, may be housed in whatever location you see fit.' Barton encompassed the shelves with a broad sweep of his outstretched hands. 'All the great works of literature are here: Chaucer, Flaubert, Stendhal, Trollope, all the poets, Byron, Keats, Virgil. And my favourite writer of all, Jane Austen.'

On the evening before I returned to Danesfort, we sat around the table after the evening meal. My father had gone to the fields to check on the day's work and plan for the morrow. We played a game called Alphabet Donkey, a relic from my mother's childhood days in Adamston. As the game deteriorated into wrangle, Felim pushed back his chair and stood erect. He adopted his oratorical pose with hands outstretched and the head thrown back.

'That's a stupid old game,' Felim said. 'Let me offer you something more sublime.' He coughed, cleared his throat and inhaled deeply. 'A poem, written by Felim Phillip Dawley, after the manner of Percy Bysshe Shelley. And for the moment untitled.'

They sheltered from showers in Glenorga bowers,
    walked in fields and streams,
Went hand in hand, through Dawley land, sharing
    whispered dreams.
They sealed their bliss with a stolen kiss, trembled with
    pangs of joy,
Basked in the cool of the clear Blue Pool, under a cumu
    lus sky.
He gasped ooh, lah, lah, at her knickers and bra, that
    picture of elegant grace.
Promise me, Roddy, on your dead body, that you love
    your Rosie Kilraish.

Mona held her splayed fingers against the well of her laughter. Hughie's brooding features transformed to a gentle suffused glow as if someone had switched on a light behind his troubled eyes. But over my mother's features came an angry shadow that filled to unbridled revulsion. She walked out of the kitchen, banging the parlour door in her wake. A dense pall of silence lowered like a weight and pressed upon us in muted aftershock.

Chapter 8

President Childe assembled the scholarship group in his study. He picked up the list of results.

'Not a single gold medal among the lot of ye. Hughes, you were supposed to be a sure thing in maths. And Dawley, you were close. Four marks off in history and geography. What do you think of that?'

'Not good enough, sir.'

'There'll be no excuse for you next time out, Dawley. We have a new man teaching history and geography this term. Wan of our own. No drinking or carousing with this man. He'll put the wind up you. A second thing, Dawley: you missed by ten points in Latin. Remember this. A gold medal in Latin is worth two in history and geography. Get my drift, Dawley?'

'Yes, sir.'

'Listen to me, all of ye. Next time round, in twelve months, if this class hasn't delivered four gold medals, then woe betide ye. There won't be wan scholarship renewed. Out now and get yeer thick heads into thim books.'

The junior competition, the Boyce Cup, was the seedbed that would produce hurlers for the senior grade. We played our first competitive game in October against Hopewell College. It was no contest. Hopewell, a Jesuit college, was a rugby school and played hurling only as a sop to its patriotic founders. In the second round we had a comfortable win over St Ita's. Then, a few weeks after the Christmas break, we were to meet St Ruadh's.

'This is it,' Akim warned us, 'by the time ye'er finished with that crowd, we'll know whether ye have guts in yeer bellies or *liatharoidi* in yeer togs.' *Liatharoidi* was the Irish word for balls.

I took my place in goal. The terraces behind me had been filled with St Ruadh supporters who rushed down to the barrier as a soon as I arrived. Missiles began to rain down on me, initially orange peel and apple cores and the odd empty bottle. It was merely the opening salvo. Soon the stones started to arrive. I felt the first pangs of fear inching up from the pit of my stomach and lodging in my throat. The mob bayed like a frenzied pack of beagles, and then miscalculated.

'Look at the cripple. Will ye look at the cripple of a goal-keeper.'

'Step and a half, step and a half, the cripple in goal has a step and a half.'

'Hey diddle diddle, look at the cripple; he should be at home with his mouth at the nipple.'

The fear ebbed and as it waned, fingers of ice passed over the route it had recently traversed. The cold sweep of a terrible anger gathered me up and took me in its frozen maw. Come red mist, follow the ice, wrap me in its blessed bounty.

'Dawley, Dawley,' Akim was saying in his tight-lipped whisper, 'are you alright? Don't let them bastards get at you. Don't do anything foolish now, you hear?'

'I won't.'

'Keep your eye on Stapleton. He's in a bad way.'

Stapleton was shivering like a leaf. His marker, Donlon, had carrot red hair and the face of a pug; what he lacked in bulk he made up in muscle and hardiness. The moment the whistle sounded for the throw in, he raced back to his post and deliberately collided with Stapleton. The mob behind the goals urged Donlon on.

Then came the first high ball and I knew by the roar from the mob that I was witnessing the first probe of St Ruadh's strategy. 'Your ball, Stapleton,' I shouted. But I knew he hadn't heard me. Stapleton put up his hand but just as his fingers were about to close on the ball, Donlon let fly. I heard the crack of wood on knuckles and the roar of the mob as the ball dropped and spun towards me. The full forward was upon me, and as I bent to gather it, his charge lifted me bodily and drove me and the ball behind the goal line. The mob roared, the umpire raised the green flag. A couple of minutes into the game and we were a goal adrift.

About five minutes later, another high ball came floating in and seemed to hang in the air for an eternity as I sought to judge its flight and the angle of descent. 'My ball, Stapleton. Keep him out.' Even if I had been alert to the danger, there was nothing I could do. The left corner forward was bearing down upon me like an express train. Out of the rim of my vision I saw his team mate coming in from my right and Halpin nowhere in sight. Their timing was perfect. Donlon spearheaded his flankers in a thrust that lifted me to the back of the net, the ball driven out of my hand with the force of the collision. In the chaos of the tumble, I saw a boot coming for my crotch and squirmed to avoid it but it caught me high up on my thigh. The handle of a hurley dug in beneath my ear and sprayed an explosion of stars. The mob responded to the raised green flag. 'Hup, you boyo, Donlon. The cripple is dead.'

Akim bent over me; Stapleton and the corner backs

grouped behind him. 'How bad is it, Dawley?'

'I'm okay, sir.'

'You sure? You got an awful pasting.'

'I'm sure, but we have to sort these fellas out quick.'

'Good man, yourself. But don't get sent off.'

I watched the ball reach the zenith and begin its descent. It would drop five yards out, give me a chance to bat it away and then take care of Donlon. I see my father's face in Donlon's leer, heard him mock me. I moved off the line, Stapleton seemed to miss a step and Donlon was free. He had turned to face me as the ball hovered above him, his splayed fingers settled into talons. They never closed for I hit down with a vengeance, the fingers flew open in a grunt of pain, the ball was picked up by Halpin and sent down the field. But I hadn't finished with Donlon. Just as I crashed into him, I raised the knee of my crippled leg and drove it into the pit of his stomach.

He slithered to the ground, and writhed and squirmed, fighting for breath, his hands clawing at the agony in his crotch. A bemused Stapleton drew near to watch. Donlon started to vomit. A couple of first aiders ran to him, followed by the St Ruadh's coach.

'That will take care of him,' I said to Stapleton.

'I could have taken care of it myself,' he scowled.

Donlon played on until half-time but his game was based on taunt and thuggery and it seemed that he had lost the will for both. Behind me the baying of the mob died away into a surly silence. Then, like all mobs, it turned to savaging its own: Donlon was transformed from a hero into a scapegoat. He hung his head; his day was over.

At half-time in the dressing room, Akim surveyed the wounded. I had a walnut- sized lump under my ear and the bruising on my inner thigh had turned a purple saucer shape. The knuckles on Stapleton's hand were invisible in the swelling that pulsed and throbbed.

'Dawley, are you alright for the second half?'

'Yes, sir.'

'Stapleton, I'm taking you off.'

'Please sir, let me stay on. My father and brother are out there. I'll never live it down, sir, if I don't take my place.'

'And I'll never live it down, Stapleton, if you make a mess of it. No more argument.'

'Sir,' I heard myself saying, 'I'd feel a lot better if Stapleton was in front of me.'

Akim contemplated. 'Against my better judgement. Okay, keep your gear on, Stapleton. But the very minute I see any sign you're not up to it, off you come.'

We began to get a grip at centre field. Cronin knocked over a couple of points in the third quarter and then we got a lucky goal when the ball ricocheted off a defender's boot. We were ahead by a solitary point with a few minutes left on the clock.

Then they began hitting the ball low into open spaces and drawing out the back line. 'Watch your man,' I kept shouting to the corner backs as their markers drifted out-field. Then Stapleton was caught dead as his opponent out-paced him and picked up a ball on the forty. He slipped it onto the corner forward, who wrong-footed Halpin and bore down on the goal. He was fifteen feet away from me when Halpin threw his hurley. The referee blew the whistle and pointed to the penalty spot. The mob bayed with a new-found energy. Akim came running along the by-line with a towel and handed it to me. As I wiped down the handle of the stick, he said. 'Well, what do you think?'

'He'll take the point.' I said. 'Go for a draw.'

'He will,' Akim agreed. 'If we let him. We must per-suade him to go for a goal.'

'Sir?'

'We want the win, Dawley. I don't want to play this shower again. You can save the shot, Dawley, I know you can. Take out the third man from the goal-line, put Stapleton in on your left, leave space between yourself and the right-hand post. The taker will go for it. Bet you he will.'

The taker saw Halpin move away and a look of gleeful expectancy passed over his face as he recognised both the opportunity and the dilemma that came with it. He could become a hero; a goal and they would win by two points. I moved closer to Stapleton, creating more space on my right. The mob started to bawl at the taker. 'Back of the net, Donie, back of the net. You've only the cripple to beat.'

The free taker stood over the ball and his body melted before my eyes and swam into a different shape. He rolled the ball onto the hurley, gritted his teeth and his eyes telegraphed the message. Move, Roddy, he's going for it, just inside the right-hand post. It was struck well but I was invincible now, floating in the capsule of the red mist. I reached it a foot from the line, took it full on the face of the stick and let it drop into my hand.

The dressing room was joy unbounded. Akim accepted congratulations with the blasé nonchalance of vindicated strategy. Childe was there, Attila at his shoulder. I saw Stapleton being hugged by his father and being playfully punched by his older brother, Justin, Danesfort's greatest hero, who captained an All-Ireland colleges winning team three years in a row. I had seen Justin Stapleton's picture in Childe's room, for he was the epitome of the Danesfort model. He was now associate professor, Moral Theology, in the Irish College in Rome.

Above the rim of the crowd I saw him make his excuses and come to sit beside me.

'I wonder if they have any idea how much they owe you for this victory?' Justin Stapleton's face had the markings of sublime kindness.

'I was lucky,' I said. 'That ball could have gone in as easily.'

'I don't think so,' Justin smiled. 'Do you always find excuses for your talent? What's your name?'

'Dawley. Roddy Dawley.'

'Where from?'

'Mount Fierna. You probably never heard of it.'

'Yes I have. I have been following the fortunes of your hurling team, St Luna's. You must be a brother of Felim's?'

'That's right, sir.'

'Call me Justin. Didn't your parents come to watch you?'

'My father wouldn't have the time. And my mother doesn't like hurling. Anyway, I don't mind.'

'You don't. Why?'

The suddenness and unexpectancy of the question surprised me, but it was dissolved by Stapleton's open-faced candour. There was nothing but frank curiosity showing there.

'Well, I have nearly always been on my own.'

'And here? Don't you have friends?'

'I don't have any, but it doesn't bother me.'

'Really? I would have found my time here very difficult only for my friends. I never liked Danesfort. I disliked the régime and its focus on punishment and religion and exam results. It must be difficult for those who don't suit the Danesfort model. Do you?'

I stowed the gear in my kitbag as the flutters of warning ran into my head. This priest beside me was the Danesfort model, cast in the same mould as Attila, whose outward appearance was the personification of all things good and beautiful. I zipped up my bag.

'I don't have any problem.'

Justin's brow furrowed. The benign friendly spokes were lost as if a shadow had passed over them.

'I'm sorry. I didn't mean to pry. I have said something you're not comfortable with, haven't I?'

'It doesn't matter. I have to be going now.'

'But it does, it matters to me. Look, Roddy, I haven't been quite honest with you. My brother has told me about you, that you've had a tough time, and when I saw you here, I thought how forlorn and sad you looked.'

'It doesn't matter.'

'You keep using that phrase! Look, I won't bother you any more. And I don't blame you for putting up the defences. I'm a priest, too, like those you've run foul of.'

'I'm sorry. I didn't mean to ...'

'Look, walk with me as far as the car. There is something I'd like to give you.'

We were a picture of incongruity, the Danesfort model and the cripple from Mount Fierna. Justin opened the car door. 'I believe you have quite an interest in geography.' He handed me three back copies of *National Geographic*.

'For keeps?'

'Why not? I have them read.'

'But people collect those.'

'I'm not a collector. But if I were you, I'd be prudent about showing them around.'

'If I'm caught with them, the magazines will be confiscated. I can't take them, sir, I'll get into trouble. But thanks all the same.'

'I've an idea. What's your address?'

He took a fountain pen from his inside pocket. It had a gold top and a barrel coloured like marble. I knew by the shape of the clasp that the pen was a Waterman. He wrote the address on the back cover of one of the magazines.

'Okay, that solves it. I'll send these to your home address. And every month from now on, when I've finished with the current issue, I'll send it on to you.'

'That's very kind of you, sir.'

'Not at all. When I come home for the holidays, I'll look you up. Would you mind?'

'I'd like that.'

That night, shortly after two, the door of my cubicle opened softly and I saw Attila framed in the dim light.

'Dawley, why aren't you asleep?'

'I was thinking about home, sir.'

'Ah, home, Mount Fierna. That cradle of civilisation, as Father Cordial puts it. Are you wearing pyjamas?'

'Yes.'

'Out of bed. Pull back the bedclothes.'

A crooked grin played around Attila's mouth. 'I see. Nothing. So we're playing, are we? Take your case from under the bed. Empty its contents on the eiderdown. Hurry now, there's a good chap.'

I emptied the case and he poked at the pile with the handle of the torch.

I emptied the case and he poked at the pile with the handle of the torch. 'Move the bed, Dawley. Let me see beneath it.'

He stood there for a long time contemplating the dust-free rectangle underneath the bed. 'My office, Dawley, two minutes.'

Attila was sitting behind his desk as before, holding the

cane at both ends, moving side to side on his swivel chair. I stood in front of the desk, staring at the floor and willing my heel to stay on the ground.

'Dawley, you know I don't like you.'

'Yes, sir.'

'Let me give you a chance to redeem yourself. What went on between yourself and Father Stapleton?'

'Went on, sir?'

The bamboo cane hit the desk with a crack of a sundering tree limb. 'Don't play around with me, Dawley. You heard me. What went on?'

My throat went dry. 'Nothing sir. I swear to God.'

'Nothing. I don't believe it. I was watching the pair of you, Dawley, I saw you go to the car. I saw Father Stapleton take something from the back seat. What did he give you?'

'He gave me three back copies of *National Geographic*.'

'Well, well, *National Geographic*, no less. Isn't that wonderful? You and Stapleton with a common interest. Where are the magazines?

'Father Stapleton is going to post them to my home sir.'

Attila made a hoop of the cane.

'Relax, Dawley, I believe you. I presume posting was Father Stapleton's idea. We couldn't be trusted with such awesome information as might be contained in *National Geographic*. We might even confiscate them. Wouldn't that be right, Dawley?'

'Sir?'

'Of course it would. I saw him write something, Dawley. Did he use the Waterman?'

'I don't understand, sir.'

'His special fountain pen, Dawley. The one with the gold cover. They presented him with that in Maynooth when he won the Cardinal Spellman prize for his moral theology thesis. We were together in Maynooth, you know. Here in Danesfort too. Same class.'

'I didn't know, sir.'

'Did he talk to you about me, Dawley?'

'About you, sir? No.'

'You're a liar, Dawley.' Attila flicked his wrist and the cane smote at a fly that had landed on the desktop. 'Did he make some reference to what he might have called my effete mannerisms. You see, Stapleton and I never liked each other. Did he offer you protection, Dawley?'

'Protection, sir?'

'You're like a bloody echo. Yes, protection. From me.'

'No, sir.'

'Pity. I would have rather enjoyed the moment when you discovered that your guardian was totally ineffectual here. In fact it would have made your state infinitely worse. Okay, Dawley, get back to bed.'

I never met Justin again. A few weeks later, when we filed into the church for night prayers, I noticed that Stapleton's place in the pew ahead of me was empty. Childe normally took the night ceremony, after which Attila would come on the altar and make announcements about the next day's schedule.

'Boys!' Attila said, 'this is one of the saddest days of my life. You all have heard of Father Justin Stapleton, a brother of Conor, who was here for the Holmes Cup match. Father Stapleton was struck by a car this morning as he was walking to lecture at the Irish College in Rome. He was dead on admission to hospital. Most of you would have known Father Stapleton by reputation. He was a wonderful athlete, a gifted hurler, but most of all, he was a brilliant academic.

Here in Danesfort we have no doubt but that Father Stapleton would have advanced to the highest reaches of the church's hierarchy. We will say the rosary now for the repose of his soul. I ask for your prayers on his behalf and for his family. Thou, O Lord, will open my lips ...'

I heard the clock in the town chime every hour until two in the morning. Justin's face swam in my vision and came to settle, like liquid in a mould, in a profile of exceptional kindness. Although he was fifteen years older than me, I imagined a friendship between us and built it into a relationship that thrived on the rapport of idealised spirituality and intellectual brotherhood.

I had started to smoke in my third year at Danesfort, though it was prohibited until fourth year. I think the habit owed more to defiance against Attila's petty régime than it did to addiction. There was a piggery at one end of the grounds, hidden by a grove of pine. Its gable, cloaked with a dense growth of ivy, backed onto Danesfort's west walk, but was seldom used because of the stench. I would climb the pine tree nearest the wall, drop down to its parapet and wriggle into a hide that I had gouged from the ivy roots. I found Stapleton there a few weeks after his brother had died.

'You may not know it, Stapleton, but this is my place.'

Stapleton hesitated. His eyes were red-rimmed, his face puffed, with a bluish tinge, like a ripening damson. 'I want to talk with you.' He rummaged in his pocket and pulled out a packet of cigarettes.

'Have one?'

I shook my head. 'What do you want, Stapleton?'

'My brother Justin, he asked me to look out for you.'

'I can look after myself.'

Stapleton struggled to hold his features in check. From

155

the corner of each eye, a teardrop formed. He covered his face with his great red hands and sobbed. I watched him ineptly, finding no words to express the odd mixture of confusion and sorrow which muddled my brain.

'It's all right, Stapleton,' I mumbled. 'Don't cry.'

He pulled his hands away and looked at me through swollen eyes. 'If Justin never asked me to look out for you, I would still want to be your friend. Please.'

I knew little about friendship. I had been reared in the hard Spartan habitat of Glenorga, a place where feelings seldom took root or, if they briefly showed, were ripped out after first exposure. 'I don't want to be anybody's friend, Stapleton. I get on fine as I am.'

'But you can't be like that. Everybody needs a friend.'

'I've made no friends since I came here. When I wanted them, they weren't there.'

'You're a strange bloke, Dawley. No wonder people don't like you.'

'That's their problem.'

'Don't you like anybody? Your parents even?'

'Oh shut up.'

'That all you can say? Let me tell you this, Dawley. I think my parents are great and I always tell them that. And my brother Justin was wonderful to me. I loved him, Dawley. I don't mind saying that.'

I watched him drop his head onto his chest and the sporadic rise and fall as a racking bout of coughing assailed him. I scrambled out of the hide, dropped down from the wall and heard Stapleton say, 'I could be your friend, Dawley. I mean it.'

All that evening in the study hall I couldn't get the encounter out of my head. It wasn't the hard man image dissipating before my eyes that puzzled me. What bothered me was that this raw-boned youth had access to a state of filial solace that I could only venture near in make-believe. In our house we never spoke of love.

Three weeks before the Easter break we played Colmans Well in the Boyce Cup final. We wore black armbands in memory of Justin. In the dressing room before the match, Childe used his death as a device to motivate us. We were the inheritors of a great tradition which tolerated no failure and if we failed this day, we would not be welcome back to the school that Father Stapleton had graced with his skill and endowed with his intellect.

As soon as we came out under the stand, most of the players hared across the field, testing muscles and sinews and running off the tension. But Stapleton held my shoulder in his great fist and walked with me to the goalposts. 'Dawley, keep an eye on me. I'd be grateful.'

He was solid as a rock that day. I watched him when the loudspeaker announced a minute's silence in memory of his brother. He stood there, head erect, chest thrust forward, legs planted wide, not a shake or a flutter of fear. When the first ball dropped in, Stapleton met the full forward bone on bone, crunched him in the tackle and tossed him in a somersault as if he were a sheaf of corn. Behind him I had it easy. I kept a clean sheet that day and was troubled with only one shot which skewed off Halpin's stick and almost sneaked inside the right goalpost. But I got to it with a flat-out dive and when I had hit it back upfield there was Stapleton to cleave my shoulders with a thump of appreciation. We won without even pulling out the stops.

Several weeks later the members of the winning team

were presented with a miniature cup. When it came to my turn – goalkeepers are always last – there was no miniature left.

'I have a spare one somewhere in my office,' Akim said. 'Dawley, come down to my room in about half an hour. I'll tell Father Rodgers you're coming.'

Akim's room was strewn with hurling gear and bottles of embrocation. A coal fire glowed brightly in the grate and beside it a built-in bookcase was filled with paperbacks, mostly adventure stories. Akim cleared a chair for me to sit down and poured me a cup of tea from a flask. He filled one for himself, stood in front of me with his back to the fire and pulled out a miniature cup from his pocket.

'Had it all along,' he said, the thin lips disappearing in the smile that lit his face, 'but I wanted a word with you. You're a funny fish, Dawley. You're probably the finest goal-keeper I've ever seen, for your age. I hear tell that you're a very clever youngster as well. But for all that you haven't a friend in the world nor do you want any.' Akim blew his breath out slowly; it made a whistling sound. 'Worse still, Dawley, you've made enemies. In high places.' He rubbed the stubble of his chin. 'Have you a vocation?'

'No, sir.'

''Tis serious then. You know, Dawley, I hate saying this. I think you'd be better off out of this place.'

'I never wanted to come here. But I'm stuck with it now. I have a scholarship and it will be renewed if I do well in the summer exams. My father would be mad if I left.'

'Worse things have happened, Dawley.'

'Maybe, sir. But I won't be driven out either. I'm not afraid anymore.'

Akim sighed and threw the dregs of the tea into the fire.

'You know, Dawley, the way I hear it, you're a marked man.

158

So, for Christ's sake, look out and don't get into any trouble.'

Easter was glorious that year. A blackbird took up residence in the pine grove behind the study hall. It sang with an out-pouring of rhapsody as if there was something in the air that provoked it. An old man spoke to me across the high wall near the piggery and told me that he had never seen potatoes planted so early. No good would come out of it, he said: fine March, bad summer.

I was reminded of him as I walked along by the gorge to Glenorga. The blackthorn was alive with blossoms. I could smell the nutrients at work beneath the soil; hear the crackle of awakening buds, feel the heat reflected from the limestone strata. I heard the tractor at work in one of our fields. Hughie was ploughing.

Then that strange warm glow started up again in my chest and stopped me in my tracks, as it had done every time I had returned from Danesfort. The glow built to a physical escape of pleasure and strained against my ribcage. This was home, the most wonderful place in the world. It needed no words to express it, no declaration of love or affection to maintain it, nothing only this savage primitive yearning that seemed to take root and hold, unaided. I suddenly knew that this was the magnet that brought Felim to work in the fields beside his brother. Felim was home a week already; he was now in Trinity College. When I had earlier walked higher up the gorge and emerged from the thicket, I saw him beside Hughie in the low field.

Mona came skipping across the Nursery Field when she saw me by the stepping-stones. She hugged and held me at arms' length to see if I had changed. 'You got thin,' she said, 'and you're as pale as the inside of a turnip. Come on, I've got a rhubarb tart cooling on the windowsill. I made it specially for you.'

She took me by the hand and pulled me towards the house. The archway of roses that Grandfather Dawley had erected over the door was laden with flesh-coloured buds.

'Mam has a migraine,' Mona said. 'We'll leave her alone for a while.' I had a glimpse of her as I passed the parlour window; her head was lowered to the book that was resting on her lap. I thought she might see my shadow, but she never looked up.

Mona sat opposite me as I ate the tart, her chin resting on the prop of her hands. She could never disguise her excitement.

'Is everything all right, Mona?'

'Everything's fine. Everything's great.'

'So what is great, Mona?'

'Me and Gene Trenchard. We're going out together.'

I stopped eating and stared hard at the radiance in her face. Gene Trenchard and my sister. I had never liked him. He aped those he thought would feather his nest and ridiculed those who couldn't. And he was a Protestant. My father would never allow their relationship.

'Mona, you can't! He's a Protestant.'

'So. What does it matter what he is, a Catholic or a Jew, a Muslim or an atheist?'

'Oh, it does matter. It matters to father. Wait till he finds out.'

'He knows, Roddy. He knows and doesn't say anything. Isn't that gas? Who'd have believed it?'

I climbed the hill of Knocknastumpa and dropped down to the valley floor of Glendign. Even before Long Pat's house came into view, I could get the acrid smell of wood burning with the sap in its veins. Mikey had been gone almost a year already and no one knew a thing about him. I had asked around, appealed to Hughie and Barton to scout for me, but nobody had heard. Mikey had done what he always said he would: be gone for all time. How I missed him. I missed his irreverence and that jaundiced eye that made minor concerns of major worries. In Mikey's world there was no Attila, no hurling coaches, no frightened young men with crooked legs who pretended they were brave and independent.

There was no sign of Rosie around the makeshift swing. The seat had split and one end of rope had broken off. It hung there like a relic from a long-abandoned garden. I waited beside the privet hedge until Lena came out onto the front yard with a basin of mash for the fowl. When she saw me in the haggard she glanced hurriedly over her shoulder and came furtively to meet me.

'There's no good looking for our Rosie. She's gone away.'

'Gone away?'

'That's what I said. Gone away. To Tipperary. Down near Aherlow.'

'Ah, come on, Mrs Kilraish. You're codding. That's miles away.'

'Faith an' I'm not codding. There's a man down there that Long Pat knows – a cattle jobber. The wife died this short while back, leaving a young child after her. Rosie is gone into service to him.'

It seemed that in a single instant the world had been frozen immobile. 'But won't she be back? On the weekends?'

'No, it's seven days a week.' Lena paused and began to rub off the dried bits of mash that clung to her fingers. 'Roddy, you'll have to go and see her. Please? And tell her for me that I love her and that I miss her awful. Go off with you now, for if that ould long fella finds out you came, there'll be trouble.'

I set out on the Tuesday of Easter week. I lied to my mother about going to visit Stapleton. A tannery lorry picked me up outside Newtown and took me as far as Cahir. The stench of half-cured cattle hides clung to my clothes and seemed to be embedded in my pores. I walked four miles along the road to Clonmel. Then a travelling salesman in a red van, who knew the countryside well, gave me a lift as far as the crossroads that led to Grogan's house in Aherlow. As I neared the house, a truck with wooden rails pulled out of the yard and passed me on the road. The driver had a florid face, a cigarette dangling from the corner of his mouth and a felt hat sloped far back over his forehead.

It was a thatched house with green streaks of lichen running down the walls. The front yard was covered in muck; slime-filled pools, like miniature oil spills, occupied the tiny islets in the midst of the ooze. The front door was ajar. I knocked on the door and called Rosie's name. I heard a child cry and a voice telling it to hush. Then Rosie appeared in the doorway. For a few moments her face underwent several emotions: puzzlement and suppressed elation, followed by a streak of fear. And then her face loosened and split into unbridled and exhilarated happiness. She spread her arms and rushed to me, burying her head in my chest, saying my name.

'Oh, Jesus, Roddy, I'm so glad you came.' Rosie began to cry, still clinging to me. Her chest heaved against mine.

'It's all right, Rosie, all right.'

She pulled away and wiped the tears with the sleeve of her cardigan. Then she manoeuvred me inside towards the table so that I was looking out on the yard and the avenue beyond. 'He's only gone to the shop for a packet of cigarettes. There is no fair today. He might go for a drink.'

'You're afraid of him, Rosie?'

'I don't want him to find you here.'

'Leave, Rosie. Pack up and come with me. I'll wait for you in the village.'

She sat at the other end of the table and traced her finger along the oilcloth pattern. The sun had gone from her face; it had vanished like the self-assured cockiness that she had often teased me with. 'I can't go home, Roddy. My father would kill me. It was him that fixed for me to come here. I think they made some kind of arrangement.' She sniffed again and inhaled deeply. 'You know what I think it is?'

'I don't want to know.'

'I'll stay here for two years. Then when I'm eighteen, Grogan will marry me.'

'They can't do that. It's a free country.'

Rosie swung a strand of hair from her brow with a sudden flick of her head.

'Aisy for you to say that, Roddy Dawley. It may be a free country for the likes of you but not for me. I can't go home, I can't run away. Where could I go? I haven't a penny.'

'You can go somewhere. Surely you can go somewhere.'

The child began to cry. I hadn't noticed the cradle in the gloom beside the open fireplace. Rosie went and lifted the child out, raised it to her shoulder and rocked it. The last time I had seen her, three months before, Rosie was a child herself.

'Roddy.'

'Yes, Rosie.'

'Will you go and see my mother?'

'I saw her before I came. She says that she misses you something awful.'

'Tell her, Roddy, what it's like for me here. She'll have to get me out, some way, Roddy. Whatever it takes. Will you tell her?'

'Of course I will.'

'Go now so, out of this place. I don't want him to know that you were here. I'll make contact with you somehow. And Roddy?'

'Yes, Rosie.'

'You said you were my boy, didn't you?'

'Yes I did. I meant it, Rosie.'

'Wait for me so. I'll get out of here, one way or another.'

I made several trips to Glendign before I got the opportunity to speak with Lena. I had a suspicion that Long Pat was expecting me for he came to the back door as I watched from behind the privet hedge. Finally Lena arrived in the yard with her basin of mash. She laid down the basin on the stones, made a receptacle out of her apron as if she were gathering eggs, and came round to the other side of the privet.

'Be as quick as you can,' she said, 'that ould Long Pat is as suspicious as a water bailiff. How is she?'

When I had finished, she caught up her apron in the gathering fold and started to move away. 'You shouldn't come near this place anymore,' she said over her shoulder.

'I'll come with you when you go to Aherlow. I can find some money and, and ...'

Lena spun round to face me. There was a fierce determination in her hardened jaw and clenched teeth. 'Have a bit of sense, you! Stay away from Aherlow. Don't make it any the worse for her. What can you offer her anyway? You're only a student?'

As we sat in our pew at mass the next Sunday I contemplated taking Felim into my confidence. Chances were that he would make a mockery of me. I saw Lionel Barton take his place in the family seat. Once it had been sited inside the altar rails but when he inherited the estate, Lionel had removed it to the front in the side aisle. Even when the church was full to overflowing, I never saw another person kneel beside him. It seemed that the Barton conversion to Catholicism had done nothing to change 500 years of deference and hatred. As I watched Lionel adjust the velvet cushion on the kneeler, I resolved to seek his help.

Father Lynch preached every Sunday. After communion he read the announcements and reminded the stragglers that their dues were still in abeyance. Then he closed the notebook, come round to the front of the altar and quoted from the New Testament.

'Allow me, my dear brethren, to paraphrase a quotation from the Bible. And so I say to you, in the words of Christ our Saviour, that it is easier for a camel to pass through the eye of an needle than for a rich man to enter the kingdom of heaven. A few days ago, I had a conversation with a fellow parishioner of yours, a man who does not regularly practice his religious duties and when he does, is usually found slouching outside the main door of this church. Which, by the way, is a habit I'm glad to say, that I have almost rooted out. So I asked this man: why it is that you don't come regularly to mass on Sunday? And do you know what he told me? I do not, he said, have a good suit to wear. As if the house of God was some kind of fashion parade. What nonsense? Do you not realise the special place that Christ has in his heart for the poor? People are not created poor at random. There is design in everything God does. So I say to you, poverty is something to be cherished; it is the hand of God. Accept it with dignity and nobility, and bear it with courage for you're ...'

My mind drifted away. But a voice cut into my reverie.

It came as loud and as clear as if it were delivered from the pew where I was sitting. 'Father, you're talking nonsense.'

For a moment I thought I had uttered those words myself. I could feel beads of sweat on my forehead and on my palms when I contemplated the disgrace I would wreak upon myself and my family. Then I realised that Father Lynch's voice had stopped and not a cough or a rustle had disturbed the terrible silence.

'Repeat what you just said, whoever you are.'

Felim's voice had the tone and timbre of his oratorical mode. 'I said, Father, that you were talking nonsense. Poverty is not a gift. There is no dignity, no nobility in the condition. If it were so, Father, how come we aren't all embracing poverty, including you.'

Father Lynch spluttered. 'You pup. You impudent cur. How dare you talk to me like that! Get out of my church. And likewise anyone else in this congregation who would countenance such behaviour.'

Felim stood for a few moments. Then he left the pew, but he didn't go alone. Hughie joined him, as did Mona and my mother. And in his seat in the short aisle, Lionel Barton hauled himself up to his full height, pushed out his chest and followed. They crossed in front of the priest, genuflected before the altar and walked down the aisle. I was on the outside of our pew and I attempted to join them as they came past. But my father put his hand on my thigh and forced me to remain seated.

Father Lynch waited until their footsteps had faded. He laid down the notebook and put his hands inside the sleeves of his alb in a gesture of nonchalant control. He cleared his throat, shook his head and said, 'I wouldn't dignify that blasphemy with a response, other than to say this. No good fortune will follow the perpetrators of such sordid blasphemy.'

Chapter 9

They were seated round the table in the kitchen when I returned alone from mass. The moment I arrived all eyes swung in my direction, anxious expectation on their frozen features.

'Where is he?' Mona asked. 'Is he in Heaney's?'

'No. He told me he was going to see the priest and he'd be home shortly. Ye are all to wait here for him.'

'Ye?' Mona queried. 'You are exempt, I suppose. You're some kind of shit, Roddy. Why didn't you come with us?'

'I tried to, but he held me back. Honest to God.'

'Honest to God,' Mona mimicked. 'You're the same as ever. You still haven't got the balls, have you, Roddy?'

'Mona,' my mother admonished, 'don't use that kind of language in this house. I'm surprised at you.'

As we waited I turned my face to the pictures above the fireplace. The *National Geographic* magazines had arrived weeks before I came home. The package was torn and wet by the time it was delivered to Glenorga and its contents were fully visible. Mona told me my mother had taken it to the parlour and for that afternoon had lost herself in the wonders of a world whose outskirts she had once come close to.

When I had finished with the magazines, Mona had the idea that we cut out some of the pictures to decorate the yellowed patch of rough plaster above the fireplace which the smoke had discoloured. One of the magazines had a feature on California and the three of us picked a picture from it. Mona had chosen a field of poppies in the Sierra Nevada foothills; mine was a flight of snowgeese at the Tule Lake National Refuge. My mother took a double page: cotton-woods in autumn in the Owens Valley below Mount Langley. We mounted the pictures on pieces of cardboard, wrapped tape round the edges and stuck them to the wall. The illuminated prayer to the stigmatist Padre Pio was removed to make way. As long as I could remember, the prayer was illegible because of the scum of grease and smoke that had formed on it.

My mother stood back a few paces from the fireplace, gazed wistfully at the scene we had created and mused, 'Mona, maybe some day we'll get to see those places'.

I wondered how many years it would be before the California feature suffered the same obliteration as the Padre Pio prayer. That patch above the fireplace was constantly smoke-bound.

Footsteps sounded on the cobbled yard and the door latch lifted. My father left the door ajar as if he were signalling that his business with us would be short. But he seemed to change his mind as he approached the table. He let his hand linger on the chair back and then he pulled it out and sat down. His gaze first picked out Hughie, who was sitting nearest to him, and then, without settling, he moved on, to traverse us all. Then a terrible change came over his face. It seemed to crumble, as if the framework that supported it had fallen inwards. I watched in a kind of fascinated horror as my father broke down; he laid his head on the table, placed his hands at each side of his head and wept.

The silence was excruciating. Every breath, every sniffle, was magnified; it seemed that the only sound in the entire world was the sound of my father's weeping.

'I have never,' my father spoke through his sobs, 'never been shamed as I have today. To think that my own family, my flesh and blood, would disgrace me in the eyes of God's priest and in the eyes of my neighbours.'

My father raised his head and swept his eyes around the table. He let them dwell on my mother. A few times he was about to say something to her but his breath caught in his throat and the sobs drowned the words.

'I'm awful sorry, Father,' Felim said, ''twas all my ...'

My father inhaled deeply and filled out his diaphragm. 'What was done today started here in this kitchen a long time ago. You turned them all against me, woman, and you did it very clever. This day in this parish there isn't a man alive who doesn't see me for some class of an eegit, a man who couldn't keep his wife or his children from making a mockery of him.' He turned towards Hughie. 'I expected more from you.'

'I don't go along with what Felim did,' Hughie said.

'Then why in the name of God did you walk out with the rest of 'em?'

'Because the priest was wrong too, Father. Very wrong. I had to support Felim; he's my brother.'

'You had to support your brother? If my father or my grandfather were alive today, and if they saw that the man who sided with my own family against the priest was Lionel Barton, God in heaven, what would they think?'

My father started to cry again. Then a chair scraped against the flagstones as Felim stood up. The self-assuredness had disappeared and was replaced by the pallid representation of sad and heart-rending regret. Felim went to my father. He threw his arms about him, buried his head in his chest and muttered over and over again that he was sorry. My father never responded; his eyes were fixed above the fireplace.

Felim went to the fields. A few moments after he had gone, Hughie rose and followed him. Mona was about to do likewise when my father raised his face and said. 'Sit down you. What happened to the picture of Padre Pio?'

'It was full of smoke,' I blurted. 'You couldn't see the prayer any more. I took it down.'

'Well, you find that picture and put it back where you took it from. Your grandmother Joanna put that picture there. She had great faith in that prayer.'

'For heaven's sake,' Mona started.

'Mona,' my mother interrupted, 'leave it alone. Roddy, go find the prayer.'

When my father left, we took down the pictures from over the fireplace and rearranged them on the back of the bedroom door where my mother and Mona slept. I found the prayer to the stigmatist, which had been thrown into the ashpit at the end of the kitchen garden. The ashes had discoloured it further but my father never passed a comment about its condition once it had been restored.

In the afternoon, Hughie and Felim took their hurling gear and walked into Newtown to join the St Luna's team playing in the intermediate championship in Limerick. Mona spent most of an hour in the bedroom, putting on what Felim called the glad rags and the artificial face. Several times she had gone into the parlour to stand before the cheval mirror.

Gene Trenchard also played for St Luna's. On occasions like this, Trenchard had use of the Barton jeep and would bring Mona to the game. Before Mona left, my mother handed her a small purse that contained a mirror and an old handkerchief. My father had no time for cosmetics. Young women should not flaunt their desirability with paint and powder. Before she returned home, Mona would wipe off the powder and the lipstick.

Shortly after Mona had gone, my mother left for her Sunday walk. I grew up believing, having it instilled in me by my brothers and sister, that this was my mother's exclusive private time. It was a tiny recompense for the routine of her days and the paucity of her nuptial partnership. My mother always looked sad and never more so than when she returned from her Sunday stroll.

When she had gone, I browsed through one of the *National Geographic* magazines. There was an article called 'The Islands of Living Fossils', which maintained that Australia, the Galapagos Islands and Mauritius offered biological evidence that Darwin's theories of evolution were scientifically credible. I had come across Darwin before, in a pamphlet that Lionel Barton had given me, but more convincingly by Felim as we once sat on the headland of a meadow while he sharpened the mowing blade of Hughie's tractor.

'Felim, do you think that Darwin is right?'

Felim laid the whetting stone on the ground and spat on it. 'There are two schools of thought, Roddy. There is the creation school, which includes the Roman Catholic Church and the Father Lynchs of this world, who support the notion that humans are formed in God's image and likeness, and therefore what we are today is exactly the way that God originally created us. God is the father of all creation. Ask our father and that's what he'll tell you. The second school of opinion is the evolution school, the scientific logical proposition. Charles Darwin and his followers tell us that the shape we have today, and that of every other creature alive, is the effect of the changes that have been taking place over millions of years. Do you follow me?'

'So the story about Adam and Eve is all a cod. We really are descended from apes?'

'Come on, Roddy, where have you been? All that stuff about the Garden of Eden is a myth, a fairytale, a way of transmitting to a simple people ideas and concepts which defy natural explanation. You know why the church is so dead set against Darwin?'

'Because it doesn't believe in his theories?'

'Not quite. There are many smart people in the church who are prepared to suspend their intelligence in favour of the myth. Fear, Roddy, that's it. Fear that if they allow the theory of evolution any credence, they might be out of business.'

After a while I put aside the magazine and turned on the radio. I found a comedy sketch on Radio Éireann; one of the female characters had an accent exactly like Rosie Kilraish. The morning events at mass had dislodged her from my mind and I chided myself for it. Tomorrow I would return to Danesfort. I had promised myself that before I went I would talk to Lionel Barton about Rosie's plight, and about mine too, for I saw us both intricately bound together.

I skirted the ruins of the Black Castle until I had full view of the front entrance to Barton Hall. There was no vehicle parked on the gravel sweep and none before the raised steps that led to the great hall door. So I doubled back, found the entrance to the overgrown track and came up through the kitchen garden to the barred basement window. It was then that I heard the music. It took a few moments for it to register in my mind until I realised that it was the same piece of music – the Moonlight Sonata – that Muirne Culhane used play for me in the parlour of her home in Ardagh.

The music was coming from the dining room and drew me towards it like an invisible cord. I doubled back from the corridor that led to the library and came to the drawing room windows by the paved terrace. The side window shutters were drawn but I was able to peep through a gap in the wood. When my eyes grew accustomed to the gloom, I could make out a woman sitting at the grand piano. Lionel Barton was standing behind her. One hand was turning the page on the music stand while the other rested lightly on the woman's shoulder. But it wasn't Muirne who was playing. The woman was older; she had black hair with a raven wing sheen and she wore it drawn straight back from her forehead. She stopped playing and turned to smile at Lionel Barton. I saw the face of my mother.

As the clock struck its night hours in the nearby town I tried to understand my mother's presence in Barton's dining room. This was the man who wanted to be my friend, who, perhaps in collusion with my mother, thought he could buy me with five-pound notes and a book about the landscape. I had stopped, maybe out of curiosity, maybe out of anger, as I passed the Giant's Grave on my return to Danesfort after the Easter holidays. There was the usual fiver under the flagstone and a note reprimanding me for not visiting. I tore the note in tiny pieces and let them fall on the red earth. Then I replaced the money under the flagstone and went away.

I knew now that I loved Rosie Kilraish. I didn't love my mother any more. I wouldn't dignify her whorish behaviour by letting her know that I was aware of it. But Barton. Him I would confront, throw his damned library back in his face. No matter how I came upon the money, I would return all he had left for me under the flagstone.

And then, that last term of the year, something strange happened to me. In the beginning, I took to staying in the college chapel after night prayers, as was the fashion of most of my peers who had aspirations towards the priest-hood. The God I discovered was kind and benign; he was the kind of deity who would sit and have a heart to heart with Darwin and uncover how much they both had in com-mon. His son, Christ, was cast in the same mould. Instead of doctrine and liturgy, there were only two command-ments: love God and love thy neighbour. In fact there were not two, but one, for should a man follow the pathway of either he had to obey both. I found it comfortable and peaceful to sit in my pew and meditate on the simple truths I believed I was discovering. After each period of solitude in the chapel, I made my way along the semi-dark corri-dors, seeing all from a different perspective. I thought I had found a meaning to my place on the earth, and maybe, after all, God was choosing me.

Danesfort began to reach out to me. I no longer heard the hissed call of Hopalong Cassidy from behind a corner. Stapleton and Halpin had become near friends. More and more, Jamesy Regan sought me out for tuition. I liked Jamesy; everyone did. He had neither the wit, the inclina-tion nor the duplicity to be anything but honest.

I had anticipated several nightly visits from Attila and was surprised and frightened when they didn't materialise. I was lulled into a kind of lassitude, as if the lighted face of inherent goodness was being genuinely offered to me and there was no need to be watchful.

My downfall came in Father Walton's class, three weeks before the summer holidays. Walton, who taught religious doctrine, looked up suddenly from the textbook and discovered a smiling Stuart, Attila's informant, whispering to his neighbour. It was a cardinal sin; there were only three possible interpretations for it: either Stuart was passing on a dirty joke, or he was bored, or the subject matter was beneath his level of interest.

'Stand up, Stuart.'

Stuart had paled. The fluster and fear was evident in his body language. No one had ever spoken to him like this before. He was Attila's white-haired boy.

'Stand up straight. Now tell me, what's so funny?'

'Nothing, sir,' Stuart said in a tiny voice.

'Nothing? Do you think this class is a joke? Or is it, Stuart, that you consider the Book of Genesis to be a joke?'

'No, sir, I believe that the Book of Genesis is the word of God. Not like some people in this class, sir.'

Walton cupped his hand to his ear as if he was trying to retrieve and amplify the words just spoken. 'Say again, Stuart. Some people in this class?'

'Yes sir,' Stuart wet his lips. From behind me Stapleton hissed, 'Shut up, Stuart.'

'Quiet,' Walton roared. 'Now you, Stuart, don't be intimidated. Say what you have in mind.'

'Dawley,' Stuart said. 'He doesn't believe in what the Bible says about the creation of the world. Or Adam and Eve. He says it's all a cod, sir.'

Walton raised the lid of his podium, threw in his textbook and banged the desktop shut. 'Dawley, up front.'

Fear beat against my ribcage. As I walked to the front of

the class, I tried in vain to recall what exactly I had told Jamesy Regan more than a year before, or to guess, in a more desperate endeavour, what Jamesy might have told Stuart.

'I only said, sir, that a person should not interpret the Bible in a literal way all the time. Many things in the Bible are symbolic; it says so in our own textbook, in the preface. The Bible was written for an uneducated people sir. The story of Adam and Eve is simply a way of explaining—'

'Are you trying to tell me that you're some kind of expert on the Bible, Dawley? What exactly did he say, Stuart?'

'I think Stuart misinterpreted me, sir.'

'He did, did he? Well, let me be the judge of that. Talk, Stuart.'

'He told Regan, sir, that Adam and Eve didn't exist. A man called Darwin has discovered that—'

'Enough, enough. Sit down, Stuart.'

Walton's face had begun to turn the colour of old parchment. 'Dawley, where did you hear of this fellow Darwin?'

'At home, sir. I read about him in a book and in a magazine that—'

'An' do you believe what that heretic is saying?'

'I think there is some truth—'

'Truth? The man is an anti-Christ!'

Walton's mouth snapped shut as if the import of his words had suddenly dawned on him. He drew back his hand and struck me across the face, and before the pain had fully registered, he hit me again. Then the red mist came; it came like a shaft of light and swirled about my head. It danced before my eyes and put words on my tongue and clarity on my mind which sought immediate and unbridled expression.

'Darwin is no anti-Christ; he's telling the truth. The account of creation in the Bible is a load of rubbish. An' the church is scared stiff of what Darwin is saying because his theories will put the fairytale out of business.'

Walton drew back his hand again, changed his mind and dashed towards the door. He yanked it open and yelled, 'Father Power, come in here and mind this class while I go and get the President.'

We heard his footsteps running down the corridor. A few minutes later the first bellow sounded. And then it grew louder and with it came the sound of the cane as Childe dragged it along the wrought iron railings of the veranda that fronted the classrooms. 'Let me at this heretic,' he was roaring. 'Let me at this infidel who casts doubt on the word of God.'

Childe came like a whirlwind into the classroom. In his wake came Attila, composed and smiling. His eyes fastened on mine the moment he entered the room and the taut sardonic mouth was like a leer of sensual pleasure.

There were four classrooms at the rear of the veranda. Childe took me into every one and caned me in a public punishment. There was a myth in Danesfort that a prolonged caning deadened the nerves and that the pain eventually subsided in a kind of anaesthetised numbness. Yet I experienced each hit, even the ones that Childe, in his manic passion, missed me with entirely.

Long hours after the beating had stopped, my hands remained on fire. It was as if my fingers had liquefied together. Then, later in the study hall, I felt a wave of clammy heat sweep upwards to my forehead, and when I put my hand on my brow, it was cold and moist. I passed out. When I woke again, I was in the infirmary and Sister

177

Gabriella was sitting by my bedside. I spent three days there. For most of it I fixed my eyes on a damp spot on the infirmary ceiling and let my hatred waft me along in its cocoon of resolve. I was done forever with men of the cloth and with their God who let them loose in rampant, unloving ferocity.

On my second morning in the infirmary, shortly before daybreak, three students went into Stuart's room. He was trussed up; his hands were bound behind his back and he was carried bodily from the room, propped against the veranda wall as the students trooped in to morning mass, but no one approached to help. There was a sign dangling from his neck. It said, in misshapen letters, 'I am a spy'.

I borrowed twenty pounds from Hughie. It was a lot of money and I thought up an elaborate rationale for seeking that much. But Hughie never asked what the money was for; he brought it out from his room in a rolled up wad. It smelled of grease and sweat and cowdung. He shrugged when I thanked him and told me not to spend it all in one shop.

Barton was nodding in his chair when I entered his library. I stood in front of him and coughed. His head jerked slightly.

'Roderick, so good of you to come. Pull up a chair. We'll have some lemonade.'

I had put the money in a brown envelope. 'It's the money you gave me. It isn't all here but I'll pay you back, every last penny.'

'Money? Pay me back? What is this, Roderick?'

I pushed the envelope closer to his face. 'Here, take it. I don't want anything to do with you anymore.'

'Heavens, man, what's come over you?'

'I saw you and my mother, in the drawing room, before I went back to college after Easter. You can keep your bloody library, and the money an'—'

'Easy on, old chap. Hey, it's nothing like what you think. Come on, sit down.'

I started to cry and I hated myself. The last time I had broken down was there, in that very room, recounting my fears of Danesfort. Three years on, I had borne the punishment and the silence, the ridicule and the shame; borne it all with obduracy and fortitude and never a tear did I shed. Now I stood in front of Barton, holding a wavering brown envelope in my shaking hand, and I was weeping like a child. Suddenly, as I remembered that I had no handkerchief, my left hand darted to my face and wiped my nose with the sleeve of my jumper. In every way I was reverting to being a ten-year-old.

'Easy on. Sit first.'

Lionel Barton vacated the chair he was sitting on and beat out its cushion until it was plump and full again. I took a deep breath, sat down, and the sobbing subsided.

'So you think there is something going on between your mother and me?'

'I know there is. I saw you both.'

'What did you see?'

'She was in your dining room, playing the piano. And you were with her. I saw the way she smiled at you and the way—'

There was an elaborate mahogany stepladder beside the bookshelves. It folded down like a deckchair. Barton stretched out a hand, pulled it towards him and sat on the bottom rung. He was hunched up like a jockey on a racehorse.

'You saw nothing, Roderick; only what your imagination

conjured. For there was nothing to see only a couple of
friends whiling away an hour or two.'

'Friends?'

'Yes, yes, I know it sounds improbable. Are you ready
for an explanation, because there is no point continuing otherwise?

I sniffed and nodded. The cuff of my jumper was wet
against my lips.

'I have known your mother for many, many years. She
comes to visit me most Sundays; that's why I told you not
to come on that day. Your mother, Roderick, is a wonderful
lady – sensitive, intelligent. She likes to read, to talk, and to
play Beethoven and Chopin. That's all there is to it. A couple of hours' diversion from the humdrum existence of her
life.' Barton pinched the skin on the back of his hand and
smoothed it out again. 'I swear to you, Roderick, that's all
there is to it. We enjoy each other's company. Let me tell you
bluntly: I have no sexual interest in your mother, nor
indeed, for that matter, in any other woman.' He hunched
his shoulders and smiled.

'Are you trying to tell me that every Sunday my mother came to your house and nothing ever went on between
you? You know what I mean.'

'You haven't been listening. I've told you there was
nothing only friendship and affection between your mother
and me.'

'But why?'

Barton unwound himself from the library ladder. He
sighed, made a circle of his mouth and slowly blew out his
breath. He began to pace the room.

'Have you any idea of the kind of life your mother has?'

'I don't know what you're talking about.'

'Roderick, for many married women in this country, especially rural women, life is one step removed from slavery. I know there are many women who would never say that, many of them, indeed, have never thought about it. But in many cases they are no better than chattels, owned and browbeaten by their menfolk. Look around you, Roderick, you know them. Are they any more than hewers of wood, drawers of water, brood mares?'

Barton's voice had risen, and his hands were gesticulating. He reminded me of Felim in his oratorical mode.

'I never heard any woman complaining.'

'Spoken like the typical man. But they will, Roderick, believe me, one of these days.'

'So what has all that got to do with my mother?'

'It has everything to do with her. Look, Roderick, your mother is going to seed on the mountain. She has an appreciation for the finer things in life – for what her father used call smelling the roses. We both know that the relationship between your parents is not good and hasn't been for a long time. Would you deny her a few moments' pleasure of a Sunday, a chance to rediscover what the roses smell like?'

I shook my head. A beam of sunlight x-rayed my hand and splashed on the leather-bound volumes with the Barton crest. 'No one else would believe that story,' I said.

'No one else need ever know. But now that I've told you, what are you going to do? It's a big responsibility, Roderick.'

'What can I do? My father would go mad. So too would Hughie. I'll have to keep it quiet, I suppose.'

'Less than enthusiastic, if I may say so. She's your mother, Roderick. You owe her.'

'Owe her.' I could feel the tentacles of the red mist. ' My

mother doesn't care for me, not in the way she cares for the rest of them. I owe her nothing. It's always seemed to me that I'm looking in from a distance, watching the rest of them; even my father is more central to things than I am. My mother doesn't talk to me. My father thinks I'm useless.'

'That's enough,' Barton said sharply. 'You're no outcast. There's a very deliberate strategy in the way your mother responds to you.'

I could feel the tears coming again. It was ludicrous, childish.

'I don't give a damn about strategy. I just wish that she'd smile at me, and tell me that she loves me.'

'But she does, she does, Roderick.' Barton threw his hands about. He started to pace again. 'Some day it will all be clear to you.'

He rummaged in the press beneath the bookshelves and brought out a bottle of lemonade on a tray. Beside it was a biscuit-holder, a miniature barrel in walnut wood with a leather lid. 'See,' he smiled, 'I have been expecting you.' Suddenly he laid the bottle down on the tray, ran his index finger along the slope of his lower lip and furrowed his brow. 'Yes, I knew there was something bothering me. I have it now. Why did you come to see me on that Sunday? Was there some kind of an emergency? And you didn't take the money I left in the Giant's Grave. You tore up my note too.'

I told him about Rosie Kilraish. Words that were always hesitant on my tongue were expressed in brimful meaning; words that were sanitised and vague were now explicit. As I talked to Barton about Rosie, it seemed to me that I had, by some strange meander of discovery, stepped outside the conventions of my time and place and found a niche that my soul had never touched or felt before.

Barton listened without interruption as he arranged a little mound of biscuits on the upturned lid of the barrel. 'I find it very hard to advise you,' he said when I had finished. 'And to be quite honest with you, Roderick, hard to go against your mother's view.' He held up a restraining hand. 'Hang on now, don't go off half-cocked.'

'What's my mother got to do with it?'

'Quite a lot. I know because she spoke with me about you and Rosie. You know the kind of reputation the Kilraishes have, especially Lena.'

'So should you.'

Barton laughed sarcastically. 'I see. Snatches from mountain gossip, eh, Roderick? Well, for what it's worth, they got it wrong. You're very young, both of you, too young I warrant to do the kind of things now that you may regret for the rest of your lives. Why don't you give it a break for a while, a couple of years? Then if you feel the same—'

'Break? What do you mean? I can't do that. I have to get her out of that awful place. If you only saw it, Lionel, only saw how frightened she is.'

'Okay, okay.' He closed up the biscuit barrel and put it away in the press. 'So what do you propose?'

'I have money – the money I borrowed from Hughie – to give you. I'll give it to Rosie. It will be enough to pay her fare to England. Her older brothers are there and Mikey. Don't worry; I'm not going to run away with her. I'll wait and finish college. But I love her, Lionel, and as soon as I'm finished with Danesfort, I'll go too.'

Barton turned from the press without closing the door. 'Capital. Tell you what. I've another idea to add to yours. It's a long way to Aherlow. Why can't we both go? I'll bring the jeep, meet you somewhere outside Newtown.'

So we went to find Rosie. But we never found her. The door of the farmhouse was bolted and the windows boarded up. We talked to a woman who lived farther up the laneway. The cattle jobber had fallen on bad times, she told us, and had closed up and gone off to Yorkshire; he had a brother in a place called Whitby. He had taken his child and the girl who was minding the house for him.

Throughout the summer of 1960, Stapleton and his father came often to Glenorga bearing copies of *National Geographic*. My father and Stapleton's got on like a house on fire. If I didn't know otherwise, I would have believed that they had known each other previously, but that was as improbable as it was curious. My father disliked strangers; he was uncertain and diffident in their presence. But one moment he was eagerly shaking hands with Stapleton's father, the next the pair of them were heading off to the fields. Seldom did my father offer the supreme accolade: a tour of his beloved land.

Felim had gone away early that summer, following the route of the building sites that Hughie had pioneered before him. He sent us a series of postcards, like signposts of his odyssey, names that found landfall in my mind and stayed: Maidstone, Tunbridge Wells, Brighton. Not for our Felim the banality of postcard messages; we were treated to mini-essays on the culture and history of the odyssey and its hinterland: Canterbury, Chaucer and the dawn of English literature, the Royal Pavilion in Brighton. They came regularly, usually on Tuesday. My mother waited by the stepping stones for the post to arrive, and then read and re-read the stories of her son's travels.

In the space of a few short years my world around

Mount Fierna had radically changed. Mikey was gone and had taken with him the fun and the gaiety, the wild madcap anticipation of discoveries still awaiting. Ferdy Culhane was in a Jesuit seminary and came home only for short breaks. I met him one day when I was hunting rabbits in the crags. He seemed troubled; his face was wan and colourless as if he had spent long hours indoors. Muirne was somewhere in France he told me; she was with a friend whose parents had a villa near Montelimar and a houseboat on the Rhone.

It was a lonely summer. My mother and Mona seemed to have entered an alliance that brooked no attempt to understand its nature. I went to the fields. We made an odd work team – my father, Hughie and me. Hughie had acquired a state of the art tractor; it had a cab and great rubber wheels, painted a vivid green and emitted a genteel trail of exhaust compared to the evil-belching column that the old one spewed forth. He seldom left the cab. Time and again I would see my father standing, hands on hips and shaking his head at the wonder of a technology that had made a quantum leap into his quiet fields. The tractor and its attachments made trivia of all those backbreaking vital workloads that had so obsessed my father when we were younger. Now my father filled a minor role, those little pieces of endeavour that occupied the preparatory rim of the major activities. Attachments had to be oiled and cleaned, blades honed, gaps opened in hedges to allow the green monster through, a spade to be worked in field corners where the tractor could not go.

The horse was obsolete. He languished in the Nursery Field because my father hadn't the heart to send him to the knacker's yard. I had a premonition of an imminent doom that the change of so-called progress would inflict on us all;

the horse was simply the first to be chosen. In the winter that followed that lonely summer, the horse lost his footing in the gorge above the Morning Star and was drowned in a shallow pool.

I honed blades in the shade of hedgerows while the air shimmered about me, mowed hay with a scythe round outcrops of rock in perfumed meadows. I thinned turnip drills and hated the eternal routine of a chore that technology had yet no answer for. We sat in the shelter of a flowering hawthorn that shed its blossoms like a shower of confetti and drank tea that Mona brought out to us. Hughie stood as he drank and wolfed down the slab of rhubarb tart. As soon as he had swallowed the last mouthful, he threw the tea dregs into the hedge, laid the cup in the basket and was gone.

'That fella will catch himself coming back,' my father said. 'I never saw a man with such a passion for work.'

'Except yourself,' I suggested timidly.

'No, no. I loved my work sure enough, but I was never driven like that man. I don't know if it's a good thing. Ah sure, maybe 'twill be all right in the end, but he bothers me.'

'Why?'

'Because he says nothing. Keeps everything to himself. Does he talk to you?'

'Sometimes. I don't be with him that often. But he and Felim get on well. I've seen them, in the fields, laughing and having fun.'

'I think the way of it is that Hughie listens and Felim does the talking. But I don't know if a man should be that quiet. And *you're* just as bad. Do you remember that story about the king of – some place in Greece – what's this his name was?'

'Leonidas, king of Sparta.'

'Tell me the story again.'

I told him. All the time he watched the tractor as it mowed the perfumed meadow. And when I was finished, he arose, nodded to me and walked away with his hands swinging. I wondered if he had heard a word. But he stopped and shouted back to me, 'Maybe some day we'll go there'. The day we cut out the pictures of California and fixed them to wall above the fireplace, my mother had said something similar. They both sounded highly improbable.

Felim came home in late August that year. He was as thin as a whip and his face had lost so much flesh that it looked skeletal. I noticed his hands shook a little and some-times his speech was hesitant. My mother held him at arms' length and wondered what sort of work he had been doing. But after a few weeks he had reverted to his old form and style and he regaled us with stories, long into the night, about people he had met on the building sites.

Then one Sunday after mass my father arrived into the kitchen flushed with excitement and lit with a grin that spread from ear to ear. He stood behind his chair, did his usual tour of the puzzled faces that looked in grim-visaged trepidation at him. He spread his hands.

'Today is the day. There were times I thought it would never happen. But it has, it has.' He paused and rested his gaze on my mother. I thought the flush had deepened. 'I said it to ye all, how many times did I say it and I suppose ye thought I was some class of an eegit. Some of ye did for sure. I said to ye: some day we'll walk down there to Barton Hall, me and my own around me, and buy those two big fields that border on ours.'

'Halleluiah,' Felim intoned. 'Praise God.'

'Do we really want his land, Father?' Hughie asked.

'Listen to him,' my father said. 'You, above all of 'em. I thought you'd be the very man to clap me on the back.'

'Father,' Hughie answered in his quiet, emphatic way, 'I'm with you all the way. I just don't want you doing it for me. I have more than enough.'

'No no, not for you,' my father shouted. 'For every Dawley that ever was and for every Dawley that will come after us. For the land that was ours by rights, for every one of my ancestors who suffered from the seed and breed of the Bartons.'

I had never heard him put so many words together before, never heard his voice rise to a crescendo of such conviction and emotion.

'Are all my sons with me?'

'Lay on Macduff,' Felim said as he kicked back his chair.

Hughie said nothing, but stood up, a half-smile playing hide and seek at the corners of his mouth, and nodded his compliance.

'And you,' my father turned to me, 'are you coming?'

'You hardly need me, Father,' I mumbled. 'I was never important to your plans.'

'Well, you little shite,' my father said. 'You're afraid, aren't you?'

'Let him be, Father,' Hughie said. 'Roddy is right. It isn't his fight.'

'It isn't, my arse. He's my son. He'll walk down there with the rest of us.'

And so we went, the four of us, striding towards a nemesis that was almost as ancient as the Celtic landmarks on our route. Our forebears had trekked across Europe in search of land. And when it had been wrested from them by a new invader, the passion for vengeance had burned and sustained the generations that had been willed the heritage of retribution. Today was retribution's day. I brought up the rear in a welter of confusion. The only living relics of that entire heritage, of the oppressed and the oppressor, were my family and Lionel Barton, my friend.

Rose Trenchard ushered us into the waiting room off the Long Gallery. It was here that the line of tenants, under the gaze of past Bartons, once queued to pay their rent. Then Felim moved from portrait to portrait ahead of us and called out the names on the brass mountings at the lower edge of the picture frames. He had a comment to make for each one: 'surly bastard'; 'face like the back of a bus'; 'Jesus, did you ever see such a sad-looking man?'

'That's Absalom Grantham Barton,' I said.

'Who?'

'Absalom. He was a Methodist preacher.'

'How the hell do you know that?'

'His picture was in a book that one of the fellas had in Danesfort,' I lied.

Felim looked at me with a dubious stare. Then he went on to examine the glass-fronted display case which held the Celtic hoard that had been recovered from Lough Cutra. As he examined it, Barton appeared in the doorway of the library and beckoned us in. He was sitting at his desk as we entered, wearing, I realised with a sudden stab of anxiety, the regalia of a landed gentleman: the tweed jacket, a Paisley cravat under a frilled white shirt and brown riding boots peeping out from under the desk. He couldn't have picked a worse time to sartorially display the Barton status. In my father's eyes it would be like a red flag to a bull.

Barton stood up. He pointed to the whiskey decanter and the cut crystal glasses that stood on the desk.

'Gentleman, could I offer you a drink? In token of your first visit to my house.'

'First and probably the last,' Felim said. 'We have business with you, Barton, but first, I would like to know something.'

'Of course, what is it?'

'In the hall, those artefacts in the display case. By what right do you hold those?'

I grieved for Lionel Barton in the silence of my sorrow and embarrassment. History had taught us little. Neither had our upward surge towards social status or the access to learning. We were still behaving like downtrodden peasants, reversing the thrusts and the cuts of triumphalism. We had failed to see that there was a new day abroad. Empires had fallen, the subjected had risen from the debris and yet in this insignificant microcosm of our country's past, we were still lost in the cul de sac of history.

'By every right,' Lionel replied. 'An ancestor of mine, Geoffrey, had sold most of that collection to a London dealer. I bought it back, at, I may add, considerable expense. It had been in my family for generations.'

'You've no right to it,' Felim said. 'It belongs to the nation.'

'Indeed it does, and it shall revert to the nation when I pass on. Now what can I do for you? Why don't you all sit down?'

'No need to sit,' my father said. 'I'll put it to you plain. We want to buy land from you.'

Barton scratched the stubble on his chin. 'What have you in mind, Mr Dawley?'

'The two big fields that bound on mine – 'long by your estate wall. I reckon there's twenty statute acres there. Say

100 pounds an acre – that's 2,000 pounds.'

'Two thousand pounds.' Barton seemed impressed. 'Would that include my right of way onto your property? I may never need it but— '

'No right of way,' Hughie said. 'You've had that for long enough. A clean buy we want; no tail ends.'

Barton nodded. 'I see. Yes, I can understand how you feel. Tell me, Mr Dawley, is that all you want, the two big fields?'

'What do you mean?' My father's words were icy. I could see the suspicion in the sudden flush within the tonsure.

'Well,' Barton said. 'I could dispose of more of my estate, and, if you were interested, I would consider less than your offer of 100 pounds per acre.'

I watched my father. He swung his head to one side and looked at Barton with glaring, outright suspicion. 'What are you saying? You'd sell me more land?'

Barton shrugged. 'It may have to be sold anyway. So why not sell it to you? You're my neighbour.'

'He's broke, Father,' Felim blurted, as if some great truth had suddenly dawned on him. 'He's totally broke.'

'Jesus Christ,' my father said. He beckoned us with his eyes and sweeping arm, turned about and we trooped out with him, down the Long Gallery and into the garden front of Barton Hall. He stood on the terrace steps that ran down to Lough Cutra until we had gathered around him.

'You should have bought, Father,' Felim said. 'You'd have got it cheap.'

'For the love of Jesus, have a stem of sense. What did you want me to do? Do that bastard a favour?' Then in rapid succession he uttered those awful soldier words that my mother so abhorred and that I had never before heard him use or never would again, 'Fuck him! Fuck him! Fuck him!'

A few weeks before I was due to return to Danesfort, a letter came for my father. It was marked confidential and bore the seal of the college. It said that my scholarship would not be extended, irrespective of any forthcoming results. It was felt that in view of my radical opinions on issues of faith and morals, and my family's attitude towards Christ's minister on earth, Father Morgan Lynch, it would be better if I did not return to Danesfort. Should I seek to contest the decision, the college would be steadfast in defence of its action. Would I please collect, as soon as possible, any items of personal property that remained in the college? The letter was signed by the Reverend Karl Roberts, Dean of Discipline.

'God, Roddy,' Felim said, as soon as my mother had read out the letter. 'I've done it again. It's my fault. I should never have taken on Father Lynch. I should have known that.'

'A bit late now,' my father said. He pointed a finger at me. 'What did you do?'

'I said some things that they had trouble with.'

'About what?

'The creation of the world.'

'We have another smart man. Can't keep his mouth shut. So they gave you a hiding, is that right? An' you never told any of us?'

'What was the point?'

'What d'ya mean?'

'Would you have believed me? You'd have taken the side of the college against me. The priests can do no wrong in your book. How did you know anyway?'

'Jimmy Stapleton told me. I knew him a long time ago. So now what are you going to do?'

'I'm going back. They granted me a scholarship. They can't fire me without seeing the results of my exam.'

'They can and they will,' my father said. 'I don't want you going back there. You can go to Adamston, where your brother was.'

'They have things belonging to me.'

'Get them then. And don't make a fool of yourself. We're in enough trouble already.'

'I'll go with him,' Hughie said.

'And me,' Felim offered.

I went with Conor Stapleton. He came to tell me that word of my expulsion was out and that he would come with me to Danesfort because he too was leaving. He told me that shortly before he died, Justin had decided to leave the secular life and enter the Redemptorist order. Conor would follow in his footsteps; it was the least he could do for someone he loved so much.

We drove to Danesfort, collected our property and passed by Attila's door as we came down the grand stairs. Conor knocked and entered without waiting for a summons. Attila started to smile and then froze in indecision when we both walked towards his desk.

'You have some things belonging to me,' I said.

'I don't like your attitude. Are you threatening me?' Attila began.

The cane was lying on his desk. Stapleton stretched a great red hand across and grabbed it. He bent it double and loosed it so suddenly that it twanged and hummed. Then he brought it down on the desktop with the sound of rending timber.

'Hold out your hand, Attila.'

'Please, Stapleton, please Conor.' The bluish tint that had fluttered many a heartbeat had paled to a sickly pallor; the cruel, sardonic mouth trembled with fear. Attila, like all bullies, was a coward beneath the façade. He opened the desk drawer and passed over my book and the torch. Stapleton made a sudden movement with the cane and Attila cowered like a chastised dog.

'Leave him,' I said. 'He's hardly worth the effort.'

I won the gold medal in Latin. The commendation and the award came in the post. I walked with the envelope in my hand as far as Waller's Point, tore the commendation to shreds and watched it float away on the surface of the water. A pair of swans glided by, poked at the pieces and then disdainfully ignored them. I threw the medal into Lough Cutra. I watched it skim the water and, with a final rippling flurry, sink to the bottom. I thought how paradoxical it would be if it came to rest beside an artefact of Celtic smiths who had cast their votives to their gods in this same spot. What uneasy bedfellows our respective offerings might make, representing, as they did, the very opposites of human endeavour and belief; the simple agrarian men of earth and the sky above and those who, in their arrogance, would have mocked and oppressed them and called them pagan.

Chapter 10

Above the fanlight window of the school's doorway there was an inscription in the leaded glass, *Nollite timere* – Be not afraid. I developed affection for the man who had put it there which was nigh to love.

Tony Villiers had a craggy face and several layers of fat above his cheekbones and beneath his chin. I spent two wonderful years in the Georgian terraced building that housed Villiers School. I'm sure he knew all about me when I arrived but he chose not to mention any of it. Villiers was a teacher born, and the school's ethos was focused on learning and the human conditions that made it possible. There were no politics, no athletic obsessions, and no thirst for medals.

I inherited Felim's bicycle. The man who sold me the wireless had repaired it and made it like new. There was yet no roadway between Newtown and Glenorga, so the bicycle was parked overnight in Heaney's bottle shed.

The countryside looked pristine, almost as if man had seldom stopped there or had never left destruction it his wake. The road to Adamston bordered fens and lakeland, rock strata exposed like a lunar landscape, meadows of wild flowers, peatbogs and pine groves. On the road to Adamston the dictum of learning's seedbed sang to me, *be not afraid*. I luxuriated in the calm that the words brought. And the hidden Roddy Dawley began tentatively to emerge into the light.

Electricity came to the mountain. Morgan Lynch pronounced from the altar that only backward people, removed from a sense of civilisation, spurned God's progress. The community signed up en bloc; even the diehards like my father and the Nevilles put their names to the order sheet. We threw out the old ways and embraced the new. The man from Adamston came across the stepping stones with a cardboard package in his hands, took away our old wireless set and replaced it with a brand new electric one. The paraffin oil lamps were cast on the ashpit at the rear of the house. With them went the metal clothes iron, the great blackened kettle that hung on the fire crane and all its companion utensils, pots, pans, bakers and griddles. It was the same as if 200 years of constancy had vanished in a puff out the door and a new day had swirled in without a whimper of wonder.

I never needed much sleep and, long after the house had settled down to its sounds of contraction and expansion, I would still be engrossed in study. I could hear my father snore upstairs, Mona and my mother whispering in the room off the kitchen, an insomniac snipe beating a flutter of wings in the darkness beyond the window.

Every evening after school I went to the fields. Work became a kind of opiate, I could lose myself in its intensity, wallow in its comfort and arrive home in the heel of the evening sated and renewed, as if contact with the soil was the power that energised the dynamo of body and soul.

My father never again spoke about the downfall of his dream: the failure to acquire Barton fields. I began to realise it wasn't the possession of land alone that fired the motivation; it was the exhilaration and pleasure of working it.

Land itself was like a bare canvas; the labour and sweat that shaped and tilled were the brushstrokes that formed the work of art. I used sometimes catch my father looking ruefully at Hughie and the tractor, and realise that he was regretting the hours of toil that the monster had claimed from him. We were all cast in his legacy: we were creatures of the soil, its drones and its worker ants; we worshipped it and did its bidding with devotion and unquestioning loyalty.

Not a day passed but I didn't think about Rosie. If she had remained in Glendign, my life would have been blissful because I felt I was finding my place on earth and learning to cope with its implications. I could accept now that my mother had grown away from me and recognise also that my sister was beginning to do likewise. Mona was in love; it was radiant in her face, evident in the eternal good humour and in the blush of sensitive acknowledgement whenever someone mentioned Trenchard's name. He came regularly to Glenorga. I still thought him brash and impudent.

I wondered why my father treated Trenchard with such tolerance. I could sense his disapproval of the liberties that Trenchard took with our long-established conventions. Why did he not make his feelings known?

And then in the summer of 1961 our world began to unravel. Trouble stalked to the summit of Mount Fierna and camped there permanently. Lena Kilraish was the first chosen. Long Pat found her lying in the cobbled yard behind the house. Her fowl basin had spilled and she had a fistful of mash in her hand. She had been dead for two hours or more: a violent stroke, the doctor said.

My father suggested that I should go to the burial with him. I think he wanted me along as moral support. It was a dismal funeral: a few bedraggled knots of people and a couple of trap carts. Long Pat sat in the front pew of the church, morose and black-faced and never once looked at those who came to shake his hand and sympathise with him. My father did not go and tender his condolences; neither did Lionel Barton.

I thought about Rosie all through the funeral mass. I had always felt she would become a carbon copy of her mother, eager for fun and merriment, tuned to the antennae of those who would brighten the gloom of routine. When I heard footsteps at the front door of the church, my heart leaped. Maybe Rosie had come home, or Mikey? I wondered if they had known and failed to arrive, or whether Long Pat hadn't bothered to get in touch. Rosie would have come; that I was sure of.

Lena made her last journey to Manisterluna without a single offspring to accompany her. I found it deplorably depressing and all the more when I saw where they had opened a grave for her. It was in the farthest corner of the graveyard, facing north, where no grave had yet been dug. Even in death, her reputation lived.

By the time I returned to Adamston for my final year, the postcards from Felim had stopped. We should have sensed the change because the last few postcards had no pictures but hastily written scrawls telling us he was well and hoping that we were too. We could tell by the postmarks that Felim had stopped the journeying and was based somewhere in London. When the cards stopped, it was strange how that familiar conspiracy of silence settled again over our house. We kept our speculation to ourselves, as if to speak about it would let loose the potential of trouble. My mother kept the cards in a bundle on the window sash, tied with a piece of string. Every now and then my father would examine the bundle to see if a new card had arrived.

Our penultimate family conference had to do with Felim. I remember sitting in the parlour and feeling I had entered a place of another time, as if I was an adult returning to the ruined house of my youth. The parlour had become my mother's exclusive place. Once, when the world was young, it had had a magical ambience; it had smelled of musk and lavender mix, the Venetian wallpaper lofted our fanciful flights into strange exotic journeys far beyond the mountain. Now the parlour smelled of dampness and old bones suddenly disturbed from their covering of clay.

'Mam is worried about Felim,' Mona began.

I stole a glance at my mother's face. Her eyes were red-rimmed and there were sallow sacs below each one.

'Felim will be all right,' Hughie said. 'I know it. One of these days he'll troop in here, throw his bag on the chair and come to the fields with me.'

My mother cried. She put her fingers before her mouth as if to dam the flow. Then she drew a deep breath that sounded like a sigh of despair.

'No, Hughie, there is something wrong. I can feel it. He's not coming back; he's gone, thrown everything away – the university, his career.'

'Mam,' Hughie stretched out an imploring hand, 'stop worrying. Time enough to do that when we know for certain what's going on. Then we'll figure—'

'For Christ's sake, Hughie,' Mona's temper flaunted itself, 'will you stop acting the smart man. Can't you see how worried my mother is? Don't pass it off as if there was nothing wrong.'

My mother, ever the peacemaker interjected. 'Mona, don't fight with your brother.' She looked earnestly at her son through half-lidded eyes. A single tear hung from an eyelash. 'There has to be something wrong, Hughie. Felim would never behave like this.'

'Mam, Felim is a university student. You know the kind of things they get up to. It'll all come right, I'm telling you.'

My mother didn't seem to hear. 'Hughie, will you go and find him. I can't bear to think what might happen if we don't make contact with him. He's my son and I love him, the same way as I love you. You have no idea how much I suffered while you were away in England. Please, Hughie, for *me*.'

Hughie gritted his teeth and looked at the ceiling. 'Mother, in the name of Christ, have a bit of sense? Do you think I have nothing better to do than to traipse all over England after Felim? Right now he's probably singing his head off in some pub? I have work coming out my ears and you want me to pack it up and go off to chase across England? Is that what you brought me in here to talk about?'

'You ungrateful shit,' Mona shouted. 'It's your own brother that's gone missing, it's you're own mother that's asking you to go and find him.'

'Right then,' Hughie turned to her, 'tell you what. I'll give you the money; you go and find him.'

'Well, aren't you the clever one? What chance would I have, a woman, going into those places that Felim might be in? Christ's sake, have a stem.'

My mother fluttered her hands before her face; it was a sign of severe anxiety.

'Stop it, stop it, the pair of you. Hughie, will you go, please? For me?'

'Mother, Felim is a big boy now. He's 21 years old; people have been married at his age and have families. Let him do what he wants. He'll be back when it suits him. So just let it be.'

'I can't stop worrying about what might have happened to him.'

'Then it's time you did.' Hughie stood up and started to walk towards the parlour door. 'And in future, Mam, don't be calling me to these conferences. I'm not a child anymore.'

The door banged in his wake. 'I'll go, mother,' I said. I was surprised how small my voice sounded, how timid were the words. My mother kept on shaking her head as if she was still hearing Hughie's refusal. She never answered me.

My father continued to search the stack of Felim's postcards. Once, when we were alone in the kitchen, he asked me, 'What do you make of that brother of yours? Do you think he's in some class of trouble?'

'Felim is too clever for that.'

'I don't know. The smartest of them make mistakes.'

'He'll be back, Father. He's only sowing his wild oats. Mr Villiers said so.'

I was relieved when my father nodded and walked away. It was all a fabrication about Felim sowing his wild oats. I had gone to see Tony Villiers in his study.

'Roderick, what do you know about your brother Felim?'

'He's my brother.'

'Which doesn't mean you know everything. He's very intelligent. But people say there's a very fine line between genius and insanity. Now, it is not as dramatic as that, but there is some veracity in the notion.'

'Are you saying, Mr Villiers— ?'

'That your brother is mad? No, not at all. But he is unpredictable. Roderick, he doesn't do things like you and me. He walks to a different tune. He hasn't attended a dozen lectures since he started at college; none at all in the past twelve months. I have friends there – students, professors, faculty members. They all tell me the same.'

'But he's been home; he never said a word.'

'Don't be naïve, Roderick. What would you expect him to do? Admit he has been missing lectures, drinking to excess, experimenting with, well, other substances, sleeping rough, dropping out? Come on.'

'Mr Villiers, I didn't know.'

'Of course. If I were you, I'm not sure I'd tell my parents. Felim will come home in due time. Of that I am sure.'

'But in what condition? Maybe my mother is right. We should try and find him.'

'Where would you look? He could be anywhere. No. I've seen this before. Felim has to work this out for himself.'

'Do you think he'll come home, go back to the university again?

'I don't know, Roderick. But that's not my chief concern. My concern is for Felim the person, not the near genius. I just hope he stays intact. For the normal Felim is one of the loveliest people on this earth. If you believe in God, Roderick, you should pray for him.'

I prayed to God. I prayed to the God of my youth, the severe God of regulation and duty. I prayed to the God whom I thought I had discovered in Danesfort, but neither of them listened to me. Felim did not come home nor did he write. A year later my mother was still watching for the postman and my father was sifting through the package on the windowsill to see if a new card had somehow arrived. And while we waited and prayed, our world continued to unravel.

I was studying in the room off the kitchen when Trenchard

came hand in hand with Mona to ask for my father's bless-ing. The moment they stood on the threshold, I had a sear-ing sense of foreboding.

'Father, Gene wants to speak with you. We both want to.'

'What is it? You never asked permission to speak with me before.'

'Hugh,' Trenchard began.

'Father,' Mona corrected.

'Out with it,' my father said; 'it must be frightful impor-tant.'

'We want to get married,' Trenchard said in a rush. 'I want to ask you for your—'

'Married? Did you say married? What kind of question is that?'

'It's something that people do all the time,' Mona said sarcastically; 'we are not the first.'

'Don't get smart with me, young woman.' I could hear the creak of my father's chair as he turned towards Trenchard. 'An' you, are you trying to tell me that you want to marry my daughter?'

'Yes, sir.' Trenchard sounded relieved and hopeful.

'An' tell me, if it isn't too much to ask you, what are your prospects?'

'Prospects?'

'Yes, bloody prospects. Have you a way of supporting my daughter? Have you a job? What age are you?'

'Hugh,' my mother intervened, 'why don't you stop intimidating and listen?'

'Why shouldn't I question him? It may be fine for you, woman, but the man that wants to marry Mona will have to be able to support her.'

'I'm 21,' Trenchard said. 'I have a good job with Mr

Barton.'

'You have in your arse. That's a tuppence halfpenny job.'

'We're not going to depend on that,' Mona said. 'We're going to America.'

'America? Be God you're not then. Look at ye, the pair of ye, a couple of youngsters, still wet behind the ears and ye're off to America. Have the pair of ye taken leave of yeer senses?'

'Father,' Mona said, 'we came for your blessing. I hope you will give it to us. But to tell you the truth—'

'Are you putting it up to me? Are you?'

'No Father.' Mona's voice had that quiet, emphatic authority that she had borrowed from Hughie. 'I'm just telling you. Gene and I are getting married—'

My father's fist smote the table with the crack of doom. 'Don't tell me what you are or what you aren't going to do. There had been enough of that in this house. I have one question for you, sir. You're a Protestant; my daughter is a Catholic. She can't marry you unless you turn. Well, are you?'

'Hugh,' my mother said, 'let them answer that question for themselves. It has nothing to do with us.'

'Did I ask you?'

Felim, I remember the story you told me. Now we are like the family of swans on Lough Cutra. We are breaking up. You are gone, and Mona is about to tell him that she too will go.

'It doesn't matter, Father. Protestant or Catholic, Jew or Gentile, what difference does it make? You knew all along that I was going out with Gene. You never said a word before.'

'I knew all along, did I? I didn't know if it were serious, did I? And when I thought about it, do you know what I said to myself. I said, they are two sensible people, the mother and her daughter. They will never let it go that far without figuring out the consequences and stopping it before it becomes too serious.'

'Well, you were wrong,' Mona said. 'But I dunno what you are making such a fuss about. Those things don't matter anymore.'

'Well they matter to me, Missy. And to all belonging to me. So let me tell you this. If you marry that man against my wishes, and he remains a Protestant, you are no daughter of mine.'

I heard the chair creak as it slid over the flagstone floor. Then my father's footsteps echoed on the stairs as he went to his room. The sound of Mona's sobbing came in my bedroom door.

On the eve of her departure, we assembled again in the parlour to bid her farewell. It would be the last time we gathered there. I dreaded that moment. Mona kept on reassuring us that emigration was very different now to what it had been in the past. America was only six hours away by plane. People made fortunes these days; anybody with an ounce of savvy and a passion for work could make it big. Gene Trenchard had all the attributes; together they would saddle the wind, ride the wild horse of fortune.

My mother was strangely animated. I had expected tears and the sacs beneath her eyes filled to the brim. But she had put on her Sunday clothes, colour on her cheeks and had brightened her lips. I had bought Mona a silver Claddagh ring with money I had borrowed from Hughie.

Mona hugged and kissed me when I presented it to her and she made me promise that I would visit her in New York after I had finished school and had earned the fare on the building sites of London. Hughie gave her a brown paper bag that rustled when he handed it over. When she looked inside, her eyes spread in wonder and she threw her arms round him, muttering thank you, thank you, over and over again against the fabric of his pullover. I knew there was money in the bag. It was probably the most welcome gift of all.

My mother had earlier built a fire in the cast iron fireplace. The firelight threw shadows on the wallpaper, giving the streetscape of Venice the same enigmatic and exotic appearance that had fired our imaginations years before. I thought how strange and paradoxical it was that this last conference – a concept that we had outgrown and disregarded – should be the nearest replica of its heyday. It would have been closer still if Felim were present.

My mother made tea in her china service and served it with Mona's rhubarb tart. We sat around the table and she took us on what she called the last leg of the journey we had begun in this very room when we and the world were young. This was no moment for sadness, she told us, nor was it the end of anything; it was simply the beginning. We were born and moulded to go out in the world, away from the narrow confines and the stultified perspective of this mountain and the people who lived in its shadow. Apart from Hughie, all of us would go. It was our destiny. We would journey the canals of the world, soar like the eagle beyond the mountain tops and exploit the talents that had been nurtured and grown in this very room. It hadn't been easy, but it had been wise. And in time, when we had all come ashore in the harbours of the world and made our mark, we would understand the enormity of what we had done and appreciate the poverty of soul and body we had left behind.

In the morning, when dawn was peeping over the rim of the gorge, the three of us walked to the stepping stones. My father was still abed. I don't know if Mona ever told him she was leaving or if he knew and chose not to say goodbye. Hughie was already astir: I could hear the tractor making its way towards Kirby's land. In the midst of my mother's harangue of the evening before, he had quietly left the parlour as if he were fetching some item from the kitchen. But he never returned and no one remarked about his absence.

I walked with Mona along by the gorge. We passed the familiar places, the core landmarks of our mountain home. We spoke no words and kept our heads fixed on the ground. I carried mother's suitcase that had accompanied me to Danesfort and would now make the flight to New York. At the front entrance to Barton Hall, Trenchard was waiting by the jeep. Lionel Barton sat in the driver's seat. I stowed Mona's luggage and went round to say goodbye. But the jeep had moved away before I got there. I watched Mona's head all the way until they passed out of sight at the bend before the gate lodge. She never looked back and as I stood and watched the dust settle along the avenue, I felt, with a terrible certainty, that I would never see her again.

In the weeks and months that followed I expected the postman would bring a letter from Mona and, if fortune really favoured us, there might also be a card from Felim. But Mona seemed to have gone to ground in the same way as her brother had. I couldn't understand it, given her relationship with my mother. And then, one day, when I mentioned to Barton that Mona hadn't written, he was disarmingly forthright.

'Between you and me, Mona has written several times.

Apparently everything is fine. They have a flat, somewhere in New York. They both have jobs. Mona is working for a woman who runs a school for children. Pre-school, they call it. Gene is a longshoreman.'

'But she never wrote.'

'So how do I know? Your mother tells me. Mona sends her letters to this address. Apparently she is afraid that your father might intercept them.'

'Jesus, and what about me? Shouldn't I know? I'm her brother.'

'Of course you should. Perhaps you should talk to your mother about it. But please, Roderick, don't implicate me.'

Then, as if to compensate for his part in the deception, he brought out the tray with the lemonade bottle and the leather-bound biscuit barrel. While he was bending at the press beneath the bookshelves, I looked out the window and noticed that the sundial, which had sat on an ornate limestone podium in the centre of the gravelled front, had disappeared.

'The sundial, Lionel, it's gone.'

'Yes. To a dealer in Colchester. There was this advertisement in *Country Homes*. Picked it up when I was over there lately.'

'You never told me you were going.'

'No, perhaps I should have.' He nodded rapidly.' No perhaps about it – I should have taken you into my confidence. You see, I went to look for Felim.'

'My mother asked you? Christ.'

'As a last resort. I should really have had more sense, like your brother Hughie. It was a wild goose chase from the start. I was short of funds and when a man is short like that, one's propensity to search is severely limited.'

'Did you find anything?'

'A pretty cold trail, I'm afraid. The last two cards, your mother told me, had a Southend-on-Sea postmark, so I took a chance that Felim was working up the east coast. I found a gas pipeline in Hockley where he had worked and a hostel where he had stayed for a few weeks. I thought I had struck pay dirt in Chelmsford. There was an industrial estate going up on the outskirts of the town and I met a Scottish bricklayer who knew Felim. Didn't like him either; said he was an Irish Paddy full of shit and fancy language, who couldn't hold his drink very well. But he did put me in touch with a couple of boarding houses where Felim might have stayed. The first landlady wanted to set the dog on me; Felim had skipped, owing a month's rent and a few days later she missed a pair of silver candlesticks that she kept in the drawer of her sideboard. The second one would have liked too to know where Felim was. Her husband was in Aden with the British Army and Felim, well, I suspect he had been a pleasant antidote to her loneliness. She had heard him mention King's Lynn but I never got that far; my money ran out.'

'I'm sorry we caused so much trouble. Tony Villiers thinks that Felim has dropped out, that he's drinking a lot and may never come back.'

'Ah, I wouldn't put it quite like that. But let me tell you something that I hadn't the heart to tell your mother. It's not so much the alcohol I'd be bothered about. That brickie intimated that Felim was taking drugs.'

'I'll be in England myself soon,' I told him. 'I'm going over there for summer work as soon as I finish my exam. I want to find Rosie as well. Will you come with me?'

His shock of white hair bounced up and down as he

emphatically shook his head. 'Roderick, forget it. It was a mistake for me to go. Leave Felim be. When I was searching for him, I kept asking myself what I would do if I found him. Apart from what he feels about me, he's an adult now, knows his own mind. Do you think for a moment he'd listen to either of us if we tried to offer him advice?'

'But it isn't just about Felim, Lionel. I have to look for Rosie too.'

'Roderick, can I give you the same advice about her?'

'No, you cannot, you're always saying something like that. As if I was some class of half-baked youngster. There is a word for what Rosie and I feel for each other, Lionel. We don't use it much in my house and maybe it wasn't very popular in Barton Hall either, for all its grandeur. We *love* each other. I'll go and find her if it takes me the rest of my life.'

I could see the suspicion grow in my father as the weeks and months passed without a word from Mona. 'What's wrong at all?' my father asked; 'surely the girl would have written by now.'

'Should she?' my mother responded. There was fire in her eyes and a sarcastic tinge to her words. She was going into battle early, deciding that offence was the better ploy. 'Why should she? To a man who threw her out of her own house and wouldn't give her his blessing. That same man who couldn't get up in the morning to say goodbye to her.'

My father went into battle too but it was an unequal struggle and he was no match for her guile and subterfuge. My father fought fire with fire, aggression with aggression.

'I never knew she was going. Was I told?'

'Of course you knew. You saw he packing her clothes, didn't you? You heard the noises in the kitchen the morning she left.'

'Ah, woman, you have an answer for everything. But in that case so, why wouldn't she write to you, or to Roddy there, or to Hughie?'

'Hughie didn't say goodbye either.'

My father looked at Hughie as if he had suddenly transformed from a conspirator into an ally. 'No more than me, he wasn't told either. Anyway, woman, have you heard anything?'

My mother looked him straight in the eye. 'No,' she said. 'I have heard nothing. It seems that I, and Roddy here, have to pay for the sins of the rest of us.' The dark sloe eyes locked into mine. In those fleeting moments that she held me so, I looked into the depths of her will and the temper of her spirit. She knew about me, she understood the nature of my friendship with Barton and how it bound me to silence. I could not reveal my mother's complicity because that would expose mine.

But they must have suspected. My mother wasn't grieving for a lost loved one. The animated blithe woman, who had appeared in our parlour on the eve of Mona's departure, fell with palpable gusto to the tasks that Mona had bequeathed by her absence. Sometimes when I came quietly to the farmyard, I would hear my mother sing snatches of songs and hum passages of music as she darted from chore to chore. In miserable contrast to her soaring spirits, I started to hate myself for the traitorous renegade I had become. And with it came a reversal of feeling, a change of heart that gathered momentum as soon as it settled in my soul and found refuge there. My father and mother began to change places in the reservoir of my tortured emotions.

Villiers called me to his office when the exam results came in.

'You know,' Villiers began, 'seeing you there, Roderick, reminds me again that I probably mishandled Felim in a similar situation to this. I should have focused on how to handle the responsibility of his exam results, rather than the glory of their achievement. Ah, well, so much for hindsight. Any news of him?'

'Not a word.'

Villiers sighed; his stomach seemed to deflate like a punctured balloon. 'So, let's talk about you. What options will your results bring? Not a university scholarship, I'm afraid.'

'University does not interest me. Never did.'

'All right. Now, let's see what's likely to come up for you. You will be offered a place in teacher training college. You'd make a good teacher, Roderick. What say you?'

'I don't think I'd like it. It's another two years of study. And it's boarding school. I've had enough of that.'

'The Civil Service? You're a certainty to be offered a junior executive position.'

'That's the city. I don't want to go there at all.'

'H'mm. What gives me this feeling that anything I suggest will be eliminated? What do you want to do – stay at home?'

'If I could. There is no place I'd prefer to be. But they wouldn't have me; my father thinks I'm useless on the land. So does Hughie. They don't talk about it anymore but I can sense it. It's there all the time.'

'What's your preference then?'

'I have none, Mr Villiers; it doesn't matter to me anymore. There was a time when all I wanted was to be like Felim and go to university. But I know now that I am not cut out for that. I don't have the confidence that Felim has, nor his other talents. I find it hard to talk to people. I can handle any problem on paper, but when it comes to putting my knowledge into practice, with the involvement of other people, then I have a difficulty.'

Villiers sat back in his chair and drummed a tattoo with his fingertips on the back of his other hand. 'Are you saying to me that you have an inferiority complex about yourself?'

'I don't know exactly what that means. I'm afraid of things, afraid of making the wrong decisions, of making a fool of myself. I feel I'm not good enough, especially in those things that really count. I'm not making much sense, am I?'

'Would it help if I told you that I understand very well what you are saying?'

I had a flash of Justin Stapleton's face. The same generosity of spirit as Villiers smiled at me and his face quivered with the effort. Few people had ever breached my external rampart and seen my inner vulnerability. The genesis of what I had just shared with Villiers I had locked in the background of my mind so long ago, it seemed to have been there forever. It all began the day the doctor told my mother that my leg would never heal. I was being punished; I had done wrong and offended God through my association with his enemy. And from there, other things came to hang like pendants from the rim of that original millstone: my place on the perimeter of the family, my father's estimation of my worth, my mother's abdication of her love. Of late I had begun to think that Rosie was another pendant. She had come into my life so that she could be snatched away again in some act of inexplicable retribution.

Villiers interrupted my thoughts.

'You know what I think? I think part of your problem is Felim, or rather the combinations of things that Felim represents. Did you ever know your grandfather, Philly Cartor?'

'No. I never did.'

'I knew him well. He was my teacher. An extraordinary man, very talented. Probably the only true bohemian I ever came across. As soon as he had acquired some knowledge or some skill, he was off again to something else, always seeking. Sound familiar?'

'Felim?'

'Felim didn't inherit his behaviour at random. It was in the genes. But it is not you, Roderick. So will you please stop trying?'

'I wish I could be like him—'

'Nonsense. Look, Roderick, you are talented in your own way. Use your ability to express yourself, to find peace with what is essentially you. And that is the greatest expression of self there is. Now where are we?'

'I can't stay at home. I have to find something for myself.'

'Of course. Can I suggest something? A former classmate of mine is running an enterprise development unit for the Peat Board. The Board has thousands of acres of land from which peat has been harvested. So they are trying to come up with ideas and products for which the land can now be used. They are looking for someone to train in, someone bright and sharp with a flair for nature and the landscape. Well?'

'I think I'd like that.'

'I think you would too. I'll fix up a meeting. And Roderick?'

'Yes, Mr Villiers.'

'There is nothing wrong with being shy and diffident. Unless it becomes a stick to beat oneself with and a bolthole to indulge one's self-pity.'

'I know. I was told that a long time ago, but I never really accepted it.'

A week later I cycled to the Peat Board's headquarters. I had journeyed with confidence. I got honours in every subject of my final exam. I had come close to full marks in history and geography. I knew *Landscape of the British Isles – Formation and Change* off by heart. I had calluses on my hands to show that physical labour was no stranger to me. But when a clerk arrived to lead me down the corridor, with his blue suit, white shirt and brown shoes polished like mirrors, the sweat of fear, my old adversary, grew so profuse on my forehead that I could smell the pungency of its presence. I would be found wanting, short of the final tally.

The clerk knocked on the door, stood aside to let me enter, and closed it softly in my wake. A thin man with a tweed jacket and open-necked shirt stood with his back to the desk. He swung around and came to meet me with an outstretched hand. For a moment the face escaped me but then I remembered it from the classroom in Danesfort. It was John Carew, the teacher with the drink problem, who had tried to give me counsel.

'Roddy Dawley. So we meet again. I'm delighted Tony Villiers persuaded you to come. Sit, sit, we have a lot to talk about.'

'Roddy,' my mother said, 'can I hold your hand?'

We were climbing the slope of Knocknastumpa, heading up into the baseline of the clouds. The bees were foraging in the heather; armies of ants were scurrying along the stumps of long dead oaks, turning the mosses and lichen that enveloped the rot into labyrinths of movement. It was years since we had been that way, a quartet of excited kids, leaping the bog-holes, rolling in the heather.

'How long ago,' Mother asked, 'since we came this way?'

'Aeons and aeons. When the world was very young. Felim had golden hair that tumbled over his forehead; Mona told us she loved us all; Hughie stood wide-shouldered on a tussock like a great adventurer. And me, well, I was able to run; I had two perfect legs.'

'And me, Roddy, what was I like?'

'You were beautiful, Mam, the brightest flower on the mountain.'

'Wow,' my mother laughed, 'you must have understudied Felim.'

My mother's hand was cool to the touch. She curled her fingers around mine and I could feel the toughened skin that her chores had willed her. Then she pulled it away and held it out to the sunlight. 'Would you believe it, Roddy: these hands were once soft and gentle; they played the piano and wove intricate pieces of embroidery.' She laughed, turned and looked back down the mountainside to our house. Its column of smoke rose like an uncoiling serpent in the heat. 'Do you remember what Felim used say, when he wanted to tell us how bored he was with our little Sunday excursions? "Tell you what, Mam, let's do something really mad today, let's climb Knocknastumpa from the north face instead of the south".'

We sat by the Blue Pool and listened to the tinkle of the rapids.

'Mona loved it here,' my mother said.

'We all did. I think that was the time when we were the happiest. Mona would always remind us how fortunate we were to be so close to each other. She used say it was the product of parents who married for love.'

'Wonder what gave her that idea?'

'Hughie was always uncomfortable when Mona said things like that.'

'He would be. And Felim, what did Felim say?

'You know Felim, Mam. He never paid much heed to something he hadn't said himself. Anyway, he was too busy swimming.'

'He was like a fish in the water, wasn't he?'

'I used think he was like an otter. He told us that if he had a choice, he would opt to die in the water. Drop there under the surface, sit on the bottom and listen to the music play, for that was the sound people heard when they were close to drowning.'

'What a terribly morose thing to say. Come on, Roddy, let's keep going. Hold my hand again.'

She took my hand and led me to Manisterluna. In the distance we heard shouting from the hurling field. Hughie was playing; my father had gone into Heaney's after mass and had not returned for his midday meal. Once it would be unusual for him to do that, but most Sundays now, after the chores, he changed back into his best suit and walked to Culhane's pub in Ardagh. When he didn't return after mass, my mother put his meal into the oven – we now had a range instead of the open fire – and asked me to walk with her by our ancient landmarks, as we had done when we were young.

'Look out over the valley,' my mother said. 'The day that my brother Roderick and I cycled up here and saw it for the first time, I thought it was the most beautiful place on earth. A long time ago. Poor Roderick. He was all against me marrying your father.'

It was territory I did not want to enter. We never referred to the state of our parents' relationship. It was exclusively their domain, theirs to share if they chose, and theirs to remain silent about if they wished.

'It is beautiful,' I said. 'There is no place else I'd rather be.'

'Roddy, don't be silly. There are other far lovelier places.'
She moved her hand in a sweep, circling the valley. 'The mountain is like Manisterluna: it's a graveyard. Don't let you get buried here, like Hughie will be. You have a job now; use it to get out. I hate the mountain, Roddy. I hated it as soon as I understood its nature. It's been like a vault, burying me alive.'

I saw the agitation pass over her face and return again like a cloud shadow in a cornfield. I could feel the tension in her gripping fingers, her rings biting into my flesh. She had never spoken to me as vehemently as now. Then she sighed, as if the moment had passed, and turned to look out over the valley again. I could see the arch of roses around our front door. I heard the Morning Star gurgle in the gorge.

'My father painted this scene,' my mother said. 'The painting hung above our fireplace until he was forced to sell it. You never knew my father? We always called him Philly.'

'No Mother, he was dead before I was born.'

'Of course, what was I thinking about? He was very like Felim, you know.'

'So I heard. Mr Villiers knew him; he was a student of his. He told me that Philly Cartor was the only real bohemian he ever knew.'

My mother laughed. I couldn't tell for sure whether it was mirthful or cynical. 'He was many things, Roddy; some good, some downright bad. But I loved him. There was something he used say about life and how to live it. You know how some, especially those from Mount Fierna, think this life is the forerunner for the next, and that what we do on this earth is to build credits for the afterlife? Philly Cartor preached the reverse. This is no dress rehearsal he used say; this life is the real thing. Make the most of it.'

We walked by Lough Cutra and Waller's Point. We

stopped by the Giant's Grave. My mother looked quizzically at me as if wrestling with a problem.

'I think you know that Lionel Barton and I are friends?'

'I saw you playing the piano in the drawing room. You know also about him and me?'

'Of course and I'm glad. He's a very good man. Do you know what his ambition is, his prime objective in life?'

'He wants to make peace with my father. He told me many times.'

'Poor man, poor innocent man. He might as well try and saddle the wind.'

My mother walked ahead, towards our secret route to the Barton library. Then walked towards me, holding out her hands, smiling the most radiant smile I had ever seen.

'Roddy, give me a hug.'

I smelled the hint of lavender in her hair and the faint tinge of camphor from her Sunday dress. She clutched at my shoulders, drawing me closer until the warmth of her cheek felt like an ointment on my skin.

'I love you, Mam.'

'That's nice to hear you say, Roddy. Thank you.'

The next day I started my apprenticeship period in the horticultural college which Carew had signed me up for. When I came home, late on a Friday evening, the house was empty. I went out to the front yard to look for my mother and found Hughie feeding the calves in the outhouse.

'The bitch,' he said. 'The bloody bitch! She's gone, packed up and gone.'

Chapter 11

My father folded his arms and reclined his chair off its back legs. I felt him make a mental inventory of his woes.

'We must think,' he said; 'think what we're going to do, what to tell people.'

'Does it matter a shit,' Hughie said, 'what people think? Let them go and shag themselves. We'll do without her; it isn't the end of the world.'

'Aisy to say. I never hear tell of it before – that a man's wife upped and left him. 'Tis a right bad thing to happen, a right shameful thing.'

My father swung round to look at me. His lower lip trembled. 'You were close to her, often here in the kitchen alone. Did she tell you anything, give you any hint?'

'I wasn't close to her, Father. You must have seen that.'

'He's right,' Hughie nodded. 'Roddy was always out on a limb.'

'Well then, that makes two of us.' My father turned away from me as if the conclusion he had just reached had no solace for him. 'What are we to do at all, at all?'

'Will you stop saying that? That's what she'd want to hear you saying. We'll manage; I'll do the farm, you look after the yard, and the cooking.'

'Cooking? I'm no cook.'

'Then you'll have to learn, won't you?'

Hughie left the kitchen and went out into the yard. I watched him move towards the outhouse and heard the back door bang as he headed for the barn. A few minutes later the tractor spluttered and a spume of exhaust rose above the galvanised iron ridge of the outhouse.

'That man's gone funny,' my father said. 'Taking over, ordering me around. Only for the way things are, I'd put him in his place.'

'The note Mother left. What did it say?'

''Twas Hughie got it. Something about having to go, about making something out of the rest of her life. She said that she had fulfilled her commitment to us all and it was time for her to move on. What do you make of that, Roddy?'

'I don't know, Father. I just don't know. 'Twas the last thing in the world I expected.'

My father held his head to one side, almost to his shoulder tip, and then picked up his boots from before the oven door of the range. While his peers on the mountain had long converted to wellington boots, my father still favoured hobnails.

From the windowsill, I saw him bend to the ground to thin out the young turnip plants. I thought again of the attraction that the land held for my father and eldest brother. In a time of great distress, when words and rationalisations were futile in the face of hurt, they went to the land, as if to the core of their beings, for succour.

Then it came to me. That walk we took on the Sunday evening, following the pathways of our youth, was my mother's farewell. She had done it deliberately; planning the route and the things she would say or cause me to say. Fool that I was, I had gone away to the college in Bruree, believing that I had passed across the threshold of my mother's affection. I searched my mind for the things my mother had said; they came to me now like ancient hiero-glyphics presented for interpretation. And I had missed the significance of it all, the journey and the landmarks, the phrases, the meanings between the lines.

When I went to bed, I found the envelope under my pillow. It was addressed to Roderick in my mother's copperplate. Before I opened the letter, I suspected that I was being drawn once again into that secret allegiance that had been set up long before when I had first made contact with Lionel Barton. The letter was for my eyes only and my mother must have known that its contents would remain forever locked in a three-way secret. My fingers trembled as I opened out the fold.

Dear Roderick,

What a lovely name you have. I should never have let them call you anything else. For many years I thought I would be writing this letter to Felim because I believed, when I decided I would leave, that he would be the Dawley spokesman-in-chief. But it hasn't worked out that way. I know now that far from being a Dawley, Felim is a Cartor to the core. And he isn't here anymore.

I wonder if you realised on Sunday that I was saying goodbye. Maybe you didn't but you should think back over what we said and talked about and perhaps you can find some comfort there. I have been thinking about it too and I am sorry for my response when you told me that you loved me. Of course I love you too, Roderick; it's just that old habits die hard. We were never much for showing affection in Glenorga, were we? But the truth is, I was deliberately never sentimental with you. You were always a sensitive soul, all the more so since your accident. I wanted to make you independent and strong, not to rely on anyone for support, especially for affection. Your father taught me that; it would have made my life much easier had I realised it earlier. I could have left sooner.

But could I? No, I am wrong. Especially not with my children to consider. You have to understand what my life was like. I had become a chattel, someone who had no mind of her own. And then compare that to what I had been born to and grew up with. I was a Cartor, accustomed to the good things in life since I was a child: literature, travel, music, what the poet called the nectar of the soul. It all died the day I married into Glenorga. But the memory lived on and with it grew the resolve that one day I would find it again.

So I made up my mind to leave. As soon as I had done my duty by my children, I would leave and seek another life. My father was right; I have only one life and it's happening here and now. I owe it to myself to smell the roses again before it's too late.

Roderick, I am leaving. And the only way I can do it is to cut loose and sever all connections. Otherwise, I will be pulled hither and tither, always feeling guilty, always trying to straddle the bridge between the two places. I have to make a complete break, but I will do it in the company of Mona, because she has been my confidante and my support. I won't be writing and I won't be returning home. But maybe in the years ahead you will come to me, when the pain of this break has dimmed and, I hope, eroded. Stay close to Lionel Barton; he's a good man. In a year's time or thereabouts, ask him to give you something that I have left in his care for you.

I will leave you, Roderick, with the words I should have said to you on Sunday. I love you.

> *Your mother, Elizabeth Cartor*

A few years after my mother left, we built a road to Glenorga. There was a bridge with a single arch over the Morning Star where once the stepping stones were. The road skirted the Barton demesne and the ruin of de Val's Black Castle. It ran by Lough Cutra and Waller's Point and a spur branched off to the graveyard at Manisterluna. We were accessible. People came by on summer Sundays, parked their cars on the verge of our front yard and made picnic trips to the mountain.

Hughie was boss now. It seemed to have happened overnight, as if my mother's departure was the catalyst that precipitated it. As sudden and complete as Hughie's ranking had grown, so had my father's lessened. The extra burden of housekeeper had been added to the role of cook.

Tony Villiers had advised me well. I was now two years into my diploma in horticultural science and deeply immersed in the subjects I was studying. But more than that – and every day I blessed the fortune that had made it happen – I was able to put that knowledge into practice and watch it take shape and grow. There is no road that doesn't have a turning, my father used say, and I was grateful for the way mine had evolved. Life had thrown many obstacles in my way; the most unpleasant had human faces. But it had also engineered some good people to cross my path: Lionel Barton, Justin Stapleton for a little while, and now John Carew for the second time.

John Carew was a typical product of rural Ireland of the 1930s and 1940s. He had gone to the seminary in Maynooth, discovered he didn't have a vocation and left after he took his arts degree. It was usual for ex-seminarians to become teachers in diocesan colleges, and Carew, as he put it, had the misfortune to approach Childe for a job when Danesfort needed a history and geography teacher.

Almost from the beginning he hated teaching. It was compounded by his lack of special training in the subject, but more so by the animosity towards those who were regarded as failed priests – the rejected of God. By the time I reached Danesfort, Carew was on the verge of alcoholism and on his last chance. Then he was involved in a serious car accident, broke both legs and spent one whole term in hospital. Childe came to visit him with a bag of grapes in one hand and an ultimatum, in the form of a dismissal letter, in the other. But Carew had already made up his mind to leave. He enrolled in the Horticultural College that I was now attending and joined the Peat Board when he qualified. He used jokingly tell me he was the only man he knew who had to break his legs to find his feet.

In the laboratory at the rear of the glasshouse we plotted and experimented. We were the first on the market with composts and peat mosses manufactured from turf mould. We raised exotic plants and indigenous trees that would replace the awful Sitka spruce. I was finding through my studies a wealth of knowledge that had its roots in the dawn of creation. I discovered carbon dating, the ages of oak tree stumps, and most wonderful of all, the remains of ancient roadways and habitations revealed beneath the layers of peat.

Carew became a regular visitor to the mountain. He would knock on the door, throw a loaf of bread and a flask on the table and order me to make sandwiches and brew tea. He had been coming there, he told me, since he was a nineteen-year-old seminarian. Walking with Carew was like reading Barton's book again. He took the skeleton of the mountain and built it up, layer upon layer, bone upon bone. He would pick up a fistful of silt from the bed of the Morning Star and analyse it for me: granules of old red sandstone, mica silicates, igneous solidification. Everything that grew and lived. Carew placed them all in the annals of Mount Fierna since time began.

Sometimes my father would come a little of the way with us. I would then appreciate the skill of the former teacher who reversed the roles, making himself deficient in knowledge and my father proficient in his. Carew probed him in a gentle easy way, until he had stripped my father's treasury of folklore. Write it all down, Roddy, he would bid me, for the time will come when people will want to know, and they will never forgive us if we haven't kept the knowledge for them. 'Nice man,' my father would say when Carew had left for home. 'It just shows you that a man doesn't have to be a shite to be smart.'

In the years that followed, I was reminded time and again of Carew's flippant remark about breaking his legs to find his feet. It held an analogy for me; I became the person who had had to lose his mother in order to find his father. Each evening, whenever I came home, my father would be waiting for me in the kitchen. My meal was either on the table or warming in the oven. In the years since my mother's departure, he had become almost obsolete on the farm. I was amazed at the docile way he accepted it. Once he would have taken his astringent anger and his bare fists to quell any slight to his position.

'What class of a day had you?'

I would tell him in detail, filtering in all the things to which I thought he could relate. My father would listen without interrupting until I had stopped. Sometimes I thought he had fallen asleep because his head had dropped on his chest and his breathing was heavy, but the signs were simply the effect of his intense concentration.

Felim, you were wrong about our father. Remember the standing joke that you invented about him: that he had the soul of a Barbary ape and all the finesse of a rutting hippopotamus? I now doubt the parlour wisdom. Once my father sent me up to his room to fetch a jacket that was hanging on the back of the door. We never entered my father's room; it was a kind of forbidden lair, redolent of his presence. I stood on the threshold, coiled my hand around the jamb to locate the jacket and then saw the chess set on its stand behind the door. The board was wonderfully intricate; the dowel joints fitted with precision, the border of the playing surface woven in star-shaped patterns within a track of diamond inlay.

Now, years later, my father was emerging from the darkness and the lair. A new shoot here, a blossom there, tentatively peering out from inside his shell, retreating again when the tractor sounded in the distance or some message of caution stirred in his brain and wafted across his face like a shadow.

'Do you think, Roddy, that the woman will ever come back to us again?'

'I don't think so. I think she wanted to go away forever.'

'Go away forever? What makes you say that?'

'I'm only surmising. Ask Hughie. He would know.'

'Maybe you're right. But there was always something strange about the Cartors. That Philly was as odd as a nine-pound note. And look at the fella that you were called after. I don't think we ever had two words to say to one another. And that mother, Mona, was away with the fairies most of the time. Did you ever hear that?'

'No, I never did.'

'Ah sure, what does it matter? The Cartors are all gone now. Half of us too. Isn't it funny how quickly things change?'

'Yes, it is.'

'Here we were a few years ago, all together. Nothing in the world the bother with us, 'cept an odd oul' tiff here and there. Felim was away in university, on a scholarship. Hughie was doing mighty with the land. You were off in Danesfort on another scholarship. Mona was here at home, herself and her mother like a pair of sisters. And then it all went haywire, up in a puff of smoke in no time at all. Three of 'em – your mother, Felim, Mona – all gone. All gone.'

I bought a car in March 1965 in honour of my twenty-first birthday. It was a second-hand Ford Consu, built like a tank, with tail fins and broad sweeps of chrome that edged its external lines. It was a time of blue suits and brown shoes, nylon shirts, hair oil and Windsor tie knots.

Before he left us to become monsignor and parish priest in Limerick, Father Lynch preached about the creeping decadence lapping the fair shores of Ireland. Men passed him without doffing their hats. Women were flaunting their sexuality and were lusted after by pimply youths and dirty old men.

The 1960s brought further changes. Electric power and its galaxy of technological products made their way to remote glen and backward wildernesses. Father had a deep-seated suspicion of electricity; no man, he said, who hadn't served time at it and been apprenticed to the skill should go next or near it. He still talked about electric power in the language of the paraffin lamp and firelight.

Hughie brought a water pipe from the Morning Star, built concrete housing for the pump and fed running water into the kitchen. A few years later the roadway ran to our front door, we had a car and the latest tractor, the house had running water and we possessed what my father called, in tones of deference and muted pride, a flushing toilet. For almost 200 years the Dawley house had grown and embedded into sameness. But in the space of a couple of years it had all changed.

Then Mount Fierna reneged on its own. At first it was barely noticeable because the pattern had always been present. But now the country moved towards industrialisation, and jobs became available. Old credos and lifestyles were cast out, the clasp of the church loosened, modern Ireland emerged from the dark of two centuries and rushed headlong into the twentieth. People began to leave the mountain, not in a trickle but in a flood. In one fell movement the Histons, the Costellos and the Donnellys, whole families, disappeared.

Five years after he had left us, in the summer of his twenty-fifth year, Felim came home. He was but a pale shadow of the young Adonis who had been my hero. His clothes were threadbare, and there was, in his sunken face and in the lacklustre depths of his eyes, some hint of long-endured suffering. But worse than his physical state was the change that had come over his personality. He used be our court jeste; he had turned our dire and ugly moments into miracles of funny trivialities. He was now no more than a visual replica of the person who once had the world at his feet.

Felim told us nothing, only those sops of information by which he indulged our curiosity and allowed him to retreat into his wasted shell. In between hauling hods and laying gas pipes, he had qualified as a civil engineer, a pass degree for the man who had potential for a doctorate. But he had never practised and never settled long enough in one place to even apply for a job. We treated him with a strange and reverential deference; we took everything he said for gospel, sought no elaboration or query. I would look at the haunted face, the dull eyes and the blotched skin and wonder if the real Felim had returned or an impostor come in his place? But he angered me when I told him about Mona and my mother. He just nodded, looked out the window as if he was searching for some distant reminder in his own horizon and never again asked me about it.

We treated Felim's case with the same retreat into silence that had been a feature of all our relationships. But we speculated about him, framing the questions and anticipating answers as if we were talking about somebody who had died or gone away.

'Something very wrong with that boy. I wouldn't be surprised if he's suffering from some class of a disease.'

'Well, there's one thing sure,' I said. 'Felim won't tell us.'

'Something awful bad happened to him over there.'

'Whatever is wrong with Felim didn't start in England. He inherited it, Father. It's in the genes.'

'Faith 'n' you might be right there. What are we going to do about him?'

'I don't know. I just can't get through to him.'

'The other man can.'

'Hughie?'

'I've seen 'em. Out there in the fields together. They mightn't be talking out loud, but I swear to God that they have some way of reaching each other.'

'I've had that same feeling, Father, for years. I used watch them too and it always made me feel that I shouldn't belong to this family at all, that I was an outsider.'

'That's a terrible thing to say. You never said the likes of that to me before.'

'I can imagine the reception it would have got. You see, there were three pieces to this family. First, there was you, Father, like an independent republic, standing aloof. Then there was Hughie and Felim, soul brothers, who seemed to be able to tune in to each other's minds and communicate that way. And finally there was Mona and my mother. When I was a child, I used think that they were the representation of the same person at different stages of their lives.'

'That was a funny way to think. I never saw it like that.'

'You didn't have to, Father; you were the boss. It doesn't matter. Most of it is in the dim and distant past, so let's forget it.'

Felim found a job on a government building site near Lackaroe. He had won it in the face of severe competition; part of the application required the submission of a design for a scheme of 100 houses. I took him in the Consul to Limerick city and rigged him out: new suit, three shirts, underwear and footwear. Hughie donated more than half the amount and told me that if the money ran short, he would reimburse me. Before I brought him to his lodgings on Sunday evening, he came into the kitchen after changing into his new clothes and I had a vision of the young man who had been my model for greatness. Since he had come home, the sun had taken some of the gauntness from his face and filled out the hollow places in his cheekbones. I thought he looked great and when I told him so he thanked me with a smile that lit his features like a torch.

A few months later Hughie and I journeyed again to bring him home. Felim had lost his job; a man came to tell Hughie that Felim was sleeping rough in Lackaroe and had been thrown in jail a few times for begging and vagrancy. When we found him, unconscious in an alley, he was dressed in rags; one shoe was missing and he had grown an unkempt beard that was caked with dirt and vomit. As we put him in the car, I had this preposterous sense of relief. I knew all along that there was something seriously amiss with Felim and I suspected it had to do with drugs. In my naïvete, I thought that drink addiction was the lesser evil.

The doctor who attended Felim was forthright and cynical. He looked every inch the country squire, wearing a tweed suit, with flaps over all the jacket pockets and a half belt at the rear. He came and sat by the kitchen table after he had given Felim an injection.

'You should take away his clothes,' he said to my father, 'and burn them.'

'Burn them?'

'Yeah. Two reasons. They smell to high heaven. Secondly, in a few days' time, when the effect of the injection wears off, he'll want to hit the road again. If he hasn't any clothes, he might be deferred from travelling, at least for a while.'

'How bad is he?' my father asked.

The doctor bit his lip and pulled at the end of his nose.

'Alcoholism is a disease, Mr Dawley, and your son is in an advanced stage. But your son was also addicted to drugs and that has taken its toll. Do you want the simple unvarnished truth?'

'Tell it as it is, doctor,' Hugh said.

The doctor sighed. It implied that we should have more sense than to pursue the undiluted reality. 'Unless your son makes a radical change to his lifestyle, gets treated, stays off the sauce, full time, he won't make it – what age is he now?'

'Twenty-six,' Hughie said.

'He won't make it beyond another year. I say that without the benefit of proper tests, but I could hear enough on my simple stethoscope to reach that conclusion.'

'Jesus, God in heaven,' my father gasped. 'What can we do? There must some treatment you can give him, doctor?'

The doctor shook his head. 'It's a pity your son ever came home. They are much better equipped to handle this problem in England than we are; they have better clinics, better treatment régimes. And of course there is this stupid acceptance culture in Ireland. Being able to hold your drink is a social distinction. Perhaps, Mr Dawley, you might be doing your son a favour if you sent him away.'

'No, no way,' Hughie glared at the doctor. 'This is his home. We'll look after him.'

'Ah,' the doctor said, as if he had solved a mathematical problem, 'now that's exactly what he had planned.'

'What are you talking about?' Hughie's voice had a rough edge to it.

The doctor's eyes sought my brother's and locked them in a cold stare. 'Let me give you some home truths. Do you know why your brother came home? Really? Do you think he wants to be reunited in the bosom of his family, to see his aged father and his long-lost brothers? Crap. He's here because he has swallowed the last vestige of his pride and is prepared to exploit his family's affection to the hilt. You are his last meal ticket. He'll use you and abuse you and the day you can't or won't deliver, he will turn on you like a cornered rat and disappear into some other hole. So he'll stay here until you drive him out, and if you had any sense you'd do that now. Because then he might do something for himself, take some responsibility for his problem and there might be a small glimmer of hope.'

'I don't have to listen to this,' Hughie said. 'Tell me how much we owe you and you can be on your way.'

'No,' the doctor said, 'you asked me here, and in so doing you committed me to a patient-doctor relationship. So I must give you the best advice I can.' He caught my father's eye. 'Mr Dawley, what you people choose to do with Felim is ultimately your own decision. I'll give you the names of a couple of clinics I know. They are the best we have. Ideally, you should persuade your son to return to England and have himself treated in a remedial institution. He knows where they are; he has been in several already. But please, above all, don't let him seduce you into being his font of mercy and clemency. He'll break your heart.'

'I think you're wrong,' Hughie said. 'Felim was off the drink for months. We can help him to stay off.'

'You can't. The mind of the alcoholic is an amazing source of conniving strategy. It knows when to recuperate and when to indulge. Sure, Felim will stay off the drink, perhaps even for six months at a time, but remember he is still an alcoholic, and in that condition devious and cunning to the nth degree.'

'Doctor,' Hughie said, 'what do we owe you?'

Time and again we set Felim up. We outfitted him, gave him money to pay the advance booking fees for his accommodation, prayed for him and stayed awake at night. And always the doctor was right. Felim drank his first pay cheque, pawned his clothes when the money ran out and lived in squalor until we heard and came to bring him home again. There were times when he never reached his work destination. At 27 he looked like a ravaged old man. The golden hair hung in lanks of streaked disarray. The eyes that had once shone with the light of exuberance and devilment were dull and dormant, as if nothing inventive strove for birth in their recesses. And then, for four months in a row, we thought that the golden god had come amongst us again.

St Luna's had never won the county hurling championship. Many of the team who promised so much at minor stage, including Hughie and Felim, had given up the game. Then one evening, in late May, Luke Heaney came into our kitchen. He had taken over the manager's role and wanted to give the championship one right good crack. He rounded up most of the team and got their commitment. Rory Costello was coming back from England, the McRedmond twins from Dublin. Peter Culhane had given up on the Jesuits and was living in Ardagh running his father's business. And a dinger of a forward called Jimmy Cronin, who had won an All-Ireland colleges' medal with Danesfort, had registered for St Luna's. If there was any chance that the Dawleys might sign up again, we would have a team that would put it up to the best.

The Dawleys signed up, Hughie at full-back, Felim on the opposite wing from Jimmy Cronin and me in goal. I was very reluctant to play again. I wasn't sure if I could lift myself off from the platform of the built-up footwear and throw myself across the goal line. But I was swept along by Hughie's enthusiasm. It was hard to believe that this was the same Hughie who could wait wordlessly in the creamery queue, repel every token of help or conversation with his closed expression. Hughie didn't need to train with the same devotion as the rest of us, since he was already hard and lean from his work on the land, but he was the first into practice and the last out of it.

Perhaps Hughie saw a glimmer of hope. If Felim could be invested with the same ardour, it might sustain him long enough to build a basis for recovery. For months I thought we had succeeded. I watched the change that came over Felim. I saw the face fill out, the handsome sculpture beginning to show again from out of the ruin, the golden hair beginning to burnish and shine. I watched the light play across Felim's face and waited for the emergence of him whom I loved.

My father's voice was heard again. He accompanied us to every game. When the rest of us were silent in the tensions and apprehensions of the approaching test, he sat by me in the passenger seat of the Consul and kept up a running commentary about the fields and the landmarks we passed by. I wondered how he knew so much. And all the time we talked, in our comings or our goings, I waited for the court jester to make an appearance. I waited in vain.

We met Thomond in the final. They were a city team, kingpins of Limerick hurling since the 1920s. In the 1940s they had won six in a row. They had it all – tradition, experience, skill; according to the lore, any other team had to be one and a half times as good to beat them. We must have been seen as a soft touch, the country yokels masquerading in a game for city slickers and hard men.

In the first few minutes of the final, Felim picked up a rebound on the far sideline, cut inwards before sending out a daisy cropper to Cronin on the other side. Felim raced on, right into the path of the return pass, and sent a screamer into the corner of the net. Thomond had hardly time to focus on what had happened before the ball was in the net again, this time from Cronin, the same pattern as before.

I have a vivid recall of that final because I had so little to do between the posts. Felim had always been regarded as the player with all the talents. Standing behind him, watching the style of his play – the way he read movement, the neat dexterity of his wrists – I realised how good Hughie was. Felim had the flash and the flair, but he was no better than his brother was.

All through that campaign I stood behind the greatest full-back I had ever seen; no one ever got a clear shot at me and it was just as well because, unlike my brothers, I had left my skill on the playing fields of Danesfort. My mind could not summon the red mist nor would my body respond to the signal to throw itself across the goal line. 'I'll look after you,' Hughie kept telling me. 'I'll watch the man, you look after the ball.'

By the time we got into Heaney's with the cup, Newtown was swarming with people. I have always hated crowds in enclosed places and would have gone home to Glenorga if my brothers and father hadn't formed a ring about me and hemmed me in. When the final whistle had blown, the players wrestled each other to the ground or kissed the turf in excitement. Even Hughie, dour, morose Hughie, had leaped in the air and wrapped me in a bear hug. We chattered like garrulous starlings as we rode home in the Consul and played the game all over again. But Felim looked silently out the window, aloof and wary.

An hour before midnight, my father suggested we go to Ardagh, as Heaney's had descended into bedlam. We left quietly by the back door in case we offended the man who managed St Luna's to its first championship. We left the Consul in

Glenorga and rode across the mountain track on Hughie's tractor. I had never seen him in such a welter of good humour and couldn't take my eyes off his laughing face.

'Dawleys, Dawleys, Dawleys.'

My father wrapped his arms around the roll bar and swung his long legs over the side of the tractor. We were skirting the base of Knocknastumpa, following a dirt track that generations of cattle and wild beasts had etched from the rocky detritus at the foot of the mountain. Below us the dark ominous lake glinted in the moonlight.

'Dawleys, Dawleys, Dawleys,' father roared into the wind.

Felim laughed. It was like watching something exquisite emerge from the essence of ugliness. The haunted features melted away and out of the fortress that had held them prisoner for so long, the features of his former self came spreading across the landscape of his face. The tractor swayed as we careered over the track. Felim stood wide-legged on the swaying axle behind his brother, and raised his hands in that mock oratorical pose that had once graced our parlour.

'Dawleys, Dawleys, Dawleys,' he roared, into the wind and the noise.

Ardagh was bursting at the seams. Cars were abandoned in the narrow street; trap carts and bicycles obliterated the front wall of Martin Culhane's pub. When we entered, there was first a moment or two of silence and then a sustained raucous whoop. Culhane came out from behind the bar and grasped my father by the shoulders. 'A proud day, Hugh,' he said; 'a proud day for both of us. Like old times.' Martin was followed by every man of his generation who came with homage and deference, as if they were approaching some ancient holy place, a forgotten shrine. They took my father's hand and pumped it, and one old man, with tears in his eyes, threw his arms around my father in an awkward embrace.

Martin clambered onto the table in the centre of the bar. 'Men, men, I want to mark this great day by buying a drink for everyone in the house. But there are four men standing here now, my own son amongst them, who brought honour and glory to this parish today. I'm not just buying the drink in their honour. I'm buying it for the best man I ever saw with a hurley in his hand. He and I played together for Ardagh. We never won nothing, but I want you to know, those of you who came after my generation, the Dawley lads that played for St Luna's didn't pick up their talent on the roadway. They got it from the king of them all – a great hurler, a great runner, an all-round athlete. Let's drink to them so: my son Peter, Hughie, Felim and Roddy Dawley and the greatest of them all—'

'Oh, that's right, boy,' a voice cut in, 'the greatest of 'em all. Well, fuck him.'

I instantly recognised that voice, though it came thick and slurred. Black Pat Kilraish pushed himself forward with a pint in his hand, a week's stubble on his cheekbones, a fiery rim to his deep-set eyes. 'An all-round athlete, you said, didn't you, Mr Culhane, sir? 'Tis true for you. Hugh Dawley was all thim things you said, the best hurler, a great runner an' a man that would ride anything with hair on it, especially another man's wife.' Long Pat came forward to where Martin Culhane stood. 'An' the sons, you know, the sons are—'

'Shut up, Kilraish,' Culhane said. 'Finish your drink and go. I want no trouble in this house, not any day and not today especially.'

I saw Hughie press forward, Felim at his shoulder and my father in front of them both. He stretched out a hand to keep them in check. Long Pat smashed his glass against the table that Culhane was on, and came for my father with the jagged end, held like a dagger. But he got no farther than a couple of steps before my father's fingers closed on the wrist holding the broken glass and squeezed until Long Pat screamed. When the glass fell to the floor, my father spun Kilraish with his free hand so that he was facing the doorway. 'Make way,' he shouted. The press of men opened like a corridor and, to whoops of encouragement, my father ran Long Pat through and fired him out the door. He returned, rubbing his hands and trying to appear nonchalant.

I could sense the puzzlement that went on in Hughie's head. If his father had been a hurler and a runner of renown, how come it had never been part of our folklore? I had asked those questions of Lionel Barton when I first found my father had won the senior cup for the mile event in Limerick. 'That's your father for you,' Barton had told me; 'a secretive man, hard to fathom.' Perhaps my father regarded his athletic youth as a frivolous phase of his life which had no consequence in the world of his maturity and he did not want his children to be influenced and driven to emulate it.

The night grew on, as did our wonder. I had no major influence in the outcome of the game, but had I been Hughie or Felim I might have been peeved at the way our father had been placed in the limelight. It was his night. Some time later, I heard a car pull onto the gravel yard that ran beside the gable of the dwelling house and saw its lights go out. Martin left and returned five minutes later, ushering

Muirne in front of him.

She looked bored and disinterested as she made her way to the battered old piano in the alcoved window. But as she passed, the silence that settled over the room, for the second time that night, was like the stifled intake of breath, a frozen gasp of wonder. When she went past me she trailed her finger under my chin and stopped to smile at me. When she was seventeen and I was twelve, she was the most wonderful creature I had ever seen and I was madly in love with her. But she was more beautiful now. I stared aghast as she passed and remembered that, once upon a time, we had swum naked in the Blue Pool and I knew every fall, line and curve of that marvellous body.

She sang her repertoire and fixed her face in a glorious smile. Felim and Hughie were standing together at the bar, but the smile was patently for Hughie. I knew then that long ago, when I was her conduit to Felim, we were both pawns in her gambit. Felim knew too for he turned away and went to order another drink. Hughie stood there locked in hypnotic trance. His eyes never left her.

When Muirne finished, the crowd bayed for my father to sing 'The Boys of Barr Na Sraidhe'. I caught Felim's glance and he was shaking his head in bemused disbelief. I had never heard my father singing but he climbed on the table that Martin Culhane had earlier stood upon, and delivered the song, in grace and harmony of note. They refused to let him down until he had encored with 'The Old Bog Road' and had recited every verse of 'The Cremation of Sam McGee'.

On the way home, in the soft balmy moonlight of a September night, we stopped beside the Blue Pool. Wordlessly, as if we had planned and organised this moment, we alighted from the tractor and threw our clothes on grass that was cushioned by moss and lichen. Felim led the way. He streaked under the water in the soft moonlight and headed for the far bank. I was last in because I stayed behind to watch my father stand on the outcrop, poised for a moment, arch his body and hit the water in a graceful dive.

'Wow,' Felim exclaimed. 'Come on then, Roddy. I have your raft of reeds ready.'

'Shag off, Felim. I can swim as well as you.'

'Nonsense, little brother. No one swims as well as me. This is my ether, or have you forgotten?'

My dive was smooth. I stroked out for the far bank and emerged to find them looking at one another in silent acknowledgement.

'Mikey Kilraish taught me.'

'He taught you well,' Felim said. Then he raised his arm and shook it at the night sky and the waning moon.

'Dawleys, Dawleys, Dawleys.'

Chapter 12

Some time in the night Felim left. He stole into my room, took the loose change that was lying on the bedside table and in my suit pockets. He rifled Hughie's jacket and lifted all the folding money he could find. He broke into the secret drawer in my mother's parlour table but found nothing. My father, alerted by the tweed-suited doctor, had moved his money to another hiding place.

Felim dropped out of sight: no cards, no letters, only the odd uncertain story filtered through. One of the Donovan brothers, coming home for an autumn break, thought he had seen him getting off the ferry at Holyhead. We had broken and sundered again. Hughie reverted to his walled up state; my father and I voyaged round each other and now and then made tentative landfalls. We seldom talked about my mother now; we never spoke about Mona.

I had lost my mother's letter; a pickpocket had stolen my wallet at a point to point meeting in Kilcolman. I constantly remembered the reference to Barton in my mother's letter. 'In a year's time, or thereabouts, ask him to give you something that I have left in his care for you.' I had a premonition that whatever had been left in Barton's care boded no good for me and, even if it were innocuous, it would open up the old sores again. So I avoided Barton Hall until I received a phone call at work from Rose Trenchard telling me that Barton was ill and wanted to speak with me.

I went in the front entrance and down the Long Gallery, those ancestral eyes following me all the way. Barton wasn't ill. He sat in his usual seat in the library, the sun warming his shoulder blades, a tartan rug over his knees.

'Roderick, my boy, how good of you to come.'

'I thought you were sick. I had the impression that it was serious.'

'I had a touch of the flu but not that bad. It seemed as good a ruse as any to get you here. It's been ages.'

'I have been very busy, Lionel, a lot of things have been happening. I meant to come but I never got round to it.'

Barton threw off the rug, put the book face down on the low table and went to a press beneath the bookshelves.

'Hardly the motivation of a friend. *I* would have gone to you.'

'I'm sorry.'

He looked round severely as he crouched before the press. 'You're a big boy now; perhaps I could interest you in a whiskey and soda.'

'Thank you, that would be fine.'

He pushed the library steps in my direction. 'Sit. Don't stand there like a stranger. Are we still friends?'

'Of course.'

'Good. Cheers! By the way, did you come in through the front entrance?

'I'm not a kid anymore, Lionel. I shouldn't be sneaking in and climbing through windows.'

'I'm not sure if it is wise to be so bold.' He sipped at his drink, and then drank a mouthful as if the sip was a primer. 'How is your father, Roderick? I don't see him around the land much.'

'He's okay. Hughie runs the farm now.'

'I can't imagine your father is too comfortable with that. And Felim?'

'Gone again. Somewhere in England.'

'Is he getting treatment?'

'For all I know, he could be lying in a dosshouse or in the doorway of a derelict squat.'

'Perhaps you should try and find him?'

'I should like hell! The doctor was right. Felim will be home again. We are the only meal ticket he's got left. I want to ask you something about my mother.'

'Oh.' Barton took another sip at his drink and studied me over the rim of the glass. I thought there was a nervous expression in his searching eyes. 'Have you heard anything from her?'

'No, but I didn't expect to. She made that quite clear when she left. I have a feeling, though, that you know something. Is she in contact with you?'

'Roderick, I gave her an undertaking. I promised.'

'So? You're supposed to be my friend too.'

'Okay. But I'd prefer if you didn't try to trade on the affections involved here. My contact is scant and scarce. That, I think, is very deliberate on your mother's part. The more I know, the more I'll be tempted to tell.'

'What do you know?'

'I have no address. Merely that your mother is now living in California with Mona. Apparently Mona's marriage with Trenchard did not work out.'

'Jesus, poor Mona. I bet he's the one that screwed it up. I never liked him.'

'Well *I* did. But I don't know the facts, so I can't make judgements.'

'It's easy. He was a shithead.'

'I don't agree. Here, give me your glass. I think we're entitled to another one, seeing as there is no lemonade.'

'Thank you.'

'When my mother contacts you – those scant sparce letters of hers – does she ever ask for us?'

'No. She made that clear to me ever before she left. She wanted a complete—'

'I know, I know. I hear it in my head all the time! She had to make a clean break; otherwise, she would be pulled tither and yon. I find that absolutely ridiculous.'

'You do?'

'How could she just extirpate all of us from her life? She was a mother; mothers are supposed to love their children. You know what I think, Lionel? She just copped out, left us all without a glimmer of remorse.'

'Stop it. You do her a vast injustice. I understand the stance she took; I believe she's doing the right thing, though I know it sounds cruel and heartless. There is no other way if she wants to stay faithful to her own aspirations. And she's a very strong woman, Roderick.'

'And you are a dyed-in-the-wool disciple. You sure that there isn't more to all this than mere friendship?'

Barton's glass stopped in mid-air. I saw the tension flit beneath the muscles of his cheekbones. He glared at me. 'I answered that question before and I'm surprised it's being put to me again. So I'm not going to respond and you can take that as you bloody will.'

'I'm sorry. I shouldn't have said that. But you can see—'

'I know, I know, of course I can see. Both sides, that's the problem.'

'All right, so what does she tell you?'

'That she is doing very well. She got a job as a

receptionist in a museum of modern art and, listen to this, she went to night classes and studied, took examinations. Your mother is now assistant curator. And ... well ... maybe I shouldn't tell you this.'

'Tell me. I can take it. I'm well practised.'

'She has a friend. Ah, a gentleman friend.'

'Do you mean a lover, Lionel? Don't use your eunuch words with me. It's 1967, people screw around, they make love, have sex. Gentlemen do it, Lionel, and apparently some mothers.'

'Fuck you, Roderick,' Barton spat at me. 'I never thought you could be such a bloody arsehole. You asked to be told.'

Into my mind came a vision of unsullied clarity. There was a great four-poster bed; the posts were shaped like the prow of a gondola. My mother and a man, whose face was blank, were writhing on the bed. My mother's face was ecstatic; there were drops of perspiration on her brow. She called out a name I couldn't fathom.

'Who is this man, Lionel?'

'OK. His name is Katchadoor Kazian. He's some kind of expert on modern art and apparently quite wealthy. That's all I know, except that she calls him Katch. Understandable – a name like that needs some kind of abbreviation.'

'Sure. Katchadoor Kazian. Not exactly Paddy Murphy. Lionel, I'm sorry. I apologise for being rude just now. You're the last person I should vent my feelings on.'

Barton made a wide sweep of his hands, beamed an expansive smile. 'Don't worry. What are friends for? Tell you what. Stay for a bit of lunch. There are a lot of things I want to talk to you about.'

'I have a better idea. Let's run into Adamston and eat

there. I'm meeting John Carew, my boss. He had an idea he wants to put to you.'

'Great, great, but aren't you being foolhardy? Adamston is a very public place. People will see us.'

'So what? Isn't it time?'

'Mmm, let's think about Adamston. I don't want a falling out between you and your father because of our friendship.'

'He has become the only one of my family that I have any recourse to. Mother and Mona are gone – forever, I think. Felim will keep on coming and going, touching my life every now and then but never as it once was. And one day he will either die or disappear permanently. As for Hughie, I will never get over the wall that Hughie has built around himself. I can't afford to lose my father, but I can try and influence him if the opportunity ever presents itself.'

'I'm glad to hear you say that. I still harbour that dream. I don't want to leave this world with that terrible enmity between us.' Barton walked towards the window and beckoned me to his side. 'Look out there; it's all crumbling like a house of cards. There's 500 years of Barton dynasty in this house and estate. And it's gone, my friend, I'm downtrodden on all sides. Twenty years from now this wonderful house will just be another shell, like the ruins of its contemporaries decaying around the countryside. Roderick. Do try and influence your father. It's so important to me.'

'I'll do what I can. Now, you have a message for me from my mother? Something she gave you before she left. I should have come for it a long time ago.'

'I have it. I had express instructions not to give it to you until you asked.'

THE BLUE POOL

I walked home by Lough Cutra and sat on a rock by the shingle shore. I took out the letter that Barton had given me, turned my back to the breeze and read.

'Roderick,
I wonder how much time will have passed before you read this. I wonder indeed if you will ever read it, if you haven't hardened your heart against me, if you have stopped loving me, for I know you did once. If things are well between us, Roderick (I love that name), this note will embrace the two of us and keep us close. I want to quote you a little poem that used to hang, framed, in the hall of our house in Adamston. I think it will make sense to you. It always did to me.

*The clock of life is wound but once, and no one has the power
To tell you where the hand will stop, at late or early hour.
Now is the only time; live, love and toil with a will.
Place no trust in tomorrow. For the hand may then be still.*

There you have it, Roderick. I will always love you.
Elizabeth Cartor

I walked back to the shingle shore and waited until the wind picked up again. Years before I had stood in this same place and cast my gold medal into the water. Out there it lay, fathoms deep, in the soft silt. I took my mother's note and tore it into tiny pieces. Then I waded into the lake and cast the shards upon the water. I had visualised the message of comfort that I thought my mother would offer me in her letter, but all it seemed now was just innocuous inconsequence.

I retraced my steps and sat on the rock for a long time, watching the pieces bob and dive in the foam-flecked swell. A lone swan drifted gracefully from under the shelter of the shallows and tested a scrap of paper in its beak. Then it spewed it out again and swam away.

Hughie was in love. I heard him whistling when he went about his chores in the yard and saw him zig-zagging the tractor through the fields as if keeping time to some tune in his head. But mostly he gazed off into space with an aspect of studied contentment. He went out two or three nights a week now, shaved every day, put on good clothes and slicked his hair with Brylcreem.

Then one evening in early summer, Hughie brought Muirne home. She came bouncing into our kitchen, her burnished hair aflame in the light, the apple cheeks rouged and toned down. She placed her index finger under my chin, lifted my mouth to hers and kissed me.

'Hey, hey,' Hughie said, 'enough of that.'

Muirne laughed. She filled the place with radiance; her presence seeped into every spot that gloom and shadow inhabited.

'You're welcome,' my father said. 'I'm an honoured man to have a daughter of Martin Culhane in my house. An' she as beautiful as the May morn.'

'Wow, wow,' Muirne gasped in mock wonder, 'there's charm and compliment for you. You should take a leaf out of your father's book, Hughie.'

Hughie scowled. Muirne beamed at my father and made a conspirator out of him with a prolonged wink. 'I'll make you a cup of tea,' Father said.

'No, let me,' Muirne said. 'It might be useful for me to

find out the run of this house.' The prospect of her words hung in the air, laden with intent. Hughie nodded and smiled at her and there was no derision in his voice, only merriment, when he said, 'Anything you want to know, ask my father; he's the head bottle-washer in the kitchen.'

She was home from France, Muirne told us. She had taken an arts degree in Dublin and had then gone on to the university in Rennes to do a postgraduate course in modern painting. She had knocked around North Africa for a couple of summers and then had taught English in a convent school in Angers. She was home for good; there was no place like Ireland, no place like the mountain. Muirne was now teaching French in a secondary school in Sluggaragh, a small town about ten miles from Mount Fierna.

'Now, girleen,' my father said, 'in the bottom press under the dresser, the one on the right, that's where we keep the tay caddy and the sugar bowl.'

Almost imperceptibly, as if each fragment of change was but a tiny piece of the ultimate mosaic, Muirne's presence began to dominate Glenorga. She came and went without leave or bidding and her movements were as natural about the place as they were to the women who had preceded her. When she stayed overnight, she slept in my mother's room. I went in there to look again at the collage of magazine pictures which my mother and Mona had fixed to the rear of the door. I found a poster of Salvador Dali in their place. But that wasn't the only change. On the windowsill there were several photos of Muirne and of places she had visited. The items of clothing that my mother and sister had left behind had been removed. Muirne was expressing her presence and her intent; she was there to stay.

I was once the twelve-year-old kid who had listened

spellbound to Chopin and Bach and gazed in silent amazement at the beauty of her naked form. But she never made a single reference to that time lest its sentiment might intrude on her design. Because now I was surplus to her requirements, a presence that might occupy her space and entangle her purpose.

'Roddy, does Hughie talk to you about me?'

'No, Muirne. Hughie doesn't talk to me about anything. But that's the way he is.'

'I know; he's a deep one. But what do you think? Does he love me?'

'Hughie is like his father, Muirne – wild, passionate, shouts his feelings from the rooftops.'

'You're being smart, aren't you? Well, I know he loves me. And one day soon he'll ask me to marry him. And then, Roddy, if you were me, what would you do?'

'Can't answer that. All I can tell you is that Hughie is a good person.'

'God, what a recommendation! Do you think you could be a little bit more enthusiastic, a little less dispassionate? And what about me, don't you think I'm a good person too?'

'Of course. But seriously, Muirne, it has nothing to do with me. If you and Hughie are happy and in love, what else matters?'

'That's rather a backhanded endorsement? But never mind. Tell me, will Hughie leave the mountain?'

'You might as well ask him to give up the land. No hope. But why should he leave anyway?'

'Because I might not like it up here. Don't know if I can take the isolation and remoteness. I need people around me, the trappings of urban life. I've grown used to them.'

'But didn't you tell my father that there was no place

like the mountain?'

'I did, but that was only in the beginning, when I wanted to create the right impression. Anyway, that's only one problem. Suppose Hughie and I continue to live in Glenorga, what will you do?'

'Do? What do you mean; this is my home. I'm not going anywhere.'

'Think again, sweetie. Hughie and I will want a place of our own. If he won't leave the mountain, then this house will have to be the place. There will be no room for you here, Roddy; we'll need space, privacy, a chance to spread our wings. In a way I envy you; you have options. You can settle wherever you want. I wish I could do that. Bet your father would prefer that too. No man in his right mind, except Hughie, would voluntarily opt to live in a desolate place like this. So, Roddy, see what I'm offering you: choice, freedom, civilisation. You'll come to thank me.'

'I will like hell. You won't fob me off that easy, Muirne. Nor my father either. If Hughie knew what your game was, he'd sort you out very fast. This is my home. I love it here and I'll stay here till the day I die.'

'Brave words, little Roddy. Don't let it come to a showdown, because I've no doubt whose side Hughie would support. Think about it.'

'This is my home. No one will drive me out, least of all my own brother. I know that for certain.'

The radiant face lost its colour; pallid specks of anger appeared amid the rouged cheekbones. Eyes blinked and glinted. 'You could be in for some surprise, sweetie.'

In the spring of 1968, Long Pat Kilraish died. Carew and I were mapping out an ancient pattern of raised earthworks when we came by his house. I hadn't come that way for years. The back door was on the latch and the moment we pushed it inward a swarm of bluebottle flies rose from a figure seated by the fire. The nauseating smell of decomposing flesh took our breath away.

Long Pat had been dead for weeks. The pathologist's report said that he had died from blood poisoning, aggravated by neglect and malnutrition. One son, Jamesy, arrived for his father's funeral; he was the only one the undertaker could trace. I talked to Jamesy. Yes, he told me, he knew about Mikey's whereabouts; he had contacted him about their father's death but Mikey was involved in something big and couldn't get away. Mikey was very big in the building game. He owned a hotel in Clacton and a pub near Wembley called The Rose and Crown. No, he had no idea what had become of Rosie. She had been supposed to meet Mikey once, years ago, but had never turned up. At that time she was living somewhere near High Wycombe, but she could be anywhere now.

Lionel Barton and I went to England that summer. We took the ferry and headed south in the car. We went west to visit Lionel's old school, Amersham Hall, that was about to be demolished; the excavators were parked in the front quadrangle and a fleet of lorries was arrayed on the front lawn.

We found a photograph of Lionel's class in the Aula Maxima, and another of the school's senior rugby team of his final year. He was taller and broader than any of his classmates with cascading hair that fell in waves towards his forehead. He was full-shouldered, upright and had a handsome, smiling face.

In a pub on the outskirts of the town Lionel named out

the students of his final year. Suddenly he threw the picture at me.

'Here, take it. I don't want to do this anymore. It was a bad decision.'

'What was?'

'Doesn't it strike you how ironic it is that the place is being torn down?' Lionel asked.

'Sorry. I'm not with you.'

'It's all being demolished, Roderick, everything that relates to my ilk and me: Amersham Hall, Barton Hall, the last bastions of our time and place.'

I took the picture, studied it for a moment and then laid it on the tablecloth upside down. I had suddenly become aware of what I had failed to recognise before and it froze the breath in my throat. The young Lionel Barton bore a striking resemblance to Felim!

We drove due east to Waltham in Essex. The founding father of the Barton dynasty had first settled near there at the time of William the Conqueror. The village that had sprung up as the estate grew was called Grantham, the family name of a Barton wife. Grantham Court had been converted to a development laboratory, servicing an industrial estate. But we did meet one Barton descendant, another Richard, host at The Dog and Badger. Lionel stayed overnight at the pub and I went down to London to meet Mikey.

As I sat waiting in the hotel lounge, I tried to put together a mental picture of Mikey as an adult. He was about a year older than me, so he would be going on for 26. Folk around Mount Fierna, who saw him serving mass on Sunday, used say that he would have been the perfect model for the Christ child. But Mikey was the antithesis of that notion: a hard-bitten combination of devilment and graft. Would he be similar, I wondered.

He had changed utterly. I would have passed him on the street a thousand times and never recognised my boyhood friend. Mikey looked in his prime. He was lean and hard and tanned to perfection. His teeth sparkled beneath the tan, the hair was as dark as a raven's wing and there was plenty of it. He wore a pinstripe suit; a dazzling white shirt with ruffed cuffs and kid leather shoes. Mikey was the only one in the hotel lounge when I arrived but I walked past him several times; he was hidden behind the pink pages of *The Financial Times*.

'Jesus, Mikey, I would never have recognised you.'

'You should have known, Roddy. I always told you that I would make out. I enjoyed watching you pass me by, and dismissing the idea that this well-heeled looking guy with *The Financial Times* could be me. Actually the paper was just a bit of camouflage; I was spying on you.'

Mikey spoke as if he had pebbles in his mouth. He had lost every semblance of a mountain accent; he could have been from anywhere in London or south of it.

'It's great to see you again, Mikey. I've looked forward to this moment for a long time. I'm so glad I've found you.'

'Was there something particular you had in mind?'

'Something in particular? What are you saying, Mikey? You were the best friend I ever had. Have you any idea how much I missed you from the mountain? I came home for holidays one Christmas and you were gone. And then I made this dream that I'd come and find you. However long it took, it didn't matter. Some day I would find you and we'd meet again.'

'Good heavens, Roddy. You've made quite a deal of it. I never thought of it like that. How did you find me?'

'James. He came home for your father's funeral.'

'He did, eh? Didn't know the old man died.' Mikey shrugged. 'Not that it would make any difference anyway.'

'James said he told you. You were too busy to come.'

'He did, eh? Conniving git. Probably thought he'd pull one over me, go over and pick up anything that was going. Well, he's welcome to what he could find. I never want to set eyes on that damn place again.'

'Did you know your mother passed on? About three years ago.'

'Yeah, I knew.'

'You couldn't make it then either?'

Mikey lowered his head and squinted. It was a habit from long ago when he was trying to extract the real meaning of what was being said.

'Roddy, what 'n hell are you getting at? Did you come here to tick me off for not attending the old ones' funerals? You knew the score. I told you often enough when we were kids. My father was a shite. Mount Fierna was like a prison, I couldn't wait to get out of the place. As far as the mountain is concerned or anyone in it, I don't want to know. I don't give a goddamn.'

'Does that include me?'

Mikey peered at me from under half-closed eyelids. I returned his gaze and saw the faint discoloration at the roots of his hairline. He was wearing a wig; obviously the cascading blond hair had begun to thin. I got the faint odour of pomade and I was sure he noticed because he leaned back fully in his chair and threw back his head.

'Roddy, it was a long time ago.'

'What was?'

'You know very well. Since we were half-arsed kids in

Mount Fierna. That's history, Roddy, it's all over. Tell you what; we'll get ourselves some drinks, for old time's sake. Then we'll have a meal, I'll show you around this town and give you a good time; you can indulge yourself in whatever takes your fancy. You just name it; I know where to get it. Let's forget about the mountain, Roddy; forget about that kid stuff. We're adults now, grown men. Say, maybe you'd like something special? You just tell Mikey.'

'I thought you'd be home for your mother's funeral.'

'Well, I wasn't, was I? Trust our holy mother church to do the right thing, even for the town bicycle! Did she qualify for sacred ground? You fellows didn't put her down on the windward side, outside the graveyard walls? Or was that just a rumour I heard?'

'You shouldn't talk like that about your mother.'

'Oh, oh, do I hear words of sanction? And from little Roddy Dawley, who was scared of his own shadow and every jacked-up shithead of authority that flourished around Mount Fierna. Draw in your horns, little boy blue, you were never any good at standing up for yourself.'

I struggled to keep the red mist in check, slivers of anger seared round the perimeter of my brain. 'You know, Mikey, for twenty years I had this notion. It was like a crusade. We were parted without ever saying goodbye and I harboured the idea that I would find you some day and renew that friendship. Well, wasn't I the prime idiot?'

'My words exactly.' Mikey snapped his fingers at a passing waiter. 'Have a drink, Roddy?'

'No thanks.'

'Don't be stupid. Course you will. Never let any class of enmity stand between you and opportunity. That's an adage of my business. Two large G and Ts – Beefeaters,' he said to the waiter. 'Carry on then, Roddy.'

'It means nothing to you, does it, that friendship? That we played, romped, created devilment, cheated and stole?'

The waiter laid the drinks on the table and pushed a chit on a silver tray towards Mikey. He signed it with a flourish and looked at me as if testing my appreciation of its significance.

'Of course, it happened. I know that, don't I? But what do you want me to do, be eternally grateful that you happened to be born in the same neck of the woods as I was? Fact is, mate, I never think about it; simple as that. It means nothing.' He leaned towards me as if imparting words of profound wisdom. 'The past is a fucking cul-de-sac. So come on, tell me what the hell it is you want and have done with it.'

'Want? What the hell are you on about?'

'You know exactly, mate. I can tell. When I was a penniless brickie, no one wanted me; now when I've made it big, I'm just so popular. So what is it, Roddy? What great and grand design of a scheme have you got?'

I stood up. The waiter took it as a sign and began to wander in our direction. Mikey sent him scuttling behind the bar with a click of his fingers. 'This is the best part of my visit,' I told him, 'knowing that there is nothing I want from you, nothing to gratify that snivelling expression on your face. So tell you what, Mikey, you fuck off and go back to your millions and into that slime pit of a personality you've become.'

Mikey nodded several times and drew his teeth over his lower lip. He beckoned the waiter. 'Sit down, Roddy; I'm beginning to like you. You might grow on me. Perhaps we might even find each other again.'

I shook my head and picked up the hotel literature I had removed from the rack beside the reception desk. 'Forget it.

The Mikey I knew is back there somewhere on the mountain. I don't think either of us will ever find him again. I'm not even sure if that person ever existed in the first place. So long, Mikey.'

He started to speak again as I approached the double door to the outer lobby.

'You did want something?'

'No,' I shouted back.

'Rosie lives in High Wycombe. Up in Buckinghamshire. Herself and the kids. That cattle jobber's long gone. Her address is thirteen Queen's Road. You'll find her there unless she's moved on again. But she won't have because I didn't send her any money, did I?'

High Wycombe was a booming furniture town. The advertising hoardings dominated the roadway as we came through in the Consul. It was Saturday but the industrial estates were working flat out and the delivery trucks were snarling the traffic around the network of roads. Queen's Road was a row of red-bricked terraced houses that fronted the park. The area looked seedy and run down. Next door to number 13 was a public house called The Flint. We bought beer and meat pies and sat on the wooden bench beneath the canopy.

'I think we're going for three losses in a row,' Lionel said, between mouthfuls.

I heard him as if from a great distance, a voice floating in the periphery of deep space.

'Don't you think that looks like a Constable sky?'

'Three in a row, Roderick. I feel it in my old bones.'

'Feel what? What are you talking about?'

'It was a mistake going to Amersham Hall. I haven't

slept since I saw that photo of my class. All that shining, glowing youth. And then, Roderick, those of us who haven't died have became the dinosaurs, out of our ambit and our time – useless, obsolete, a case study in history. See what I mean? One down.'

'It will pass. Brighter days ahead.'

'You're getting too damn glib, young man. I don't like to hear my own phrases thrown back at me.'

'Okay, maestro. From now on only original expressions. So what was the second mistake?'

'Wasting your time on that scamp Kilraish. I had always a bad feeling about that fellow. Selfish little scoundrel he was, trading affection for opportunity. You should have listened to me. I kept on telling you it was a mistake to go?'

'Wrong, Lionel.' I scraped away the last of the encrusted mashed potato from the bowl and saw that Barton had only half-finished his pie. 'I wouldn't call it a mistake; it was well worth the visit. Now I know. I can forget the legend. I can see the bare truth of it now and isn't that better than living a fabrication?'

Barton took a deep swallow. 'Don't know which is worse, my old friend. Sometimes I think it's better to cling to the myth than to discover the truth. Reality is no substitute for shattered dreams. And I, in the winter of my days, am a past master of that experience.' He paused, threw back his head and followed the drift of a swirl of cloud. 'So despite what you say, I take it we're going for the hat trick?'

'Rosie?'

'Yep. We could leave now. I've always wanted to visit the Lake District and the Yorkshire Dales. We could be in either place by the morning.'

'We could. But as soon as we finish the beer, I'm going

down to Queen's Road to find Rosie. Will you come?'

'What the hell would I be doing at a lovers' meeting? No, no. I'll amble along in the park. But first, Roderick—'

'Please. Don't say it. Que serra, Lionel. I must see it out to the end.'

'What age were you when Rosie left?'

'Okay, okay. We were kids, we didn't know our own minds. It was childish puppy love. And all the other things you say are probably true. If it were to be, if we really loved each other, we would have found a way. But let me tell you this: I must find Rosie again. Even if all I can do is tell her I'm sorry, that I let her down, that never a day passed that I haven't thought about her and regretted my failure. Perhaps she hates me; perhaps she had no feelings for me whatever. But I know mine. I must put them to the test, vindicate or exorcise them.'

The woman who answered the doorbell had a smudge of flour on her forehead. She was middle-aged, with lank hair that had a damp hue and continually fell into her eyes.

'If you're sellin', don't want nothin'.'

'I'm not selling anything. I am looking for Rosie Kilraish.'

'Don't know nobody by that name. What you want her for anyway?'

'I used know her, a long time ago, back in Ireland. She was Rosie Kilraish then.'

'Well she ain't that now and she ain't here. Say, how do I know you're not some weirdo, out to do her some harm. All sort of strange things happening these days. A body can't take nothing for granted.'

I took a five-pound note from my wallet and handed it to her. 'Just to show you I'm on the level. You are quite right to be cautious.'

The woman looked at the money and several times unclasped her fingers as if the temptation to accept was getting the better of her suspicion.

'She owes me rent,' she said: 'two full weeks, ten quid.'

I handed her three fivers, which she stuffed down the front of her blouse. She smiled at me, but it only exaggerated the hardness of her features. 'Nice girl, Rosie. Rosie Gubbins, that's her name. Hard done by and all, bastard of a husband upped and left her with three kids and not a penny to support them. Good girl; works night shift in Gommes, the furniture place. But she ain't in.'

'Where can I find her?'

'Took the kids to the park, she did. Always does when she's free on a Saturday. 'Ere, I'll show you. Go along by the canal; see them blokes playing cricket. Park swings around there; you can't see it from here. There's a small lake beyond and a children's playground. And a small pavilion with a band. That's where Rosie'll be.'

I skirted the rear of the cricket ground. The band had stopped playing. An ice cream van had entered the park and was edging its way towards the pavilion, its jingle plying for trade. Then I saw Rosie. She was sitting by the lake dangling her feet in the water, watching three children sail a makeshift paper boat. I could hear the squeals of argument and the tinkle of small laughter. As the van approached, I saw the eldest boy grab her handbag and take out some change. He went to the van and returned with three cones. He gave one each to the other children. It seemed as if he knew I was watching him for he began to walk in my direction, scrutinised me intently over the rim of the ice cream cone. I beckoned and without a moment's hesitation he came closer.

'Like to do me a favour, son?'

'Depends. My mum says I gotta be careful.'

'Your mum's right. What's your name?'

'Jack.'

He was about twelve years old. He held his head to one side as if he was constantly on the alert for some opportunity.

'Would you go down there and tell your mother something?'

'Tell her wha' then?'

'Tell her that Roddy Dawley is standing 50 yards behind her. He used knew her a long time ago and would love to meet her again. Will you do that?'

Jack inclined his head even further so that his head seemed to be listing at right angles to his neck.

'What's in it for me?'

'A pound.'

'Could you make it thirty bob?'

'Okay.'

I gave him the money and he ran to the group at the water's edge. I saw him grasp his mother by her arms and speak animatedly with her for several moments. Then he took her by the shoulders and turned her about so that she was looking in my direction. I saw her shake her head, wave her hands and push him away. The boy loped towards me.

'Well, what did the lady say?'

'Never heard of you. Don't know nobody with that name.'

'You sure you gave her the right name?'

'Sure. Roddy Dawley. Know something, mister?'

'What?'

'I think she knows you. She was all upset when I mentioned your name. Say, why don't you try again?'

'No, forget it.'

'No problem, I'll set it up for you. Call round tonight when the youn' uns are gone to bed. Couple a' quid is all it will cost you. Mum gets callers like that every once in a while. Two quid, mister. I'll see you right.'

Involuntarily my hand pulled back. I wasn't aware of it until I saw its shadow out of my peripheral vision. Jack stepped away a pace or two and I could see his muscles tense as if he were priming himself for a quick take-off.

'You're a nasty little piece of work, aren't you? Get the hell out of here before I drive my shoe up your arse.'

He backed away a couple more paces and began to leer at me. In a swirl of movement he had turned and was galloping away, but before he was out of earshot I heard his parting shot.

'And fuck you too, mister.'

I picked up Barton, pointed the Consul west and drove out of High Wycombe. He talked for a while about the places we might divert to as we headed west, and then settled into a grim silence as he studied the road map. I knew I should tell him what had happened but I found myself once again wallowing in that waterhole of misery and self-pity, which, long ago, Miss Horgan had counselled me to avoid. I grew more morose with the passing miles. Now and then I heard the sounds of annoyance that bespoke Lionel's impatience and tried to ignore them as they grew in volume and frequency. Suddenly he threw the road map he was studying onto the back seat with a hiss of anger.

'Christ's sake, Roderick. What the hell happened?'

We stopped at a pub and I told him about Rosie. When I had finished, he kept shaking his head as if it were all as patent as daylight and needed no question or query.

'You were right, Lionel.'

'About the three in a row. Oh sure. But hardly acute judgement, was it? The cards were stacked against us. I take it that we are now going home.'

'We could stay here. Head up for Cumberland in the morning.'

'We could, but we won't. I doubt if either of us would want to stay here any longer. If we get cracking, we could be in Fishguard in a couple of hours. We take the night mail from there. What do you say?'

'Sounds good. Home by midday tomorrow.'

'For you, yes. But it would be a dead giveaway if we arrived in Mount Fierna together. Ever hear me talk of Riddlestown Park?'

'I would have remembered a name like that.'

'The Blenners live in Riddlestown. We were great friends when I was growing up. Thought I was in love with Marcia when I was twelve, but I knew for certain that I was in love with her brother Foster when we were both eighteen. We were together in Amersham Hall. I didn't point him out to you in the class photograph; still too painful. Foster rammed his roadster into a railway bridge when he was home on leave. He had a leg blown off in Monte Cassino.' He paused and let his breath out slowly. 'I've a mind to stay in Riddlestown for a few days, maybe longer. You can drop me on the way. It's near Rosenalis in County Laois.'

The house was less pretentious than Barton Hall, three bays and a pedimented central window above a Doric doorway. There was decay everywhere. The box hedge labyrinth was trampled and gapped and in many places rotted away. Great patches of damp showed on the walls, chimneypots were missing and the windows on the third floor were boarded up.

'Lionel, are you sure you want to stay?'

'Perfectly. Two of my oldest friends are here, Marcia and Philippa Blenner. Why do you ask?'

'I don't think you'll be very comfortable.'

'Nonsense. I came to be with my friends. That's far more important, Roderick, than creature comfort. Would you like to come in? Meet the sisters. They know about you from our correspondence.'

'No. Your lifestyle, Lionel, or that of the Brenners was totally removed from mine. I don't know its language or its mannerisms. I'm afraid I'd be rather gauche.'

'I see sounds quite plausible. But the truth, of course, is that you don't want to witness up close the demise of other dinosaurs. Okay, run along now, drive carefully and come to see me as soon as you can. And thank you, thank you, for sharing your time with me, even if we did leave part of us buried back there.'

Before I drove away, I heard a holler from the house. An old lady stood framed in the Doric doorway, beckoning on someone behind her. Then the two of them appeared, Miss Marcia and Miss Philippa. They were almost replicas of each other, yellowing hair, print dresses, a book in one hand as if they had just looked up from the library window and seen their visitor in the driveway. They hobbled down the broken flight of steps to the broad sweep of gravel. They were shouting out Lionel's name, waving the books aloft, stopping now and then as if to savour the luxury and wonder of the moment. Lionel put down the suitcase and walked towards them, arms outstretched.

I drove home to Newtown and called into Heaney's for a drink. Every time I went to the pub, he accosted me with the same preamble. There's another championship in us. Would you and the brothers be game for it again? I was halfway down my pint before I realised that he hadn't said anything to me this day. Eventually he moved towards me, wiping a glass as he came and making clicking noises with his tongue against the roof of his mouth.

'You were away?'

'I was.'

'Foreign parts, I suppose.'

'South of England.'

'Ah, sure, only across the pond. An' you're only coming home now? Your first day back?'

'Yeah. What is it?'

'Ah nothing. I'll be up to the house one of the nights now.'

'I see. We're going to have another go at the senior championship.'

'Stranger things have happened.'

I left the Consul at Heaney's and walked home to Glenorga. The road, the new line, as people called it, ran along beside the gorge and the Morning Star. Ever since I was a child, the gorge had been a mystical place, made more mysterious by the sheer drop and the roar of the river over the rocks.

As I walked, I was assailed by a bout of despondency. All that wonderful promise of my youth and time, the brave new world of my future, had been smashed. What small talent we Dawleys had for affection or filial love, our family graces, especially that bonding of siblings and parents, were little removed from the social acumen of primates. We had drifted like flotsam in a turbulent tide ever since my father had announced his mission and my mother had set her face against it.

I sat on a flat stone that edged the water and took stock of myself. Much as I wanted to, I had no skill for making friendships. It seemed that there was some collusion of forces that thwarted me at every turn. I felt as close to Lionel Barton as I had ever done to another living soul, but I could never profess it. Once I had loved Rosie Kilraish, I probably still did, but she had turned into a shapeless dumpling, who sometimes whored at night and did not choose to acknowledge me. And Mikey had changed into an ogre and killed the crusade that sustained me.

I thought I heard laughter. It came tinkling above the music of the waterfall as if it were a snatch of fairy song from the depths of a cavern. Then I heard it again, louder now and human, brimming with the pleasure of stolen happiness. I followed the sound until I rounded an outcrop of rock and saw a couple who had suddenly risen from the mossy edge and were dashing along the shingle of the gorge. Echoes of their laughter, like a windblown crystal chandelier, lingered in their wake.

When they had gone, I wrestled with the impossibility of what I thought I had seen. The young woman was Muirne. But the young man with the flowing hair and the bronzed rippling body was my brother Felim.

Chapter 13

He was sitting in the reclining chair that my mother had bought for Joanna Dawley. The archway of roses above his head was in full bloom and the perfume filled the air. He heard me coming, but the dramatist in him waited until I was almost by the chair before he lifted the straw boater from his face.

'Say welcome home, Felim.'

He looked the picture of health. The ravaged face had smoothed out, the hair had bleached in the sun, the eyes twinkled and shone like pinpoints of light in a sallow landscape.

'Welcome home, Felim.'

'Don't shout it from the rooftops, little brother; someone might hear you. You were never one for exuberance, were you, Roddy?'

'I'm delighted you're back, Felim.'

He leaped from the reclining chair, planted his legs wide and bunched up his muscles. 'Ah, but just not back, Roddy. Look at me, man! I've beaten it, kicked the hell out of it. I haven't had a drink in ages. You're looking at a new man. I can move mountains.' He came close to me, locked me in a bear hug, squeezed, and in a moment had extricated himself again. 'Sorry, I shouldn't have offended the Dawley masculine ethos.' He pointed towards the Nursery Field. 'My motor car. What do you think?'

It was a Triumph with a British registration plate. The chrome sparkled; the white-walled tyres lifted the gloom beneath the tree's shadow.

'I bought it for a song from a bankrupt dealer in Smithfield. Say well done, Felim. And while you're mustering the right balance of envy and admiration, let me tell you I have a job as well. Starting Monday, site engineer with Sisk's; they're building a factory in Kilmallock.'

'I'm delighted for you, Felim. It's wonderful news.'

'I'm relishing this moment, Roddy. You and my father, you never thought I'd make it, did you?' Felim came close to me and held his hands aloft, the palms pointing outwards, 'All is forgiven. Your model brother was never one to bear a grudge. You were away on holiday?'

'Yeah, took a break. I went to England for a few weeks.'

'Where exactly?'

'Wiltshire, Salisbury Plain, High Wycombe, Amersham.'

'Amersham? A bit off your route, wasn't it? I was holed up there for a few months. Used to be a famous public school in Amersham. What took you there?'

'Nothing special. Just kept on driving.'

'Alone?

'Say, am I getting the third degree about something?'

'Of course not. It's just that you're defensive about something. It's patently obvious. You were with Barton, weren't you? Dangerous game you're playing, little brother. Thought no one knew about that, didn't you?

'Felim, are you trying to start a row with me? What's this about Lionel Barton?'

Felim pursed his lips, made sucking noises and returned to the reclining chair. He looked up at me with a face of glowing innocence. 'Sorry, Roddy, it's just my way; I get flippant and caustic in my exuberance. Sorry. About Barton: I've known for ages. When I was working the fields, I used see you go into his house, along by the old cattle track and through the kitchen garden. The wonder of it was that no one else ever saw. If the old man knew, it would be the death of him, and you. What do you see in that old geezer, Roddy? It's hardly sexual, is it?'

'Don't be stupid. Lionel Barton is one of the finest people I've ever met. He has always been very good to me; you've no idea. He practically paid my way when I was in Danesfort. And he's always been a friend, in good times and bad. But Lionel Barton is broke. Most of the best things in the house have been sold off – furniture, statues, antiques – all to keep his creditors from the door. But bad as that may be, he does not see it as his greatest problem.'

'Which is?'

'The enmity that has existed between the Dawleys and the Bartons, generation after generation. Whatever about the destruction of his home and his estate, he would regard himself a success if, at the end of his days, he and our father had made peace. It's an obsession with him.'

Felim began to snigger.' Jesus, Roddy, that's as good as I ever heard. Our father making peace with a Barton. You might as well go catch a moonbeam ...' He stopped suddenly as if some other absurd thought had entered his consciousness. 'Hey, you're Barton's ally in this stupid notion?'

'You could say that. Maybe you'd help us, Felim.'

'Jesus, you're mad, Roddy. I wouldn't get involved in some venture like that against Father for all the tea in China. Neither should you. I don't carry any torch for Lionel Barton. The fact is I'm on my father's side. So, my advice is, forget it. Must be off. Hughie is working in

Kirby's. I promised him I'd help. I owe him.'

'Don't we all?'

'I don't mean in a monetary sense. In the worst of times I kept on seeing Hughie, working in the fields. It was the part that never died, this vision of home.'

'I know it well. How is Hughie?'

'Great. Say, how serious is it between him and Muirne?'

'You must have seen yourself. Hughie is head over heels.'

'Well, I don't blame him. She's a beaut, isn't she?'

'You didn't like her. You gave me short shrift one day when I came bearing messages.'

'I was a twit then, Roddy, full of pretentious claptrap. You know what we did this morning? Cleaned out the entrance to the Blue Pool. We got it looking like old times. She had some interesting stories to tell about you. Not at all the sweet innocent little chap we all took you to be then, eh?'

'Long time ago, Felim. Is Muirne still here?'

'No. She went off to work about ten minutes before you arrived. Father is in the kitchen though. What is it, Roddy, that makes me feel sorry for him? He's like a bird in a cage. Our father was never cut out to be a housewife.'

We had two cycles of Dawley happiness in the lifetime of my generation. In neither case was it a full complement, shared by all the family. The first, the Grand Canal period, was formed around our family conferences and the Blue Pool days, activated by my mother. We saw nothing of its strategy, only the completeness of its warmth. It was natural that our father was missing from the core of happiness that surrounded us then. He was outside the circle.

Many years later came The Reformation, the period that began when Hughie fell in love and Felim returned home, having conquered his affliction. It too was fragmented and incomplete. It flared briefly in a brimming of cohesive spirit and then faded away so that we were unaware of its passing. And perhaps the most wondrous thing about it was that it was my father who seemed at the centre of it. We allowed him become the patriarch of the house and deferred to him in a way that he found no resentment for. But of course it wasn't my father at all or any of his sons who were at the core of The Reformation. It was Muirne.

My father was enthralled by her. Most evenings she came by Glenorga on her way from the school in Clonaslee. When I arrived home early or took time off to complete some task away from the workplace, I would hear them going about the work in the yard and catch echoes of their laughter. There was an ease and naturalness about their relationship that surprised me.

Muirne was a born strategist. She nurtured the worth of her supporters and isolated the sceptical. My father stood tall and favourable in one corner of the triangle that she had consigned us to. Felim and Hughie stood in the other, twin pillars of advantage, so resolute that they sometimes acted as a single source. I was well aware of my placement in the angle of misgiving, but I was absorbed like the others in the bliss of The Reformation and prayed that it would last forever.

It was a time when I was fully occupied. In the month after Felim returned, we stumbled across the remnants of a Neolithic settlement beneath the millennia of peat deposits. It was a farming system: fields of cultivation and grazing, low stones walls, a network of timbered roadway, beaten clay floors with post holes. I started to write an account of the excavation and my interest grew. With Carew and Heaney, I pieced together the story of Mount Fierna: formation, topography, human colonisation. I began to write for specialist magazines, did broadcasts on radio. I was the mouthpiece of my colleagues, putting their thoughts on paper and exposing the prints of pre-history.

I worked beneath the central light in the kitchen. The light was a relic from my mother's time. When she had first come to Glenorga, she had brought with her a paraffin lamp with a mottled green shade that was designed to hang from a pulley. When electricity reached the mountain, Hughie installed a bulb in the globe's fixture.

'What are you writing now?' my father would say. 'Don't you ever get tired of it all? You should be off out with your brothers and Muirne and maybe finding yourself a woman.'

'Time enough. I'm only 25. You weren't married at my age.'

'Well, I asked you, what are you writing about?'

'Rock composition in Mount Fierna.'

'Read it out to me.'

'Okay, here we go then. "The sandstones are the commonest sediments of the Old Red Sandstone formation. But there is another type. If you walk along by the gorge, above the Morning Star, you will see the other main rock type. This is red siltstone, fine-grained sediment that is almost a dark wine colour. These siltstones were not laid down in the riverbed itself, as the sandstones were, but on the flood plain when the river overflowed its banks. There are other formations in the siltstones—"'

'"Tis like double Dutch.'

'It would be a lot easier if you'd let me show you.'

'Faith an' I might take you up on that. If Heaney can make sense of that class of thing, I don't see why I shouldn't.'

So he started to come with me and listened intently when I showed him the rock formations exposed by the river as it gouged its way through the valley and formed the gorge and dingles. He made clicking noises with his tongue against the roof of his mouth, a forerunner always that he had questions to ask.

'You're telling me that all this happened of its own accord. That long before the Morning Star existed, other great rivers carried the sand over the land and left it down here and there? Then the Morning Star came along and exposed it once more. Is that what you're telling me?'

'Something like that, yes.'

'And are you saying that God didn't make those stones and put them there.'

'I'm saying that it all happened from natural causes, over millions and millions of years. You have to see it over an enormous expanse of time.'

'But God didn't have anything to do with it? In the same way as he made the birds of the air and the beasts of the fields. I thought that was the way it was; my father thought so too and all before him. God planned everything – what kind of stones he was going to make and where he was going to put them. I learned that at school; God's infinite wisdom my teacher called it. You're saying now 'tis something else entirely.'

'I'm saying that there's a natural reason for most things. And most things happen by chance.'

'Get along with you. See that tall thin tree growing out of the bank across the water? You trying to tell me that tree grew there of its own accord?'

'No, the rowan grew there by chance; some accident brought the seed to a place where it could germinate. Perhaps the seed came down in the river. Maybe it was shed from another tree far up the mountain. Or maybe it fell out of a bird's beak or came through in its excrement.'

'In its what?

'In the bird's shit. It was taken along in the current until it was swept in there and left in the mud.'

'Ah, that's a handy way of explaining things. Chance or accident. That's the class of thing that got you into trouble.'

'Sorry?'

'Don't sorry me, boyo. You know well. The bad time they gave you in Danesfort. It all began with that class of stuff you've been telling me. You didn't think I knew that, did you?'

'No, but so what?'

'You remember that man who came here once with his son?'

'Stapleton?'

'The very man. He told me that you had the quarest of ideas, even as a youngster, and 'twas no wonder you got into trouble. But mind you, that was no excuse for the treatment they gave you.'

'It was a long time ago.'

'Aye, some things are best forgotten. Anyway, that man Stapleton: his son is a Redemptorist, off out somewhere in the wilds of South America. He's always asking about you, so the father tells me. You should write to him.'

'All right. You get his address, I'll write to him.'

'Fine. I'll tell the father. He'll be delighted about that.'

I brought him to see the Neolithic farm system that we

had unearthed in Lackaroe. He was enthralled. He examined every twist of the field boundaries, marvelled at how the stones were fitted together, and pumped me for information. I had never seen him so intently interested. As he sat, I imagined he saw his ancient forebears move their cattle along the tracks between the fields, saw them make harvest and store it away, watched them grow old and die in that inevitable cycle of life, as constant then as now.

We came home by Ardagh. Martin Culhane greeted my father with his usual effusion, and without bidding, placed three whiskeys on the counter top.

''Tisn't often a man comes in here with his son and they drink together.'

He raised his glass.

'Here's to good company. Martin, have you ever been to see that place they dug from under the bog in Lackaroe.'

'Indeed I haven't.'

'This boyo here knows all the ins and outs of it.'

'So I've heard, so I've heard. An' I'm glad of it. You've come a long way, Roddy, since you used to be knocking around with that shagger Kilraish. Jaysus, Hugh, that was some prime bucko. I wonder whatever happened to him?'

I could feel the question on my face, the slight shuffle of my father on his stool as his curiosity thrust him forward. 'He's in England,' I said. 'I hear that he did very well for himself; made a lot of money.'

'Isn't it the like of him that does?' Martin said. 'They were some family, weren't they, Hugh? They were all the same; where would they be got? Although, mind you, I've heard the youngest one, Rosie, was a nice little girl.'

Culhane looked at me over the rim of his glass and his eyes twinkled. My father made clicking sounds in his mouth. They were like pair of hoary old schemers baiting a callow youngster.

'True,' I said. 'Almost as nice as the mother, though I'm not too sure if Rosie had her generosity. According to the tradition of my youth, the pair of you had many an outing with the village—'

'That's enough now, that's enough,' my father said. 'Don't speak ill of the dead, especially when you don't know what you're talking about.'

Culhane wore a mask of studied concentration. Then slowly, he began to laugh; the hand that held the whiskey glass had the tremor of a leaf in a young breeze and the sound of breaking merriment peeled from his throat and then burst through his lips.

'Jaysus, that's a good one. Faith, Hugh, you got your answer there. Poor old Lena.' Culhane furtively looked towards the kitchen door as if someone might be listening in its shadow. 'She wasn't the worst and, as that boy there tells it, she had a generous streak in her body.'

'You should be ashamed of yourself,' my father rebuked him, 'going on with talk like that. I want it to be known right here and now that I never—'

'Father, we're only joking. We believe you! But seriously, I knew nothing about Lena's past. I only knew her as a lovely and gracious lady. She used bring me into her house, feed me with cold rabbit and apple tart and make me pay for them with stories. I think her life was a misery; she was dreadfully unhappy and that Long Pat hadn't an ounce of humanity. She was dealt a bad hand in life and deserved a lot better.'

My father was looking at me with his mouth open and head askew as if the shock of what he was hearing had arrested his faculties. Then he raised his whiskey glass.

'That was a great spake,' Culhane said.

My father put the glass down. 'Never knew you were that fond of her, Roddy, but I'll tell you this. I found her that way too. That was what I saw in her and not the other thing that people remember her for. If the world had been any way good to her, she might have made some man bloody happy.'

'You should have married her yourself, Hugh,' Culhane said.

His words hung in the bar like some long-silenced secret suddenly enunciated.

'Jaysus, Hugh, I never should have said that.'

'You said it anyways, Martin. An' who knows what's right or wrong until 'tis all accounted for. Give us the same again. I want to see what this boy here is made of. We might even get a song out of him before the day is through.'

'Ye'll have to count me out,' Culhane said. 'I'm the only one at home today and there's a few jobs to be done in the yard. If ye fancy another one before I get in, pour it yeer-selves.'

'You're a trusting man, Martin.'

'Aye I am, when I know my men.'

We heard the clatter of pails and the lowing of calves alerted to his coming as Culhane went about his chores. My father threw back his whiskey with a sudden jerk of his elbow and went behind the counter. He refilled his glass and topped up mine.

'You're falling behind, boy.'

'I'm not much of a drinker.'

'No more than myself.'

'I heard it differently. I heard you could put away ten

pints and a few small ones and walk out steady as a rock.'

'You heard ould rubbish. People hereabouts are always exaggerating like that. You tell 'em 'tis four and immediately it becomes eight.'

'I've noticed.'

''Twas the same with Lena Kilraish. People made her out to be something she wasn't at all. If you listened to them, you'd swear every man and garsoon on the mountain had a cut off her. 'Twas all wrong. It ruined her. By the time they were finished, the only man who would look at her was someone like that shit Long Pat.'

'You must have been very fond of her.'

'Ah well, I liked her. I wouldn't say now that it went much beyond that.'

'Martin Culhane seems to think that it went much deeper.'

My father leaned closer as if to check for some unspoken censure in my face. Then he nodded, satisfied that there was none. 'Martin's mouth always worked faster than his brain. We got into many a scrape over that. He should never have said it, about me marrying Lena.'

'Were you in love with her?'

Immediately I said it, I was sorry. I could see the knuckles whitening round the glass and the sudden intake of breath that long ago used to strike us youngsters with dread.

'What class of a question is that?'

I should have read the signal but the whiskey was loosening my tongue and flustering my brain. 'If you loved her, you should have married her.'

'What's he on about?' My father looked around him as if evoking the sympathy of some invisible person. 'Loved her? What does he know about love?'

'As much as you obviously. And while we're talking about love, did you love my mother?'

My father slapped his glass on the counter with such force that the spirits slopped over the rim and formed a pool. 'Who in Christ's name do you think you are? Messing around with things that you have no right to. That's enough of it. Keep them kind of questions to yourself.'

'It's a very simple question, Father. I don't see why it should provoke such a response. Did you love my mother, yes or no?'

My father moved his head violently from side to side, like a terrier shaking a rat. I could hear his teeth clench and the jawbone clamp.

'Jesus Christ, did he hear anything I said? Did he?'

'Answer me, Father, answer me.'

He drained the last of his drink and spluttered as if it was driven pell mell down his throat. 'I'll tell you something. I'm off. I didn't come in here to be roared at and cross-examined by a whelp of a son that thinks he knows it all. Stay here if you like. I'm going home.'

'You didn't answer me. Did you love my mother?'

My father paused with his hand on the door latch. The wind blew and rattled the spars of the plastic chandelier that hung above the counter.

'You can't leave well alone. You have to know, don't you? All right then, I was very fond of your mother, very fond of her. Is that good enough for you?'

My father banged the door behind him. I saw him pass the window, hands in his pockets, his head held down, the shoulders hunched as if he were walking into a storm. I went behind the bar and poured myself another whiskey. It seemed that the liquor was laced with a terrible remorse that filled me with nausea. I put my head on the countertop and started to cry.

By the time I caught up with him, my father had crossed over the summit and was sitting on a tussock of heather that bounded the narrow white road. He was still hunched. I stopped and pushed out the door on the passenger side.

'Are you coming home?'

'I told you I could walk.' There was a slight rasp to his words as if something had lodged in his throat.

'Come on. Sit in. We'll go back to Culhane's and finish our drinks. Martin will be wondering what became of us.'

My father turned a blackened furrowed brow to me as soon as he had settled himself in the seat.

'You shouldn't be asking me questions like that. 'Tis none of your business and it makes my head addled.'

'I know but I find it sad that you could not answer, just couldn't get yourself to say the words. And somewhere in all that, Father, is the Dawley cross that you have willed to your sons. We have no finesse with the language of mature relationships. We can't say "I love you", can't say "I was wrong", can't say "I forgive".'

My father made a half-hearted attempt to open the door again. He blew air on the glass and watched as it misted up. Then he drew a smudged line with his index finger and wiped it away with his jacket sleeve.

'You know something. You shouldn't drink at all if it affects you like this.'

'Okay. Maybe I am out of step. But now that I've come so far, would you listen to something else for me, please?'

'What do you want now?'

'No lecture, Father. Just a simple request. About

Lionel Barton.'

His fingers closed round the door handle.

'What about Barton?'

'Isn't it time that you stopped the hatred? Time you made friends with your enemy. It doesn't make sense or reason any more. Close the enmity, Father, put an end to it.'

My father wound down the window until it disappeared in the framework of the door. Then he wrenched the handle, kicked the door open when the lock disengaged and banged it shut with such force that the car rocked as if it was caught in a gale. He leaned in through the opening and there was a terrible anger in the face he thrust at me.

'You bloody shit. I swear to Christ, you have been scheming with that bastard behind my back. Lionel Barton if you don't mind.' And then as if the face was a profile that a portrait artist had brushed over, the anger dissipated, the eyes smoked with sadness and the hands that a few moments before were reaching for me through the window fell limp at his side.

'Would you take that from me too?' he half-sobbed. 'The one thing that kept me going and those who went before me. All through life the Dawleys and the Bartons have been enemies and it is right that it should be that way; you know the history as well as I do. Make friends with Barton? I'd give up my religion; turn my face against God before I'd do that. You haven't an ounce of sense, boy, to think that I'd make peace with that man and renege on everything that I stand for. Do you think I'd let down the past generations of Dawleys?'

My father gathered himself to his full height. He threw back his head, hunched his shoulders and marched past me into the gathering twilight.

The years of absence had compacted the closeness between my brothers. If there was still light when Felim arrived home, he went immediately to the fields. As I approached the place where they were working, I could hear the laughter that would suddenly float across a hedge, as it had been twenty years before. And Felim was still the court jester, except that now he mostly focused on entertaining Muirne under Hughie's approving eye and silent acquiescence.

That was Hughie's downfall, because it was never him that Muirne had set her cap for. The time I first saw Muirne and Felim together in the gorge of the Morning Star, I interpreted it as simple friendship. But I caught glimpses of trysts in various parts of the mountain in the weeks that followed until I could no longer doubt the evidence of my own eyes. I didn't need to surprise them swimming naked in the Blue Pool or see their frenetic coupling in the heather swarth of Knocknastumpa to know it. I had only to lift my eyes from the table and catch the glances that passed between them to realise that Felim and Muirne were in love. Even my father saw.

'I have to say something to you. I think Felim has wiped Hughie's eye.'

'I think so too.'

'There will be blue murder. Hughie will kill him. 'Twill be a bad day for all of us.'

'I'm very worried about it. It will break Hughie's heart.'

'I know that. Isn't she some class of a hussy now to do that to him, right under his very nose? Wouldn't you think he'd have noticed it by now?'

'He hasn't because he doesn't suspect anything. I'd hate to be around when he does. But I don't think the pair of them care anymore, I get the impression that they wouldn't mind if it was out in the open.'

'God help us when that happens. Roddy, talk to Felim, will you? Try and get him to see a bit of sense. We'd all be better off if he had never come home.'

'Why don't *you* talk to him?'

'Go way with you. What good would I be at that class of thing? I wouldn't know what to say. I wouldn't have the words for it.'

It took me weeks before I could muster the courage or find the right opportunity. In the meantime I had prepared and rehearsed several ways of broaching the subject.

I brought Felim tea to the meadow where he had been making silage. The whiff of new-mown hay hung like a per-fumed incense above the shorn ground as if it had absorbed every other scent into its all-pervading mixture. When we were kids, we had rolled in the mown swarths so that the smell would cling to our clothes.

'Felim, I want to say something to you. I appreciate that it is very delicate and maybe you might think that I have no business raising it—'

'Roddy, get on with it.'

'About Muirne.'

'What about Muirne?'

'It's really about you and Muirne. She's Hughie's woman; they are going to get married.'

'What's that got to do with me?'

'You know damn well. 'Tis as plain as day that she has fallen for you. Everyone can see that except poor old Hughie. Felim, stop it, give over. It will break his heart.'

'I can't; it's gone too far. I never meant anything like this to happen. Neither did Muirne. But we can't help it, Roddy.

What can I do?'

Felim stood up from the boulder he had been sitting on. He threw the dregs of the tea into the hedge and rolled the greaseproof paper that the scones were wrapped in into a ball. Then he kicked it away.

'Tell me, in Christ's name, what should I do?'

'Go away, Felim. Go back to England. Muirne will get over you. And even if she doesn't and follows you, it won't be as bad as if you were both here when Hughie finds out.'

Felim's expression changed. He looked at me with hooded eyes. Then he took a step towards me, made a fist of his right hand and thrust it under my chin. 'Well, well, well. Aren't you the conniving little bastard? Get rid of me and Muirne and you'd have it all to yourself again. Isn't that right, my clever little brother? You have no time for Muirne, have you? She told me that. Get stuffed and mind your own fucking business.'

A few weeks later I heard a commotion in the yard. It was mid-afternoon on a glorious Saturday in early September. What I had first heard was the heavy door of the outhouse being pushed so violently on its runners that it ran off the rails and clattered against the wall. I heard Hughie roar; it was like a bellow of anguish from a mortally wounded animal.

'Come out, you bastard,' Hughie screamed. 'Come out and face me, you treacherous fucking rat.'

Instinctively I knew that Hughie had found out. And so did my father because he came running around the gable of the house and stood in front of Hughie with his arms outstretched. Hughie pushed him aside as violently as he had torn the barn door off its runners. Before my father had stood erect again, Felim appeared in the doorway of the outhouse, wisps of straw in his hair, the leather belt of his trousers untied about his waist. A dishevelled and wide-eyed Muirne appeared over his shoulder. She tried to push forward, but Felim stayed her with his hand and walked boldly to the centre of the yard where Hughie stood splay-legged on the cobbles.

'I'm sorry, Hughie …' Felim began.

I had once seen Hughie in a fight. We had played a team called Tour and he had had words and a brief skirmish with the opposing full forward. That night, during a dance in Creeves, the full forward came after Hughie with two of his cronies in support. It was no contest. Hughie stood wide-legged on the dance floor as he now stood on the cobbles and took them with ease. He planted the full forward with an elbow in the face and stretched the nearest crony with an uppercut; the third turned tail and scuttled away. Hughie wasn't even angry then. Now the colour had drained from his face; his teeth had bitten though his lower lip and there were flecks of blood in the hollow beneath it.

I hardly saw the blow that stretched Felim on the cobbles. But I heard, and still hear the awful crack of bone on bone and knew that the impact had done damage.

'Get up, you bastard. Get up and fight me. Or I'll kick the shit out of you where you lie.'

It was a terrible beating. For a little while, though his jaw must have been broken, Felim tried to make a fight of it. But even in the full of his health and strength he would never have been a match for Hughie. My father and I tried to keep Hughie away but he just squared his shoulders and pushed us aside. Behind us Muirne was screaming: Felim moaned with every blow that made contact, Hughie roared his demented anger. Finally Felim lay motionless. Hughie drew back his leg as if to kick him and then he seemed to suddenly realise that he had caused the carnage that was curled on the cobbles.

'Aw Jaysus, Jaysus, Felim,' he sobbed. Then he ran across the yard, vaulted the low wall that led into the Nursery Field, tore madly across our youthful playground and through the hedgerow at its other end. We lifted Felim and carried him into the kitchen. Muirne washed his face while I searched in vain for a particle of flesh that wasn't bruised and discoloured.

'Go, Muirne,' Felim mumbled. 'Go from this house.'

A few nights later I heard him moving about the room that he occupied next to mine. I thought I heard the sound of sobbing and the patter of bare feet on the kitchen floor as he shuffled across it. Beyond the parlour was Hughie's room; I heard the door open and a few moments later the footsteps retrace their patter. The pacing continued for a little while as if there was no pattern to his movements. Then I heard the front door open and gently close. When I looked out my window, I saw Felim cross the yard in the moonlight. He was carrying a small cardboard case; his walk was an old man's shuffle. He stopped beside the Triumph, seemed to contemplate for a moment and then walked on. He made for the pathway that would take him by the gorge and the Morning Star. And when he had faded away in the haze of that autumn night, I knew that I would never see him again.

Rumours abounded in Felim's going. There were sightings from all over the country but none of them led to anything. When I discovered what he had taken with him, I was convinced more than ever that he would never return. He had taken no clothes and when I searched for clues in the pockets of his suit, I found his previous month's pay cheque. I wondered what he had stowed in the suitcase until I went into the parlour and saw the outline on the wall where the family photograph had hung. It was a picture taken by a stranger whom we had met on the slopes of Knocknastumpa. My mother was seated on the root of a 5,000-year-old pine and we were grouped around her. Hughie had a huge smile that lit the picture. Felim had a tooth missing; Mona looked the essence of studied gravity. I had two perfect legs and wore two perfect shoes. It was a beautiful picture, a snapshot of guileless fortitude in a brave young world. Gone also was the picture of the St Luna hurling team that had won the senior championship.

Muirne disappeared too. Her name was rarely mentioned in Glenorga. I heard that she had left her teaching post in Clonaslee and found another in Dublin. Later, someone told Lionel Barton that she had returned to France and then I heard no more. Like Felim, she just vanished and because we never spoke of her again, it was the same as if she never existed.

Hughie stayed on in Glenorga but he too soon left us. He became like a standing stone in a field that marked the spot where life had once flourished, played, made dreams and fell in love. Day by day, he went farther and farther away into that dark tumulus that had no exit. He worked every hour of light and into the darkness at the end of each day. He avoided contact with my father and me, but when he had no option, he spoke with graceless belligerence. He resented any spark of relationship that we tried to establish with him as if it were an attack on his fortress.

Hughie bought a motorbike after Felim left. The Triumph remained in the shade of the apple tree until winter set in. Then Hughie made space for it in the out-house and frequently worked on it when he came from the fields. He lavished a lot of his time on that car, as if in there, beneath the bonnet, was some connection with Felim which he was able to reach out to. The engine ran perfectly. It should have because Hughie was a gifted mechanic. When he drove it out onto the yard to do his test exercises, you could hear the way the engine purred as if it were exulting in its perfection. Hughie rode off on his motorbike when most people on the mountain would be thinking about going to bed. He must have journeyed far from Glenorga for there was never a sign or mention of him in Newtown or Adamston. He came home in the dead of night; often the worse for wear, cuts and bruises on his cheekbones and with half-closed discoloured eyes. My father and I knew enough not to comment on the state of his face. Most times we never got the chance, for no matter what time Hughie came home, he was up again at the crack of dawn.

I tried to take Felim's place, going into the fields and falling into work beside him. Hughie resented me there. He would rev up the tractor and drive off to another part of the field when I arrived, or look at me with downright animosity before turning his back and marching off. Then his behaviour took a strange and frightening twist. When I came along the hedgerows that bordered the fields where Hughie was working, I heard laughter and talk. He was standing beside the mudguard of the tractor, as I had seen him with Felim many summers before. Hughie was run-ning a make-believe conversation with his brother, playing both parts. Every now and then he would slap his thigh with pleasure and peal into laughter.

And then there came a day when we were thinning

turnips together in Kirby's field. Hughie was at one end, I at the opposite, and I suspected that as usual my father was lurking about somewhere. Suddenly I heard Hughie shout, 'Felim, Felim, wait for me'. He walked up the furrow towards me, arms outstretched, his eyes on some distant point on the horizon. Then he broke into a shambling run, stumbling across the drills, still shouting Felim's name. 'I'm coming, Felim. Hang on for me.' He tore through a gap in the hedgerows until he passed out of sight.

All that day we searched for him. When he failed to come home that night, we called in the police. A sub-aqua team from the garda station in Adamston found Hughie in the Blue Pool. His clothes had snarled at the bottom on a strand of barbed wire that had come away from the fence on the bank. The young diver who found him thought that Hughie had ripped off the wire deliberately and wound it round his body to keep himself grounded on the riverbed. But the strange thing was, the diver said, that Hughie seemed deliberately to have chosen that spot. He was in a sitting position, there was no sign of a struggle, his arms were folded, and there was a great smile on his face.

Felim had been gone for a couple of years when Hughie drowned. My father bought a new grave in Manisterluna, which would, he said, be big enough for all of us when our time came. 'Where's the need?' I asked him. 'Our mother and Mona will never come home, and Felim won't ever—'

'Felim will come home. I can feel it in my bones. It will be the way it should be: a father and his sons in the one plot of ground.'

The new grave faced Glenorga, the same vista that Beth Cartor saw when she came that way with her brother

Roderick. It looked out on tiered slopes, on ancient fields. Down on the valley floor was another graveyard: the resting places of broken dreams, of primitive emotions, of the puny, petty schemes of men, which life and the world had trodden upon and snapped underfoot. I thought about all those things that day as the gravediggers filled in the hole in which my brother was lying. I could feel my father shiver beside me and hear the sudden intakes of breath as he sought to stop his anguish spilling over. But stop it he would, for the Dawleys never showed emotion in public. We were the race of strong, tough men inside the tumulus of our anguish.

But of course we weren't. We were failures, who had failed each other and ourselves collectively. In my generation it had begun with my mother. Hughie was the only one of us who had seen and understood the position she had taken. She had diverted my father's aspirations and his role, had planned and executed it coldly and deliberately until we thought it was a natural process. We could have reached out to him, brought him into the circle, but the wisdom said that he was beyond all that, a primitive man who could not say the most basic human phrase of all, I love you. But none of us could, not even my mother. Perhaps in some ways she was the greatest Dawley of us all.

And perhaps I was the fortunate one. My father and I grew closer in the days and the months after Hughie had left us. By then he had leased the land to a son of Paddy MacAdastair's, for whom there was never enough hours in the day to satiate his quest for work. We traded off the Consul, the Triumph and the motorbike and bought ourselves a new car. He had become as ardent an admirer of the landscape and its prehistory as I was and together we toured the countryside for its story. Sometimes we fell into long and deep troughs of silent sadness because we had a lot to be sad about. And sometimes we laughed, if not in Heaney's pub on a Friday night, maybe Culhane's on Sunday, when some words of merriment tweaked across the anguish and lighted our souls.

We knew we were the last of the Dawleys. 'I'm glad you never married,' he used tell me, 'because a woman might come between us and set us against each other.' But then he would apologise for what he called, 'tarring all women with the same brush' and go on to wonder about the mysterious ways of God, who had solutions for the ills of ordinary mortals that they could not appreciate until proved by time. It was God's will that none of his sons ever married because there was something in the genes which should never be allowed to escape. Mona Cartor, he told me, had not been accidentally hit by a passing train. She had walked right out in front of it, as deliberately and as single-mindedly as Hughie had pulled the strand of wire from the fence and lowered himself to the bottom of the pool. A man whom he trusted had told my father; he had seen it happen.

Hughie was dead many years before I plucked up the courage to test the suspicion that had haunted me, day and night. On a quiet Sunday afternoon I dived into the Blue Pool and squirmed over the sandstone ledge that blocked the route to the cavern. I was certain what I would find and when my eyes became accustomed to the shimmering water and refracted light playing on the walls, I could see Felim's skeleton with remnants of his clothing still attached. It was lying just inside the entrance; the eddy must have been barely strong enough to carry him through. Parts of the skeleton were beginning to come apart so I found another

THE BLUE POOL

ledge at the rear of the cavern and rearranged it there. The cardboard case was beside Robert Kilraish; it was water-stained but still intact. Inside I found the picture that the stranger had taken in Knocknastumpa, and the photograph of the hurling team. And there too was a picture I had never known existed: a newspaper cutting of my father holding aloft the cup, which he had won at the Limerick athletic meet.

I never told a living soul about finding Felim. I believed then, and still do, that he had found the perfect repose and it would have been wrong to deny him the eternal relevance of it. I went frequently to visit him in his watery grave, choosing those hours when there was no one about. I sat by the limestone ledge and talked to him. I knew it was silly and probably macabre but I didn't care; indeed I revelled in it. My life and the mountain that contained it had always been populated with stolid, serious people. That was my way too but it wasn't Hughie's way, despite all the ramparts he raised around himself. And, of course, it wasn't Felim's, our court jester. He was as unconventional as laughter in a place of sorrow.

So I sat and talked to my brother, feeding him the embellished titbits of life on Mount Fierna and how things were between my father and me. Then years later, a winter flood brought a great boulder to fill the space before the entrance to the cavern and I could no longer swim through. But for a while, round the edges of the boulder, I could still make out Robert Kilraish's skeleton on his resting-place and Felim's foot bones farther in. Eventually the entrance silted up until the time came when nothing at all was visible.

Then I was glad because no one now would ever know. Had my visits to the cavern and what it contained been discovered, I would have been vilified. It was unthinkable that a Christian should lie in an unhallowed pagan grave. My visits would have been seen as the morbid actions of a twisted soul and my father would never have forgiven me for withering away the vision of his hope. Felim will come back, he would tell me time and time again; when we least expect it, that man will come in here to the kitchen, he will throw his bag on the couch there and we'll carry on the self-same way as if he had never left. Mark my words, Felim will be home. And though my mind would want to shout the truth of it, I didn't have the heart to shatter the hope or the dream.

My father emerged from his cocoon, displaying unexpected pieces of humanity and losing the baggage of tradition that bared the inner warmth inside the outer carapace. Or perhaps it was simpler than that; perhaps in the end there was nothing left to maintain the outer layer for. It had all washed away, the restoration of Barton fields, strong sons tied to his ambition, principles and aspirations and the puny little vanities of life that evaporate in the first surge of death or parting. Some of it died when my mother left; it all died with Hughie. But now and then they stirred, the tentacles of the former man that sought to touch and feel the crumbling dreams.

'Isn't that a strange thing?'

'What is?'

'In all the years, they never tried to contact us. Mona or your mother. Isn't that a strange one?'

'Not so strange. You threw Mona out. You could hardly expect—'

'You don't have to remind me. But wouldn't you think,

some time, in all the years past, she would say to herself, I wonder how my father is. Maybe I should contact him.'

'She might, Dad, if she weren't your daughter.'

'Ah, you're always saying that. An' the woman, not a meg from her either. You heard she was doing well?'

'I heard she had a job in an art gallery, or a museum. She went to night classes and has a big job now.'

'How did you hear?'

'Someone home from California told Carew. You asked me that same question many a time.'

'Suppose I did. I forget things now. I'm an old man. Time I was gone to my bed.'

'Little you forget. I presume you have something in mind when you bring up this topic. You have been nibbling away at it for a long time now. You think I should go to California and find out for myself, isn't that it?'

'Wouldn't that be grand. When might you be going?'

'Maybe next month. Would that suit you?'

'Will you listen to him? Sure it has nothing to do with me. 'Tis you that's going.'

'You have no interest?'

'Lord God, man, what would I be doing, getting on a plane, going to America? Ah, not at all. Travelling's for young people. I'll be off to my bed so, but I'm glad you're going to see them.'

'Goodnight, Dad. I love you.'

'Good, good.'

'Did you hear what I said? I said I love you.'

'Oh that's grand. Grand. Don't forget to quench the light when you're finished.'

Chapter 14

Mona and I crossed the corridor that led to the barred window by the kitchen garden and I unlocked the library door. This was the only room in the house that was closed to the public.

'All mine,' I said to Mona, 'a gift from Lionel Barton to a Dawley friend.'

Mona grinned in puzzlement. 'I knew there was some connection between you guys but never thought it was as deep as this.'

'We had a long-time illicit friendship. He was the warmest, gentlest man I ever knew.'

'What will you do with this place, Roddy? Fine and all as the gesture was, it's a bit impractical, isn't it?'

'Oh, I don't think so. He left me the room as well as its contents. And a right of way through any part of the house or the land. I come down here often; it's a great place to write and to think and there's an enormous amount of reference material here. Lionel, and old Amos before him, were very well read. So I'll hang on to my bequest until I too pass on, and then I'll give it to the state. There is no one else to give it too, is there? Like everything else I'm left with.'

'God, and to think of all the fighting, all the bitterness and hatred that went into amassing this estate and our piece of the mountain. That too will go to the state, I presume?'

'Yes. It's all part of the Theme Park trust. Do you know

what Lionel's ambition was?'

'That one day he would shake the hand of Hugh Dawley in friendship. God, he must have been naïve. He told that to Mother. I think she tried to wise him up. Did our father ever find out about your friendship with him?'

'I don't think so.'

'He would have been as mad as hell if he had known.'

'Sure, and worse still if he knew about our mother and Lionel.'

Mona looked at me with a quizzical set to her Dawley jawline as if she was being compromised by a question that had several potential consequences. 'What was there to know? There was nothing at all to it only that they often met and spoke to each other. And of course Barton was the conduit by which she kept in contact with me after I was thrown out. Are you saying there was more?'

'You remember how mother used ramble off on her own on Sunday afternoons? She would be gone for hours, walking – as she said, finding time for herself. Well, I solved the puzzle of where she went when I stumbled into Barton Hall when I shouldn't have been there. She was playing the piano for Barton, the Moonlight Sonata.'

'Christ's sake, Roddy, there was nothing to it. Mother would have told me. She never hid anything from me.'

'Lionel said the same thing. They were just two lonely souls who shared a love of books and music. But can you imagine Father's reaction if he had found out.'

'Doesn't bear thinking about. Say, Roddy, any place around here I could get a cup of coffee. I haven't had anything since I got off the plane. I'd murder a cup right now.'

'Let's walk up to Glenorga. I'll rustle up something. I make a good cup of coffee.'

'Oh great. I'm dying to see the place.'

Several years before, the local authority had built a walk-way along by the river. Rustic wooden bridges and stiles led through hedgerows, over dividing walls and connecting streams. Along the trail, on signs etched into embedded tree logs, was information about the surrounding habitat and the birds and animal life that populated it. The road that ran beside the trail was now smooth and tarred, weaving out like a slimy anaconda all the way to the house. Across the river, where once there had been stepping-stones, there was now a hump-backed bridge with a single arch.

Mona and I walked in silence, and that surprised me. This was the route we used take to school in Newtown. We went in single file, Hughie to the front, as befitted his status, and me in the rear, as befitted mine. Once we had passed the stepping stones and turned inland from the gorge, the house was hidden from our view, and so was my mother, who had come out as far as the ford to watch us safely across. The simple change in direction freed the restraints of Glenorga, took away the fear and loosed the secrets of our hidden places. We spoke our dreams out loud, our conjecture and our wonderings, our feelings, emotions and our anger. And then the court jester amongst us would bound upon an outcrop of stone as we passed, spread his hands in a theatrical pose and intone my father's voice in exaggerated dramatics, 'Some day, some day soon, I'll walk down there to Barton Hall, me and my own around me. We'll buy the two big fields that are bounded with ours. Won't that be the day? I can't wait to see his face. A Dawley buying land from a Barton robber.' We laughed outright, even Hughie, through his glare of caution.

'Mona, you're strangely silent.'

'I'm impressed, Roddy, but I must tell you too that I'm disappointed.'

'Why?'

'All through the years I've kept this vision in my head of Glenorga, of Mount Fierna, all the places that I knew. I know it's stupid, but I expected to find them as they were. I wanted to see them that way. But this isn't the country that I left. There has been so much progress. I find it sad because I wanted to see it as it was. Even this.' Mona threw out an arm to encompass the bridge. 'I hate it. Why the hell did you take the stepping stones away?'

'Because I couldn't drive a bloody car across them, could I? Are you saying that we should have stayed rooted in the last century just to satisfy your sentiment? I bet you wouldn't put up with those primitive conditions in California.'

'Okay, I suppose I was just being silly. Am I witnessing a new Roddy, just like all the other changes?'

'I think it's too early to be making those kind of judgements. Come on, I'll rustle up the coffee.'

I had restored the cobbled yard and edged it with flagstone from the riverbed of the Morning Star. In front of the house, opposite each of the bedroom windows, we had planted a flower garden. My father had first frowned at the idea; he saw it as some kind of frumpish ostentation that real mountain men and their women would have no time for. Mona ignored the flower garden; perhaps she had not expected it and so failed to see it. But she did see the arch of roses over the front door. It was fuller now, supported on a trellis, and its scent wafted about us. Mona clapped her hands. 'Oh, my God,' she gushed, 'the roses. They're still above the door.'

301

'That was Dad's work of art. He used spend hours here, training the brambles to twine round the arch, pruning and shaping.'

'He never struck me as a man for roses.'

'Perhaps you weren't around him long enough.'

'Are you implying something?'

'For Christ's sake, Mona, don't be so touchy. Do you know the origin of those?'

'Someone gave the cuttings to our grandfather, light years ago.'

'They had taken root and were in full growth before Father found out where they had come from. He wanted to pull them up, but his mother prevailed upon him.'

'Am I missing something here?'

'Just this. When I was doing research for the Theme Park, I came across something odd about our grandparents and their relationship with the Bartons. There was little of the hatred between them. Joanna, as a young woman, had worked in Barton Hall and apparently was quite friendly with Lionel's father, Amos. It seems that the hatred had waned in our grandfather's time.'

'Until Hugh Dawley took up the cause again.'

'As did Hughie and Felim, but to a lesser degree.'

'Well,' Mona sighed, 'it's all over now. And what was it all for?'

I pulled off a rose and gave it to Mona; I put another in the lapel of my jacket. 'Every morning, while they were in bloom, I wore one of those in my buttonhole to work. It became a kind of Roddy Dawley trademark. When my workmates asked me about it, I told them that there were several kinds of roses, many species, many hybrids. But this one was unique; this was a rose for peace. Lionel Barton wore one too; they still grew along the estate wall. It was our badge of commonality.'

Mona traced the rose petals along my cheekbone. 'Nice touch, Roddy. Perhaps you are a sensitive soul after all. Now let's get that coffee.'

She stopped just inside the threshold and I watched her survey the room. The old solid fuel range had been changed for an oil-driven model and a suspended ceiling hid the spars of the thatched roof. Our mother's hanging lamp was still centred over the kitchen table and the cord that worked the pulley was fixed to a hook beside the windowsill. And still in place, as smoked and as veneered as if it was worked over with a daily application of furniture polish, was the picture of the stigmatist Padre Pio. Several times it had broken loose from its nail and once a hole had been burned right through when it fell on the middle ring of the range. I had thrown it several times into a biscuit tin that was a cornucopia of discarded mementoes, but always my father had replaced it over the fireplace.

Mona walked to the middle of the kitchen, still sweeping her gaze about the room.

'You've left it almost as it was. You've changed so little. Jeez, Roddy, how come? Where has all the progress gone?'

'This kitchen is perfect for me. And, anyway, if I changed it, it wouldn't be authentic. Remember that this house represents a typical mountain home.'

'With running water and a toilet?'

'Sure. We've had those since Hughie's time. When electricity came, Mona, it changed everything. But the basic structure remained the same. Here, sit down and I'll make the coffee. Would you rather stay here or go into the conservatory?'

'Conservatory? You've got to be kidding?'

'No, we have one. Straight out the back door there that used lead to the Nursery Field.'

I filled the kettle and put some delph on the table. 'It's our only gesture to ostentation. We had become reasonably well off, our father had leased the land and was making good money from it, I was doing very well at work, including some earnings from a product that Carew and I had patented. We could have built a new house, moved down to Newtown. I had bought a site there. But wild horses wouldn't drag him away from here, and frankly, when I thought about it, me neither. So we built on the conservatory as a kind of sop to our comfort. And Dad got to love it; he spent all his time in there. You know why, I think? The conservatory was new; it had no association whatever with his past, with the things that had blighted his life and which in the end he brooded and fretted about. Everywhere he looked in the house there was something to remind him.' I pushed the biscuits towards her. 'Cookie, as you folks say?'

Mona leaned back on her chair and put her feet on the under-rails of the table. 'I hardly thought he was that sensitive.'

'He was many things, Mona, that we never realised, or never searched for.'

'Roddy, can I ask you something? Don't get me wrong about this. You know what my feelings were and are for our father. But I'm getting the impression that you're trying to influence me. It's almost as if you're presenting another side of him for me to consider.'

'Sorry. I didn't realise I was doing that. It's just, well, I lived with our father for almost twenty years when there was only the two of us. I discovered a man that I never knew existed. Father was a good man, Mona. The problem was we never believed it might be possible, never took the effort to find out.'

'I never thought he had converted you. But, of course, you didn't always follow the same route as the rest of us.'

'Knock it off, Mona. It's a great day; I'm absolutely delighted that you came, so don't let's get off on the wrong foot.'

The microwave sounded; it was like the ring of an old-fashioned telephone. Mona took the cake of soda bread, knifed off the crusted end and plastered it with butter. That was a Dawley habit, as widespread as if it too was enshrined in the genes. When we began to keep a dairy herd, we bought butter at the creamery and its cost was deducted from the monthly cheque. My father railed at us. We ate butter, he said, like a pack of wolves. Butter came in 28-pound wooden boxes; when it was used up, Hughie converted the boxes into kitchen seats, milking stools, vegetable containers. Every time a new one appeared, my father would draw his breath in a hiss and give vent to another tirade.

'You can't buy this kind of butter in California, or this kind of bread.'

'I must send you some. You can buy vacuum-packed food in the supermarkets, ready for shipping abroad. That is, of course, if you decide to go back.'

'No decision, Roddy. I couldn't live here now. But we should see each other a lot more often. You and I are all we've got. Why don't you come and live with me? What's here for you?'

'I couldn't live anywhere else. That's another legacy that seems to have been embedded in the genes. Hughie had it. I think if he had been taken out of here, he would have wasted away. And Felim, he had it in spades. He told me that in the worst of times, when he was literally lying in the gutter, he used summon a vision of Mount Fierna to sustain him. He heard it call to him, voices in the wind, like echoes of some forgotten song. Come on, bring your coffee with you, I want to show you the parlour.'

'Jesus, Roddy, I'm not sure if I can handle it. The parlour represents most of what I hold dear about our life here. It was our happy place, it and the Blue Pool. It was the way Mother saw it too; the parlour was some kind of sanctuary to her, a haven surrounded by a state of perpetual hassle.'

'I'm sure it will please you. It is as it always was, nothing has been changed. Come on.'

No matter what I did with the parlour, I could never get rid of the smell of must and the cloying remains of long-departed camphor that seemed to be locked into the very walls. That morning, before I left, I had sprayed a scented air freshener in the room and polished the furniture with a product that was supposed to contain the scent of lilac and wild flowers. But neither had made the slightest impression; the old odours announced their presence again the moment I opened the door.

'Christ, do I remember that smell?' Mona said. 'I came into this room the night before I left, for a last look and got that odour of must or dampness, I couldn't make out which. But I've never foprgotten it.' Then her eyes lifted to swing about the room. 'Oh sweet Jesus, Roddy, it's marvellous. Not a thing out of place. Look at the wallpaper. What did you do with it?'

'I had it restored by a Dublin firm that specialises in old period furnishings. Several times the guy who came here offered to buy the wallpaper from me. It made me suspicious, so I contacted an antique dealer that my friend Jim

Carew knew. He valued the wallpaper at somewhere in the region of 15,000 pounds and thought his estimate was on the conservative side. It is probably now worth more than the house itself.'

'You're kidding.'

'Phoebe Jackson gave that wallpaper to our mother as a wedding gift. What none of us knew was that it had been bought in Florence almost 100 years earlier, probably intended for the Brigadier's villa. Yet for some reason it was never hung. It lay there in its wrappings until Phoebe gave it to our mother.'

'Would you credit it – something destined for a gracious drawing room, winding up here on those crude walls? Isn't that so ironic?'

'It sure is. I wonder what our father would have made of it, if he knew.'

Mona mimicked my father's voice: 'Whatever class of antique it is, it doesn't cut any ice with me. One roll of wall-paper is the same as the next.'

'When our mother left, he never came into this room. He took his money from the drawer, along with his receipts, and kept them in his bedroom. When I asked him why he never came in, he told me that there were too many reminders in this parlour of the children he had lost. So he locked the door in case he entered without thinking.'

'You're a sensitive soul, Roddy. You've kept it exactly as it was.'

The room was not exactly as it had been but it was so long since Mona had last looked at the parlour that I was sure she wouldn't notice the difference. I had to trawl through back issues of the county newspaper until I found the picture of the St Luna hurling team that had originally hung on the wall opposite the fireplace. I couldn't find an exact match for the frame, but its replacement was very close.

'I must get a copy of that picture,' Mona said. 'Do you know, I haven't a single photograph of my brothers.' She stopped, leaned forward and peered intently at the wall beside the picture. 'Say, Roddy, wasn't there another picture there? We were all in it as kids, with our mother. Some man took the photograph when we were coming down from Knocknastumpa. You remember?'

'I remember well. I thought you might have it. Maybe Mother had given it to you. I noticed that it was gone shortly after she left and I assumed that she took it. She must have.'

'I never saw it, and I would have because she lived with me when she first came over.'

'She must have lost it,' I said. 'Pity. I was going to ask you for a copy.'

Over the rim of the wooden weir and through the cracks that the years had etched in the wood, the river flowed. As it fell, the light played in the swirling water, sending iridescent light into the gloom of the pool below. The water gurgled as it left the boulders; it tinkled like the breaking of ice on some distant frozen shore. The soft summer breeze entered the space between the gorge cliffs; it sighed there and seemed to whisper as if it had found a haven and wished to stay.

I took off my shoes and stuffed my stockings into them. Mona sat on the tartan rug, idly turning the capsule in her fingers.

'Are you happy about this?' I asked.

She shrugged. 'I had never thought about it, Roddy, until

you came up with the idea. Mother herself had no great preference where I should scatter her ashes, other than it be somewhere in Mount Fierna that was connected to herself and her family. I thought it might be an idea to put this capsule somewhere in Manisterluna, perhaps in Hughie's grave.'

'She never liked graveyards.'

'You're right. She hated the idea of people being put down in the earth and worms gnawing at their flesh.'

'This was our happy place,' I said. 'Perhaps the happiest of all. I think she might want to be associated with that.'

'Felim especially loved it here,' Mona said wistfully. 'Remember what he used say. If he had the choice, this is the way he would go, down there with the water about him like an embrace, hearing the music of its journey playing in his ears. Poor Felim. Do you think, Roddy, that he is still alive somewhere? It's been so long.'

'No, I know he is not alive, Mona. Last night I made up my mind to tell you the truth about him. You're the only family I have left and you should know.'

Her brow furrowed. 'Tell me what?'

'Felim is here, Mona, in this pool. Over there under that far bank.'

'I don't get it. Jesus.'

'Years ago, when I swam here as a kid with Mikey Kilraish, we discovered a cavern under the rock at the far side. It had been gouged out by the river thousands of years ago. It's a wonderful place, like a cathedral. The light comes in part of the way and lights up the cavern roof and the stalactites that hang from it. Years before we found it, Mikey's uncle had drowned in the Blue Pool and his body had been washed into the cavern. He's still inside there, lying on a ledge.'

'Is Felim there too?' Mona whispered. 'Is that what

you're saying?'

'I came up here one day, long after Felim had disappeared. I sat where you are now and it suddenly dawned on me that he too must have found the cavern; you remember the way he used dive in and be submerged for so long that we feared for him. So I went in and found him, lying on a ledge like Robert Kilraish. He must have swum across and lay on the bottom, as he said he would, just in front of the entrance. There's an eddy there and it would have swept him into the cavern.'

'Oh God.'

'Something else I didn't tell you – about the picture that's missing from the parlour wall. When he left after his fight with Hughie, Felim took a small brown suitcase with him. It contained the missing picture from the parlour. The original of the St Luna's hurling team is also with it; the picture on the wall is a replacement I put there. When Felim walked out of Glenorga, that last night, he knew where he was going and what he was going to do. The pictures were the fondest mementoes of his life on this earth. I think it is so fitting, so profound. A modern Stone Age burial in the valley of ancient Neolithic men.'

'Holy Christ, Roddy, it's awful. You kept it to yourself all those years? Why didn't you tell somebody?'

'You know what would have happened? They'd have gone in there, my father amongst them, and taken out his skeleton. I couldn't do that to Felim; that's his special place in there. Let him lie in peace.'

'You're right, Roddy, that's the place for Felim.' Suddenly she covered her face with her hands and started to sob. When she took them away, her eyes were bloodshot and the tracks of her tears ran down her cheekbones.

'I knew he was dead. I always did. So did Mother. We had sketchy information about his alcoholism and his comings and goings. Barton always implied things rather than said them outright. I suppose he was trying to make it easy for us. From the moment Mother heard that Felim had had a fight with Hughie though, she had this Doomsday premonition. "Felim is dead, Felim is dead", she kept saying to me.'

'Felim was her favourite, wasn't he?'

'For a long time, I thought Hughie was the white-haired boy. But you're right; she had a special yen for Felim. He was the personification of her father, the unfettered intelligent bohemian who followed his own way.'

'I think we'd better be getting along with it.'

I cast around until I found a suitable length of stick on a hazel shrub. I dived in, feeling again the tightness of chest and the stifled breath of foreboding that had always assailed me as I looked at the gun-barrel sheen of the water. As I surfaced, I heard the water sough under the far bank and a shout from Mona telling me to be careful. I ducked under again when I reached the bank. The boulder was still shutting off the entrance to the cavern and had grown tighter around the place where it had lodged. The space around it was beginning to silt up. In 50 years it would have grown round the boulder as a natural part of the rock shelf above it. It would seal Felim's and my mother's burial chambers as if they had been placed in a Pharaoh's pyramid. I poked at the silt with the stick, gouged out a hole and pushed the capsule through.

Mona was sobbing anew when I returned. After I had dried out and was putting on my socks, she came to me and grabbed me in a tense, tight embrace. I could hear her sobs beating against my heart.

We stood by the ruined gable of Manisterluna watching the sunbeams catch the valley floor like titanic lances and then flatten out as the light drifted in the clouds. Below us was the valley of Glenorga. I had pondered, time and again, what the first colonisers must have felt when they breasted this hillock and looked out over the mountain, on tiers and flat plains, on sparkling streams and valley floors as pristine and lovely as if they had just been shaped and painted.

It was warm and sultry in the graveyard. The last time I had been here, when my father was being laid beside his son, the burial ground was rank and overgrown. Some of the tombstones had fallen to the ground; others were so pitted with fungus and lichen that the lettering was indecipherable. My father had showed me where the Dawley family grave was. Generations of my ancestors were lying under the mound but no one had ever raised a flagstone or a monument to their memory. When his time came, my father had said, he wanted a gravestone to mark his place. It had never occurred to either of us that Hughie would go before him.

I had enclosed the grave with a wrought-iron railing, and raised a large tombstone to the memory of my paternal grandfather and grandmother. Later, my father's name and Hughie's were added.

Mona knelt by the railing and her lips moved in prayer. In the last few years the local authority had cleaned out and restored the graveyard. They had cut out the creeping brambles, the ragwort and the nettles and had stood the tombstones upright again. The lettering on ancient stone was etched out anew.

'Mona, look here, the grave right beside ours.'

She peered and squinted at the sandstone Celtic cross that had been raised above a low wall of black Kilkenny marble.

'I don't believe it. Christ, Roddy, did our father know about this?'

'No, Lionel Barton lived on for another ten years after Dad died. He spent the greater part of it in a nursing home. He'd had several strokes and his last years were dismal. I used go to see him regularly. He just sat there, in the day room, staring into space. He hadn't a notion who I was.'

'How come they let him in here?'

'Why not, for God's sake? He was a Catholic, the same as the rest of them. By the time he died, nobody cared; hardly anyone remembered.'

'But they're all here, Roddy, every Barton that ever was. Look at the names: Richard, Godfrey, William, Geoffrey, Amos.'

'I know. I think I'm responsible for that. When we were kids, Mikey Kilraish and I broke into the Barton vault. The place was falling down; the coffins had split open and some of the skulls were lying on the ground. Lionel had little money to spend on repairing the vault, so I suggested that he buy a grave in Manisterluna and re-inter his ancestors here. He jumped at the idea, but I think for an ulterior motive.'

'Like?'

'If he couldn't get near my father while he was living, he would do so when he was dead. I know it sounds far-fetched, but Lionel was obsessed to make peace with the Dawleys. He probably knew that this was as near as he was ever going to get to it. Doesn't it all seem so silly now? Here they are, lying side by side, and no one gives a damn about their hatreds or their passions.'

'Our father would turn in his grave if he knew.'

'He would. Come on, let me show you where Lena Kilraish is buried.'

'Rosie's mother? Our mother didn't like that family.'

'I know. Let's walk; the grave is over at the far side.'

A sudden flash along the stone wall grabbed my attention; light glinted off a brass plaque mounted on the wall.

'Jesus, will you look at that plaque? I've never seen that before.'

'I can't read it without my glasses. What does it say?'

"Sacred to the memory of Lena Kilraish, RIP. 1929 to 1989. Erected by her loving son, Michael."

'Mikey?'

'I didn't think he had it in him. He turned out to be as big an asshole as old Long Pat, if not more so. Fuck him. Come on, let's go.'

Mona put a restraining hand on my elbow. 'Wait a minute. You brought me over here for a reason.'

'I just wanted to show you how, even in death, the stupidity of status lives on. The people of the mountain were almost destitute. Yet we considered ourselves a cut above other people. Someone like Lena Kilraish was at the bottom of the pile. There are no other graves in her part of the graveyard, as if she might contaminate the good people elsewhere. Those who did that to her believed in a just and loving God and they professed to follow in his footsteps. They did like hell!'

'Hey, you sound like an admirer too, Roddy.'

'No, Mona, not just an admirer. I loved her. Lena fussed over me: she gave me choice bits of food, she titillated my ego. She made me sit at her table and tell her stories. But above all, she was Rosie's mother.'

We sat in the conservatory and watched the darkness creep across the foothills of the mountain. One Christmas Eve,

Mona and Mother and I had walked to the tip of Knocknastumpa to see the lights that pierced the blackness of Mount Fierna, in mountain slopes, in valley floors, on tiered plateaux. The night was as black as ink, a bitter wind came out of the north from the direction that Red Hugh O'Donnell had come on his way to Kinsale and by a random innocuous stroke of fate made us mountain people. All over Mount Fierna the lights twinkled; it was like the view of a distant galaxy from a speeding starship. On a star-bright, frost-laden night when no wind blew, we counted twenty-seven Christmas lights guiding the Holy Family to Bethlehem.

Mona rummaged in the biscuit tin, that cornucopia of sentiment that carried all I had collected of family tentacles. In there were Felim's postcards, the few letters that Hughie had written when he was in England, a school photograph of Newtown, grainy and blurred, newspaper cuttings. Every time I came across some memento I stored it there, laying it on top of the pile and never looking beneath.

'Here's a picture of you. The St Luna's minor hurling team, 1962.'

'Yeah. I know the one. Would you believe, Mona, that there were seven of us from the mountain on that team, including Ferdia Cahill from Ardagh and, of course, Gene Trenchard? And Mikey Kilraish, the star of the show.'

'Didn't ye win the championship?'

'No. But we won the senior five or six years later.'

'Is there any team now?'

'None. And never will be again. There is almost no one living on the mountain now. The era of the mountain has come and gone; people won't put up with the isolation and the hardship now, and who can blame them? They can find much better lives away from here.'

Tom Nestor

'What became of Mikey Kilraish?'

'I prefer not to talk about him.'

'Okay. So let's talk about Rosie.'

'I told you when I was with you in California. Rosie wrote me out of her life.'

'I always thought that was puppy love, an infatuation that would evaporate when you grew older or someone else appeared.'

'You're right, Mona.'

'Don't try to con me, Roddy. You never did grow out of it, did you?'

'I never did. Talking about the minor team, did you know that Trenchard came home for a holiday a few summers back?'

'Did you meet him?'

'No, I avoided him like the plague. I never liked him, but I think you know that. He was a frequent visitor to Heaney's, throwing money around as if there was no scarcity. He owns a construction company in Boston and apparently has made another fortune playing the futures market. You could sue him, you know. He married again.'

'Roddy, if I never see Gene Trenchard again, it will be too soon. You have no idea what that bastard put me through. All I ever was to him was the price of a ticket to New York. We lasted no more than a year together. He seldom came home, he flitted from job to job, and when I accosted him about it, he told me that if I didn't like it I could lump it. I was working for a lady who ran a Montessori school, and I liked it so much that I went to night classes and took my diploma. Then I split with him. It was easy. I just walked away.'

'So what brought you to California?'

Mona took a newspaper cutting from the biscuit tin and laid it on her lap. She put the lid on and turned to me with a curious expression of mingled sadness and appreciation. 'You did. And our father. And of course, Mother.'

'Explain please.'

'Remember when we decorated the wall above the fireplace in the kitchen. You had gotten some *National Geographic* magazines and in one of them was a feature about California. We all chose a different picture and pasted it onto the wall. Our father ordered them down when he arrived home and made us look like idiots for trying to put a little colour into our lives.'

'Padre Pio is still on that wall.'

'I saw it, looking as browned off as ever. I never forgot that feature, and especially my choice of picture. When I walked out on Trenchard, I bought a ticket on a Greyhound bus, headed for Los Angeles and found a job in a school in Anaheim.'

'And you never looked back?'

'Several times. In the early days I hardly made enough money to keep body and soul together. Eventually, with financial support from some of my students' parents, I set up my own school. By the time Mother arrived, I had gotten on my feet. She was something else, Roddy. You should have seen her. She blossomed as if she had been released from some kind of prison. Her first job was as a receptionist with the Soames Museum for Contemporary Art. She went to night school; became Assistant Curator and could have made the top job there if she wished. But by then she had met Katch.'

'If you're finished with the biscuit tin, I'll put it away.'

'What's wrong with you, Roddy? Every time I start to

talk about Mother, you change the subject.'

I was never comfortable talking about my mother's other life in America. It seemed to me that she had packaged her previous existence as a mountain wife, loaded it with concrete and cast it into the depths of Lough Cutra, never to surface again. When I met her in California, it was as if Mount Fierna had never existed, that my father had never been, that my brothers had never walked the earth. That last part was the hardest to understand. I knew there were different shades in the way she loved Felim and Hughie, but it was love nonetheless, deep, warm and apparent. I remembered the way she had mourned when Hughie went to England, how she used walk out to the stepping stones to wait for the postman. I tried to talk to her about it as we sipped a glass of wine in the front room of Katch's house – why she never referred to Mount Fierna. We were alone and for almost an hour she had regaled me with the story of her American period, from the moment she stepped off the aircraft. 'Roddy, there's a line drawn in the sand. One side is Mount Fierna and all belonging to that time. I don't go there any more.'

My mother had undergone a metamorphosis. A vitally different person, in dress, decorum and mind-set had emerged. She made me feel that I too, like Katch, had walked into her life from the side of the line in which she now existed. I felt diffident and unsure in her presence. She knew this and exploited it. Every now and then something I said was put down with an abrasive dismissal or I got that quizzical frown which reduced my opinion to nonsense. Then she would look at me as if my ignorance had nonplussed her. It was all impossibly complex and convoluted. Back home in Mount Fierna I was finding the other man who co-existed within my father's outer shell; in California I had lost the woman who had once been my mother.

And then there was Katch. From the moment of introduction I disliked him. He was handsome and well preserved; he worked out every day and what the exercise didn't achieve for him, he supplemented with male cosmetics. Katch always looked robust and tanned, as if he had stepped off a plane from an African safari. He was a third-generation Armenian, with Slavic face lines and a Jewish nose. When he discovered that I was going to mass the Sunday after I arrived, he gave me a lecture on the evolution of various credos and concluded that religion was for simple, ignorant people. He spoke to me as if he was talking from a podium. Katch was a specialist in western American artists, the likes of Frederic Remington, N.C. Wyeth and Charles M. Russell.

Mother and Katch had an extraordinary arrangement, an apparent testimony to the axiom that opposites attract. What in effect happened, however, was that Katch compromised. He was deeply in love with my mother – he never ceased to tell me that during the few weeks I was in California, and what an amazing woman she was. He stayed on the American side of the line she had drawn in the sand; never once did he talk to me about our lives in Mount Fierna. Around my mother he was gracious, well-mannered and gentle. That was why the relationship was so exceptional. Katch was the cynic of cynics; he belittled every opinion, sentiment and belief which didn't match his.

We fought, Katch and I, teeth-bared rows. At least that's how I felt. My mother maintained that Katch held no animosity towards me and was surprised and disappointed that I hadn't gone to him, after each dust up, with my hand outstretched, bearing the offer of renewed friendship. Renewed friendship! I needed an excuse and was glad he had given me the opportunity to cross swords with him. To this day I can remember the opening words that had sparked the first confrontation. 'Beth and Mona, I know you both are familiar with the concept of déjà vu. But for the benefit of Roderick here, who probably has not come across the expression ...'

Katch had made a fortune from a collection of early original cartoon art and from the property portfolio that his father had willed him. When he died suddenly from heart failure, he willed everything to my mother. She became a very wealthy woman. I went to see her once more only after that first visit, after my father had passed on. By then she was dying. She was comatose by the time I got there. We never spoke again.

'Roddy, did you hear what I said to you?'

'Yes, Mona.'

'And?'

'I find it hard, very hard, to talk about our mother. Like her, I have a line in the sand too. California, Katch, all that wealth, they are all on the side I know nothing about. I didn't like what I found there and I don't feel like going anymore.'

'For Christ's sake, Roddy, *I* belong to that side. You can't shut me out too.'

'No, Mona, I could never shut *you* out. But you straddle the line: days of the Blue Pool, parlour days, all those core elements of our youth before you went away.'

Mona got out of her chair, placed the biscuit tin on the table and came and hugged me. 'I love you, Roddy.'

A well of emotion built in the well of my stomach and

rushed into my throat. It stalled there, like floodwater about to overflow its banks. And then it burst through my fingers, wringing out sobs and gulps of grief that I thought had been buried forever. Mona looked at me with the same manifestation of deep compassion that I had once seen in Julian Stapleton's face.

'What was it, Roddy?'

'All my life I waited for my mother to say I love you. She never did. The day before she left, she took me for a walk by our old stomping grounds. We went to the Blue Pool, climbed Knocknastumpa, along by Manisterluna, by Lough Cutra and the Giant's Grave. She offered me advice and guidance; I had to grow independent she told me, must learn to take care of myself. After she had gone, I realised that she had been saying goodbye that day, but she never told me she loved me. She did later; she left me a note with Lionel Barton. But, Mona, the thing is, I never heard it from her lips, never heard it from my father either.'

'That is not to say she didn't love you, Roddy.'

'Then why make such a bloody secret of it? Why couldn't she have told me then? That was the perfect time.'

'Roddy, I can tell you this with certainty: Mother loved all her children. But she had to cut loose, had to sever the connections.'

'Yeah, yeah, I've heard that so many times. Mona, what a bloody strange family we were. We just adopted positions and stayed there. It didn't matter how polar they were, how distanced or obdurate.'

Mona twined her fingers across her chest and stared out of the conservatory window, as if she were searching for some response. That was unusual for her. At least it was unusual for the young woman of long ago who wore her feelings on her sleeve and plucked them into combat at the first opportunity.

'Well. What would you expect? We were the children of our father, or rather of him who sired us. Sometimes I wonder did I invent him, did I create him out of my worst nightmares. I have never forgiven him. If he was here right now, it would give me great pleasure to tell him what I think.'

Her eyes bored into mine. It was as if she was daring me to contradict her. Katch, I thought, your pupil has regressed.

My father was the last person I had expected to see at the airport when I arrived home from California. I had called Heaney from Heathrow, asked him if he'd walk up to Glenorga, find the key of the car hanging from a nail above the picture of Padre Pio and pick me up at Shannon. Not only was my father standing beside Heaney when I cleared customs but he was wearing his best suit and his shoes were polished. He was, in his own expression, all dickey doo.

I was shocked to realise how old he looked, something I hadn't noticed before I'd gone away. It was now strikingly apparent; as if our separation had thrown the cumulative effect of what I had missed into stark relief. As he grew older, his face had thinned and narrowed towards the chin in a wedge shape, the facial skin was a network of wrinkles and broken veins and sometimes, when the light was dim and the beard shadow dark on cheekbones and upper lip, his features had a hominid cast.

I sat in the rear of the car as we drove towards Newtown. My father was strangely garrulous. He had pulled down the windscreen visor and several times I caught him looking at me in the mirror. Each time he smiled and gave me a lascivious wink as if he were privy to some lusty secret. When we reached Newtown, Heaney invited us in for a drink but my father shook his head emphatically. 'The boy here will be worn out from all that travelling.'

'You were wound up,' I said to him as we started off again.

'No one is entitled to know anything about us if we don't want to tell. If I hadn't kept talking, questions would have been asked.' He paused, just enough to let his strategy be appreciated. 'Don't turn for home when you get to the cross. We'll go to Ardagh and have a drink. I'm right glad you're home.'

'Are you?'

'What class of a question is that? Course I am, and you the only one I've got under the sun.'

Ferdia had grown into a younger version of Martin, but he had none of the warmth and affability that marked his father's character. He greeted us with a watery smile, told us in response to my father's query that Martin was as well as could be expected at his age and that his mother was as spry as ever.

We took our whiskey drinks to a table in the far corner. 'So tell me,' my father asked as soon and we were seated, 'what's it like in California?'

'Lovely. Beautiful climate, beautiful people, loads of wealth.'

'That's not what I meant.'

'So what did you mean?'

'Stop sparring with me and answer the question. You know well. How are they?'

'All very well. It would take me ages to fill in all the details; they've been gone a long time. Fifteen years almost since Mother left.'

'Tell me the main things so.'

'Mona owns her own school now; it's very successful. She has a teaching staff of ten; there's a two-year waiting list. She's a wealthy woman, in her own right. The piece of ground on which the school is built is worth over a million dollars.'

'Holy Jesus! Well, fair play to her. Tell me, any sign of her getting married again?'

'I don't think so. And maybe just as well, given the Dawley genes.'

'Ah, don't be saying things like that. But,' he held out a monitoring hand, 'time enough to talk about that another day. Go on with your story.'

'Mother is fine. She is the Assistant Curator in a museum of modern art. There is something you should—'

'I heard from Paddy Heaney that she got married again. That fella Trenchard was telling him when he was home a few years back. Sure she couldn't do that, could she, Roddy? She was married to me in the eyes of God.'

'Trenchard was wrong. Mother never got married. But she has what they call out there a partner. A man called Katchadorian something or other. They all call him Katch. He's a big art dealer.'

'Ferdy,' my father shouted. 'Bring us the same again. An' be starting two pints.'

'You must be planning on a long session. I don't think I'm up to it.'

'That fella Ferdy is a bad hand at pulling a pint unless he gets plenty of notice. Are you saying that my wife is knocking around with someone else, maybe living with him? That it?'

'That's the way of it. No point in telling you anything else.'

My father held his whiskey glass to the light and watched the amber pinpoints that glanced off the crystal as he turned it. He veered off the topic with a suddenness that surprised me. 'Would you live out there? Are you going back?'

'That's two questions, Father.'

'Well, make one out of it and answer me.'

'I couldn't take the lifestyle. I'm sure it's wonderful for those who were born and bred there or those young enough to adapt. It's not for me. But I might visit again.'

'That's grand so. Do you know, son, all the time you were gone, I had this bad feeling. As sure as God made little apples, I kept telling myself, the boy won't come home at all. Sure what's here for him to come home to?'

'You.'

'Ah, that's nice. That's grand. Did they ever talk about me?

'Of course they did.'

'And what class of things did they say?'

'They asked how you were getting on, how you were managing the land. All the things that had happened since the time they left here.'

Ferdy ran a wet cloth over the table surface and then laid the drinks down. 'Back from the States,' Ferdy said. It sounded more like an affirmation than a question.

'California,' my father answered for me, 'just home from California.'

'Ah, California,' Ferdy said wistfully. 'I spent a summer there long ago. Out in Orange County.' He sighed. 'Those were the days.'

325

'He should have stayed there,' my father said when Ferdy was out of earshot; 'he hasn't a scrap of the common touch that Martin has. I suppose we'll never see the pair again? Mona or your mother.'

"Fraid not. I don't think either one of them could adjust to Mount Fierna again. They're perfectly in tune with America. You should see my mother, she's like someone who grew up there.'

'I wonder if she ever thinks about me?' he whispered.

'Of course she does. She talked a lot about you.'

'An' you're a damn bad liar.' My father took a long swig from his pint and stared steadfastly at me over the rim of his glass. 'Maybe now you have some class of a clue for me, because in all those years I could never unravel it. I was awful fond of that woman; okay, we had our rows and our ups and downs. But I thought, in the long run, that she felt the same way about me. She told me so before we were ever married. I was never one for writing, Roddy, but your mother was. Never in all the years a single word, not a single word on a scrap of paper or a message through someone. As for Mona, she must hate me terribly. What is it, Roddy? In the name of Jesus, tell me. I have to face my maker one of these days. What did I do that my wife and daughter would turn their backs on me for fifteen years and more? 'Tis the same as if I never existed.'

'They were asking for you, Father.'

'They were like shit! The same as if I never drew breath; never knew them at all.'

'Let me tell you something. There's two of us in it. I felt that I was a stranger to my mother. Do you know what she told me? She said she had drawn a line in the sand. It separates her life in Mount Fierna from her time in America, and since the day she arrived there, she has never crossed the line. Now you riddle me that.'

'I don't know the answer. It beggars belief.'

'In a way, I'm sorry I went.'

'Aye, I know what you mean. Will we have another small one before we go down any farther in the pints? Sure we might as well. Will you go and get them? That fella Ferdy will be wiping away with his ould rag if he comes down.'

I remembered the time we had won the senior championship and came to Ardagh to celebrate: Hughie and Felim in the prime of life, my father in the early autumn of his days. I thought about my mother and Mona that night and wished that they had been with us. They would have seen my father's alter ego breaking through in a manner that belied the ascetic personality that we sought and found.

Ferdy filled the glasses and I brought them back to the table. My father was turned round in his chair, his face to the window. His shoulders were slumped and he was absorbing the sound of his sobs in the hands that pressed against his mouth. When he came round to look at me again, the eyes were red rimmed and there was a tear stain along the lantern jawline. His words were barely audible.

'Here's something that enters my head every day of my life. Tell me, Roddy, what did I do wrong? Where did I go astray? It must have been a terrible sin to punish me like this.'

'We all did wrong, Father – Hughie, Felim, Mona and I, and our mother too. We never gave you a chance. We took your faults and your failings, your aspersions and your dreams, found you guilty for having them and set ourselves in a contrary alignment. It never occurred to us to negotiate or to influence, to show you another way, to try and change your perspective. No, we decreed you wrong and set ourselves apart from you. We were all at fault.'

A bluebottle entered the open window and buzzed loudly. My father threw off the whiskey and drained the remnants of the pint. He had two more shorts and his head dropped farther towards his chest. Suddenly he shot upright and fixed his fingers round my wrist.

'I was as good as the next man, Roddy, aye and even better. I could walk behind a plough all day and not a stir would it take from me. I could pitch hay day and night, work in all sorts of weathers; there wasn't a man on the mountain could stay with me. Aye indeed. An' I could run like the wind. I won two cups below in Limerick for the mile; they wrote about it in the papers. For ten years I hurled with Ardagh; there was no man better liked. And once, Roddy, I made a chess set. The man over the carpentry class told me that he had never seen anything like it.' He stopped and the head dropped again. 'Aw, shit, what's the point of talking? What the hell does it matter what I did? I haven't a thing to show for it. My wife shagged off and left me. My daughter hates the ground I walk on. One son in the grave, another God knows where. What the fuck was it all about?'

He was drunk when we left. I took him home and put him to bed. As I unlaced his boots, his eyes opened and he smiled at me.

'I love you, Dad,' I said.

'Ah, that's grand. Grand entirely.'

Mona put the lid on the biscuit tin and then removed it again when she noticed the newspaper cutting still lying on her lap. She folded the cutting and put in on top of the pile in the box.

'You should read that,' I said.

'Why?'

'Read it and see.'

She unfolded the piece of paper and smoothed out the folds. 'He was handsome in a strange sort of way; if he weren't so gangly and the hands didn't dangle so much.'

'He reminded me of a chimpanzee the way he walked.'

'Bet you never told him that.'

'I did. Before he died. We had a very good relationship.'

'How did he die? Was he ill for long?'

'No. I came home from work one evening and found him sprawled over the kitchen table. He always prepared my tea and when he had the table laid, he used stand at the conservatory window and wait for me. That particular evening I never looked at the window, but the moment I entered the house I had this terrible premonition that something bad was afoot. He must have been dead for hours, perhaps since he had got up that morning. There was a stocking dangling off one foot and the other he had grasped in his hand. And the most curious thing of all – there was a scrap of paper on the table and a pencil as if he knew that the pain was going to kill him and he wanted to tell me something before he died.'

'Did he?'

'No.'

From the top of Knocknastumpa a curlew cried. It sounded remote and melancholy as if it carried the secrets of mountain sadness and the cry was but a forerunner of all the unhappy things it knew. When we were children, we thought that the curlew was the avian form of the banshee, that terrible hag of doom who went abroad in the night screeching its message of impending death.

'Sweet Jesus,' Mona said, 'I never knew he was an athlete. Two titles in successive years. Well, what do you know?'

'Hang on, let me show you something else.'

I went upstairs to my father's room and brought down the chess set. I placed it in her hands. She made an attempt at a whistle of surprise. 'You're going to tell me he made this?'

'Yes he did. Isn't it absolutely lovely? It's impossible to believe that the man who created this had no soul, had no love. I find it—'

'Roddy, stop it. Stay on your side of the line and I'll stay on mine. But don't try to put an aura of goodness around this man. You're all I've got, Roddy, so don't let's fight, please.'

'I've no intention of it. Mona, there's another picture in that box. Probably down at the end. A photograph of a school class.'

'I'm warning you, Roddy, if this is another angle in my father's rehabilitation ...'

'Take it out and see.'

Mona peered at the picture that Barton and I had removed from Amersham Hall.

'What am I supposed to be looking for?'

'Go along the back row. Study them carefully. Anything familiar?'

'Nothing, so ... Hey, Jesus, the guy in the middle looks like Felim. But it couldn't be, could it?'

'No, that's an eighteen-year-old Lionel Barton.'

'No way.'

'That's Barton. I was there when we took that picture from his old school. Nothing, but nothing represents the terrible stupidity of the Dawley-Barton feud as much as that picture does. I couldn't explain the similarity when I first saw it but I suspect Lionel could because he wanted me to have it. I didn't know until I began to work on the Theme Park project. Have you heard of the right of *prima nocte*?'

Mona shook her head.

'When tenant subjects of a landlord were getting married, he had the right to claim the first night with the bride. In the great majority of cases, that entitlement was seldom demanded but in Barton ancestry it was. It was well known in the folklore. William Grantham Barton and his wife were childless, but he had fathered a son through *prima nocte* with a Dawley bride. The child was brought up as a Barton and was named Geoffrey, Lionel's grandfather. So you see, Mona, we're blood relations, the Bartons and the Dawleys.'

Mona shook her head, over and over again and several times brought the picture closer to her face to scrutinise it. Then she put it away in the tin, placed it firmly down in the bottom as if to shut its significance away forever.

'Roddy, I'll ask you again. Why don't you come and live with me? This is a terribly lonely place. You have no friends here.'

'I love it here. I will never leave Mount Fierna. It would be like walking over the graves of all those who have gone before me, my father and my brothers, even Lionel Barton; he had a great yearning for this place too. And I do have some friends – one in particular: a person called Conor Stapleton.'

'Never heard of him.'

'He's a missionary priest in Chile. As poor as a church mouse. He comes and stays for a month every year. I pay his way and feel privileged.'

The rain began to patter against the window glass. It filled me with comfort. It always did. In a corner between the crumbling walls of de Val's old castle, I had made a shelter with sheets of corrugated iron. I used go there when it rained, with a book inside my jersey, and sit on a lintel that had fallen from a mullioned window. It was the safest place on earth; I heard neither voices nor the sounds of anger or argument. The rain filled the channels of my makeshift shelter and formed a pool that stripped away the earth and bared the pebbles beneath. I pushed out my foot and watched as the spatters moistened the toecap of my boot.

'And you, Mona, will you visit again?'

'No, Roddy. I will never come again. I came for your sake this once. But you must visit me often. Promise.'

'Because you're my sister and I love you, I promise.'

The curlew cried again. It filled the world with loneliness. I thought of Felim. He loved the curlew's call because, he said, it was like the fanfare to an opera, like an overture. It opened for him the sounds and the sights of Mount Fierna, a conduit to reach out to in the black days of despair. And suddenly I envied Felim. Not for him the bleak cold days, the interminable hours that beckoned me onward into feeble old age. Felim was like the eagle that once had flown over the top of Knocknastumpa, free and graceful. He went out in the flowering of freedom, in his own choosing. I wished I had such bravery.

The eagle soars no more. I will sit and dream and fall asleep. I will be alone. And when the curlew calls, and the sound probes my mind, I will hear what Felim heard. I will hark to the Dawley dirge, the chant of a dead race. It will come to me out of the wind and the heather, like the echoes of a forgotten song.